THE MURDER ALGORITHM

WILSON KINCAID

Thanks to all the beta and early readers who helped bring this book to completion. Thanks to Danny Klein for his support and advice. Thanks to my friends and family who encouraged me to keep going. And especially, thanks to Rebecca Robinson of First Write Editors, who patiently took the time to work with me to make this novel better. It was a pleasure and I'm grateful for the guidance.

FOREWORD

Wilson Kincaid's "The Murder Algorithm" is a masterfully crafted story with a deliciously futuristic and thought-provoking premise. Kincaid transports us to a world where social media reigns supreme and everyone's lives are a 24/7 reality show. This gripping novel is an exciting combination of science fiction, mystery and thriller that will keep you guessing until the very end.

The characters are well-drawn and complex, each with their own motivations and secrets. Roman Glass, the protagonist, is easy to root for as he fights to clear his name with the help of his friends after being charged with the murder of one of the greatest stars in history. Rae Dettmer, the social media investigator tackling Roman's case, is a favourite of mine as well, and is a tenacious and intelligent character who fights to uncover secrets a tech giant family would rather keep buried. Together, they must race against the clock to uncover the truth.

Kincaid captures the essence of a future Los Angeles, where scorching flames dance on the edges of society, reflecting the precarious balance between progress and destruction. Amid this backdrop, the StarSee towers rise like glittering sentinels, dominating the skyline of a city teetering on the brink of chaos. As we follow the narrative, we catch glimpses of the enigmatic billionaire founders' luxurious yet sinister world, a place where power and influence are intertwined in unexpected ways.

Kincaid's writing serves as a timely warning, shedding light on the dark corners of our tech-obsessed world. He dives headfirst into the consequences of our digital lives, raising important questions about the toll it takes on our mental health, lifestyle, and the rampant spread of misinformation. The writing is top-notch, with crisp dialog, vivid descriptions and a plot that keeps you guessing until the very end. But what really sets "The Murder Algorithm" apart from the rest is its genre-bending style. This is a book that will keep you on the edge of your seat with thrilling action scenes while also exploring big ideas about the role of technology in our lives and the consequences of a society preoccupied with social media.

Wilson Kincaid is a writer to watch, and "The Murder Algorithm" is a must-read for anyone who loves mystery, sci-fi or just a damn good book. Be warned though, this tale will have you flipping through its pages well into the night.

By Daniel Klein, acclaimed author of the international bestseller "Plato and a Platypus Walk into a Bar," as well as the Elvis Presley Mystery series and many more.

CHAPTER
ONE

Monday, 6:30 p.m.

The world watched with a million digital eyes as Roman Glass entered the luxury penthouse suite of the beautiful Miss Starla Devine. Watchers of Roman's never-ending live StarStream hoped to catch a glimpse of the statuesque blond. Even Roman knew that tonight, she was the main attraction on his own feed.

She had been his highest profile client when he had scanned her a few years ago, and he felt a touch of shame that he was still trying to break into show business after all these years.

He took a deep breath of the filtered air, absent of the smell of smoke that permeated Los Angeles. The large open Marina del Rey condo was clean, bright and modern. Like a physician's waiting room.

"Welcome, Mr. Glass," said Starla's Digital Assistant. The male voice was warm and came from everywhere.

"Hi Charlie." As he looked around the room, Roman's Geosense unconsciously flashed in his mind, and he instantly had a three dimensional mental picture of everything he saw. Unique to

Roman, anytime he entered a new area, a neurological calculation exploded in his brain and every object, distance and angle was known. He pulled his large camera bag off his shoulder and put it near the white leather couch. The view from the top was amazing, ocean as far as the eye could see on one side, sparkling city lights glowing through a thin veil of smoke on the other.

"Hi Roman!" She stepped out from behind the privacy screens. Initially, he thought she was naked, but quickly realized she was wearing a hyperthin body suit. The picture of beauty, smiling broadly and posing playfully.

"Hi Starla, nice to see you again."

He couldn't help but admire her. She was number one, the first StarStreamer, zero degrees of separation from everyone, the Tom to Myspace, the Mark to Facebook, the Jack to Twitter. Though not a founder, she was the face of the global platform called StarSee.tv, in a world where marketability kept fans watching and stars streaming.

There was another big difference between her and those other firsts; people loved her. In a social media landscape where most stars grew in popularity and fame based on how much drama and conflict they created, she was different. She somehow created attraction without promoting negativity, and her employer was lucky she made the splash she did, so that they could ride her wave to tremendous success.

StarSee.tv was now the king of the socials, a unique combination of Hollywood, social media and reality TV, and the regal blond was the queen. She was an authentic studio star with a social media reach like no other human being on the planet.

StarSee.tv. Where stars are on 24 hours a day, and everyone is a star. Some are just bigger than others.

She stayed on her side of the room as Roman set up his equipment for the new scan. As she walked over to the shiny black bar, Roman resisted the urge to watch her. She was the very definition of attractive. Starla was not always real in her StarStream, sometimes she appeared as a photo-real behaviorally driven digital person, but her avatar was always true to the real Starla Devine, and people loved the real Starla Devine more than any other.

Tonight, she had her privacy filters on, so she was invisible to his StarStream viewers, and was not broadcasting to her own. His image would be clear, but if his StreamBugs inadvertently turned towards her, she would appear soft and blurry. The rich could afford to control their own StarStreams, and Starla Devine was very, very rich.

As Roman grabbed his bag of drone lights from the foyer, he glimpsed himself in his augmented reality StarStream. *I should have dressed better.* He ran his hands through his shaggy hair in a useless attempt at vanity.

"I have a new signature vodka for you to try." Her StreamBugs silently hovered over her, even though they were not broadcasting.

"Okay," said Roman. "I can't get drunk, so why not?" his voice cracked as he laughed.

She moved a small stuffed gift bear holding mylar balloons out of the way to pour the drinks.

"You must get a ton of gifts from your fans."

"I wouldn't know, they get intercepted before they get to me." She handed the drink to Roman, walked back to her large armoire, and stood waiting, sipping her martini. Something was off. She seemed anxious.

The drink was delicious. It took him back to a time when alcohol affected him. He gulped it down faster than he should have. Old habits die hard. He unfolded his gear.

"You'll need the lights off again, right?"

"Yeah, my drone lights will provide lighting for your capture."

"Charlie, blackout the condo windows." The curtains silently slid closed. No more Pacific Ocean. No more city lights. No more Free Agent StreamBugs outside the windows trying to see in.

His capture camera drone lifted out of the center of the eight-foot diameter circle of scanning gear and waited for her to step in.

She put her drink down, stepped into the circle and walked towards him.

"Ready babe?" asked Roman. *What the hell? Why did I call her that?*

She stepped closer to him, a little too close. "Are you still mad about the award?" She whispered.

Roman froze. His eyes narrowed as he turned towards her. "Why would you ask that?" Something about her felt threatening.

"There it is." She glanced at the shelf that stood next to them. On it was the coveted award, gleaming. "Is your name on it?" she whispered so quietly he strained to hear her, even though she was mere feet away.

What the hell? Roman looked at the award. He already knew his name wasn't on it. She nodded, prompting him to pick it up. She looked different.

"Something feels wrong," he said. *Why am I dizzy?* The swirling cloud of StreamBugs watched as he grabbed it.

"Sorry pal."

He looked at the award. Why was she messing with him? A flash of anger and a wave of disorientation swept over him as if he had stood up too quickly.

"All lights out," she whispered.

It was dark now, all he could see was spots. He reached out to steady himself, felt her shoulders, then her neck. *What am I doing?* She screamed. Her hand wrapped around his hand, which was wrapped around the award. Something hit him in the head. He was falling forward. "Roman! Stop it!" *Why is she screaming?*

As the floor approached, he tumbled into the inky blackness. He heard her scream again, but she was very far away this time. Everything was very far away.

Monday, 9:23pm

Sitting in his cell in the MobiJail bus, Roman had emerged from the darkness of unconsciousness into the world of modern interrogation several hours ago. He had already been through a very thorough medical exam, and an actual living public defender who assigned him his personal Defenderbot. Despite the extreme stress of being accused of murder, he still felt groggy. The bump on his head wasn't bad enough to cause it. She had drugged him, he was sure of it.

Homicide Detective Travis Clark had been pleasant to him so far. A little too friendly. The kind of friendly a nurse shows a patient that is about to have a surgery that they might not survive. Roman knew it was part of the shtick, get the perp feeling comfortable, achieve a rapport, they'll talk more that way. But despite insisting that Roman call him Travis, Roman knew Travis' allegiance was to the authorities and nobody else. Not the truth, not Roman, not fairness.

The windowless cell in the MobiJail smelled of disinfectant. It was empty, except for the white table and chair, and the portable Magnetic Resonance Imaging Truth machine which sat behind Roman, clicking like a zombie's teeth, waiting to get his head inside its open maw. In the corner stood a dark gray Sedationbot, a sinister reminder of what would happen if Roman became agitated. The interview would come to an abrupt end at the point of a needle.

His black and gray twelve inch wide Defenderbot sat on the table next to them, legs retracted into its body, smiling male face on the little display screen, propellers off, recording the entire session. It would beep loudly if it detected Travis asking anything that crossed the line, or Roman saying anything self incriminating. The Defenderbot could beep so loudly that it could effectively end an interview, but it had been quiet thus far.

Travis wore iBrowse, the thin gray plastic device which wrapped around the back of his head, and terminated at the two glowing dots sticking out next to his temples just in front of his eyes, providing an overlay of information to his world via projection and bone conductive sound.

Roman felt naked without his own iBrowse on. He just wanted this nightmare to be over.

"Can we just get on with the test, dude?" He could feel his Admiration Points slipping away.

Travis nodded, "I'll take that as confirmation," and he tapped the touchpad on his chest. Roman automatically slid backwards into a white padded machine and his chair clicked into place. A large magnet wrapped around the back of his head like a memory foam donut. Pads pressed down on his shoulders, forcing him to remain staring at Travis. The machine only cared about his head, that's where the truth was. The clicking sound went from being outside his skull to inside.

He tried to adjust his position to be more comfortable. There could be no cheating, no lying. This MRIT machine saw thoughts, leaving nowhere to hide. Years of mapping brain patterns and machine learning had resulted in a 99.95% reliable lie detector.

Two displays sat on the small table in front of Travis, who leaned forward. "Don't be dancin' around the truth. Just let it out. The quicker you tell me what really happened, the quicker this is over." He nodded in an attempt to get Roman to agree, then looked at something in his AR.

Travis' slight southern accent made Roman wonder what brought him here to Los Angeles.

"Address?"

"7001 Franklin ave, Apartment 5," Roman replied.

He thought he saw Travis flash a smile. Few people would notice that he lived in the Magic Castle apartments. Roman loved old fashioned magic, and he wished he could disappear right about now.

"Y'all are related to Roman Glass Sr., right?"

He got asked this all the time, and quickly deduced that Travis already knew he was the son of the famous exobiologist and was fishing for an emotion. "Yeah. He's my father. Was my father." *Until he was murdered. By someone like you.*

Travis nodded. "Why'd y'all go over to Starla's condo tonight?"

"I was hired to do a new scan of her at a higher resolution, to update her geometry and sculpt." Roman wanted to itch his face, but knew he should sit still. "The records of me being hired to scan her will be in StarSee's database."

"We'll gain access to that if we see fit," said Travis. "Thanks for letting me know how to do my job."

Roman clenched his jaw and pushed on. "I figured the extra watchers might get me more Admiration Points, which could boost my crappy StreamBug subscription to a better quality."

"But why tonight?"

"I didn't ask questions. It was Starla. It's been a few years since I last scanned her, maybe she'd lost some weight or something. I don't ask why stars want new scans, you know? It's usually because they've had some work done."

"You two had bad blood. Why'd she want you to do it?"

"We don't have bad blood, man. That was all blown out of proportion."

"Regardless, why'd you want to work with her again?"

"Admiration Points. Working with her would have gotten me thousands. Besides, I've been trying to get more involved in entertainment, you know?"

Travis glanced at the readouts. His expression remained perfectly neutral. "Afraid I don't know, Mr. Glass. But go on, what happened after you arrived?"

The machine continued softly clicking in Roman's ears. It was a form of torture that alone was enough to make him want to tell the truth. "We chatted, she poured us drinks. It's a nice place, top floor, pretty views. She mostly stayed to her side of the room. She had on a skintight bodysuit."

"Aint it better if she's naked?" Travis raised an eyebrow.

"Nah, hyperthin body suits can actually help with scars. This is L.A. after all." Roman attempted a smile.

"Why no intimacy coordinator?"

"She refused one, used her modesty filters instead."

"You keep a copy of the scans for yourself?" Travis smirked.

Roman knew what he was implying. "Of course I do. I'm the only person other than her that's allowed to have a copy, and it's locked to me."

Travis nodded casually. "Anything unusual about the session?"

"Not really. The only thing of hers was a little stuffed bear holding plastic balloons on the bar where she poured the drinks." Roman struggled to remember. "Everything else looked set up for a catalog shoot, except for that."

Travis looked blankly at his display.

"Place was pretty big," Roman continued, "the main living area was 1,827 square feet. She told me where to set up, eight and a half feet away from a big armoire."

"That measurement is oddly specific," said Travis. "Oh yeah, you have that mental ability. What's it called, Geomapping?"

He took a deep breath. "Geosense. I instantly measure out 3 dimensional space in my head." Roman mumbled.

"Do it on me. Unless it's just your own self-promotional marketing bullshit."

Dammit. Circus monkey time.

His ability wasn't something he had to summon like a demonic power, it just happened in his brain. "Fine. This table is just slightly off level by one point three degrees to the left. You're six foot three and three-quarters inches tall, but half an inch of that is your shoes. Your arm span with your arms spread out is two inches longer than your height, which is slightly unusual. Your natural stride is about four feet, your neck size is seventeen inches, your pupils are two and five-eighths inches apart," he paused and stared at Travis, squinting, "as for what's between your legs, I can't measure what I haven't seen."

Travis chuckled and sat up straight.

"You have special cameras?"

"No, just a special code. Celebrities, anyone rich really, usually buy the rights to their own likeness in any StarStream. Their NIL. That means regular StreamBugs and cams don't work on them without authorization. So if you're gonna scan them, your camera or StreamBug subscription has to have an authorization code that allows it."

"But celebs are always being captured on other people's StarStreams."

"Yup, and all those StreamBugs and paparazzi get authorization codes. Not everyone knows that, but you do."

Travis stared defiantly at Roman.

"So, like, to scan her, my cameras grab the data and imagery and immediately securely save it to my personal Vault files. It's all very secretive and I'm under a strict NDA. Anyway, I open the kit, and my camera rises where she's supposed to stand. She steps into the area where I'm going to scan her, and then she shut off the lights."

"How detailed are your scans?"

"Super close, down to the pupils."

"Did you start scanning?"

"I dunno. I barely remember anything after bending over to open the camera case. Like I told you, I think someone drugged me."

"Are you suggesting drugs made you do it? That's your defense?"

"I don't know! I just know how I feel."

Travis examined the readout more closely. "Afraid the lab work doesn't show any drugs, Mr. Glass, other than booze. And there've been problems in that area before, am I right?"

"I've had the shot. I can't get drunk now."

"Maybe you swapped one addiction for another? Now you're addicted to Admiration Points?"

Roman sighed. *Cheap shot.* "Anyway, I blacked out, and I don't know what happened."

"You committed murder's what happened."

The Defenderbot flashed red and beeped so loudly that both Travis and Roman jumped.

"Let's watch the stream." Travis rotated a display around so that Roman could see it. This was the part where the authorities showed the perp the crime to see how their brain reacted. It was a slam dunk in most cases, because the perp can't help but recognize the events, which means the perp is guilty. Then it's off to HardJail.

"Have you previously seen or heard any recordings of the events that occurred between you and Starla Devine this evening?"

"Nope."

"A simple yes or no will do." Travis tapped a keyboard that only he could see.

Roman watched as the volumetric playback of his low rent StarStream fast forwarded, slowing down at the point where she turns out the lights. On the display, in the darkness of Starla's condo, Roman's cheap StreamBug subscription could barely make out anything.

"Your geomapping makes it so you can get around, right? Even when it's dark?"

"Geosense," Roman corrected him again. "And yes, as long as things don't move once I have the mental picture."

"Convenient." Travis' lips curled slightly.

Shadowy figures move around in the murky darkness on the recording. The sound of a scuffle, Starla screams. "Roman, stop it!" The sounds of a struggle continue. *I don't remember any of this.* Grunting and thumping, glass breaking, something being dragged. A thud. Something falls. Hard. A long stretch of silence. Too long. Roman tried to imagine what was happening. Starla screams a blood curdling cry. A loud crash. The sounds of broken furniture settling. Everything goes silent.

Roman looked up at Travis, who was watching Roman's brain for any sign of recognition. Despite Travis' poker face, Roman could tell that he knew Roman was experiencing all of this for the first time.

Travis fast forwarded the stream. The lights flickered and came back on. Charlie, Starla's Digital Assistant, had detected trouble. Roman lay on top of Starla, the bloody award in his right hand.

Travis stopped the playback. "Roman Glass, did you knowingly cause the death of Starla Devine?"

"No! You're watching my brainwave analysis! You know I'm telling the truth, man."

Travis shook his head like something was broken. "I found you there, lying on top of her dead body. And your StarStream tells the story."

"Come on, man." Roman's frustration was growing fast. "This is crazy! I would've gotten thousands of Admiration Points. I have zero reason to want her dead!"

"Except for your history."

"I didn't care about that!"

Travis' face tightened. "There were only two of you in the room, and now only one of you is alive. I reckon maybe you cared a lot."

The Defenderbot beeped and flashed bright orange on Travis' side. He switched off the MRIT. "We'll solicit the stream from Starla's StreamBugs that were set to privacy mode and find out what they saw during the blackout. That'll probably take at least a day or two to get out of StarSee, but it'll come out. Even if she didn't have night vision on, we'll be able to rebuild the entire scene once we have it."

"Yeah, I know all about rebuilding scenes. And I promise you, it'll also show I'm innocent."

"We'll see about that." Travis' iBrowse chirped. He swiped the touchpad on the left side of his chest to answer the call. His eyes flitted. "Yes, I thought the same thing... Yes, the social media division asked those questions... Yes, I will... Okay." He tapped his touchpad again. Roman couldn't know if he was talking to someone in the next room or the next state. "That was my partner, Detective Mascon. He corroborates the findings. Because you passed the MRIT, and your brainwave patterns indicate you're not a threat, you'll be released to HomeJail. You'll be given full instructions on the way home." Travis stood up, "but then, you already know them, don't you?" He straightened out his shirt. "Enjoy the next few days, Mr. Glass. You better hope once we see the clean stream from Starla's StreamBugs that it shows a ninja sneaking in, and killing her with your hands while holding the award you wanted."

The Defenderbot shrieked.

"Yeah, yeah." Travis yelled at the device. He glanced at the floor and then straightened himself out. "Sorry Mr. Glass, I'm in a piss poor mood. The amount of murders I'm dealing with lately is crazy, and I just got word of another one." Detective Travis Clark spun on his heel and walked to the door.

His stride was in fact four feet and two inches.

Roman sat in his chair, trembling with clenched fists. To be accused of something he didn't do was one thing, for there to be proof that he did it in this day and age, when cameras are everywhere all the time, felt like a nightmare.

He would soon be HomeJailed. His mind was already planning what to do next. He desperately needed help. *My team is loyal, but will they believe me after they see a recording of what appears to be me killing Starla Devine?*

CHAPTER
TWO

Monday, 9:45 p.m.

Social Media Investigator Rae Dettmer surveyed the grizzly tableau. A decapitated body sat slouched forward on the couch like a teapot having just finished pouring blood on the floor from her open neck. The woman's head lay next to her body on the couch, eyes fixed in a dead stare, watching StarSee streams still playing on the giant quantum dot living room display. Small gray clouds of StreamBugs that broadcast everything on StarSee swarmed around the dozens of blue and red lights that flashed through the evening haze outside the windows of the yellow tape wrapped house. There were no crowds gathered outside on the cracked Los Angeles suburban street, everybody was inside watching on their live StarSee streams. They would not know the stink of the fresh blood that permeated the air inside the house, even through the ever present smell of distant fires.

On her department issued iBrowse, Investigator Dettmer could access all the details of the neighborhood; who lived in the home, nearby sex offenders, recent purchases made by the deceased, etc.

Every detail appeared in her vision as she carefully stepped through the open home, careful not to get any blood on the cuffs of her navy blue pantsuit. She wore hyperthin gloves and had her dark hair pulled up and back.

These scenes of bizarre violence and tragedy were becoming more frequent. The Lake Balboa area would not have been the kind of neighborhood Dettmer would expect someone to break in to a home and chop off a woman's head, but that was changing now. The real-time mayhem was becoming commonplace as people grew more numb to the onslaught of violence in the city.

Being here at the scene of the murder brought back her days in the Homicide Division and made her stomach churn. But nothing replaced being here in person, not even the very best AR money could buy.

Homicide Detectives Mascon and Travis watched Dettmer carefully, as if she were an eight year old among priceless artifacts. Mascon, an older detective with a beer belly and gray hair, stepped forward.

"Shouldn't you be off investigating Totalfake scammers?" he said.

Travis Clark, a recent transfer to the department, was younger and taller. "Yeah, the phrase is *stay in your lane*," he said.

Dettmer turned slowly to face the two of them. She was used to this treatment. She had heard it a thousand times that her department was a play division that did nothing but delete mean posts and fine people for hate speech. The Social Media Division was originally created with the blessing of the social media platforms, to investigate cases of fraud and harassment, people scamming others out of Admiration Points, but she was increasingly being called upon to help Homicide Detectives figure out the relationships between people in apparently random crimes connected only by their social media accounts.

"Unfortunately, this is my lane now." Her unmistakable Dutch accent came through. She turned to Travis, the second fiddle.

"These two did not know each other except through StarSee. Is that right?"

Mascon rolled his eyes. "Guess that's why you're here." He walked over to the body on the couch, careful not to step in the large puddle of warm blood. "Victim, female mid forties, Lucia Morales. She was on the Land Management Council for the Hollywood Hills. No iBrowse, was watching the streams on her main screen here when the perp, Justin Kelling, entered through a sliding door, snuck up behind her and swung a medieval battle ax at her neck, cleanly cutting off her head." He pointed to the front door where a five-foot long double-sided battle ax leaned against the wall as if a knight had just come home after a hard day's work, a smear of wet blood across the blade.

"Has the murder weapon been touched?"

Mascon turned to Travis, who shook his head. "I was first on scene and it was right where it is now."

"First on scene again, Travis?" Asked Dettmer. "You were first on the Starla Devine scene too, right?"

"I'm new. I have to try harder."

"Where is our perpetrator now?"

"In the MobiJail," said Mascon. "Admitted he killed her, immediately regretted it and called 911. Not that he needed to call anyone. Three hundred streams worth of watchers had already notified us as soon as they realized it was real."

"How did he get here?"

"SDV. Solo. Said nothing the whole way. We checked the car," said Travis.

"Apparently he was a LARPer and had quite a few watchers," said Mascon, who stood with his hands clasped over his belly.

Dettmer glanced around the house. "Live Action Role Play? Pretty gigantic leap for someone to go from LARPing to murder."

"Doesn't surprise me," said Mascon. "He already pretended to kill people. This was just one step farther."

"The thing is, that is not how it works. LARPing releases

tensions. It allows for a sense of recreation and role playing that lets steam out of the pressure cooker. In all the years I was in Homicide, I witnessed no one who played at LARPing actually kill someone."

"Well, now you have." Mascon smirked.

"If you know your shit so well, why'd you quit Homicide?" asked Travis.

Mascon grimaced and shook his head as Travis entered into dangerous territory. "Her old partner, Carmen, had... issues."

Travis got the hint and changed the subject. "I came straight here from testing the accused killer of Starla Devine. He passed."

"Really? I thought he was broadcast doing the deed live on stream?" asked Dettmer.

"He was, but no recognition neurons fired during the playback test. It was unusual."

"Starla Devine, Queen of StarSee." Mascon tilted his head at Dettmer. "Guess since it's the socials, your team will be involved, right? You'll be hobnobbing with the rich and famous?"

"I am quite sure I will find my way around," she sneered. "Speaking of which, I am going to visit our ax wielding man's home after this."

"No need, we sent bots in. It's clean," said Travis.

"Oh really? You looked at his StarSee history?"

The two detectives looked at each other like siblings being asked if the dog had been fed. "Everything we need to know is right here, covered in blood," said Travis.

"I did not think so. You should not judge the book by how it looks."

"By its cover," said Travis. "The phrase is judge a book by its cover."

Reflected in the pool of blood on the floor, the display still glowed with a dozen StarSee streams. Several were the outside of the house she was standing in right now, others were outside of Starla Devine's condo. It was a busy night.

"Did he own iBrowse?" asked Dettmer, assuming he could not afford iRiz.

"Yep, in evidence," said Mascon as the two Homicide Detectives headed for the door.

Dettmer spent fifteen minutes looking through the victim's computer. After inserting a simpin and running the code that sorted through the files and streams of the victim's systems faster than any human possibly could, aggregating and comparing data and watcher networks, it immediately determined that the killer knew her, but she did not know him at all.

Another one.

The crime scene crews would finish up, and then the cleanup crews would come in. So much blood. There was little more to see here that would help her understand why this happened. She headed out into the hazy suburban night. Uniformed officers leaned against their SDVs as various bots documented the scene. StreamBugs quietly hissed as they picked her up and followed her to her car. She got in the back passenger's seat of her departmental Self Driving Vehicle.

Dettmer said, "Digital Assistant, warrant for personal computer data, first forty-eight hour window, case ID Justin Kelling one one seven, district of Bellflower, CA."

The display on her iBrowse chimed green. Warrant approved.

Monday, 10:41 p.m.

After investigating Justin Kelling's home, Dettmer rode through West Los Angeles on the 405 freeway, a route she had taken so many times she barely even looked out the window. But tonight, the massive white, glass and steel StarSee Towers, lit up like three large fingers in the distance, caught her eye. Highway traffic was always busy, an unsafe mix of gasoline, electric, self-driving and human-operated vehicles. The car did not find it worthwhile to connect to other cars in the SDV Connect lane, therefore, it navigated through normal traffic. She spent so much time in the rear passenger's seat of this vehicle that it was like her second office, and it looked like it.

She was filing the reports to wrap up the night and had as many questions as answers. Kelling lived with his mother, worked at the shipping depot, and loved LARPing. She had her software dig into his accounts and run a quick analysis before locking them up. There was no manifesto or confession. His Stream was hours of him trying to attract attention by dancing, making weapons, pretending to be a medieval knight and rambling on about freedom. He was on the side of the fence that insisted any government regulations, no matter how small, were tantamount to Orwellian authoritarianism.

He had barely any direct on-line interaction with the victim at all, but had lengthy conversations with someone named Larpers-Friend393 in which the victim's name came up repeatedly. The discussions all took place on a dedicated page called *#FunIsNot-ACrime*, a page with only a handful of members. A scan of his entries on the page revealed a pattern of intensifying anger toward the victim. Earlier today, he was worked up into a rage over the idea that the victim wanted to make LARPing illegal since it was a dangerous practice ground for criminals. It took Dettmer no time to do a quick search on her own iBrowse to find out that none of this was true. Neither the victim, nor anyone on the council, were considering making LARPing illegal. Justin's last entry had been *"Wish me luck friend, I'm doing this for all of us. Dieu et mon droit!!"* Her iBrowse translated the text for her, *"God and my right!"*

Her iBrowse chirped with an incoming call. She made a hand gesture similar to grabbing her eyes and throwing them at the display, as if there was a hair in front of her face that she wanted to grab and toss away. As a result, her partner Mo's image appeared on the display in the center console between the two front seats.

His face looked larger and more round than it would in reality, which meant his display was live 3D mapping from his own iBrowse cameras. Her image, with the two glowing iBrowse dots by her temples, appeared in a smaller window. Seeing herself, she adjusted her hair tie so that her hair was pulled back into her ponytail more evenly.

"Crazy night. Where y'at?" he asked, the New Orleans version of "how are you?" Lights played on his face. He was also riding.

"Good. Headed home. Just got done with Justin Kelling's home, the ax-wielding man."

"Why waste your time? He already admitted that he did it to stop her from passing laws against LARPing."

"The thing is, I did not find any evidence that she was engaged in any such thing. Lucia Morales was on a land management council for the Hollywood Hills, but the two of them had no inter-action. She did not appear to even know who he was. He posted to her Stream, but she did not reply or block him. He and someone named LarpersFriend393 were somehow convinced that she was going to eliminate their pretend games. That boy took someone else's life and threw away the rest of his own, believing that killing someone was the best course of action for some greater cause."

"It's always the greater cause that justifies the worst behavior."

"True, but not very helpful," she said. "I am making use of the forty-eight hours I have to analyze his StarSee data before it goes to the Vaults."

As usual, she would have to work within the confines of The Lisa Lam Law, which was passed to help real investigators by reducing the number of amateur internet sleuths on a case. Before the law passed, homebodies would pour over every detail of a case on line and spew out hundreds of theories, creating a mob-like opinion of the case, flooding investigators with crazy leads that had to be pursued, and often ruining actual investigations by tipping off suspects. But in reality, the byproduct of the law was that it also made it harder for Dettmer and her colleagues. Forty-eight hours after a serious crime, all the StarSee data would go to the StarSee Data Vault, and she would physically need to go to the Towers to investigate it.

"Something strange is going on, Mo. This is different. I feel it."

"Sure seems like it's been gettin' worse."

Outside her window, the streetlights went from light blue solar lights to amber, signaling that she had turned off the highway. "If I just had access to StarSee metadata, I could run full analysis code and track the patterns."

"Ha!" Mo burst out a laugh like it was a single shot from a cannon. "Getting access to StarSee metadata is like pulling out King Arthur's sword. The Blakewells have nearly completely walled off their internal data. But hey, if you want to buy some aggregated data, I'm sure they'd be happy to sell you that."

"On my salary? I could buy a few lines of buying preferences, maybe."

"That's how they get ya," said Mo, smiling. "The first few lines of data are cheap…"

She chuckled. "Busy night. Let me know if I can help with the Starla Devine stuff tomorrow."

"Yeah, there's already a hundred theories floating around about why he did it."

"But he passed the MRIT. So maybe he is innocent?"

"Too much evidence to the contrary. It's his brain playing tricks."

"I keep telling you that cannot happen. Even dissociative amnesia caused by trauma would be revealed in the tests."

Mo looked unconvinced.

"Is he safe from mobs?" she asked.

"He's headed to HomeJail now. He'll have extra security bots at the doors for tonight."

"What are the next steps?"

"We requested Starla's clean StreamBug recording. As soon as StarSee releases it, we'll have more answers."

Her car rocked up and down over a speed hump. "I am almost home. See you in the morning."

"Don't work too late again, cher." replied Mo, as he disconnected.

She would still sit in her SDV for another half hour, finishing up her paperwork. *Funny that they still call it paperwork when there is not a piece of paper in sight.* Mo was right, she was already working too late again.

CHAPTER
THREE

Tuesday, 9:52 a.m.

Roman watched helplessly as the murder of Starla Devine reverberated around social media like the echo of a gunshot on an empty Los Angeles street. Every watcher watched it, and every streamer re-streamed it. Anyone that hadn't witnessed it happening live, had seen the recording by now.

Is it possible I killed the queen of StarSee? He wished the interrogations would've extracted some knowledge from the dark void of his own memory. But there was nothing there. The struggle in the dark either did not happen, or the drugs someone used on him had wiped the experience from his mind, which should be impossible.

While he was being interrogated, they had installed the Home-Jail system at every entrance, exit and window in his apartment, which could deliver a shock that was the equivalent of being tased. Now he was locked in until the hearing, tormented by the fact that he could not remember what really happened, but knowing in his heart that he would not, and could not, have done what they said.

Pacing his twelve-hundred-square-foot apartment, he

continued trying to work out a problem in his head for which there was no solution. He walked from one end of his place, his geosense envisioning where every wall, every piece of cheap furniture and every barely functioning appliance sat as well as any StreamBug volumetric representation could.

He stopped, opened his eyes and glanced at the clock in his iBrowse display again. Almost time.

Orange sunlight poured into the room through the thin gray cloud of StreamBugs gathered outside the windows trying to peer inside. Those particular StreamBugs, called Free Agents, were not subscribed to by any one person or group, but were provided by StarSee free of charge as a way to capture reality and get people hooked. Because they were not assigned to any Streamer in particular, random watchers could look through them and direct them. They were controlled on a first-come first served basis, but watchers could always view whatever they were broadcasting. The popularity of reality voyeurism quickly overrode any privacy battles that arose.

The Free Agents might catch glimpses, but Roman's subscription StreamBugs were the only ones allowed inside his private residence. His own StreamBugs were always there, hovering near the ceiling, following him from room to room, broadcasting his life to the watchers. As he watched them swarm like a microscopic flock of birds, he began to wonder about the watchers on the other side of his StarStream, and whether they believed he was guilty or innocent. The thought that they might abandon him forever sent shivers down his spine. To Roman, the combination of watchers and Admiration Points were what gave him confirmation that he was valued by his friends and society. Without them, he was just taking up space in an already crowded city.

An angry mob was already forming at the end of the driveway. Living in the Magic Castle Apartments had the advantage of having a long driveway that was legally private property, keeping the raucous gathering at a distance. He could hear them shouting his name from the street, two-hundred-forty-three feet away.

Closing his blinds, he sat down in his office chair. Behind him, the antique poster of his favorite classic science fiction movie, *2001: A Space Odyssey*, hung on his wall. He gestured in front of his iBrowse, making the throwing motion to his display, and then removed his iBrowse and tossed them on his desk.

His StarSee app popped up on the far left side of his giant ultra-thin desktop monitor. His favorite StarStreams were all highlighted with a green border, and there were a few new ones highlighted in yellow that were suggested based on overnight interest polls and who he already watched. Every box was a 3D window into someone else's life. Several were going about their business as the StarSee software popped up text balloons containing interesting facts about where they were and what they were doing, such as what they were eating or where they were going. Turn on "Star's Say" and the most popular "caption this" responses were displayed over the actions of the participants.

Fully-digital AI generated entertainment, as completely photo-real as it was, had enjoyed its time in the sun, but now, possibly because of StarSee's popularity, the pendulum had swung the other way. Real people, real lives. That's what everyone wanted now.

Roman tended to stay away from Streamers that were always putting on a show, dancing wherever they went, hugging random people, or dressing outrageously. He preferred to watch people with interesting professions, like a pilot, a firefighter, or a stripper.

Roman had been on the verge of earning enough Admiration Points to level up. More watchers equaled more StreamBugs, which meant a better quality Stream, which meant more watchers. He felt the pull. He wanted to rejoin the real lives of the real people that he was voyeuristically addicted to. Pulling himself away, he tapped his touchpad on his chest, navigated the menus, and turned on his Digital Assistant.

Because HomeJail was not technically incarceration, he was encouraged to keep working. The loophole was that they hadn't specified what he could work on, so proving his innocence was at the top of his list.

"Hal, start team meeting." The window popped open on his huge display, waiting. He nervously tapped his hand on his leg while he waited for his team to log in.

He saw his own photo icon and was reminded that he wanted to change it. His shaggy hair, blue eyes and slightly crooked smile made him look like he wasn't serious. Sure, he was basically a happy twenty-eight-year-old surfer dude, but he needed to project an air of professionalism if he wanted his business to grow.

Switching to his live Stream, all his StreamBugs swarmed in front of him. Upon seeing his Stream displayed, Roman immediately realized that after last night's lack of sleep, he looked awful, despite his colorful Hawaiian shirt and shorts.

At exactly 10:00 am, Seven, Tek and Pete, his three closest colleagues turned friends, blinked into existence within 10 seconds of each other. Except for Pete, who was new, this team of people had been assembled years ago as Roman's top picks to work in the high-tech entertainment field in which he was endeavoring to succeed.

Seven sat in a tropical paradise, her curly red hair and freckled dark skin providing a striking contrast to the lush green and blue scenery in which she sat, wearing a white bathrobe. It was impossible to tell whether she was actually in a tropical paradise or was just placing herself there. Knowing Seven's financial status, she certainly could be jetting around the world to the different locations she frequently appeared in. Roman felt a pang of envy.

Tek, in contrast, sat in his home office, a high-tech junkyard of old and new monitors and tables covered with disassembled equipment. Roman did not know whether Tek was his nickname or birth name, and he didn't care. The mid-thirties South Korean with blond hair could have been in a boy band, but was genuinely brilliant at solving technology issues. Roman was lucky to have hired him. Tek wore iRiz, the most expensive contact lens AR devices available. For audio, Tek had the two telltale dots sitting just in front of his ears.

Roman started speaking abruptly. "Thanks for jumping on, I appreciate you guys."

Seven was the first to reply. "We're here for you, Roman, whatever you need. After what you did for us, me especially, we owe you."

"I keep telling you, there's no debt owed. Where's my sister?" he asked.

"On location for a photo shoot." Seven's bright red frizz framed her dark face like a halo. "She sends her love and says to keep your head up."

"The evidence looks bad, but I don't trust it," said Tek.

It wasn't the first time someone had accused Roman of a crime. His name attracted a lot of attention. But this time was different, and this crime was worse. "Thanks guys, it's crazy, right?" he said. "I don't like to ask for help, but I think I need it. I'm being framed, and we need to figure out who's doing it and why." Roman was a tilt-a-whirl of emotions, spinning from pissed off at being falsely accused, through to scared that the charges might stick, and then, deeply saddened by the tragedy of Starla Devine's death. "Pete, you're new, if you have reservations about helping me out, man, I completely understand, you know?"

"Not a problem, I'm happy to do what I can." Pete reminded Roman of a Labrador puppy. Blond hair, unmanicured scruffy beard, always smiling and excitable. "You really can't remember anything?" Pete's resting smile face made it seem like he was always thinking that what he said was funny.

"No, nothing. I totally passed the MRIT, so this whole thing is a setup. I just dunno why."

"First of all, let's all remember we're monitored, as always, so think about what you want to say before you speak," said Seven.

"Second, let us do some ground work Roman. I know people who can help." She leaned closer to her camera, smiled and nodded reassuringly. Roman realized her green eyes were glowing slightly, which meant she was also wearing iRiz.

"If you didn't do it, I'm sure the authorities will figure out who did," said Pete.

"The authorities?" Roman chuckled. "They don't care about us, the little guy, the innocent people! They're all in bed together, cops, corporations, politicians. They're all part of the same system designed to make the rich richer!"

The meeting went quiet. *Jeez, I sound like my dad sometimes.* Even though his parents were scientists, they were also what most people would call hippies. Roman took a deep breath and exhaled slowly through his nose, determined not to lose his cool. Pete could be forgiven for trusting the authorities, since he likely didn't know Roman's full history.

Roman cleared his throat. "So... Starla Devine," he announced, his voice quivering. The Defenderbot in the corner of the room lifted itself a few inches higher at the sound of Starla's name, as if on alert.

Out of the corner of his eye, he saw his watcher numbers start to rise. Like the Defenderbot, his watchers must have had his Star-Stream set to tune in on certain keywords. "I don't like to ask for help, but I need you guys. I want to figure this out, not just for me, but for Starla. Whoever actually killed her is getting away with it, and she doesn't deserve that."

"You know her family, right Roman?" asked Seven.

"Yeah, after the first time I scanned her, I became friendly with her and her mother. She was a military kid. Father passed away a long time ago. Has a brother, Paul. He's older, I think. Him and her mother both live in Massachusetts. Good people. Extremely unlikely that they had anything to do with this."

"Money can be a potent motivator," said Tek. "And as the

number one StarSee Streamer, she was very, very rich. We can't dismiss that someone was after her money."

"If someone was just after her money, why frame Roman for her murder?" asked Seven.

Roman unconsciously bit his lip. His emotions were dangerously close to the surface. "We gotta figure out who would want her dead, and why."

Pete chimed in. "Have you reconsidered giving your T-fake tracing token to the cops so that they can contact-trace you? Maybe the real killer had some interaction with you, you just don't remember."

"I dunno, man."

"I know you're leery of giving your data to the cops, but they already have your history from every Stream on StarSee. This is purely protection against Totalfakes," said Tek.

Roman thought about it. The Totalfake laws were fairly simple and universally accepted. If you were not physically in the place that the Totalfake showed you to be, at the time that the Totalfake showed you to be there, a large T-fake icon was placed as a watermark on the screen. That way, someone could not show the president kicking a puppy at the airport at 2:04pm when the President's actual location at that time was in a meeting at the White House. But users had to allow the software to track where they were at all times.

"It's not the tracking that bothers me," said Roman, "it's just another piece of hardware and software that another company extracts subscription fees for. First, someone invents the problem of Totalfakes, then we have to pay for the solution, and it's not cheap."

"If you don't have a token, is there a chance that the recording of the murder was entirely Totalfaked?" asked Pete.

"Even if I did, the problem is, I was there. And it's my actual Stream in the recording. Whoever's framing me knew I would turn off the lights, knew I have a cheap StreamBug subscription. It's like the opposite of a Totalfake."

"And the fact that you hit her with that particular statue doesn't help either," said Tek.

"I didn't hit her, dude." Roman sighed. "Plus, that whole thing went away years ago." He paused and took a breath, looking from person to person. "Look, guys, I know it looks like I hit her. And you're right, that specific weapon makes things look even worse, but you gotta know it wasn't me."

"I didn't mean for it to come out that way. I'm sorry," said Tek.

"Maybe the fact that it was that particular weapon means something," said Pete.

"Yeah, they know it makes me look guilty."

"I'll do a search, connections to the award, just to see what I find," said Seven. "Someone obsessed with the awards maybe, who thinks you tarnished the show or something." She leaned a little closer to her screen. "Roman, we'll figure this out. We always do."

"Thanks Sev, I appreciate it."

"Listen Roman, in a couple of hours, I'll have more information and then we can talk about a plan, okay? We all know you're not capable of killing anyone, especially not Starla, and we'll figure this out if we don't panic." Her tone changed and became more upbeat. "Let's talk about something else for a minute, okay? Sometimes answers come to us when we're not trying to think of them."

"I guess it would be best to keep working." He put his hands on the sides of his head as if he had to hold his brains in. He shook his head back and forth quickly, blew raspberries, and gave himself a couple of gentle slaps on the cheek. He put his iBrowse back on so he could see the AR keyboard on his desk and tapped a few keys. A chart popped up on everyone's displays, showing a timeline for Roxy's House Project.

Most of Roman's bread and butter business was in removing, sculpting and adding logos to AR and VR scenes, but in his sister's case he was using his team's skills to help her with an insurance case. It was a far cry from what he hoped to become involved in, which was entertainment, but he would do anything for his twin sister.

"Let's talk about her old house," said Seven. "The insurance company is still saying the damage from the fires was because Roxy didn't clear the brush behind her place." A volumetric display of Roxy's previous rental property popped up onto the screen.

"Did we provide the insurance company with the three simulations, proving that she couldn't have prevented the house fire without cutting down the trees herself? Which she was not permitted to do?" asked Roman.

"Not yet. Licensing the burn data from the city is going to cost us. I'm not sure how we can pull this off without a paying client," said Tek.

"Roman," said Seven, "if you transferred some of your Admiration Points over to the Atlantis Project, we could take out an advance, and we'd have money for your sister's project now."

"I know, and I want to, but not yet. We'll find another way to fund my sister's case," said Roman. He sniffed the air. Sometimes it seemed that as soon as he started talking about his sister's project, the smell of smoke in the air got stronger. It was probably psychological, but fire season was no longer a season so much as a euphemism. Fires in the hills of Los Angeles were so common that reporting on the fires had replaced a segment on the weather on the news.

Roxy, was lucky she wasn't home when the house she was renting burned down. He had tried to warn her landlord that three trees created a bridge that fire could cross and make its way to the house, which is exactly what happened. His warning had become a double-edged sword however, since the insurance company now tried to say that since Roxy knew the trees might be a problem, she should have trimmed them herself.

"I know we're doing this project without pay, so I really appreciate it. She's always looked out for me, and now it's my turn to return the help," said Roman.

"Absolutely," said Seven.

"By helping you, she's helped us," said Tek.

Pete nodded.

"And Seven, she digs that townhouse you found for her. Thanks for that." Roman glanced at his watcher count on his StarSee page. It was slowly going down. The watchers must be getting bored. He had been watching the short-term counts too much lately. Much like the stock market, he knew he should pay attention to the trends, not the minutes. But the StarSee award on his shelf for having a million watchers for one week was now two and a half years old, and he would love to get another one soon.

"I just can't figure out why all this is happening," said Roman.

"It's bad enough getting arrested for things you did do, right?" Seven wore a smirk on her face.

"Have you been arrested before?" asked Pete.

"Just for stupid stuff like protests, and I hit someone at a bar that was badmouthing my late father. But this time is different. They might just take the next step of Legal Sedation. And that is damned petrifying."

"I've done it. Just to see what it was like. It's actually not that bad," said Pete, smiling as usual.

"Then you can take my place, because I'm not going under. We've got to figure this out before it comes to that."

"Pete'll do it for you, right Pete?" said Seven. "We didn't tell you, but part of the initiation is that you take the place of your new boss who has been accused of murder and then get sedated!"

The group chuckled. Roman leaned back and checked the time. "I'm supposed to call the lead Social Media Investigator back in ten minutes. I'll let you all know how it goes."

"Keep your Defenderbot nearby," said Tek.

"You kidding? It won't leave me alone." Roman looked at the

small hovering device that had set itself down on his reading chair in the corner. "It's like an overgrown StreamBug."

"Let your Defenderbot do its job, especially when you talk to this investigator," said Seven.

"Not to worry, gang. I, of all people, will not trust the authorities when I shouldn't."

After planning to conference again if any of them found anything, they disconnected one by one, leaving Roman sitting alone with his StreamBugs. He expanded the StarSee page on his monitor. He had time for a few minutes of watching before his call, it would be a quick little distraction. He just wouldn't get drawn into posting anything. Not this time.

CHAPTER
FOUR

Tuesday, 12:40 pm

Maddox Blakewell, the obsessive, brilliant programmer, the incredibly rich man who could have and do anything he wanted in life, was pissed off. He stood in the large darkened StarSee Gray Room at the head of his conference table, berating the virtual image of one of his young programmers, who stared back at him like a wide-eyed anime character. Maddox Blakewell was not happy. But Maddox Blakewell was rarely happy.

The son of Owen Blakewell, the founder and CEO of StarSee, Maddox may have inherited his father's business acumen and his mother's dark curly hair, but where he got his height, or lack thereof, was a mystery. Standing only five feet four inches, Maddox's short stature in real life was not visible to the programming team's virtual conference room display, since he had programmed his own stream to make himself appear taller than everyone else in the room. Everyone knew his image was augmented, but it still empowered Maddox to carry on like a tyrant.

The Gray Room, as it was called, where the meeting was being held was the Blakewell's favorite room in the massive StarSee Towers headquarters. It was the ultimate display of the company's power, looking out through floor-to-ceiling glass windows over the entire City of Los Angeles. On one side of the room stood the very heart of the technology that drove the company. The Machine Room. Glass enclosed the room of quantum computers that maintained the real life reality show of the StarSee world. He took advantage of any excuse he could to use this room for meetings, especially public facing ones. They even held banquets in this room so that as attendees enjoyed whatever function was happening, they would be wowed by the blinking, humming presence of the company's awesome computing power.

Currently, he had the exterior city view blacked out, so that the room was dimly lit except for the massive floating displays. The displays updated him every minute on everything to do with the company, from who was the most watched stream of the day to the stock value, to who was gaining the most Admiration Points, to any news broadcast where the mention of the word StarSee, Maddox or Owen came up.

Maddox was the only real person in the room, and, in order to keep the employees having the same experience as most of the public, the only one allowed to wear iRiz. The team of programmers appeared in the virtual space via their company issued iBrowse, which only supplied limited connectivity in order to keep workers from surfing the internet while at work.

He had started the meeting with explicit instructions not to talk about the murder of Starla Devine. "Let the authorities complete their assignments. You may post about your sorrow on StarSee at home, but do not speak about it with colleagues or let it affect your performance. None of you really knew her, and I did. If I'm capable of not letting it trouble me, then you should do the same."

Then he quickly moved on to why he was mad. A member of

the team had dared to analyze his work. He pointed his finger at the virtual image of Vahid, a young Iranian programmer. "Don't you ever address me like you're my superior. You're not my fucking superior in any way."

Maddox turned and looked down at each of the five programmers sitting around the table and then came back to Vahid. "If you don't like that fact, then you can take your entitled ass out of this company and never be allowed to wander through my doors again. Not into this company, and not into this industry, because when I discharge someone, it ripples through the socials like a nip slip at an awards show. You will never recover."

Vahid had made the mistake of questioning whether one of Maddox's lines of code, in which he made a username password pair request, could cause a security problem later in the software for the massive company. He sat unmoving, looking unsure if he should apologize or just stay perfectly still, like a hiker confronted with a roaring bear.

Maddox grabbed a clump of his own hair as if trying to control his own brain. "I will not allow you subordinates to push me into letting my emotions get the better of me!" He couldn't stand that some junior had assumed that Maddox hadn't thought his code through, but he had to keep a level head. None of them knew the Erlang language like he did, and it was his code that made StarSee what it is today. He glared at the young man, and for a moment wasn't sure if the programmer's stream had frozen. *Perhaps he switched it to freeze frame and ran out of the real room crying. Wouldn't that be fun.* But then he noticed the StreamBugs hovering around the programmer's real space creating a swirling light gray cloud, and as the programmer glanced down at the table in capitulation, Maddox couldn't help but curl his lips into a slight smile.

"Anybody else want to assume that they know more than I do about using Elixir within the Erlang virtual machine? I fucking learned it from one of the authors' students, you morons." He leaned on the table, brows furrowed, eyes darting from one face to another. "God dammit, do you have any inkling how discouraging it is to realize that I could do any of your jobs more effectively than all of you if I had the time? You're my extensions, my surrogates. I require you to remember that, and to step up and try, at least fucking try, to do better. You are lucky to be here. Act like it."

Maddox sat back down in his chair, having exhausted his tirade. He noticed out of the corner of his eye that one of his senior programmers, Kelly, was indeed frozen, which meant she likely turned off her AR stream and went about her business while Maddox finished his outburst. Of the group, she had been with the company the longest, so Maddox would forgive her for getting work done while he flexed his authority for the newbies.

Kelly's image flickered back to life once Maddox had been silent for a few moments. She blinked and waited.

He needed to keep this team motivated. The streams into the conference table were coming from three different locations, including his, and the fact that one of the locations was only sixteen stories below, where Kelly and Vahid and the others were sitting, gave him a sense of power. He didn't even have to go down and join the plebeians.

Maddox turned his attention to one of the other programmers at the table, a young woman. "Did you at least tighten up the face replacement audio synchronization, Ashley?"

"Yes, the speech synthesis is on target now. We just have to stay within the Totalfake code of ethics and add the audio watermark if the impersonated was not at that location at that time," she answered.

"Fuck ethics!" said Maddox. "If it's legal, it's ethical." The room went quiet for a moment, waiting to see if another outburst was brewing.

"Yes, legal. That's what I meant. We need to stay within the Totalfake laws," she said.

"The reason this company is a triumph is that we go into unexplored territory. Twenty-four hour stream Channels? Meme

Factory? Admiration Points? The list goes on. We're here because we push forward and nobody blocks us. Let my father take the punch if we step over the line. It's not our concern."

Kelly cleared her throat. "Your father does a good job of getting the courts to rule in our favor, but we still need to tread lightly in certain areas."

"He could do better." Maddox caught himself. "God damned laws. We'd have billions more subscribers if it wasn't for these ludicrous laws." He thought for a moment. "Ashley, do me a favor..." he smiled his creepy smile at her, "... test out a voice synthesis cadence emulator as if the Totalfake law does not apply to audio. Just bypass the geolocation and time check routines temporarily. I just want to see the plain code first, and then we'll incorporate the Impulse Governor, okay?"

He could count on her not to push back on altering the boundaries, regardless of what she was comfortable with. Ashley nodded.

He abruptly leaned forward and glanced from person to person. "In order to get this vital code push completed on time, I'm introducing a contest. The deadline is only a couple of days away. Here's the game. You ready?" He smiled his best friendly boss smile, hoping it didn't appear to be a mask, which was what it felt like. "You each have your section of code that is required to run in the main system by midnight on Friday." He made a drumming noise with both his hands on the table as if building up to something, and finally slapped both hands hard on the table. Even though they were not actually in the room, the programmers flinched. "Whoever finishes their sandbox test LAST, gets to find another job! Got it?"

He watched as each of the programmers winced again. *Perfect. Now maybe they'll get some fucking work done.*

And by not firing anyone in the end, it would make him appear a gracious and forgiving leader. Sure, it was a little twisted to be the one who put someone in front of the firing squad to begin with, only to be the one to take credit for pardoning them, but the code would get done faster.

"Meeting adjourned." He pressed the disconnect button that only he could see. In a snap, the five chairs became empty. "Ouch," he said. He was certain it pissed them all off. Anger was a great motivator.

"Maria," he called on his Digital Assistant, which he had named after his mother, "Open front view blinds and get me fucking HR!" he shouted into the room and stomped toward the giant black panels on the front side of the cavernous room, his slippers slapping the rubber antistatic textured floor. Six-inch slats that covered the windows turned, revealing the view of Los Angeles from the eighteenth story of StarSee Headquarters. He stood looking out over the city in the distance as the sunlight poured into the space.

A woman appeared in his iRiz display, sitting at the conference room table where one of his programmers had just been. "This is Denise from HR. What can I do for you, Maddox?"

"Vahid. I want to report a digression. He received a warning this morning. I want it on his record."

"What was the infraction?" she asked flatly.

"Sexual misconduct. I observed him suggesting something of a sexual nature to one of my female team members during a team meeting."

The woman paused for a long moment. "Vahid is gay, Maddox."

He gritted his teeth and grimaced. He had forgotten that. "Gay people can't say inappropriate things and cross the line?"

"Of course they can. Did she report to you that she felt uncomfortable?"

"It made me uncomfortable."

"So you want to put on his permanent employee record, that you are a witness to potential hostile work environment infraction, which may affect his visa, is that right? And let me remind you that if you answer yes, I will not only have to interview her, and the team, to find out if it really happened, but I will also notify your father, who hired Vahid to begin with."

Denise was tough. This was a losing battle.

He laughed an unauthentic laugh as if it was all a joke. "No, it must have been my misunderstanding, Denise. I'll monitor it though and let you know if I witness something like this happening again, okay?"

"You do that, Maddox." She pursed her lips and raised her eyebrows. "Take care, now."

The last thing he needed was to have his father notified that he was trying to file another complaint against one of his father's personal picks for the team. He slammed his fist on the table in frustration. *I need to keep my cool. At least until our client is happy with my new product. Then my father and his trophy girlfriend will be free to go and live on a tropical island and leave the company to me. Finally.*

CHAPTER
FIVE

Tuesday, 4:30 p.m.

Rae Dettmer's fingers twitched as she sat at her little black desk. The office in the old Hall of Justice building was intended for one, but had been divided into two. Sunlight from the long horizontal windows that stretched the length of the building just above eye level filled the small dull office. A gray, eight-foot high cubicle panel with a sliding window between them divided it. She saw the size of the office as a sign of how much importance was given to the Social Media Division, and how much money in general was given to crime investigation in Los Angeles.

She looked over the data from the decapitation in Lake Balboa and added it to the data from the other recent crimes. She couldn't figure out why yet, but clearly there was a trend happening. Two people who have never physically met, almost always single and lonely, get into some kind of on-line feud, watchers increase, and one of them gets riled up enough to either kill or attempt to kill the other one.

Perhaps it was a sign of the times. People were just more prone to take what used to be a normal problem and turn it into something to kill over. Like a deadly tornado in the midst of a hurricane, it was concentrated anger that was hard to separate from the overall chaos. Watchers behaved like rubberneckers on the 405, slowing down to catch a glimpse of the carnage. Drama begets more drama, with watchers acting like a cheering section and awarding Admiration Points, until the aggressor snaps and shoots, stabs, poisons, or in this case, chops off the head of the victim.

StarSee's public position was that they should exercise as little control over their subscribers' free speech as possible. They repeatedly pointed to their adherence to the law and their voluntary use of Impulse Governors, which would kick in at signs of hate speech and threats of violence. But Dettmer sensed that there was something else going on. Some reason the Governors were not doing their job.

The data she reviewed from Justin Kelling's digital accounts was inconclusive at best. Clearly, someone was instigating Justin and feeding him lies while a crowd of watchers cheered him on, but the identity of LarpersFriend393 was hidden behind a digital wall, and she would need to access StarSee data directly to get anywhere. For access to the StarSee Vaults, she would need a warrant. And for that, she would need permission from the man with the railroad tracks on his shoulder.

Captain Rennick's corner office wasn't that much bigger than hers, but there was only one desk in it, which made it feel roomy. He held up a finger while he finished a conversation on his iBrowse. Dettmer stood patiently in his doorway, trying not to look at him.

His hair looked particularly black today. He must have just re-dyed it.

Finally, after tapping his touchpad on his chest to disconnect the call, he turned and looked at Dettmer, eyebrows raised, but not making a sound. It was passive aggressive to withhold the verbal acknowledgment, but she was used to the middle-aged man trying to assert his dominance in cheap psychological ways.

"Captain, I need to gain access to the StarSee servers."

"So pitch it at the meeting." He tapped something several times on his desk that only he could see.

"Yes sir. I know. But if I can get ahead of this, I can pitch something much bigger. There is a pattern emerging and I need access to who is behind the usernames on the killer's streams."

"Dettmer." He leaned back in his chair, his close-set eyes peering out from between the two small glowing dots of his iBrowse. "Have a seat."

Not a good sign. She tried to smile, nodded, and sat on the edge of a hard wooden chair that faced his desk. She now sat lower than him, and the late afternoon sun glared, making him a silhouette. She still could not get used to American power dynamics, even after all this time.

"This division is short on money, you know that," he stated.

"Yes, but I..."

"One way we could get more revenue into our department would be to allow StreamBugs into the offices. People would love to see what we do. You're an attractive woman, I'm sure you'd get a ton of watchers who would enjoy seeing and learning from what you do."

"The thing is, it is a total conflict of interest, sir. Allowing StarSee StreamBugs into our station just seems like letting the fox into the chicken house."

Captain Rennick slid his chair out from under his desk and stood up. "That's where you're wrong, Dettmer. You see, StarSee isn't our focus. Our focus is the subscribers." He came around and sat on the corner of his desk. "StarSee is just a platform, and we should use and benefit from that platform just as much as anyone else. It would be good publicity, and StarSee is offering us a nice chunk of the ad revenue generated by allowing the StreamBugs in. I honestly think you should consider it."

"But what if StarSee should be the focus?"

"If StarSee needs investigating, then that's up to the Financial Crimes Enforcement Network, not us." He stood back up to return to his seat.

"I do not mean a financial crime, sir..." she argued, and then realized the conversation was getting off track. She still needed to get what she came for. She cleared her throat. "Maybe I can think about it." She paused as he sank back into his chair. "Since StarSee itself is not our focus, then the warrant for end usernames should be no trouble at all." This time, she stood up. "All I need is to trace some identities."

"Denied. For now." He tapped some invisible keys on his nearly empty desk. "Bring it up at the pitch meeting. Think about what I said, talk it over with Mo. If we allow StreamBugs basic privacy protected access, we could start seeing revenue as soon as next week, which would allow me to say yes to more requests like yours."

"Yes sir." Dettmer stopped herself from saying anything further, turned and walked back to her desk. There wasn't much to think about. StarSee was already infecting people's lives, and she was dead set against letting them seep into her workplace.

Tuesday, 8:17 p.m.

Dettmer and Mo grabbed a small table near the back of the dimly lit bar. It was busy as usual. The swarms of microdrone Stream-Bugs made it easy to imagine what it was like in the days when people smoked. Due to the multiple automated safeguards, the StreamBugs stayed high enough that there was no danger of being accidentally swatted or inhaled.

She liked to observe the behavior of the groups of people drinking and laughing. A few had no AR devices, as evidenced by having normal eyes. Some had slightly glowing eyes, the sign of iRiz, but most wore iBrowse. She squinted. All she could see were dozens of pairs of lights dancing around the room. She thought of fireflies in the fields of Holland when she was a child.

The ones with the most watchers, who also had the most StreamBugs allocated to them by StarSee, acted normally, like there wasn't a camera in the room. They behaved with the confidence of someone used to being watched. The wannabees, on the other hand, were always glancing at the StreamBugs and posing, or adding comments to their StarStreams to stay engaged with their watchers.

She took her hair out of her ponytail and let it spill on her shoulders. She was on to her second glass of red, and Mo was on his third stout. Dettmer was glad to have the man as her partner. The fact that he was married kept things comfortable, and it was good to have a confidant.

"I don't think it would be that bad," said Mo. "Shit, we're already on camera everywhere we go, cher."

"Not my point." She had to talk a little louder than usual even though Mo was sitting right next to her at the sticky little two top. "The problem is with the department making money off it. It creates a conflict of interest."

Mo tapped the touchpad on his chest, the two glowing iBrowse lights at his temples dimmed. "It'd help my watcher count. They wouldn't have to stop watching us just because we went to work. Wouldn't that be cool?"

"I don't think it would be cool at all. Who cares about my watcher count? I would copyright my image if I could, so they could not show me without my permission."

Mo laughed. "Shit, you couldn't do that even if you could afford it, you're law enforcement! We have to be visible outside the office. Why do you think we don't have to wear god damned body cams anymore?"

"I just don't understand why normal people would give up their privacy just to get watchers." She shook her head.

"Everybody secretly wants to be a star."

"The thing is, it was a great trick," she said. "Getting people to sign away their privacy in exchange for fame that never really happens. Everybody thinks their own stream is suddenly going to go viral and they are going to get rich, but really we are just watching each other play house. And then, ironically, only celebrities can afford to turn off the cameras?!"

"I dunno what we can do about it."

"One case at a time, I suppose. Tomorrow, I will investigate LarpersFriend."

"Was he the shit stirrer?"

"I believe so. There has to be more to Justin Kelling murdering that woman."

"Maybe he was just bat shit crazy. Lots of peeps get worked up over stuff, but they don't go kill someone with a god damned battle ax."

"That is exactly why I am curious. He is not the first, or even the second or third."

"Well, you got the scent now, and I know you. You won't let it go. Just let me know what I can do to help. I'm your man." Mo was the guy that liked everyone when he got intoxicated, and loved everyone to the point of crying if he got hammered. "How you gonna hold on to the case though, ain't it going back to Homicide?"

"I filed a rider to the case since the victim and the perpetrator only knew each other through StarSee. Homicide is so chaotic that I will be able to solve the case before they even notice I am still on it. Speaking of which, what do you know about Travis and Mascon?"

"From Homicide? What about them?"

"Something is off about Travis. He is always first on the scene and wants to close cases quickly."

"Like you said, Homicide is chaotic and underfunded."

A commotion was happening at a table near the bar. A man wearing a purple hat was looking up at the StreamBugs and yelling something while pointing at people at another table.

Mo turned. "Everyone's so damned angry. We have everything we need, but peeps is still pissed."

"The more things are different, the more they are the same," she said.

Mo chuckled. "Almost. It goes *the more things change, the more they stay the same*." The shouting was rising in intensity. "I don't get it. I mean, I'm happy. What the fuck is there to be pissed at?"

"You are also on your third stout." Dettmer raised her wine and clinked glasses with Mo. "Proost," she said.

The argument across the room was getting more heated. The young man in the purple hat was shouting to his StreamBugs. "Fucking Iranians! They should never have been allowed to get nukes to begin with!"

Dettmer shook her head. Everyone was on different sides now, and alcohol quickly brought it to the surface.

A man from the other table stood up, Middle Eastern, tall, and shouted back, "We're not even Iranian, idiot!" He turned to his own StreamBugs. "These racist morons are what's wrong with our country!"

Nearly every StreamBug in the place, including the Free Agents, were soon hovering in the vicinity of the two men, creating a patch of dim shadow like a dark cloud for the altercation to play out beneath.

Mo and Dettmer sat like everyone else, including the bouncers, watching the mini drama unfold for the hundreds of hissing cameras. Dettmer instinctively felt for her weapon, an instant disabler. The two men advanced toward each other. No sooner had they had gotten within striking distance than a bouncer grabbed the instigator by the arm, twisted it around his back and began pushing him towards the door like a large take-out order. Another bouncer had his hands on the other man's shoulder and was clearly letting him know to take it down to zero quickly, or else he would get thrown out as well. The man put up his hands.

Applause broke out. The tall and not Iranian man waved, first to the people, and then up to the StreamBugs.

"Things are getting worse." She downed another gulp of her wine. "Where does this end?"

Mo downed the rest of his beer. "Shit, I don't know." He belched. "I'm glad we're on the same side, cher." He ran his hands through his dark hair. "I'm just thankful for how good I have it. How lucky am I that you're my partner, right?" He was stumbling headlong into crying territory.

Dettmer finished her wine. "Time to end this evening." Watching the brief bar fight almost break out gave her an idea of where to begin an analysis of the data. It wasn't much, but it was an angle, and every successful investigation resulted from looking at what was right in front of everyone from a slightly different angle.

CHAPTER

SIX

Wednesday, 8:40 a.m.

The front door sensor chimed. The strip of glowing security tape lining the opening of the door changed from red to yellow. Roman placed himself at exactly six feet away, the minimum distance he was legally allowed to get, while the HomeJail bot pulled open the frosted glass door.

It was entertaining to watch the choreographed motion of the bots as he received his groceries. Twelve feet away, in the hallway outside, was a yellow four-legged Mulebot holding two bags of groceries. Three-foot long probes extended from both bots, allowing them to touch like E.T.'s finger, a required form of authentication for anything crossing the HomeJail barrier. The security device surrounding the door flashed green, the HomeJail bot's arms extended past the threshold of the door and small hooks flipped open at the end. The Mulebot placed the bags on the hooks. The HomeJail bot scanned the bags, and finding nothing but the groceries Roman ordered, retracted back into the room.

Then the Mulebot turned and sped out of the building like an odd-looking dog, off to make another delivery.

As Roman put his groceries away, his streamBugs followed him, reminding him of his watchers. Since he was currently accused, he was instructed by his Defenderbot not to say anything directly to his watchers, and it was eating him up. He couldn't even bear to look at his Admiration Points.

His previous team meeting had been valuable, but they had spent so much talking about his case, and not about work, that Roman had been sent an automated warning from the public defender's office after reviewing the meeting, about refraining from discussing his case with those not involved. If he was caught doing it again, the Defenderbot would recommend to the courts that Roman be placed under secluded HomeJail, which would mean limited outside contact.

He would be more careful now. Not about who he talked to, but about who was listening.

Seven messaged Roman that she had managed to get in contact with Starla's family and convinced them to have a meeting with the team. Roman could listen in, but neither the Devines or his Defenderbot could know about it. Hiding it from the Devines would be easy. Turning off the Defenderbot would require the skills of Tek.

Roman navigated to his StarSee settings menu in his iBrowse, where he had to click several confirmation tabs to prove that he really truly wanted to disconnect from his streamBugs. It was the quickest way to lose both watchers and streamBugs. After clicking the final *"are you sure?"* button, his streamBugs all flew into his bedroom, which was where they landed on the docking station. "Done."

Five minutes before the meeting, Roman called Tek on his iBrowse, who popped up in Roman's view, smiling.

"StreamBugs off? We can't broadcast this."

"Yup. Feels wrong, but I did it."

"Did you physically turn off the closed captioning Line 21 sidecar data on your devices?"

"Really? That seems like overkill."

"It's not. I have software that can peek into the text record of recordings by opening the closed captioning data file. So, better to be safe."

"Okay," said Roman. He swiped through a few menus to make sure no active AI closed captioning was on. "It's off."

Tek spoke clearly and deliberately. "Now, don't say anything out loud yet. Just go over to your Defenderbot and put your hand on the ID scanner. I'm going to send the signal, and together, we're going to disable it."

Roman anxiously followed Tek's instructions for disabling the watchful eyes and ears of the Defenderbot, which included a combination of voice commands, proof of identity and waivers of liability. The Defenderbot quietly retreated to a corner and awaited reactivation.

"Thanks, Tek. I always knew I made the smart move hiring you."

"And after what you did for us, I'd be willing to do anything to help you out. I'll get Seven on here, and we can get started."

Roman swiped his touchpad, set his own display to *non-participating anonymous listener* and joined the meeting. He made the *throw to display* gesture in front of his face, and the call with Seven, Tek and Starla's family appeared on his large panoramic desktop screen.

Starla's brother, Paul, and mother, Ruth, were sitting on their black leather couch in their small Massachusetts home. Judging from the angle, looking slightly down on them from above a fireplace, Roman guessed that they were using their home entertainment display as their monitor, since Tek had requested that they turn off their streamBugs before the meeting began. Roman immediately and without thinking mentally mapped the eight-by-twenty foot room with eight-and-a-half foot high ceilings.

Starla's mother looked older than he remembered. Her brother, Paul, whom Roman had never met, was an average-looking forty-something year old with brown hair and a goatee. Roman could not tell from this distance if Paul had Starla's special heterochromatic eye color gene. Neither was wearing iBrowse.

Seven was thanking them for taking the time. She had thrown out an ice breaker about the temperature in Massachusetts, and the Devines had strained smiles on their faces, like they were pushing through their grief.

Seven continued, "Ruth, Paul, I know this is a difficult time for you, but we felt it was important to talk. We were hoping you could help us figure this out." Seven appeared to be in what looked like a luxury hotel room.

"I don't know how we can help. We don't know much about what happened at all," said Paul.

"But you know Roman, and you know he wouldn't do this," said Seven.

"I don't know..." said Ruth, "... I've been hearing on NewsCann that he was still angry about her not giving him credit for that award a few years ago."

Roman was already pushing the button requesting to join the conversation as himself.

Seven did not acknowledge Roman's request in any way. "Mrs. Devine, did she ever explain what really happened with that?"

"I'm hearing that Roman resented her for not giving him credit, maybe even enough to kill her."

Roman couldn't stay anonymous. He unmuted his audio but left the anonymous voice encoder on. "Ruth! You know that's just the media trying to make something out of nothing!"

Both Seven and Tek grimaced.

"Is that Roman?" asked Paul as he stood up. "We can't be talking to you. I'm turning this off."

"Paul, wait! Please, give me just one minute. Ruth, we've met a few times over the years, you know I loved Starla." Roman was leaning into the display even though they couldn't see him yet. "We disabled my Defenderbot. They can't use any of this conversation in court, and my stream is off. If you turn off your StarStream then this is just us talking." He unconsciously ran both hands through his shaggy hair, as if trying to flatten it out.

Seven jumped in. "Roman didn't kill Starla, and we just want to figure out who did and why they're trying to frame him. Whoever did this is still out there and getting away with it."

After a long moment, Ruth mumbled something to Paul, who said "Okay, perhaps."

"Let me switch us over to an Ultraviolet connection, so we are completely off the network," said Tek. The connection flashed purple three times as the connection became securely encrypted.

The display shifted to a slightly lower quality stationary view, like a security camera. Paul sank slowly back into his couch.

"Thank you," said Roman. He turned off the voice changer and turned on his little desk cam. "I'm sorry, I'll be calm. It's just that the whole feud between me and Starla was, like, a totally fabricated thing. I was never angry at her for not giving me credit. The reality news streams were just looking for something exciting, so they misconstrued my comments. We both said publicly that there was no argument, but we got completely ignored, because that meant there was no conflict. No conflict, no story. You know?"

Everyone sat quietly until the silence began to feel awkward.

"Okay," said Ruth. "I believe you."

Seven's window highlighted green, indicating she was about to speak. "The first question is the obvious one. I'm sorry if it's a little morbid, but did you receive confirmation that it was her body?"

"Yes," said Paul with a sigh. "DNA identification was positive. It was my sister."

"Could someone have used a Vyle to simulate her DNA ID?" asked Roman.

"No," Tek jumped in. "A Vyle can work for impersonating

someone for common DNA ID scans, but when a person dies, they do a marrow check."

"Did the autopsy reveal anything unusual?" asked Seven.

"The only things they said about the autopsy were that she was positively identified, and the cause of death was blunt force trauma to the head," said Ruth.

"Because it's a criminal case, it's standard practice to withhold information," said Tek. "In the hopes that the killer reveals themselves by letting on that they know some detail that hasn't been released yet."

Paul was suddenly uncomfortably silent. Roman sensed the chill.

"Paul, pretty much everyone loved your sister, rightfully so, but was there anyone that had bad blood with her? Not media-fabricated, but real? Maybe someone from where you are?"

"No," said Paul. "At least not publicly."

"She was so popular and pretty." Ruth's bottom lip quivered. "And then when she was signed by StarSee, back when they were a startup, it just confirmed what we all knew. She was special."

Paul grabbed his mother's hand and squeezed it.

Ruth continued, "And since she was the first StarStreamer, as StarSee kept getting more popular, so did she. Her appeal drove StarSee and StarSee drove her popularity. It was because she was so genuine, so real." She was clenching her jaw to hold back tears. "Well, you know, Roman."

"I do."

Paul stiffened, as if a bad memory had come to the surface. "But then, a couple of years ago, she became distant. Stopped calling, never flew home. Like she got completely sucked into the Hollywood glitz and glamor."

"I know she got super busy around that time," said Roman. "As StarSee leaned in on fewer recordings and more live StarStreams."

Starla's mother let her anger and confusion show in the tone of her voice. "There was all that talk about her plastic surgery. I never understood why she needed it." She shook her head. "It's like Hollywood turned her into a different person. She disappeared for at least two months and didn't even tell us where she was going. We were worried sick. She completely missed the birth of her nephew, didn't call or anything. It wasn't like her at all."

Roman would understand if they blamed the whole industry for her death. There were times he hated being part of the Hollywood socials machine, and this was one of them.

"At least you'll be taken care of," said Seven. "She must have been quite wealthy."

"We wouldn't know," said Ruth.

"Turns out, we're not in her will. We don't know who she left her money to, but it's not us," said Paul.

The team couldn't help but look confused.

"The lawyers reached out specifically to tell us we weren't named," said Ruth. "Far as I'm concerned, it's dirty money anyway."

"And we can't find out who she left it to. That's locked away under some kind of conservatorship. Her name and likeness, or her 'NIL' as they call it, is owned by StarSee. Something about them having an ownership stake in her name and image in life and death."

Roman's brow furrowed. "That's terrible. I'm so sorry."

"I thought conservatorships were only put in place if the person was deemed mentally unfit," said Seven.

Roman gently shook his head. "These giant corporations get away with so much, man. Tek, could we try to look deeper into that? Into her accounts? To help them?"

Tek cocked his head. "How?"

"Like, if Mrs. Devine gave you their family passcode, could you use it to run one of your ghost subroutines that analyzes past transfers of Starla's funds?"

"Yeah, that could work. Maybe we could see a trail that would tell us more about her estate. But..." Tek was squinting. "I'm not sure I should be the one to do it. If StarSee detects someone running a ghost subroutine, it might get them a warning and a temporary block, but I'm way past that stage. They would ban me for life. Again."

"It's obviously going to be some StarSee shell that the money is going to anyway. What we really need is to piggyback a StarSee monitoring routine and ride it back out, then overlap multiple subroutines and find out when it happened, how her will was changed, and who changed it."

"I'm telling you, I don't think I can do it," said Tek.

"Actually, it has to be me. I'm almost certainly being monitored." Roman glanced at the disabled Defenderbot. "Tek, you flip me the software through VenPin, and if the Devines will give me the family passcode to back into Starla's account, I'll risk it."

The meeting went quiet for a moment. Roman could hear his own heart beating. *This is a way forward.*

Ruth broke the silence. "Let's do it. Whoever took her money is probably the reason she stopped calling us."

"And maybe the real killer," said Seven.

"You know what they say," said Roman, "in Hollywood, the graves are shallow."

A sour look flashed across Ruth's face. "I don't know what that means."

Roman blushed. "It means skeletons, secrets, don't stay buried very long around here."

Seven's nose was scrunched up, as if smelling something bad.

He changed the subject quickly. "I promise we'll help you sort this out. And maybe we can figure out who's trying to frame me."

The meeting wrapped up with the Devines providing their family passcode. Roman was already lost in thought about how Starla's estate might be a clue that could lead to his exoneration.

After the Devines signed off, Seven, Tek and Roman stayed on the unmonitored chat.

"I know it's difficult, but try not to obsess. I'm sure the authorities are figuring out that there's no reason for you to have killed her," Seven said.

"Their job right now is to prove that I did it, not to prove that I didn't. And they have everything they need: motive, even if it's false, and a StarStream recording that is very incriminating."

"It is a lot," said Tek.

"You should call Roxy. I'm sure she's worried sick about you."

Roman leaned back. Seven was right. Plus, connecting with his twin sister often had the side effect of bringing things into focus.

After closing the call, his apartment was silent, and for a moment, it felt nice to have his streamBugs off. But then it quickly felt odd, too quiet. Like getting used to hearing white noise while going to sleep and then not having it. He went onto his page and turned his StarStream back on. He heard his streamBugs lifting off from the base and head back into the room, the sound somehow gave him comfort.

CHAPTER
SEVEN

Captain Rennick stood at attention, hands clasped behind his back, slicked back hair lit by the overhead light, waiting for the meeting to begin. The group of investigators, eight men and women who were physically at the office, were all on the right side of the room. Another six virtual people sat at tables on the other side of the room. Using a technology intended for larger meetings called *Ionic Displays*, they each appeared underneath two thin black sticks that stood about six feet high and created a volumetric display that radiated downward. Though slightly transparent, it was a near perfect illusion, unless you looked at the lower half of their bodies, which was where they faded away and disappeared under the table.

Dettmer felt unprepared. The pitch room was like a game show in which the investigators were there to sell their colleagues on the merits of their investigations, as if they were contestants competing against each other, instead of being a team. She hated having the focus on herself and was leery of how American entertainment had infected law enforcement.

One of the virtual attendees, Lucas, a young investigator from another office, was finishing up his pitch. He had found a scam that was targeting nursing home residents by getting them to purchase an AI avatar that their loved ones could visit after they passed. But there was no avatar ever made, and the fake company would change its name overnight and move on to a new aging community. Everyone voted by tapping their chest touchpad, and the results were immediately displayed on the monitor behind Rennick.

"Okay, Lucas, you're approved for three additional units for thirty more days," said Rennick, like he was handing out stuffed animals at a carnival.

"Moving on. Dettmer and Mo, I see you have both Starla Devine and random murders listed?

"Yes," replied Dettmer.

"I saw you put a rider on so you two could stay on the Devine case?"

"Yes."

"But the accused killer, one Roman Glass Junior, knew the victim. They had a history. Other than the fact that she was beloved by all of us for her StarStream, there's no need for us to be involved. It's a straight Homicide case."

"Yes, but I think it is a door into what is happening with the random murders. Unfortunately, Homicide is trying to keep primary control of that case and reduce our involvement to second tier."

"Which would mean we'd never hear 'bout it again," said Mo, sitting across the table. "Homicide calls us back into a case about as often as a camel takes a piss." The room chuckled and nodded.

She waved her hand in the air. "I want to use it. I need to investigate StarSee directly."

Captain Rennick was not alone in looking puzzled. She knew

he would not want to use the department's resources to investigate what he considered to be a benefactor.

She continued. "It is the only way to investigate the random murders. I believe StarSee has more information and may even be directly involved somehow."

"How?"

"At the very least, the Impulse Governor is failing."

The room murmured. Arguments on social media resulting in real life attacks had happened for decades. As a result, Impulse Governors were put in place that identified escalating tensions between users or groups of users and put a temporary hold on all communications. This was almost always enough to keep people from acting out of emotion, and the governors were considered extremely reliable.

"And at most, StarSee is directly involved," said Dettmer. "I can feel it."

The room full of investigators broke out in chatter. She heard the words "directly involved?" Several green lights popped on, indicating questions. Rennick pointed to Lucas, his favorite of the day.

Lucas stood up. "Maybe the Impulse Governor software needs tweaking, but to suggest that StarSee is directly involved in murders is a stretch! You're the motive hunter, what's the motive? If simply being connected in some way to a crime was itself a crime, we'd have to investigate every vehicle manufacturer that was used as a getaway car."

"Well, that's not..."

Rennick cut her off. "I agree." He held up his hand to quiet the mumbling. "We're on the verge of getting an enormous boost in funding from StarSee. There's no motive, and there's no reason we should publicly implicate them."

"But," she almost shouted, "that funding is tied to us letting streamBugs into the office, and if we let streamBugs in, then we may as well let criminals know exactly what we are investigating.

It makes no sense!" Everyone sat, blank faced, watching her. The green question lights went off. She bit her bottom lip and took a breath through her nose. "Listen, that is not important. What is important is that if StarSee is inadvertently involved in these murders, not on purpose, but somehow something is happening by mistake, I need more resources to continue looking into it." She glanced at Mo, looking for backup.

"Give us another couple of weeks, guys," said Mo, "just to be safe. We're still in discovery on all this. We're just spitballing here. We've got a responsibility to find out what's going on, right, cap?"

Captain Rennick nodded reluctantly. "Okay Dettmer, what's your pitch?"

Dettmer tried to sound enthusiastic. "One month, six units, with warrants for StarSee proprietary."

The room full of men and women, both real and virtual, guffawed. Captain Rennick smirked.

Dettmer knew she wouldn't get everything she wanted, but by setting the bar high, she might end up with something reasonable.

Rennick swiped a few times at his chest pad. "Okay everybody, let's vote." Each person looked down at their individual voting device and chose from the four options Rennick had allowed, ranging from *Drop the Investigation* to *Full Dettmer Ask*. It took about thirty seconds.

Rennick looked at the display, and the results appeared on the big screen. "You have two weeks, two units, you and Mo, with limited warrants." The room applauded politely as she sat back down. It was a partial win, and probably the best she could have hoped for, given her weak pitch.

"Moving on," said Rennick.

Wednesday, 12:14 p.m.

Mo slid the small window in the partition open that separated their desks. "Well, it's a little tricky, right?" he said. "I mean, we kind of do work for the companies, helping them keep their subscribers from stealing each other's Admiration Points, or creating public health risks or selling drugs. It's not StarSee's fault that people are wacky."

"The thing is, we do not work for the companies. That is exactly the problem. It seems like we do, and the social media giants love that the public thinks we do, but we are not supposed to for real. What if the companies themselves have something to do with what appears to be low level criminal activity? Not the big stuff where they have to go before congress because of some shady business practice, but something that seemed small but isn't? Something that might only be noticed by us?"

Mo leaned back in his chair, which made him disappear from Dettmer's view. "Like what?" he asked.

"I am just saying hypothetically if they did, who would investigate them? That should be us, right? Our job description is not to work for them. It is to work for the people. That is why this division was created." She thrummed her fingers on her desk and leaned forward so that she could see Mo's reaction through the opening in the thin partition wall.

"Yeah, you might be right," said Mo, "but Rennick sure as hell doesn't see it the way you do."

"Rennick is too close. He is motivated by the idea that we could have a StarStream like everyone else, get Admiration Points and get extra funding from ad revenue."

"Would that be so awful? He's just looking out for what's best for the division."

"By letting streamBugs in? No. It makes zero sense. I am buying my copyright if that happens."

"On our salary? Good luck with that." Mo stuck his face into the hole. "Why exactly do you think StarSee itself is involved in the murders instead of just being the vehicle? We all know they go through pretty strict testing these days to keep from driving groups of peeps down rabbit holes like they used to."

"I do not know for sure. There is something odd happening, and I struggle to find a good explanation. When I was investigating in the virtual padded room, I saw correlations between the publicly available daily ad revenue figures and the murders, and then there is all the hidden data I could not see without a full warrant."

"That's all pretty normal, cher."

"But the other weird thing is, at exactly twelve hours after the random murders, all of them, there are packets of data that are overwritten. Not erased, overwritten. Like tracks being covered."

He pulled his head back out and slipped his iBrowse back on. "Code's updated all the time. Nothing odd about that."

"That is true. The thing is, the code updates did not correspond to any other events or any other people. Only when a crime was committed, and only the accounts involved in the crime."

"Sounds like you found your answer right in the question. It's automatic. There's something that happens to a person's account if they're involved in a crime, probably part of the StarSee data going into a data vault because of the Elisa Lam Law."

Dettmer unconsciously itched her eyebrow. "Huh. Possibly. It was just odd that the update was generated directly from the StarSee core."

"Where else would it come from? Probably part of the protocol. A timer goes off, there's verification that a crime occurred, and then the process of vaulting the StarStream begins."

"The thing is, that process is not usually triggered from the inside. Usually it is imposed by us. But in this case, I observed the ad revenue increase, triggering the code update from the inside. Those two things should not correspond."

"How'd you figure that out?"

"By using a temporal diff routine on the ad revenue and comparing the angle of the revenue curve to the timing of the updates."

Mo adjusted his iBrowse. "Pretty slick, but let's keep digging. We got limited warrants. That code update is as good a place to start as any. I'll prep the warrant forms."

"Okay. preparation is the key to winning."

"Success. Preparation is the key to success. Also, regarding the Roman Glass case..." Mo sounded suspicious. "... how do you see us using it to get into StarSee?"

"I am not sure yet, I just know there is more to it. I can feel it."

"How so?"

"They knew each other, okay, but a minor altercation around credit for an award leading to murder years later does not add up."

"You know better than anyone that peeps often have shitty motives."

"But the son of a famous murdered exobiologist kills one of the most famous celebrities ever? Why? Does he have anything in his past that would make him snap?"

"I read up on our boy before the MRIT interrogation. Lemme bring up his file."

Mo got up from his desk and walked around the partition, leaning against the wall in front of Dettmer. He tapped his touchpad and glanced up into space, reading from his iBrowse. "When his dad, Roman Glass Sr. discovered the fossil evidence of alien life inside a meteorite, it was a big deal. Most of the attention was positive, but it also attracted the attention of some right wing evangelicals, who were none too happy 'bout it. Several churches collapse under the weight of the truth, others take a deep dive into crazy and focus their anger on Roman Sr. Eventually, because of the constant threats, his father leaves the family and goes into hiding.

"Cut to when Roman Jr. and his twin sister, Roxy, turn eighteen, Roman Sr. contacts the family and decides he wants to meet up to celebrate. They get together, and afterwards, Roman's father dips his toes into rejoining society by posting birthday wishes to StarSee. But even though Dad was careful, a sleuth-like StarStream watcher figures out where he is. Suddenly, the nut jobs are back, and a week later, Roman gets notified that his father has been taken into custody for his own protection. The next day, Roman Jr. finds out his father has been killed by a zealot who was on the force. Poisoned his father's food with a concentrate of the drug used for HomeJail sedation."

"Holy cow," said Dettmer.

"Yeah, another case of no good deed goes unpunished. Presently, Roman Glass Sr. sits on Ice, waiting for medical science to figure out how to bring him back."

"So, to Roman, for all intensive purposes, StarSee and the police killed his father."

"It's intents and purposes. But yeah, that could be."

"When I was sifting through the data, I saw he had been in trouble once or twice, maybe the result of his having a problem with alcohol? Hard to say what is really going on with him."

"Junior's got issues, and he killed StarSee's top star to get back at 'em. That's what's goin' on, cher."

"What about his family?"

"His older sister also lives in Los Angeles. His Mother left the country and is currently in Greece, remarried."

"Okay. I think we need to talk to him. Something seems too simple about that whole award explanation."

"Copy that," said Mo. "I'll pass you the warrant forms when they've gone through the system."

"In the meantime, regarding the random murders, I am going to let the pattern recognition algorithm chew on the data to see if it finds anything else."

"Using algorithms to find the patterns in algorithms. It's a strange world we live in."

CHAPTER
EIGHT

Wednesday, 2:15 p.m.

A modern tycoon of the digital industry, Maddox Blakewell sat on the upper deck of his tower looking out over Los Angeles. The Southern California sun shone through the multiple dimmable Sun Shades hanging over the luxurious deck of what was a private resort, which was connected to the multibillion dollar business that was his life. The business that would be nowhere without him, that he should get more credit for having masterminded. Behind him, his vanity project, the world's largest private aquarium, glistened. Maddox Blakewell's philanthropic cause was saving the oceans, so to make sure that was obvious, he had constructed his living quarters surrounded by the largest, highest, saltwater aquarium in the world. An incredible feat of engineering that at once showed true dedication to a cause, while also demonstrating that there were virtually no limits to his own wealth.

StarSee Headquarters' three cylindrical towers of varying heights, built into the side of the mountain overlooking Los Angeles, sparkled in the California sun. His father Owen's living and working quarters were in the tallest tower on the left. The word "StarSee" was displayed atop Owen's tower. Maddox's live-work tower on the far right was the next tallest, and the slightly shorter middle tower, which contained the machine room, as well as the tourist area and much of the business, conference and other functions, sat between them. The middle tower was also where the tram stopped and the tourists were free to roam.

Maddox took pleasure in knowing that many city residents considered the three tower superstructure to be a grotesque blemish on the hills bordering the north side of downtown. Grotesque or not, the StarSee facility had become as much a landmark as the Hollywood sign, and that nobody could look at the Hollywood sign without also having their eye drawn to the StarSee headquarters was no accident. It was his father's monument to social media's power, saying in no uncertain terms, StarSee was the new icon of mass entertainment, the real-time reality show that was now Hollywood.

Air-purifying fans blew soothing air on him, filtering out the smell of wood smoke and increasing the humidity to a tolerable level. From his vantage point, Maddox could look down on the multitude of mourners holding vigils for Starla outside the facility, and yet remain invisible to the masses below. He reclined in his lounger, in shorts and a StarSee t-shirt, sipping his second John Daly, while two young personal assistants waited in the wings like living Waiterbots. It was difficult for Maddox to slow down his thinking about the multitude of company issues he obsessed over, but a few drinks in the sunshine helped. He was determined to enjoy this day, his fortieth birthday.

Today, Maddox pushed his private no-fly zone back far enough that he couldn't even tell the streamBugs were there. It felt good to be free of the constant noise. He took pleasure in the fact that regular people could not increase their personal space at will, but he could.

At 2:20, his iRiz audio dots chimed in his head with an

incoming call from his father. He blinked twice while looking at the answer icon.

Owen Blakewell emerged in Maddox's vision, hovering about six-feet away. Owen's immaculately styled white hair did not reflect the sunlight the way it should if he were really there. Maddox also noticed that, as usual, Owen did not have any of his other filters on, so he appeared as his natural, overweight, extra-tanned, seventy-year-old self. Maddox often wondered how a man so incompetent at using the latest technology could be in charge of a company in which groundbreaking technology was such an integral part.

"Happy birthday Maddox," said Owen.

"Thank you, Father."

The pause grew awkward faster than the internet spreading a lie.

"What's happening on your end?" Owen sat at his desk. He spoke as if this was just another business meeting.

"Everything is proceeding with no significant disruptions," said Maddox.

"That's not what I heard. I heard there's a Social Media Investigator who's been asking for access to deep warrants." Owen's lower jaw jutted out like a pointing finger, as if Maddox had personally invited the investigator in.

"Not an indicator of any miscalculation," replied Maddox. "Even if she gains access to the Vaults, she won't find anything that doesn't add up."

"Good. Keep it that way. Managing this entire Starla thing is in your purview, and we don't want to inconvenience our primary with the need for a cover up."

"Of course, Father." He turned and looked up at his father's tower. He was tempted to wave, but knew the only person who might see him, the only person who ever looked out any windows from that tower, was Lara.

"Why is this detective so interested? Have you checked up on her?"

"Yes," said Maddox. "Her partner was that woman that was killed while attempting to confront Zuckerberg."

"I see. Keep an eye on her."

"Of course, Father."

"This is a big day, eh? Forty years old?" Owen raised his eyebrows as if he should get some kind of recognition for having known that it was Maddox's birthday. "I want to give you something special."

You're finally retiring?

"I'm giving you the increase in ownership in Acquisitions and Expansion you requested."

"Is that so?" This caught Maddox off guard. It was unlike his father to give up control of anything. The last time he had been given a major increase in power, Owen reneged on the promotion at the last minute and took it all back. This left Maddox unable to steer development the way he wanted to with regards to their new and largest client, whom Owen liked to refer to as their primary, or *Client M*. It was a few years ago now, but Maddox Blakewell did not forget. "Does the increase include the associated value increase in the allocation of voting weight?" It wasn't a genuine gift if it didn't, and Maddox knew he had asked the right question at the right moment.

Owen shifted uncomfortably and then smiled his perfect, large, white-toothed smile. "Obviously. You're forty years old. Of course, by the time I was forty, I was hatching the idea for this entire company."

While I was learning how to code so that it would actually function. And recruiting Starla.

Owen virtually leaned in. "This comes with the need for absolute loyalty, of course. I still want you to check with me before you do anything."

Maddox paused and leaned back, squinting at Owen. "Well, if I have to run everything by you, then you're not, in actuality, handing it over to me, Father." He raised an eyebrow. "For me to accept the gift, I'll also require that you entrust me with it."

Owen bristled. "No, no, of course I trust you." And then, as if he couldn't leave it at that, he said, "I trust you to be loyal to my interests and to the interests of the company."

"When have I not, Father?" Maddox's lips curled up in a smile, but his eyes said otherwise.

Something gauzy swished in front of Maddox's AR vision for a moment, and then Owen's new beautiful young assistant Lara appeared briefly in the image, handing something to Owen. Owen mumbled something, and she leaned in, her dark hair falling around her face as she bent forward, exposing her cleavage. "Happy Birthday Maddox." She smiled.

"Thanks, Lara."

"I hope your wishes come true. But don't say what it is, that ruins it," she giggled.

My wish is that you will cause my father's heart to explode during sex and the emperor with no clothes will be gone for good.

"Thank you, that's very kind."

Lara gave a wave and backed out of view.

You got yourself into this. He waved back.

"Now that I've given you your gift," said Owen, "I need you to do something for me."

Of course the gift was going to be transactional. To Owen, there was no reason for a gift to exist without the expectation of getting something in return.

"I just finished a meeting with Gabe…"

This could be trouble. Gabriel Lazarus, Owen's lawyer, both personal and business, sometimes had very disruptive ideas. Once Gabe had put a notion in Owen's head, it could be good, or it could end up falling onto Maddox's shoulders to figure out how to repair it.

Owen's chest puffed out as if he was proud of the accomplishment he was about to describe. "We have a new Attorney General, and let's just say he's now a fan of StarSee. Maybe because he left his streamBugs on when he shouldn't have." He flashed his signature grin, which disappeared just as quickly. "You've been quietly inserting new code, which is not only satisfying our primary, but driving up our value, so we're on a good positive upward trend."

"Alarms will blare if we do anything big."

"Oh, it's big, and I don't give a shit about alarm bells. Did you not hear what I just said about the new AG? There's always a way to quiet the alarms, and now there's a way to keep them from ringing at all, which you would know if you paid more attention to me. But that's why you do the tech stuff and I do the business. Don't make me regret my gift to you."

"Proceed," said Maddox.

"Gabe recently came across some insider knowledge. There are rumors that somebody big, a certain news organization, might be ready to sell." Owen had gotten remarkably good at speaking in veiled language when he needed to. Unlike Maddox, Owen insisted that streamBugs follow him around and remain on, as a demonstration of his fundamental belief in the mission of the company. "Gabe thinks we should absorb them. I want you to get with Gabe, and then get them in for a meeting. Apparently, it will all have to be done very quickly."

Maddox smirked, but kept his self satisfaction hidden. "Who is this person we need to meet?" Maddox sipped his drink and was momentarily caught off guard that there was alcohol in it, which reminded him that it was supposed to be his birthday.

"First of all, it's a man, not a person. Women like to... hold onto things."

"Does this *man*, like us?"

"He already offered to sell to us once, and I didn't like the deal, so I rejected it. But Gabe says we should give it another look. Apparently, there's some way we could use it to keep our cards closer to the chest. Which could be useful with our primary."

Maddox's brow furrowed. The previous offer was news. *Why does nobody realize that it is imperative that I am consulted and fully informed about everything? Imbeciles.* "You never revealed that they made an actual offer before."

"Well, I'm mentioning it now."

Exactly what I've come to expect, mentioning strategic moves after the fact, asking for neither permission nor forgiveness. It's like playing chess in the dark.

"Run with it Maddox. Happy birthday." Owen disconnected without waiting for Maddox to reply.

Maddox sat for a moment, pondering the fact that his father knew he had just given him more work as a birthday present. It was a curiosity that confirmed what he already knew. He was becoming more valuable than ever, and even his father could no longer ignore it. What he was doing; all the new subscribers, the success of Admiration Points, the rising stock value, and the fact that he was turning the world into a giant reality show that StarSee owned. It was Maddox who was making all of it happen.

One of the young assistants behind Maddox spoke. "Mr. Johannsen is waiting in your office, in person," she said.

Maddox got up out of his lounger and put down his drink. He shook his head, his black hair spraying sweat in all directions like a wet dog. He was a little buzzed, and usually wouldn't do any work under these conditions, but in this case, he was too excited to wait until tomorrow. Stealing efficient coders from the competition accomplished two goals, it gave him an advantage while simultaneously leaving the other company weaker, and this particular programmer would accomplish both goals well. Karl Johannsen's specialty would be put to use right away, enhancing the StarSee "Totalfake" code. The forty-eight-hour window before Starla's stream went into the Vaults would close soon. The timing was perfect.

CHAPTER
NINE

As the hot brown blanket of evening settled over the city, Roman sifted through data like a beachcomber hoping to find a gold coin. Only family and authorities that had been given proper passcodes were permitted access to a victim's StarStream for the first forty-eight-hours after a crime. Ruth and Paul Devine had passed theirs off to Roman for the last couple of hours of access. Soon, even family would be barred from poking around her StarStream, and would have to visit the Vaults if they wanted access.

The search for the money trail, and for clues to the identity of the real killer, had thus far turned up nothing. The only thing he knew for sure was that someone was keeping her finances a secret. Probably someone in StarSee.

It was easy to go down empty rabbit holes, and with so little time Roman was reluctant to get sidetracked. But he needed to learn more about StarSee. He knew a little about the CEO, Owen Blakewell, who was always in the press touting his accomplishments. But he knew very little about his son, Maddox, the man referred to as the brains behind the operation. Roman visited the Wikimedia page about the Blakewells and clicked to watch the first of the narrated videos about the father-son team.

The male narrator spoke. "Maddox Blakewell is the only son of Owen and Maria Blakewell. While Maddox was growing up, Owen worked for Facebook, which was the largest social media platform of the time. Owen generated ad revenue in the marketing department and won several internal performance awards. Having excelled in sales and marketing, Owen had a reputation for not involving himself in the actual technology, being quoted as saying, 'Technology will change, but what people want stays the same.'

Owen and Maria divorced when Maddox was sixteen years old. Maddox became involved with politics during his early years at Stanford, and even majored in political science. However, he very publicly supported a politician that failed in his election bid. Maddox was obsessed with winning, and this dealt him a great blow, causing him to switch from political science to social media programming.

With the advent of perfectly photoreal Artificial Intelligence driven content, Facebook found itself taking a backseat to instant artificial entertainment. AI generated content quickly rose to total domination, however, when literally everything and anything found on line could be faked with AI, there was no ground truth, and soon everything became suspect. The tides turned to a desire to see real lives, real world people doing real things, and Owen had his big idea. He would combine the latest micro-drone technology, reality television, and social media. He started a new platform with a twist: anyone who wanted to could become a star, by being 'on stream' all the time, and it would all be verified. Subscribers would become streamers and watchers.

Owen founded StarSee just as Maddox graduated from Stanford University with a major in computer science. Maddox developed the source code for the platform and created the first StarStream, a real woman named Starla Devine. StarSee met with great success, seen as a new reality-based alternative to several other existing AI social media platforms. When the site tied Admiration Points to real digital currency, the platform became a worldwide phenomenon.

StarSee was born, and the age of non-stop twenty-four-hour a day reality streams began.

As StarSee grew, Owen gave Maddox little public credit, and a public feud ensued. Maddox threatened to leave the company. Eventually, Owen dedicated an entire tower in the massive three tower StarSee corporate campus to his son. To this day, Maddox Blakewell is largely considered the unrecognized genius behind StarSee's success."

Roman wanted to dig deeper, but he didn't have time. He closed the window and navigated back to Starla's stream while it was still accessible.

In order to hide exactly what Roman was investigating from StarSee's prying eyes, Tek's software compressed and transferred large blocks of Starla's streams into an air-gapped computer. Once cached locally, it ran an analysis on those pages without StarSee's knowledge. The code searched for outlier behavior and actions that could reveal unknown connections or activity. So far, it had not turned up anything unusual, but that wasn't surprising. She was a celebrity with handlers that made sure she had a squeaky clean online image.

It was like looking for a needle in a haystack, without knowing what a needle looked like.

She had the usual mix of obsessive fans that followed every moment of her life, some who even had plastic surgery to look like her. There were also haters who would put together mashups of her worst work. But haters and lovers all agreed that she was undeniably attractive.

As he examined footage of an interview before her release of "The Tears We See Through" three years ago, he noticed her eyes again. They had a remarkable look to them. Her eyes were two slightly different blue and green colors, a condition called hete-rochromia. Very few people even noticed it, and those that did would likely mistake it for wearing iRiz. Roman was aware of it because he had scanned her eyes himself.

He felt himself being drawn in and felt the pang of her loss returning.

After the language and behavior pattern analysis, the AI software determined that something happened around two-and-a-half years ago that drastically changed her mood. Though nothing overtly changed, the software was able to analyze various aspects of her behavior, like body language and vocal tone, and the results showed that she suddenly was less comfortable with her fame and possibly depressed. This might not be that unusual, except that this was Starla. She had always been positive and outgoing.

Maybe she was secretly so depressed that she decided to take her own life? The thought vanished when he realized she wouldn't be able to kill herself by hitting herself in the head, and she would never have framed Roman for it.

He remembered Mrs. Devine saying Starla began acting strangely a couple of years ago, and what she said about missing her nephew's birth. He searched for her nephew and found his StarSee page. Even two year olds had their own streams now. There was barely any communication from Starla with anyone during the time surrounding his birth. The posts she made could have all been auto-posts or re-streams.

It was getting late. Roman set the time frame to two months on either side of her nephew's birthday, set the compression to high, and waited. Three minutes later, all the streams and data were copied to the air-gapped analysis machine.

Tek's algorithm flagged several data points as unusual. The first was a trip she took to Japan with the Blakewells, unusual only because it was not to promote anything, and there was nothing in the press about it. The second was a fall she took on the red carpet in which she twisted an ankle when she stumbled in her high heels, something she had never done before or since. And last were three different fans who exhibited strange behavior even for Star-See. A young man claiming to be entering law enforcement to free her from captivity, who was attempting to create a *#FreeStarla* movement, a little girl from France that kept posting pictures of herself with Starla, even though her speech analysis revealed she was a grown man, and a fan that was irrationally furious at Starla for not taking a stand against the mistreatment of intelligent cephalopods.

Roman squinted at the streams. The resolution was too low to identify any of them. The Free Starla man, going by the name Kevin Will, was a lead worth pursuing. The little girl from France seemed to have lost interest and stopped posting. The angry cephalopods woman, Mina Batin, lived here in Los Angeles, 8.3 miles away, or at least she did almost three years ago. Her account was no longer active.

He put his fingers on his temples and rubbed. This was not going well, and he was tired.

Suddenly a notification popped up on the active Starla Star-Stream. "Data lock executed." Roman watched as red *X*s popped up over all the other data from Starla's stream. *"For further access, please visit the StarSee Vaults."* Time was up.

The data he had analyzed using Tek's algorithm on his air-gapped machine had only gotten him more questions.

Roman waved his hand at the corner of the screen like he was brushing away a bug, which turned off the monitor. Looking around his apartment, he saw his streamBugs sitting on the flat surfaces pointed at him. No need to fly around if he wasn't moving, and he hadn't moved for several hours. Disappointed by his lack of results, he would call the team in the morning and let them know how little he found. Maybe they would have some ideas. He needed rest before trying to dig deeper.

• • •

Thursday, 6:50 a.m.

Morning came abruptly. His iBrowse chimed, which meant someone was using priority mode to bypass his *do not disturb* settings and try to get a hold of him. It was a priority, but not an emergency, so a cup of coffee first, and then he would call them back. He stretched and padded his way to his bedroom window. As he opened the blinds, a small swirling gray-black cloud of stream-Bugs floated outside. There was way more than there should be.

Roman quickly shut the blinds. He threw on some clothes, splashed his face, and brushed his hair. Yes, he needed to shave, but that would wait. Something had happened.

He retrieved his iBrowse from the nightstand, put them on, and headed out to his tiny kitchen. He looked up to see far more streamBugs than usual, broadcasting his morning to the world. This meant he had been allocated more by StarSee, despite his lower tier subscription plan. Roman felt a twinge of excitement that his popularity had gone up enough to get more streamBugs, no matter the reason.

The Defenderbot rapidly flashed bright blue lights, meaning it had an urgent message. Looking at his iBrowse calls, he saw there had been several attempts to reach him. He realized what must have happened. *They found the actual killer!* His heart pounded.

He raced to the Defenderbot. "Play message." The smooth robotic voice of the Defenderbot spoke through the synthetic man's face on the display. "Recent events that affect your case have been revealed in the press. Do not speak to journalists or media outlets of any kind. Setting streamBugs to highest privacy mode is recommended. This is for your own protection. We also recommend you do not speak with anyone regarding your case, except the PD team. Please follow all HomeJail guidelines, and the PD office will be in contact after reviewing recent developments and advise future action. Please confirm you have received this message by DNA ID."

Roman waved his DNA ID card in front of the scanner and said, "Confirmed." *That doesn't seem like good news.*

He grabbed his coffee and sat down at his small dining room table for two. "Hal, set streamBugs to full privacy mode and call Seven. Private." After a few rings, Seven appeared in his vision, her frizzy red hair pulled back into a bushy ponytail, sitting at what appeared to be a large wooden kitchen island in a brightly-lit kitchen.

"Holy crap, Roman." She was not smiling. This was not a good sign. "What the hell's going on, Sev?"

"You don't know?"

"Know what?" His palms were sweaty. He gulped his coffee and walked into his office.

"I'm going to bring Tek and your sister on," she said. "I hope you're sitting down." Her image froze for a moment as the other two images popped up along the top of Roman's vision. Several streamBugs landed on the top edge of his monitor, acting as multi-angle streams of Roman for the conversation. Even though they were set to the highest privacy setting, so would not be broadcasting live, they could still provide volumetric video. Roman made the *throw to display* gesture. The images went from his iBrowse to his wraparound monitor. Seven, Tek and Roxy were all sitting very close to their cameras.

Roxy, Roman's twin sister, looked exactly like him, except her hair was long and tucked behind a baseball cap. When they were born, they were both male, but Roxy quickly began to express as female. Over the years, it became clear to everyone, especially Roman who was closest to her, that she was not the gender she was born as, and she underwent gender affirmation to present as her true self. The question surrounding identical twins with different sexual identities was cause for much debate in the scientific community, but Roman was thankful that those days were long gone now.

Roxy wore makeup that was as artistic as it was beautiful, making her eyes look bigger, her cheekbones higher, and her lips fuller.

"Why am I getting a bad vibe, guys?" asked Roman.

"I'll play the NewsCann stream. Oscar, share my display," said Seven to her Digital Assistant. The window appeared with the headline, *"Starla Devine's Murder Recording, New and Updated."*

Roman's heart jumped into his throat. It was Starla walking around her penthouse suite, as seen from her unprotected stream, no modesty filter blurring. She had a drink in her hand, and she was wearing the hyperthin bodysuit that she wore the night of her death. This was the part of the recording that didn't show up in Roman's original stream. StarSee had released her side of the night of the murder.

Seven started to say, "I think the only smart-"

"Wait," said Roman, "I need to see this."

The 3D volumetric display currently featured Starla, smiling and talking to Roman, doing as he had described to the authorities. Roman's geosense flashed, and he internally created the layout of the room again. It was all correct, exactly as he remembered it. This was real.

The mini-drone lights flew out of their case and formed the eight-feet diameter circle. She was stepping into the middle of it to begin her scan, but this time, Roman could also see her in the recording instead of just himself. Her skin-tone bodysuit showed off her near perfect figure, and her blonde hair was up in a tight bun to keep it off her shoulders. She leaned in to Roman and whispered something unintelligible. The award seemed to catch Roman's attention. She said, "All lights out," and the image went dark.

There was a moment of pitch black, and briefly, there were the same sounds of the struggle, but this time Starla's night vision came on. Roman's geosense flashed again, this time something was off.

In the slightly greenish footage, everything was moving quickly, but Roman was clearly grappling with Starla and had her by the neck. Starla elbowed Roman in the side, and he stumbled backward. He lunged at her again, and she yelled, pushing him back. The sounds were the same as what had been on Roman's recording, only this time, what was happening was visible. Starla fell backward and grabbed her tumbler from the table.

Suddenly the stream stopped and turned black, and white text appeared that said, *"The following recording may disturb some viewers due to its violent nature, click here to continue."* Below the warning was a pharmaceutical ad for cholesterol medication.

"Christ on a bike," said Seven. She clicked again, and the play-back resumed.

Roman lunged at Starla, but she swung at his head with the glass and hit him. Hard. The glass shattered, and Roman stumbled. A small spot of blood appeared on his head. He shouted, enraged, held up the award and struck her in the head with the heavy golden statuette as he passed out, and they both fell to the ground. The stream went silent, no motion as the two bodies lay on the floor. A piece of furniture outside the view clunked as it settled. Starla's Digital Assistant said, "I've detected a medical emergency. Agencies have been notified and are on their way."

After a few minutes, the lights came back on, the streamBugs switched from night vision to regular vision, and sirens echoed in the distance. The playback froze with Roman laying on top of Star-la's dead body, murder weapon in his hand.

Nobody said anything. Roman, Tek, Roxy and Seven exchanged nervous glances. Watching the recording made him ill. Seeing Starla brutally murdered was a shock. He could only imagine the grief and outrage her fans were now feeling.

"You did do it," said Tek.

"Christ, Tek, that wasn't me."

"Roman," said Roxy, "it's pretty much-"

"That wasn't me!" Roman was shaking. He realized he'd been squeezing the arms of his chair with all his might. "That whole night vision sequence was someone else. The arrangement of the furniture was slightly different. The way she was fighting, the body mass of her assailant was off. My body was inserted. My DoppleMe human was stitched into the actual murder scene!"

"The anti-Totalfake algorithms would show that, wouldn't they?" said Roxy.

"They were doctored somehow. Tek, display the timecode of that section of the stream," said Roman.

"I looked, there's no timecode."

"Aha! See?" said Roman.

"But the Snopes verification graph shows it as mostly certain it's authentic. It says location analysis authenticates that it was her condo, streamBug analysis authenticates that it was really Starla, real-time chronological analysis authenticates that audio correlation is 100%. It shows that there are minor fluctuations on the time passage of the volumetric recording analysis that are within the margin of error, and that geolocation analysis authenticates that you were physically there during the time the recording claims you were there."

"Jesus," said Roman. "Why would they do this?"

Seven jumped in. "Tek, why would there not be any embedded timecode?"

"I don't know. NewsCann is dismissing it as a technical glitch caused by the night vision. Without the continuous timecode, the Snopes Totalfake detection algorithm turns to all the other methods I just mentioned and still verifies it at 95%. Given everything else, no news media is even questioning that one little bit of unverifiable data."

"It's a fake," said Seven. "Somebody absolutely wants to pin this on you, Roman."

"I don't understand who, though," said Roman. "Could it be another zealot who hated Dad?"

"That's probably it!" said Roxy.

"But who could doctor Starla's recorded stream in the last forty-eight hours to that level of realism?"

"Someone who had actual root-level access to her StarSee stream and personal authorization. But that seems impossible, unless it was someone deep inside StarSee," said Tek.

"Or a cop with the right clearance," said Seven.

"Somebody spliced in the murder and Totalfaked me in. The couch was four feet from the chair in the night vision, but in my full spectrum recordings it was three and half. And there were a ton of other physical distance and size differences, too, like the way they fought."

"Maybe we can share that information and anything else you uncovered last night using my software," said Tek.

"I didn't find much. Your analysis software said she's been depressed, starting about two-and-a-half years ago."

"Starla Devine? That seems odd," said Tek.

"I know, I thought so too," said Roman. "I only found a few things that were outliers around that time. A guy trying to start a Free Starla movement, an angry little girl from France that was actually a man, big surprise. And a woman angry about octopuses. Other than that, I couldn't find anything."

"You should tell the authorities anyway," said Roxy.

"They won't care, especially now," said Roman.

Roman's Defenderbot hovered into the room, flashing blue and red, which meant it had an important police message. "Speak of the devil." He spun around in his chair, put his hand on top and said, "Play message."

"Roman Glass Junior, because of recent developments in your case, ID SD7992 dash CA 4257, and your continued attempts to contact others to influence the case, you are hereby notified that you will be put under Legal Sedation until your pretrial date to eliminate the risk of attempted flight or suicide. The Medbot will arrive at 8 p.m. this evening to administer your sedation. If you refuse sedation, you will be transported to an incarceration facility for the remainder of your holding time until pretrial. Please state your intention."

"Holy fuck." Roman was trembling. "Sedation."

"Please state your intentions."

Roman's eyes were wide, welling up with tears. They would almost certainly murder him in HardJail. "I agree to sedation," he said, his voice quivering, as Seven, Tek and Roxy looked on from the display in horror.

CHAPTER
TEN

Thursday, 11:52 a.m.

As Roman waited for Tek to set up the double-blind VPN so that they could communicate without anyone listening in, he again paced through his apartment with his eyes closed. He could hear the faint hissing of his streamBugs following him back and forth. The thought of escaping crossed his mind. Anything to avoid sedation. To him, agreeing to legal sedation felt like signing his own death warrant. For his father, that's exactly what it had meant.

His iBrowse chimed, and he opened his eyes. A single word floated in his vision: *Ultraviolet.* He raced into his office, sat at his desk, opened the command prompt, and typed on his light keyboard, "run: ultraviolet." The interface popped up, just an empty white box with a blinking cursor. He squeezed the button on the side of his chest touchpad and said out loud, "Voice ident Roman Glass. Passcode, victor two nine."

The screen flickered from white to purple, and then Tek, Seven and Roxy all appeared in his display. Since they were using the Ultraviolet meeting platform, the crypto of meetings, and not the StarSee platform, the interface was different. The usual StarSee full 3D volumetric display was gone as well. Now, his people were just flat 2D video streams. The usual GUI displaying watcher counts, Admiration Points, Meme Factory memes and favorited StarStreams were all gone. Just a plain white box around each person's plain 2D video. It felt strange, but refreshing in a way.

He had already used Tek's method to override the Defenderbot again. It did, however, continue to display the time until the Medbot arrived to sedate Roman. That display could not be turned off. He had eight hours.

"Hey gang, I can't turn off my streamBugs completely anymore. They are monitoring the video feed, but I've enacted the highest privacy I legally can, so they can't see what's on our screens and the audio is muted."

They nodded. They had all turned off their own streamBugs as well.

"I'm so screwed, people," said Roman.

Seven appeared to be sitting in the lounge of a high rise suite or admiral's club. Her piercing blue eyes glowing slightly from wearing iRiz.

"Seven, where the heck are you now?" asked Roman.

"Not important," she replied. "Your threat level has been elevated. That's why we had to migrate our conversation to the Ultraviolet network, which is invisible to authorities." She looked off screen and shook her head no, as if declining something.

"I'm at a loss, people. I've been reviewing the recording over and over, and the only real thing we have to go on are the changes to Starla's room when the murder recording changed to night vision," said Roman. "Especially the armoire, it got significantly smaller in the night vision, even though it was the same one, you know?"

Seven's face contorted. "I don't know. That sounds very strange. You're saying that during the section of the recording that we think was faked, her armoire was smaller than it should have been?"

"Absolutely, man. It sounds bizarre, I know. It changes sizes in the course of five seconds. I wish I could get back in there and know for sure. I have both geometries in my head, but I'm not sure how I could even prove it. Also, the way she's fighting, the way her body mass shifts, she was fighting someone smaller than me in real life."

"So someone spliced in the night vision sequence for sure. How do we prove it?"

"You have to go back to her condo, get the proof you need of the scene of the crime that you have in your head, give it to the cops and post it online," said Tek.

"You have to escape," said Roxy. Everybody went quiet. "Should I not say that out loud?" Her hair was down today and her make up had an Egyptian flair to it.

"You can say whatever you want," said Tek. "This is completely private."

"I'm inclined to agree with Roxy," said Seven. "Somebody has it out for you, and once you're sedated, you won't be able to figure out who it is. In fact, once you're sedated, it's likely that you'll be on the fast track to HardJail."

"Probably a slim chance you could get a real defender, right?" said Tek.

"I looked into it. There aren't any available. Too many cases. Totally sucks for us who can't afford personal attorneys."

"I could - " Seven started to say.

"Nope," said Roman. "We've already discussed the money thing."

"But this is different."

"Nope. Keeping you guys on the payroll during the downturn was the right thing to do. I didn't do it so that you would feel like you owed me."

Roman and Seven looked at each other. It was an impasse.

"In that case, let's get you out," said Roxy.

Roman looked around the room. Even though the streamBugs were in a dumbed down state, it still felt like he was being watched and shouldn't be talking about this out loud. "I can't just escape, and the Medbot will be here this evening."

"We've been talking. There's a way, but it involves you not running," said Tek.

Roman tried to understand the logic. "What the hell does that mean? Running but not running?"

"It means you have to escape, but it can't look like you escaped."

"That sounds pretty much impossible," said Roman.

"It's not," said Roxy.

"I think it is. I've never heard of anyone escaping and fooling the system to make it look like they didn't escape."

"But not everyone is like you," said Tek calmly. "You have something most people don't have."

"Hear us out, Roman, it'll work," said Roxy softly.

"I could get you out," said Seven. "We'd have to get someone else in at the exact same moment to take your place. And then they would be sedated instead of you."

"There's no way we could make that work, and no one could take my place anyway," insisted Roman.

"I'll do it," Roxy said again, this time loudly. "I can take your place. Our DNA is identical, and I'll do my makeup, so I'll look exactly like you."

Roman paused for a moment, then thrummed his fingers. "No way." He shook his head. "Not gonna allow it, sis. There has to be another way."

"There isn't," said Tek.

"We'd make the swap exactly when the Medbot shows up tonight. I'd fire off a silent dark market HomeJail video system disruptor to hide the swap."

"The cops would notice a video stream disruptor right away, guys," said Roman.

"So I put disruptors in front of three or four other people's doors that are also HomeJailed. Those people won't even know the disruptors have gone off, so they won't do anything, let alone try to leave. After three minutes, everything returns to normal. Nobody has left their HomeJails, not even you, and nobody's the wiser. It'll be considered a glitch, and you'll be out."

"Only you can do this," said Roxy. "You're the only one who has the memory of that night buried somewhere in your subconscious. You're the only one who knows what to look for in her condo."

"I'll use my contacts to gather the list of addresses of people that are HomeJailed. Tek can get the disruptors from the dark market. You and your sister can work out what to wear," said Seven.

Roman sat motionless. Faced with an impossible choice, he said nothing. He continued to shake his head back and forth as if another option would reveal itself. The risk was too great.

"I have the time, Roman. I don't care if I spend the next couple of days zoned out, watching old movies."

Roman was used to Roxy wanting to take care of him, but he hated relying on her.

"We're family," she said. "It's what we do, right?"

Roman put his head between his hands. "This sucks." After a moment, he looked up at the group. "I can't. Whoever has it out for me, they still have it out for me. I'm not putting anyone else at risk."

"In fact," said Tek, "if that's true, then there may be no safer place for your sister than to be sedated in your place, fully protected and monitored."

"Tell that to our Dad," said Roman. "He was in protective custody when they killed him!"

"Roman," said Seven, gently. "If you don't want to run, that's completely understandable. We'll continue to work on your behalf while you're sedated. I promise."

The silence that followed was uncomfortable as Roman considered the option of running versus sedation. He knew that if he didn't do this, his sister would likely go out and investigate anyway, which may be an even worse choice. "If I do try to escape, and succeed, I'd have to disguise myself, wouldn't I?" Roman had a sour look on his face.

"Yes," said Seven. "Tek and I will help you with that. I can pull in favors and get you in and out of places."

"You'd certainly be continuing the family tradition," said Roxy with a crooked smile.

"That's not funny," said Roman. "Dad had to hide who he was to avoid the zealots, and it still didn't help him. It's pretty damned scary that I would walk in our Dad's footsteps when he ended up dead."

"Your dad was an inspiration to scientists and reasonable people around the world. That he got killed just because his discoveries ran up against other people's worldviews is no reason for you to give up on saving yourself. In fact, I would argue, it's the one reason why you should try."

"Defending my father's name has gotten me into trouble more than once."

"But this time it's your name. And you could go to actual HardJail."

"This is a lot bigger than getting arrested for protesting or fighting," said Roxy.

"Someone's trying to frame you," said Tek. "It might even have to do with your dad, but you'll never know if you sit in HomeJail and get sedated."

"I'll be okay," said Roxy. "I'm not scared of sedation like you are. It's kind of pleasant, I hear."

Roman stared down at his desk, analyzing the situation. He

looked up at each of the three life-size faces on his monitor. Seven, Tek and Roxy all stared back, saying nothing.

"If I do this, there's no turning back. I have to go out there, hide who I am from a million watching streamBugs and solve this, or else I don't come home. Ever. I go to HardJail, and you guys probably end up in serious trouble too. Are you sure you want to do this?"

"You know me, as long as we think it through, I'm willing to take the risk," said Tek.

"You know I'll support whatever you decide," said Seven.

Roxy just looked at Roman. She seemed to know that there was nothing more she could say that would help him with this decision, except for one thing. She held up her right hand and wiggled her pinky finger. "Pinkies, brother."

He slowly lifted his hand and made the same gesture back to her. They had been seen holding pinkies in the womb, and now it was their love signal. "Pinkies," he said. He could hear the angry mob outside. The news window on his entertainment display in the living room barked about the latest recording of the Starla Devine murder.

"Okay guys, let's say I'm willing to step over that HomeJail threshold, totally illegally, explain to me how we would do it. I want to understand exactly how we're going to pull this off."

CHAPTER
ELEVEN

Thursday, 3:22 p.m.

The back of Dettmer's SDV looked more like an office than her actual office. There was a traditional driver's seat, just in case the vehicle needed to be operated by a human, but there was no passenger's side seat. There were three displays surrounding her, one on the desk-like area next to her, behind the driver's seat, and two in front of her on a flat surface where the passengers seat normally would have been. Her darkened windows allowed her to work without the glare of the afternoon sun.

Displayed on one of the screens directly in front of her was Mo's live face. "Where you off to?" he asked from the back of his own SDV.

"To talk to Roman Glass before they put him under sedation tonight."

"What are you hoping to find out?" Mo was looking at a different screen off to his right, and not directly at Dettmer.

"The motive. There is something going on here that does not add up."

"You couldn't find that out by calling?"

"He would not talk to me. Seems to have a strong distrust of authority."

"I wonder why."

It took her a moment to realize Mo was being sarcastic. Sometimes she still did not pick up on the rhetorical questions in English. "The thing is, why did it take StarSee two days to release Starla's stream?"

"How is Roman going to help you with that?"

"Unclear, but it makes me suspicious. There is something about his case that does not fit together. I know it."

The sunlight poured in from the left side of the car as it turned to drive north on the 405. The windows on that side automatically tinted to reduce the light and temperature.

"We heard back from another city." Mo had his iBrowse on and momentarily looked like he was watching a fly buzz around his head that wasn't there. "Jeff, from the Social Media Division in Austin. He said to say hi to Travis, thought he was part of our division. I told him Travis was in Homicide."

"How does he know Travis?"

"Austin is where Travis transferred from."

"Interesting. What else did he say?"

"They're continuing to see a rise in crimes between peeps who don't know each other except through StarSee. Wants to know if we have any info."

"Tell him it appears this is happening everywhere, Boston, Houston, Philadelphia…"

"Yeah, but how can you tell with Philly?" Mo laughed.

Dettmer smirked, and they both looked at each other for a moment before turning back to their other monitors.

She continued, "The underlying cause is unknown. Is it the political climate, the latest economic crisis, or perhaps even the actual climate causing people to just snap more easily? Or is something else going on?"

"Times are crazy. I'm not surprised peeps are losing it."

"The thing is, and this is a weird thing, the violent crimes, I will call them the *StarSee Murders*..."

"Good lord, do *not* call them that! Cap'n Rennick would have a shit fit if that nickname got out to the press." Mo shook his head and laughed.

"Okay, fine, I will call them the random but interconnected crime wave of killings between people who do not know each other and have no reason to kill each other aside from what they see on the world's largest social media platform."

Mo made a sleepy face, eyes half closed and partly crossed. "Don't call them anything. I know what you're talking about."

"Anyway, it appears that these crimes are rising at the same time across the nation. If more of them are happening here in LA, then more are happening everywhere. And they are all increasing at a faster rate than ever right now."

"Could be proof that it's just the mood. After the last elections, it seems like half the country wants to kill the other half."

Dettmer turned and glanced out the darkened window as the car exited the freeway. "Not just the last one, every election. It has been like that for decades. But this is different."

A chime sounded from Mo's side of the conversation. "Let me know what you find out with Mr. Glass."

"Will do." She looked directly at Mo. "I understand the goal of the sedation thing, and it does cut way down on people trying to escape, but it just seems wrong."

"Can't be more wrong than what they used to do, locking peeps up in an actual jail with other criminals just because they're accused of something. Something they might be innocent of."

"I suppose." She rolled her head around her neck, stretching her muscles. "Still does not feel right."

As the SDV turned from La Brea onto Franklin, Dettmer started folding up her gear and putting it away. She put her iBrowse on, and tapped the car's console, the tinting on the windows reduced so she could watch the hot Los Angeles streets pass by.

Thursday, 4:07 p.m.

He sure does look like the pictures of his father.

Roman stood inside his open doorway, arms folded, glaring at Dettmer while she sat on her folding stool in the dark wood paneled hallway. She had to sit on the other side of the barrier for security. The glowing rows of yellow lights that surrounded the doorframe presented him in a flattering light, like a makeup mirror. He looked comfortable in his loose-fitting cargo shorts and t-shirt. His iBrowse poked out of his temples through his shaggy brown hair and glowed dimly in front of his eyes. StreamBugs were blocked from broadcasting legal interviews, but Roman's Defenderbot sat nearby.

"It's harder to say no to you with you physically at my door," he said. "So, what do you want?"

"I realized there is something weird about StarSee taking two days to release the footage from Starla's stream. I intend to ask them why, but I need leverage in the interview. Can you tell me anything they might not know about that night?"

"Look, nothing personal, ma'am, but I know you're just trying to get me to reveal some detail that only the murderer would know."

"Roman, I am much more on your side than you think." She leaned forward on the stool with her elbows on her knees and her hands clasped in front of her. She wanted to win him over, but knew it would not be easy. "There is something going on, and I am not sure what it is, but you are a target, and you need help."

Roman stared at Dettmer, unflinching.

"The thing is ... timecode is missing from the important section of the new recording. Why is that? It passes all the other verifications, but that is odd, right?" She raised an eyebrow and tilted her head.

"Yeah, it's odd."

"Can you think of anyone that might want you to take the fall for this? Someone from your past, maybe someone still angry at your father?"

"Nope."

"Is there anything new you remember from the night of the murder, anything out of the ordinary?"

"I already gave my statements while in the MRIT. You know I'm telling the truth when I say everything was fine until the lights went out."

"And then everything went to hell."

"Yeah."

She shifted her weight and straightened up, the stool was uncomfortable. "Before that night, was there any StarSee messaging between you two that was adversarial? Like you were getting messages from her that made you angry?"

Roman shook his head. "No, like what?"

"Provoking messages. Do you have a watcher that goes by Larpersfriend393?"

"Larpers friend? Like, Live Action Role Playing? No way, man." Roman chuckled. "Why?"

"Just following a lead. I currently have several cases of murders where people who did not know each other are, for some unknown reason, driven to attack each other."

"Isn't that like, Homicide's problem?"

"The antagonism is starting on social media, so I am involved, even if there are those that want me to leave it alone."

"Whoever wants you to leave it alone is probably who's benefiting."

"The thing is, it seems nobody benefits. No Admiration Point boost or anything. One person is dead, and the other is in HardJail for life." She realized immediately after saying it that it was probably not the best reply. "I think that there is more to this than meets the view. Which is why I am here. I want to know what made you go to her place on Monday night."

"That's simple, I was hired."

"By who?"

"StarSee? Starla? Her Digital Assistant, Charlie? I don't know exactly, it was done through my form."

"Have you spoken to her recently?"

"We hadn't communicated much in recent years."

"Since the ... feud."

"It wasn't a damn feud." Roman sounded exasperated. "Why do I have to keep telling you people that?"

Dettmer stood up from her stool, walked closer to the invisible barrier around his door and looked him in the eyes. "Because you were recorded murdering StarSee's biggest and most popular moneymaker, and I do not understand why you would have done it. Therefore, I am going to do my job and ask questions."

Roman's Defenderbot was blinking orange and the synthetic man's face said to Roman, "You are not required to continue the interview."

She was losing him. "I want to help, Roman."

"Look, lady, I get why you're here. This is probably part of some pre-sedation test or something."

"Roman, can I tell you why I do what I do? Why I am a Social Media Investigator?"

"It's your time. I can't go anywhere. Soon, I won't even be able to speak very well."

She took a deep breath and sat back down on her stool. "Pull over a chair. It makes me uncomfortable with you standing there like that."

Roman rolled his eyes, but he pulled over one of his kitchen chairs and sat down.

"About five years ago, I was working Homicide with my partner of three years, Carmen. She was a wonderful woman and an avid user of social media. She was tough and had strong values. We got along well." Dettmer smiled a sad smile. "Anyway, we were on a drug trafficking investigation one night when we entered an active lab. It was booby trapped, and it blew up. Carmen was severely injured, with burns on her face and body."

"Well that sucks." Roman's shoulders sank a bit.

"They hailed her as a hero at first, but that quickly faded, and she was just left with scars. The online bullying started, and instead of ignoring it, she responded by getting defensive and becoming addicted to the conflict. The angrier she got, the more vicious the attacks became. It was an awful cycle.

"Finally, she decided that it was the CEO of the platform's responsibility to do something, and in a fury, she went to confront Zuckerberg at a public event. As she approached the stage, security detected that she had a gun. It was her department-issued weapon, but they didn't know that. She started yelling and screaming at him, and when it looked to them like she was going for her weapon, they shot her. She died three days later."

"I'm sorry," said Roman.

"Eventually, I left Homicide to join the newly-created Social Media Division, hoping I could get platforms to respond to issues of addiction and bullying. But I have found that the department moves very slowly and are more interested in controlling subscribers than changing the platforms themselves. Now, here I am, trying to figure out why you are accused of killing Starla, and why other people who do not know each other in real life are killing each other. Homicide does not care, and my division is confused about its purpose. They are even considering allowing streamBugs into the office."

Roman looked for a moment like he was about to open up, but then he went cold again. "I know how this works, the games you people play, the manipulations. You don't really want to help me, you want to get a conviction—"

"That is not true, I do want—" she tried to interrupt.

"And I'm not going to help you get it, lady. The only people that are on my side are my friends, and we're working on it."

She paused for a moment. "What do you mean, 'working on it?'"

"Nothing. I'm just trying to sort this out."

"That is understandable. But if you find anything that might help the investigation, please, do not do anything that could hurt yourself in court..."

"The bear. The little gift bear with the balloons." Roman raised his eyebrows like he was stating something obvious.

She did not understand.

"Did your people test the gift bear in Starla's condo? The one I told your partner to look at?"

Dettmer tapped her touchpad and looked at the case notes in her iBrowse. "I see nothing about a gift bear."

"See? You guys don't even have the courtesy to investigate the clues I already gave you. You're not interested in solving my case."

"I know nothing about—"

"How about Mina Batin, the octopus lady? Or Kevin Will, the Free Starla guy?"

"I do not know—"

"And then there's the condo layout question in the new footage..." Roman stopped himself. "I'm sorry, but you and your team are not even trying. Goodbye Investigator Dettmer, please don't come back, I'll only be sedated." Roman closed the door, and the lights surrounding the door turned red.

Unable to see in through the door anymore, she sensed he was watching her through the one way frosted glass from the other side. She collapsed her stool and threw it over her shoulder. She was more convinced than ever that there was something going on here, but she couldn't help someone who did not want to be helped.

Thursday, 7:55 p.m.

Dusk settled over Hollywood, sucking the color out of the world like a 20th century sepia-toned photograph. The Medbot would arrive in five minutes. Roman stood in his kitchen, dressed in the gray sweats and a hoodie that had just been delivered from Amazon, ordered less than an hour ago by Seven. It was a trendy look, unisex, nondescript. If the plan worked, he wouldn't have far to go, only 780 feet from the front door of his building to the waiting SDV. The car would pick him up and automatically take him to his sister's place. That same car should be dropping her off right about now.

Law enforcement had instructed Roman to create a comfortable area to sit and watch entertainment, with an unobstructed path to get to the bathroom and bedroom, so his leather easy chair was now sitting precisely in the middle of the room covered with blankets and pillows. HomeJail sedation was detainment without suffering. Though it was called sedation, there was no loss of consciousness. It was more like a potent dose of Valium, but

without the pleasurable side effects. The feeling was one of numbness. It was harder to move quickly, or think, or care. There was no
perfect solution to temporary incarceration, but this was a proven
99% safe way to greatly reduce the number of daring escapes and
attempted suicides while in custody.

This escape attempt wouldn't even be possible if human med
techs still accompanied the Medbots on the sedation assignments.
But after several HomeJail prisoners jumped the techs, stole their
clothes, or used them in some other creative way to try to escape, it
was decided that having only the Medbot administer the sedative
was the safest method.

His streamBugs sat along windowsills and countertops, a few
hovered mindlessly waiting for the show. There was not much to
see, but he was a criminal in custody about to be sedated, so there
was always an audience that would get some sort of morbid satisfaction from watching the process unfold. Roman needed to keep
cool until the moment Tek's disruptors went off, shutting down all
the streams in a 600 square foot radius of his front door for three
minutes. There were lots and lots of highly technical people in
Roman's industry, but he was glad he had hired one that was also a
good friend.

The doorbell startled him. "Hal, front door, see outside," he
said. There, on the other side, was the Medbot, the small white
unassuming cylinder with the red cross on the side of it. It
displayed the face of a female doctor on its small screen. The
Medbot's main drone propellers collapsed back into the body, so it
stood like a bumpy super clean white can at 2.6 feet tall. It sat atop
three carbon fiber legs, each four and a quarter feet long, with large
rubber wheels for use when not flying. The bot was a minute early.
"Hal, front door, 100% opaque." It couldn't see inside, but it felt
better not seeing it standing there, waiting.

Behind Roman, his Defenderbot stood at the ready. The two
bots would physically need to touch in order to exchange permissions, document the event, and allow the entry of the Medbot past

the HomeJail barrier. When it comes to transferring sensitive data, there is little that's more secure than a hard physical connection unconnected to the internet.

He watched the clock in his iBrowse display, waiting. Seven should appear any second via Ultraviolet.

Outside, in the hallway, the Medbot spoke in a soothing female voice. "Roman Glass, you are directed to allow the administration of your legal sedation. There is nothing to fear. Any attempt to prevent entry or to disable this Medbot will be considered an additional crime, incurring additional fees and possible additional sentence time. You have three minutes to comply."

He watched the seconds tick down. His hands were shaking.

Seven popped up in his iBrowse using Ultraviolet. "It's time, you ready?" Judging from her background, she was in a stationary vehicle in a parking lot somewhere outside.

Roman knew he was not supposed to speak out loud, so he nodded affirmatively, which Seven could see by watching his video.

"Ultraviolet will also shut down from the disruptors, so you'll be on your own for a bit. Let's do this," she said.

Roman took a deep breath and then pushed the big green acceptance button on his Defenderbot. The Medbot touched the entry button outside. StreamBugs lifted off and hovered in anticipation. The frosted door disengaged its locks and clicked open. He pulled it all the way open. His Defenderbot rolled up to the entrance. Roman took a step back. A small panel in the Medbot opened at the same time that a small panel opened in the Defenderbot. The two stood directly across from each other at the threshold of the door. The physical contact that was required to exchange the permissions and validate that each bot was the bot it was digitally identified as was about to occur. As the two arms extended, the red lights surrounding Roman's doorway turned green, and the two robot arms touched.

Roman heard Seven say, "Now, Tek!"

Nothing happened. The two robot arms reached each other and began the verification process.

"Shit! Wait! I can still see your feed. The disruptor didn't work!" Seven shouted.

"Everybody freeze!" yelled Tek.

Roman saw Roxy's head around the corner in the hallway. She stood perfectly still, eyes wide.

Time was running out, the fifteen seconds it took for the bots to exchange verification was rapidly disappearing.

"Okay, I see," said Tek.

Suddenly, both bots stopped making any sound. All the streamBugs froze in place, ceasing their video feeds.

"Go!" said Seven.

Roxy stepped out from around the corner, wearing the same sweatpants and hoodie as Roman. She waved him out frantically but silently.

Roman vibrated with anxiety. He stood motionless. Maybe he shouldn't do this.

Seven shouted a whisper in Roman's ear. "Now Roman!"

He couldn't do it. The next instant was too important. Roxy ran up to the door. She looked exactly like him. She had cut off her long hair and changed her makeup. It was weird seeing her like this. She grabbed him by the shoulder to pull him out. His leg bumped the Defenderbot, and it wobbled. They both froze for a moment, but the bots remained silent. This was it, now or never. He slid sideways past the two connected bots, sucking in his stomach to avoid touching them again. He hugged Roxy.

"Love you, sis," he whispered.

"Pinkies," she replied, as usual. "Get going. I have some sedation to enjoy." She pulled off her shoulder bag, yanked off her iBrowse and face mask, unclipped her touchpad from her chest, and exchanged them with Roman for his identical items. She pulled a wig out from her bag. "Put this on, quick."

Roman put the mask with the facial recognition blocking QR

code on it on, pulled on the wig, quickly put her iBrowse on over it, threw what he had packed into Roxy's bag, and swung her bag over his shoulder. They had very little time. The three minutes the disruptors would provide was a ballpark estimate.

Roxy was already squeezing past the bots into Roman's apartment. She smiled at him, waved and stood behind the bots, waiting to be escorted to take a seat in the chair Roman had made up as his comfortable place.

He waved back and quickly darted away. He stepped down the stairs, ran outside and out to the street, where he started jogging to the car. The good thing about wearing sweats is that people can't tell if you're running from something, or just running. Roxy's iBrowse popped back on. Either the disruptor must have worn off or he was out of range.

He found the car waiting exactly where Seven said it would be, on the corner of Hillside and Outpost. The side door to the SDV unlocked as he approached, sensing Roxy's DNA FOB in his backpack. He jumped in to find Roxy's streamBugs perched on the dashboard. She must have put them in *wait here* mode. They would not go back online until he gave the command through Roxy's iBrowse, which he now wore.

As the car pulled slowly away from the curb and headed for Roxy's townhouse, he looked out the window and saw people on the streets with their clouds of streamBugs following them. He wondered if this was how his father had felt all the time. Hiding in plain sight, surrounded by the watchful eyes of people who considered themselves citizen journalists, peering out from behind cameras that invaded everyone's privacy under the guise of free speech, all making it impossible for him to live a normal life.

He dimmed the car windows. Since he was now Roxy, Roman could tune into his own StarStream, and like all the other snooping voyeurs, watch the sedation. He saw his sister, looking exactly like him, sitting in his comfortable chair, with the Medbot nearby. The patch that contained the tranquilizer was being placed on her upper arm. Because fingerprints were the one way they were not identical, she wore a hyperthin fingerprint glove prepared by Seven's dark market ID friend, Keith. Having already passed the DNA ID test, she sat there looking quite comfortable and turned on Roman's living room display. She would remember little of what she was about to watch. She was Roman in sedation now.

The indicator next to the Roman Glass Junior channel showed the number of watchers dropping. The main show was over. Other than a weird glitch, nothing had happened. People were not very interested in a StarStream of someone, who was going to be high for a few days, watching other streams. Roman sifted through the comments to see if anyone was concerned about the glitch caused by the disruptor and saw only one person who seemed to have gotten worked up about it. Someone named *watchmewatchyou909*, but they seemed to have lost interest and disconnected.

He felt a pang of guilt. He was letting his watchers down. They were his fans, and he was losing them. He was not providing them with the entertainment they deserved, which was the experience they could only get from watching him. They were his admirers, and they were going away. He would have to win them back.

He sunk into the back seat and thought about what lay ahead. If he got caught, not only would he be in significantly more trouble, but now his sister would be considered an accomplice. There was also a very good chance that his team would get caught and charged as well. There was no going back until this was over, until they had what they needed to prove his innocence. He had to find direct physical evidence exonerating himself. Then he could swap places again with his sister before his virtual court hearing in four days. He watched his Hollywood neighborhood shrink on the rear view display as the SDV pulled away. If this didn't work, he would go to a HardJail this time, for a very long time.

CHAPTER
THIRTEEN

Friday, 9:38 a.m.

As usual, Owen led the small tour group consisting of himself, Lee Hoffman, Maddox, Gabe and Lara through the facility like a carnival barker pointing out the sights. Maddox watched from the back, keenly aware that Owen never mentioned that Maddox handled this entire department's inception and layout. The Meme Factory, as it had become known, played a key role in attracting early subscriptions, when people logged onto StarSee not just to watch other people's lives unfold, but to see what StarSee creatively did with everyone's streams to make them funny, poignant, political and interesting. Subscribers loved getting to choose which StarMemes would get permanently added to their own stream.

As they walked through the facility, Maddox had tuned his iRiz into the same informational Augmented Reality presentation that Lee Hoffman, owner of the massive NewsCann Corporation, was seeing through his own iRiz. Another thing no one would ever know was that it had been Maddox who had surreptitiously been the one to bring the opportunity to purchase NewsCann to the forefront of Gabe's awareness, who, in turn, brought it to Owen. Maddox wanted it that way. After the last massive deal with client M, when Owen simply yanked the rug out and went back on his word to give Maddox what he was due, he would never make the mistake of drawing acknowledgement to himself again. He would also, somehow, make his father pay for that, but not just yet.

Owen led the tour through the rows of cubicles that lined the open modern industrial warehouse space. Each eight-by-eight cubicle had a full volumetric display wall at the back, a very large monitor on the desk and a green office chair. One way frosted glass extended from the top of the cubicle wall to the ceiling, creating a small soundproof booth in which to work. Almost every chair had a twenty-to-thirty-year-old meme maker sitting in it, surfing the StarSee site, watching streams and scrolling through messages, oblivious to the fact that the owners of their livelihood, the kings of their digital world, stood mere feet away, plotting the future.

Seeing his father standing next to Lee Hoffman, the difference in height was striking. Sure, his father was wearing lifts as usual, but Lee was Maddox's height at five feet four inches, and Owen seemed to tower above him. Instead of making Maddox feel small, it made him feel empowered, as if he was part of a special group. Lee Hoffman, the cowboy hat and vest-wearing Houston native, had built the NewsCann empire against all odds, in much the same way that Maddox had built StarSee.

Though there were no streamBugs around the cubicles, there was a cloud hovering above the small group, as per Owen's standing order to always let streamBugs follow him around. His blue suit and perfectly coiffed white hair looked completely out of place, given the casual vibe of the Meme Factory. "The workers rarely need to record themselves at all in order to make the memes, since AI does most of the work, but when they do need to–" he turned on his shoe heel to Lee Hoffman and grinned as if selling a new car "–in order to add some extra pizazz–" he wiggled his fingers in the air as if doing magic "–it saves time if they can add the flair to the meme right from their desk. Their display wall backgrounds can become anything."

"You got 'em well trained to ignore us," said Lee. "Feels a bit like a zoo." He sounded like any mid-western newscaster when he spoke, and while his left-leaning politics were no secret, creating a news empire that appealed to everyone, from the coastal elites to middle America, was no easy feat.

"They're not trained to ignore us," said Owen. "The cubicles are one way frosted glass. We can see them, but they can't see us. It makes them feel more comfortable doing strange things and making a few mistakes while they come up with the memes if they can't tell anyone is watching."

Maddox bit his tongue. Putting the meme factory workers behind one-way glass booths also lead to depression and suicide for some workers for whom the one-way isolation had the opposite effect.

Owen continued to speak while walking. "We do it all for the subscriber. You see, most subscribers love it when a meme gets created using something they did, since it brings them quick notoriety, an increase in watchers, and therefore, extra Admiration Points."

"And it doesn't hurt that our company stock goes up too, right?" said Gabe. He was wearing a light khaki suit with a form-fitting black t-shirt that instantly let people know how in shape he was for a man in his fifties. He was the picture of a hip corporate lawyer, always impeccably dressed with salt and pepper hair and a handsome face.

"That's exactly right, Gabe." Owen slapped Gabe on the shoulder. "That's what this is all about, increasing value. For everyone." Owen grinned.

The bright rainbow-colored lines on the floor stopped when they reached the large glass doors to a giant courtyard outside. In the open space beyond, workers sat on benches and around tables, some eating, some talking, some playing. Everyone wore company provided iBrowse. There were outdoor ping-pong tables, foosball and pool tables. Electric bicycles by the dozens were either parked in racks or being used to get around the large StarSee campus. On the surface, it looked like an idyllic place to work.

Owen turned to Lee. "This is where my part ends. My new assistant, Lara, here will see you the rest of the way back to the main desk." He reached out for Lee's hand and grabbed it firmly with his fat fingers. "I trust you can see the kind of loyalty I've built here, the kind of thing that earns more than simple respect. A win-win for everyone." Owen continued to shake his hand, a little too long. "Gabe'll be waiting for your call. You're a good man, Lee. I feel a synergy here. I can tell we share the same values, and I look forward to our partnership."

Maddox felt nauseous. He stood silently, watching the routine he had seen play out dozens, if not hundreds, of times before. Owen thought of himself as the best salesman on the planet, and Maddox was still surprised by how many people bought the act.

After some cordial goodbyes, Lara smiled in a slightly flirtatious way and put her hand on Lee's arm. She was like dessert, and her role was to make Lee feel comfortable enough as the two of them strolled through the campus on his way out that he would let her know what direction he was leaning, and then she would report back. They headed out through the courtyard into the sunshine. Maddox, Owen and Gabe began walking back through the Meme Farm.

Owen double-tapped his chest. Now that the show was over, his streamBugs would continue to follow him but would no longer be broadcasting.

"Insiders say that he is also talking to Zeitgeist about selling to them," said Gabe.

"Let him sell," said Owen. "I hate his God damned company. Old-school journalists who don't like me and the success I repre-sent." Owen's turn around from the way he was talking to Lee mere seconds ago was not unusual. "I've already turned him down before."

"I know, but I've looked at the language," said Gabe. "Turns out his original offer is still legally on the table. We could accept it along with the newer terms right away and scoop the competition."

Owen shook his head. "Hit pieces, that's what they do. Lefty earth-hugging hit pieces. They don't admire me, and they don't understand business."

"So, wouldn't you like to take them over and be able to influence the stories they do?" asked Gabe.

They were both missing the point, unable to see the big picture. Maddox realized he had to make a choice, take charge, or watch things unfold incorrectly. This was the moment to take control and put his latest plan into action. "You don't understand," he said as he abruptly stopped walking, forcing both Owen and Gabe to stop and turn to face him. "This is huge. Most news is citizen journalists now, but NewsCann is one of the old-school news-gathering organizations, and because of that there are certain laws still in place that protect only them. If we, rather than some other major tech player, take on NewsCann as a partner, we could use it in a very important way."

"We don't need a goddamned news stream," barked Owen.

"Yes, as a matter of fact, we do," said Maddox. "If we can structure the deal so that StarSee becomes legally covered under the umbrella of being a news channel, we can use the Shield Law to protect our data by interpreting the code as journalistic source material. It would allow me to increase the testing, deliver the product quicker, and continue to drive up our value without the threat of someone coming poking around our code."

"If that were possible, why the fuck wouldn't someone have done it already?" asked Owen.

"They tried, but there wasn't core programming that used AI before." *And they didn't have me to suggest highly-intelligent ideas.*

Gabe put his hand to his chin. "That's an interesting angle. We'd need to redefine the key AI code as being a proprietary news-gathering method entitled to the same protections as a journalist."

"I don't see how we could do that," said Owen. "AI is not sentient or self-aware. It can't be classified as a person, at all, ever."

"We won't say it's intelligent or sentient, we'll simply say it's a proprietary news source," said Maddox.

"It would become protected as long as we fed the news division with information from it," said Gabe.

"You put me in charge of acquisitions for a reason, Father, and I'm advising you, this would be an extraordinarily worthwhile move." He paused for a moment, realizing that any suggestion that he was advising his father was a mistake. "And ... NewsCann would never produce another piece that made you appear bad."

Owen remained silent, but he had won him over. Maddox knew it.

Gabe was mulling it over. "Modifying and accepting the existing offer, and then filing the NewsCann takeover with the FTC is a big step. There will be a period where objections could be filed. Once we do this, it sets lots of other dominoes in motion." He looked back and forth between Owen and Maddox to make his point, "I need you guys to understand that if we do this, and then fail at the filing to absorb NewsCann, it could draw attention to how large we've become, and the things we've done. We risk being broken apart, or worse, our client list could become public, which could expose Client M."

"Then we make sure no one files an objection. How long would it be if we file this morning, three days?" asked Owen.

"Yes, three and a half minimum, Monday night at midnight," said Gabe.

"Okay, we keep it a secret and hope no one notices," said Owen, in his know-it-all voice.

"No, we can't avoid drawing attention," said Gabe. "The press will know the instant we file the papers. Saying nothing will attract investigation, and then the press will own the story. We'll lose control of it."

"I don't understand why we don't control the press already," said Owen.

Gabe looked confused. "You do realize that's exactly what Maddox is talking about doing, right? We become the press so that we control it."

Maddox bit his tongue. Sometimes his father's intellectual myopia was shocking. "I say we announce it, present it as a major positive advance for the company and our services, a win for everyone, but especially for the subscribers. If we get the court of public opinion immediately on our side, then we've practically won already."

Owen fidgeted for a moment, and then said, "Fine, do it. I'll tell Lara to cancel his flight."

Gabe still looked concerned. "But acquiring a company exactly one week after losing our biggest star, maybe we should take a beat."

Owen snapped, "I didn't get to where I am by waiting. Every important thing I've ever done was a point of no return." He started walking again, but before Maddox and Gabe could start following, he stopped and turned back to face them one more time. "Swallow Lee Hoffman and his *do the right thing* news organization whole. And then you–" he pointed at Maddox, "–can step up your game for client M." His scowl twisted into a repulsive smile as he turned and began his awkward walk back to his tower. The discussion was over. Gabe hurried after him.

Maddox was left standing alone in the middle of a sea of cubicles, watching as Owen and Gabe walked away. He had won again, by making his father think he had won again. Once the StarSee data was even more legally protected, Maddox was one step closer to his goal, something his father would never see coming.

CHAPTER
FOURTEEN

Friday, 11:28 a.m.

Dettmer looked at Mo through the opening between their two cubicles. "But what would cause all those HomeJail systems to stop transmitting at the same time for almost three minutes?" she asked.

"Dunno," said Mo. "Seems like it was just a glitch. If it was disruptors, then we would have seen one of 'em try to escape, but every single perp is right where they should be."

"There was nothing else unusual about it, other than the timing with Roman Glass' Medbot?"

"Not that I noticed. And once everything came back online, all the bots reported everything was normal, all security measures had passed, and Roman got his patch. You can see him right now sitting in his living room watching streams."

She was already watching his StarStream. Mo was right. Roman was sitting still, temples glowing from his iBrowse. Completely zoned out. "Shame. Maybe I should interview his family. His sister is local, right?"

"Yeah." Mo was distracted by something in his vision. "Oh, speaking of killers, the Justin Kelling case is ready for bed. Every single real person he knew checks out and says he killed Lucia Morales because he was convinced she was going to ban LARPing. And the person he was chatting with on StarSee, Larpers-Friend393, the one who worked him up into a murderous frenzy? It was an untraceable fake account."

"Every StarSee account must lead to a real person or company. It is in the terms of service."

"Well, this one broke that agreement, because I followed the digital trail through three other dummy accounts until it finally looped back on itself between two accounts originating in China and disappeared into Ultraviolet."

"Huh." Dettmer hung her head. "So someone smart enough to hide themselves works someone else up into a killing frenzy. Why?"

"If solving social media crimes was easy, everybody'd do it."

"Everybody used to try."

Mo stood up and went to the door of their shared office. "Gonna join us in the conference room?"

"Fine." She followed Mo into the same gathering area that they had their pitch meetings in and sat in her usual seat. Mo sat across from her at the cafeteria style table as usual. All the screens displayed either the NewsCann stream or the StarSee live stream. The channels that were tuned to StarSee all had smaller windows with popular amateur reporters giving commentary and scrolling text down the right side. StreamBugs created the full volumetric environment of the courtyard of StarSee headquarters, decorated with an official looking platform, in real time.

Captain Rennick sat in his usual spot on the small raised platform at the front of the conference room. He held a controller that allowed him to remotely fly around the volumetrically recreated press conference environment.

Flanking the stage were two large flags which bore the StarSee logo. The abstract shield with an image of the three towers on the Cahuenga Peak mountainside with a sword under it, was said to signify protection of on-line freedom of speech. The stage was empty, except for a podium with the same logo on the front of it. The podium looked presidential. The blurry line between what appeared to be governmental and what was corporate messaging was likely no accident.

In front of and facing the StarSee stage sat a large group of white folding chairs, arranged ten across and six deep. Only the first two rows contained IRL, or In Real Life reporters. The back four rows were all physically empty seats but had virtual reporters sitting in them. Atop the Ionic display posts, the same kind of displays creating investigators in the pitch room, were not only the transmitters that created the images of the reporters, but also a light which the reporters would turn to orange if they had a question, and green while they were allowed to speak.

A small group of people walked into the courtyard, Owen Blakewell and Lee Hoffman leading the way. Everyone at the conference stood and applauded. It was like watching royalty come to address the peasants. The crowd continued applauding as Owen's new assistant, his lawyer and the StarSee Chief Communications Officer climbed the small stage.

The CCO, Sasha Abioye, walked to the podium. She was a strikingly beautiful, dark-skinned woman. Infographics filled the lower portion of every stream, displaying facts about who she was, how long she had been at StarSee, what StarSee's stock value was, how to follow her on StarSee, etc. It was obvious to Dettmer that she was the CCO because, in more ways than one, her looks made it difficult to be critical of what she was saying.

After the cursory introductions, Sasha got to the point. "Today, we are officially announcing the merger of NewsCann and StarSee. This melding of the two organizations will result in an unprecedented level of service for StarSee subscribers." She paused and stretched out her arms as if to say you, my people, my friends. "All of you –" the reporters and bystanders' faces lit up like puppies about to be given a treat, " – you will have a new journalistic news stream that is dedicated to bringing you the information you want, in real time, using StarSee proprietary core code, and relying on the active participation of our unprecedented number of subscribers. The highly regarded NewsCann fact checking service we have all grown to trust will be added to our list of truth analysis algorithms, so you can rest assured that what you are seeing is accurately labeled fact or opinion. StarSee subscribers can now think of themselves as reporters, even if they are simply reporting to the world about their own lives. Isn't that exciting?"

The courtyard of mostly fake reporters applauded.

Sasha beamed as a large panel lit up on the platform, unveiling the new slogan, "News travels faster with StarSee!"

Some of the reporters now stood and whistled and clapped.

"And for our friends who love NewsCann, the great thing is that NewsCann will continue as it was, but now with access to the StarSee streams and algorithms in order to bring you the most complete, up-to-the-minute information possible in full volumetric real time. And as viewers, no more waiting for the recording of the mass shooting to get to the news, StarSee will put you right in the middle of the action as it is happening, live, and StreamBugs will now be allowed in crime scenes, since they will be legally designated Press."

The courtyard of people was applauding. Dettmer turned to Mo. "Holy crap, they are completely manipulating their way into our world."

Mo looked concerned. He nodded once.

Sasha continued, "As you can imagine, we are very excited by this opportunity, and thanks to our amazing CEO, Owen Blakewell – " she gestured to Owen who stood up, waved and smiled, "and Lee Hoffman, CEO of NewsCann – " Lee remained sitting and just nodded, "this great opportunity will be finalized in just over three short days."

"Hoffman does not look so happy about it," Dettmer whispered to Mo.

"Maybe this was more of a hostile takeover than a friendly merger?"

Sasha smiled broadly. "These two incredible men have busy schedules, so we have only a few minutes for questions..." She scanned the rows of reporters. Several had orange lights on, both virtual and IRL, reporters.

"Yes, Cindy." Cindy's light pole turned green.

Cindy's chair moved slightly when she stood up, a giveaway that she was there IRL. "You mentioned the deal would be complete in three days. Why the delay?"

"That's when the deadline to file objections passes. Midnight on Monday night. Yes, Carl?"

Dettmer took note of how quickly Sasha moved on from the question.

A new virtual reporter stood. His pole went green when Cindy's turned red. "I wanted to help investigate a crime recently, knowing I only had forty-eight hours, but I had to wait – "

"I'm glad you asked that, Carl," interrupted Sasha, nodding. Given that Sasha was answering before he even finished his question, Carl was almost certainly a StarSee plant. "This is an example of how great it will be when this merger is complete. Because you, the public, will get to see that recording as it happens, instead of having to wait several hours for StarSee to go through legal channels to release it. It's this opportunity to bring you newsworthy events in real time that will help the public and law enforcement."

Dettmer turned to Mo and whispered loudly, "Is she suggesting that people will be able to see the crime recordings at the same time we can?"

Mo shrugged his shoulders.

Sasha was continuing on, "We all know the Lam Law, which keeps the public from interfering in an investigation, actually slows everyone down. So this will allow us to share our information with the NewsCann branch quicker, and for you to learn the truth as we do. What could be better for our democracy than allowing the public instant access to the truth as it happens in real time?"

"That is bullcrap," said Dettmer, a little too loudly. "If they want to help, they should open the records up to us without a warrant, not just choose what recordings they want released straight to their own news organization!"

Her colleagues sitting near her in the conference room turned with scowls on their faces and shushed her.

Another virtual reporter, whose name was displayed as Nemma Carter, was already asking another question, "... you've suggested that StarSee wouldn't directly benefit from the new watcher goal incentives, because StarSee doesn't make money directly from Watchercoin, even though Watchercoin is tied to Admiration Points, but isn't it true that the higher the value in Watchercoin overall, the higher the stock value of StarSee is? Can you speak to the direct correlation between Watchercoin value and StarSee stock?"

Sasha seemed a bit confused that someone in the StarSee press corp would ask a tough question. Nemma was not following the corpospeak press conference script. Sasha glanced around uncomfortably for the briefest of moments before Owen stood up behind her and came stomping to the podium. Sasha moved out of the way quickly.

Owen smiled a slick smile as he spoke. "The American economy works because businesses benefit from each other, people benefit from each other, and people benefit from business. If our stocks are rising, it's because everyone is winning." He made a sour face and shook his head. "That's a terrible question to ask at a wonderful time like this." He turned and went back to his seat.

Several reporter's lights that had been orange switched off.

Sasha returned to the podium, applauding slowly, as if Owen had just spoken some sage words of wisdom. The standing audience surrounding the reporters immediately picked up on the cue and also started clapping. Soon, the reporters were also applauding.

But Sasha had neglected to turn off Nemma's green light, and Nemma started speaking again. "Won't this merger make you precisely the size of the giants that the DOJ broke up already? Why should you – "

Nemma's green light went red, her mic went silent, and in the flicker of an eye, her image went from standing and asking a question, to sitting quietly.

Sasha pointed to another orange light. "Last one for the day." She smiled at the crowd and the cameras.

A young woman wearing a purple beret, a junior reporter, stood up. "Tragically, we recently lost Starla Devine, one of our beloved StarSee heroes, to a senseless act of violence..."

Dettmer cringed. This young girl's question would be designed to humanize the company by capitalizing on tragedy.

"... yesterday you released the tape of Roman Glass Junior murdering Starla Devine in cold blood. Do you think justice can finally be served? And as a follow up, do you have someone in mind to take Starla's place in the upcoming production of *The Eternal Road*?"

"We at StarSee are as happy as anyone, especially the family of our beloved star, that the murderer is under sedation in HomeJail. StarSee always has, and will continue to, provide law enforcement with assistance in the matters of catching criminals. If you use our service in the process of committing a crime, Social Media Investigators will find out, and you could even lose your StarSee privileges for life." She said it as if it were a punishment worse than going to jail. "And when it comes to replacing Starla Devine in The Eternal Road, there are some exciting developments. All we can say right now is that it's difficult to replace such a wonderful icon, but we are watching thousands upon thousands of StarStreams to find just the right person. So keep 'em entertaining. You never know.

We might be watching yours, and you might become the next Starla Devine!"

Applause broke out, and the stock ticker for StarSee jumped three points.

Dettmer rolled her eyes. This was too much. "Why do I watch these things?" she mumbled to no one. The "press conference" wrapped up to more applause, plastic and flashing lights, as if an announcement of some importance had just been made. Captain Rennick turned up the lights and the giant display reverted to the checkerboard of StarSee streams they were watching for potential criminal activity. The conference room filled with murmuring as everyone stood up to return to their desks.

"That StarSee announced the deal even before it is final is a good sign, kudos to their transparency," said Rennick, a bit too loudly.

Dettmer stopped and turned. "They did it to control the story! That is not transparency, that is obfuscation disguised as transparency."

"Agree to disagree," said Rennick, as he quickly turned to another group of investigators and began chatting them up. As she walked out of the dull conference room, she overheard him say something about how once streamBugs are allowed in, they could feature the investigators on the new StarSee news stream for solving crimes.

Annoyed, Dettmer returned to her desk and resumed browsing the StarSee financial data, looking for clues.

Mo slid the divider between their desks open. "I don't get why they even made that announcement. StarSee merges with other companies all the time."

"Maybe they had to because it is a news organization." Something flickered in the back of Dettmer's mind like a distant spark. *That it is a news organization is important.*

"You have that look on your face, cher."

"I am just thinking. Since they eliminated The Fairness

Doctrine last century, the line between what is news and what is propaganda has been blurred. Old-fashioned news does not exist anymore. There is only real time opinion and reaction, not even bothering to masquerade as researched facts. I do not mean to throw out the baby, I know there is some good, but it is hard to see it lately."

"Throw the baby out with the bathwater. That's the saying."

"Ah, okay."

"But I hear ya. There's no accountability for what peeps say anymore."

"Maybe that is our job, to hold the executives accountable."

"I know you see it that way, and I know you are still fighting for Carmen, but be careful not to muddy the issue. Her death was partly due to bullying, no doubt, but don't blame the platform for the user's actions."

"They may not be as separate as we think."

"Are you condemning a technology for what users do with it?"

She rubbed her eyes. "Possibly, but it is a fact that the companies themselves are making billions of dollars while hiding behind free speech arguments."

"That's the system we live in, cher," said Mo.

"Maybe that system can tell us something. I'm digging deeper into Blakewell's financial involvements." She turned to her display.

Looking inside the semi transparent StarSee 3D bubble, she saw Owen Blakewell's connective strands reaching out from the middle of StarSee's protective sphere. Like a cell within a cell, his tendrils extended out into a myriad of investments. She zoomed in and saw that among the many financial connections he had, he owned shares in an exclusive fund that invested heavily in medical devices. Zooming in closer, one caught her eye, Truth Be Told Inc. They made the MRI Truth Detectors.

She turned to Mo again. "What do you know about the companies that make the MRITs?"

"Not much. I don't like 'em, but the manufacturers are extremely well regulated."

"Why would the head of StarSee be invested in an MRIT manufacturer?"

"Probably because it's a good investment. I hope my retirement fund has money in 'em."

"I wonder..." She stared at the floating Truth Be Told logo. "If there are more crimes, there are more MRIT tests, right?"

"I suppose. But what are you suggesting?" Mo looked at her like she was crazy. "Blakewell is making crimes go up so an MRIT manufacturing company he's invested in can sell more machines? That's pretty far-fetched."

She had to agree, but there was not much else to go on yet. She swiped her touchpad a few times and brought up a request form. "I am going to check out the MRIT thread." She began filling out the request for level two access to personal financial information of shareholders in the company. "I am going exploring. I need to research any possible motive that jumps on me."

"Out. Jumps out at me," said Mo. "Anyway, while you go spelunking for financial information, I'm gonna find out what she meant in that press conference by having a deadline to file objections. I'd like to know what that means. Who can object? Could we object?"

"If we had cause, probably," mumbled Dettmer as she sent off the request form for access to Owen Blakewell's financial data. "Keep me in the loop on that one."

"You got it, cher," said Mo. "And good job, you said keep me in the loop correctly." He smiled and gave her a thumbs up.

CHAPTER
FIFTEEN

Friday, 12:05 p.m.

The townhouse off Ventura Boulevard was comfortable and spacious. Seven had gotten Roxy the place fully furnished, and at an excellent price, which was unheard of in Los Angeles. All Roxy had to do was put her personal touch on the interior by decorating. Roman wandered around, looking at photos that were sitting out on shelves that displayed knick-knacks and mementos of the trips she had taken. *This is what a home feels like. Memories of real life on display.* As he walked into the open and airy living room, lit up by the scorching late morning sun, he saw the picture of their father pop up in one of the digital picture frames. Roman Glass Senior, standing in front of his suburban garage laboratory, grinning while holding up a piece of a meteorite encased in a vacuum-sealed cylinder. *He didn't even know yet.*

Roman hated the situation he now found himself in. He had promised himself he would never pretend to be someone else. His father had masqueraded for years, and look where it got him. And now Roman found himself pretending to be his own sister.

Even though he set all the streamBugs off, effectively shutting down his sister's StarStream, he had to be careful not to inadvertently reveal himself through any of the other connected devices by speaking to them and having them alert authorities of an unauthorized intruder. He had to log in through his sister's refrigerator by hand to get instructions for using the hot waffle sandwich maker. All he had to do was put the ingredients into their respective holes in the top of the machine and out popped a fresh breakfast sandwich between two waffles. It was delicious. He would never buy something like this, but his sister loved kitchen gadgets.

Fiddling with the media center controls using his chest touch pad, he navigated through the display in his AR vision until the big screen in the living room came on. He took off the iBrowse and set them on the table while he ate his waffle sandwich. Seven would be calling soon with instructions to go get his fake DNA ID made on the dark market by her connection Keith. Then Roman would be off to Starla's again. If the cops wouldn't thoroughly investigate her condo, then he would have to do it himself.

The local weather report was finishing up. Sunny and hot, just like yesterday. And just like tomorrow. The fire report quickly followed. An attractive woman stood inside of a 3D display, pointing at maps showing where fires were burning in Calabasas and Santa Clarita. It was a high-fire danger day, just like yesterday. And just like tomorrow. *It's amazing there's anything left to burn.* As the woman rotated the maps in her virtual set, he couldn't help but paint his own picture of the geography on display. The hills and valleys formed a complete model in his mind's eye of forest density, open areas, roads, peaks and valleys. The wind vectors she described became a layer in his mental map. He predicted where the fires were likely to go, which hillsides it would crawl up in mere minutes, and where the natural blocks would slow the burn down. *I can't wait until this murder thing is over, so I can get back to winning my sister's insurance case.*

Roxy's iBrowse chimed, the caller ID popped up on the living room display. It was Seven. He tapped his chest pad to answer. He left his privacy settings high, added the voice changer to female, and set his own video off just to be safe.

"G'morning Roxy," said Seven, smirking. She appeared to be sitting outside in a garden, surrounded by greens, flowers and dappled sunlight.

He waved and then realized she couldn't see him because of his privacy settings. "Morning," he said.

"Hope you slept well, you have a busy day," she said. She was looking down at a device she was holding in her hands. "I've transferred what my dad used to call "walking around money" into Roxy's iBrowse chip."

"Thanks, Sev." He felt awkward about taking help from her, but she insisted that her success would not have happened if not for Roman keeping her employed during the big economic downturn.

"I've done everything I can to help you with getting around and getting back into Starla's, but there's something else I should mention. The announcement that was made by StarSee yesterday about the merger between them and NewsCann, there's more to it than it seems. I figured out that once it goes through, and they pass the deadline for objections, they're going to use it to wall off StarSee data from prying eyes using the Shield Law."

Roman swallowed. "How does that affect us?"

"If there is information that we need out of StarSee, like Starla's recordings, and we don't get it before then, there's a good chance that it will be much more difficult to obtain, if not impossible. So we have fifty-four hours to figure out exactly who's doing this to you and why."

"How can they get away with that?"

"They're pushing the laws as far as they can. They always do."

"That seems outrageous. Who can file objections?"

"Other than law enforcement, only stakeholders in the transaction. But nobody in the Blakewell's proximity would go against them."

Roman blew out a sigh. "Fifty-four hours."

"It's not much."

"I guess I better get going then, right? You set me up with Mister DNA?"

"Yes, get yourself to Keith's place in Hollywood. I've told him you're coming. Listen, there's lots of dark market tech guys out there now, but it's hard to know who to trust. Keith is a little rough around the edges, but I think he's one of the good ones. Just be careful."

"Thanks Sev, I'll touch base later and let the team know what I find."

Roman got dressed in Roxy's unisex pants and shirt in the bathroom where no prying electronic eyes could see. He put the wig back on, then the iBrowse, donned a sun visor from Roxy's closet, and put the QR code invisibility mask back on. The disruptive mask was usually worn as a political statement. Ironic that in order to hide from digital surveillance, he wore something that could attract attention from real people.

Just as he was about to turn off the living room display, another call came in. This time, the ID said Verified Caller: Social Media Division. He let it go to messages, but watched on the screen.

Investigator Dettmer popped up against a blurry background. Her face was distorted and flat due to the lack of streamBugs. "Hi Roxy, this is investigator Rae Dettmer. I am working on your brother's case. He may have told you I visited him yesterday. I would like to chat with you today." She paused for a second. "Listen, if your brother asked you to do any investigating, we would like you to know that we are already on the case. We do not want anyone doing anything that could jeopardize a fair trial by mistake. Please talk to me before you do anything." She disconnected.

Roman stared at the blank screen. Dettmer was persistent. But what if she was right? What if breaking into Starla's condo, even if he found evidence of who did the crime, somehow hurt his chances of winning in court? Admittedly, he didn't understand all the ins and outs of the legal system, and he had no Defenderbot with him to yell at him when he crossed a line.

He glanced up at the photo of his father, happy to be alive. *He trusted authority when he shouldn't have. I won't make the same mistake.* He shut off the display, closed every blind and door, instructed the streamBugs to stay put, and left the townhouse.

Friday, 1:10 p.m.

It was a quick trip to the address Seven provided. This section of Hollywood was a mixture of old and new. The streets here were mostly bright, clean and well mapped so that SDVs and delivery bots could easily navigate them, but if Roman looked just off the main roads down the alleys, the decay of the city was apparent. The alleys were bumpy and broken, with sections of old cement shifting like tectonic plates. Roman got out as far away as possible from any bots that might have facial recognition and avoided any people walking by with hovering streamBugs around them.

He stood before the big two-story white box on Sunset Boulevard, squinting in the sunlight. He saw nowhere obvious to enter. The corner building looked like it could be an incognito strip club, or an underground gasoline auto repair shop. Three-foot wide half cylinders, the same flat white as the rest of the building, ran down the outside walls from the second story roof to the ground at twenty-foot intervals. No windows adorned the building at all. Roman navigated the interface on his iBrowse and called the number Seven had given him.

Before he could connect, a man's voice began speaking from somewhere inside the building. "Go to the alley. Stand between the yellow posts."

Roman walked around the corner of the building. There was an eight foot by eight foot white rectangular outline on the ground with four yellow posts at the corners, as if this was a parking space for a very small flying vehicle.

"Hello? Keith?"

"Into the rectangle," said the man's voice.

He stepped between the yellow posts. The ground started vibrating. He started moving downward, sinking into darkness.

After descending some distance, the elevator-type doors opened into what appeared to be a dimly-lit reception area. It took a moment for his eyes to adjust. Roman stepped off the elevator, which immediately closed behind him. The air smelled clean and fresh, a sign of a good filtration system. Black walls made it feel like a Burlesque waiting room, with a reception desk and a red velvet curtain behind it. The only door burst open, and a short bald man, probably in his mid-seventies, rushed toward him with his hand extended.

"Roman Glass! Seven said you were coming. I'm Keith." The man beamed with energy as he vigorously shook Roman's hand. He had neck tattoos and large hoop earrings in both ears. He was five foot six and an eighth, and dressed in blue jeans and a black t-shirt. That he was not wearing iBrowse or iRiz was a bit worrisome, given that he was supposed to be a dark market tech guy.

"Thanks," said Roman.

The heavyset old man grabbed a metal box from behind the reception desk and held it open for Roman, smiling.

It only took Roman a moment to figure out what he was supposed to do. He removed his iBrowse and touchpad and dropped them in the box. Keith closed the lid and put the box behind the desk.

He gestured around the room. "Place used to be an intentional speakeasy. One of those well advertised secret places that everybody knows about," he said, holding up air quotes as he said the word "secret". They went down a hallway and into another room, well appointed with comfortable looking furniture, a wide open floor plan, and more dark walls. Curiously, sunlight streamed through the curtains in each window every twenty feet, even though they were underground.

Roman's Geosense immediately mapped the room's dimensions and layout. "How is it so bright down here?"

"Fiber optic cables from the roof, that's what the cylinders on the outside of the building are, magnified and diffused through controllable frosted glass tubes, you know, like doors." He pressed a button on a wall, and all the windows went dark and then bright again. "Pretty great, right? I love it down here. It's all reinforced above, so earthquakes, fires, zombie apocalypse, whatever, I'm good!" He grinned.

An open surface that could be a dining room table rose to counter height, and they each sat on stools on opposing sides.

"Seven told me about you," Keith said. "Said you were good people."

"We've been good friends for years. She's part of my team."

"She said you connected her to her benefactor who helped with her patent, even though the economy was in the shitter."

"Yeah, anybody would do the same. She earned it."

"But you dig her?"

"Yeah man."

"Romantically?"

"No, we're not like that. We quickly figured out that we're not, like, chemically compatible."

Keith leaned forward. "Speaking of chemicals, she said you needed a DNA fob so you can get back into the condo of that big star you killed."

Roman stiffened, and his eyes widened. "I didn't kill her, dude."

"Doesn't matter to me, but that is why you need it, right?" Keith's eyes remained locked on him.

"Yes, I need to look around and check some dimensions in my

head, and also try to find a little gift bear that I think might be important."

Keith stared at him, and slowly, his face warmed. "Actually, it does matter. Never a good thing when the system takes down a good man." He reached out his arm and put his hand on Roman's arm. "And I think you're good people, like Seven."

"I also need it to get into the Vaults and check Starla's stream again before some deadline happens. I'm pretty sure the recording that was just released was Totalfaked by somebody very skilled."

Keith stood up and started fiddling with a piece of equipment on a long bench against one wall. "Ah, the Vaults, that's trickier. Her DNA key fob for her apartment will only use mitochondrial DNA, but to access her streams at the Vault will require a multi-factor nuclear biometric ID with an onsite live test to prove you're related. Either that or a governmental passcode. And since you're not a cop..." He flashed Roman a glance with his eyebrows raised, and then turned back. "You won't have a passcode. That means you need both a biometric ID, and a way to fool the live test."

"I have her hair for the key fob," said Roman. "I dunno what to do about the other stuff. What could we do to fool a biometric scanner?"

"Nothing."

"It's kinda critical that I get back into her StarSee account. What should I do?"

"We can't fool the actual biometric scanner, that's what makes them secure. So we have to hack the software system and make the scanners think they're seeing what they should. It's sort of the difference between using a fake fingerprint versus making the software think the wrong fingerprint is the right one."

"Can we do that?"

"Probably not. That would require somebody who can code an insertion of biometric updates into a database."

"I have a guy, Tek. I'll have him help you."

Keith momentarily looked offended at the offer of help, but

then relaxed. "Okay, in the meantime, let's make your fob. While you're snooping around her condo, we'll work on the biometric problem."

Roman pulled his pack off his back and snapped it open. He fished out the small baggie with a lock of hair in it.

Keith grabbed the baggie like a kid being handed a lollipop. "Ah, so she was a natural blonde. Did you know that they once thought blonde hair was disappearing from the gene pool?" He ran over to the long empty table. "That would only be true if there was a genetic advantage to getting rid of it, which there's not! Therefore, the population of blonds stays basically stable." He pushed a button on the front of the table, and the lid popped open and slid back against the wall, revealing an entire contraption that looked like a high-tech medical device, which flipped up and raised into place. "Same goes for red hair, like Seven's. It's still rare, but it's not disappearing. Now Seven, having red curly hair and brown skin, that is rare. But it's all in the genes." He opened the baggie, reached inside with tweezers, and pulled out a single hair, placing it under a microscope. He peered into the viewfinder. "Nope," he said, and placed the hair back in the baggie. He grabbed another hair and placed it in the machine. "Nope." He reached in for another one. "Bingo! There's a good root." He took the hair out of the microscope and placed it into a small flat box, which he slid into a slot on the machine's side. "In order to detect the specific nucleotide sequences, I use DNA probes tagged with a radioactive molecular marker for identification, which bind to the complementary DNA sequences in the sample, which is your root from Miss. Starla Devine."

"I don't know what any of that means, dude."

"Ah, well, the long and short of it is, this creates a distinctive pattern for each individual, which is then used by the DNA readers, the very thing you, good sir, want to get past. The reader has to compare the pattern to the rather large database of samples in order to verify that the markers are *mostly* the same as the person it claims to be, and also to check that it is not a closer match to any of the other existing samples in the database. It's a quicker way to identify people than trying to do a full three-billion point DNA sequence every time someone uses a DNA fob."

It sounded complicated to Roman. "How long will this take?"

The machine clunked and a plastic laminated card slid out. He handed the card to Roman. "Your very own Starla Devine DNA ID. You may now get into her door, or vote as her." He grinned. "But that would be illegal."

"If it's that easy, why don't more people make fake DNA IDs?"

"For one thing, what I just did is highly illegal. Secondly–" he gestured to the machine "–I'm not supposed to have this."

"I gathered."

"Definitely don't tell anyone."

"Definitely won't, man," said Roman, examining the mostly plastic ID. It had Starla's smiling photo on the front. Roman recognized it as a publicity photo, plus a holographic seal of authenticity, and a piece of metal in the middle that Roman guessed contained Starla's DNA code.

Keith stood up and reached out his hand. "Good luck. I hope I don't have to see you again."

Roman shook his hand. "Thanks Keith, I'll have Seven give you Tek's contact info to help you with the biometric stuff."

Keith flashed him side-eye.

Roman put the new DNA fob card in his pocket and grabbed his sister's iBrowse on his way out. Since he had to wait to go to the Vaults, he would go directly to Starla's condo from here. It should only be about an hour away.

Friday, 2:19 p.m.

It was a sunny afternoon, and the ocean air was refreshing. The Marina was an upper class area, and Roman felt out of place already. Walking through the Marina was like being allowed a peek behind the curtain of the one-percenters. The light sparkling off the water cast dancing reflections on the multi-million dollar yacht bows lined up one after the other. Older people dressed in white clothing, wearing sunhats and shorts, walked their purebred dogs to the park. Few people wore iBrowse, most wore iRiz. Free agent streamBugs mingled with others in the public areas as people online peered into the lives they wished they had.

It was easy to overlook the homeless man laying on the sidewalk holding a government issued pad that displayed the sloppily drawn words "please help." He needed the pad to accept money, now that cash had been almost entirely eliminated. The contrast between the wealthy and the unhoused may be a common sight on the streets of Los Angeles, but here, amid the beauty of the Marina, it seemed even more pronounced.

Roman shivered. His fear of becoming homeless gave him goosebumps. It was a short road to economic despair these days, despite all the attempts at safety nets. One bad business move, and Roman might find himself on the streets, unable to afford a subscription to StarSee or even a pair of iBrowse.

It occurred to Roman that he was in fact homeless right now, if not for the people in his life that were close to him and willing to help him.

Having connections with real people, that's the key to getting through hard times.

His iBrowse chimed. It was Seven. Audio only.

"I'm almost there," he said.

"Okay, Tek informed the condo tower's security company that an investigator is coming to inspect Starla's personal security system as part of the court case, so if you inadvertently trigger any alarms, it'll look normal."

"Excellent. Do I need to stop at the desk?"

"No, just walk right to the elevators like you own the place. I guess I don't need to tell you where they are."

"No," said Roman. "I know every inch of her condo." *Including where they found me on top of her dead body.*

"Another important thing, because you have Starla's DNA fob, her streamBugs will think you're her. Hopefully, her copyright protection and full privacy mode was never turned off, which would mean any streamBugs still lingering in her place should not be broadcasting. But we can't know for sure until you get inside."

"What if they're still active?"

"You have a limited range micro-disruptor in your bag. Set it off, and then you'll have to make it quick, like three to five minutes."

"Copy that. I'll call you after. I have to shut down my iBrowse now, so that there's no signal coming from me that doesn't belong to Starla." He pressed and held the button on the side of his touchpad and powered his iBrowse down. He stuffed them in his bag and tightened the mouth covering with the anti facial recognition QR code.

He arrived at the semi-circular condo building complex and marched right past the desk, into the shining brass elevators, and pushed the PH button. Thankfully, no one else got in with him.

Stepping off the elevator, he saw the twenty-three steps down the hallway to Starla's door in his mind before taking them. A single stripe of yellow crime scene tape crossed the doorway at chest level. Standing on four thin legs next to the door was a police guard bot.

Shit! They must have stationed one there for longer than usual because she was a celebrity.

Roman now stood in the long hallway, just him and the guard bot and the one door. Surely it had detected that he had gotten off the elevator, so he had to think quickly. He reached into his bag and felt around. The micro-disruptor should work on the bot without triggering any alarms, hopefully looking like a system glitch. How he would get past it on his way out is a bridge he would have to cross later.

Roman pulled out the tiny drone and flipped it on. The display counted down from 10. It lifted itself to the ceiling. Roman counted... 4, 3, 2, 1..

He had no way of knowing if it had worked, since it only disrupted the signals, not power. Stepping forward, he walked toward the door. He felt for Starla's DNA fob in his pocket. As he approached the door, he heard the audible click of the locks as the DNA ID card reader detected it. The bot stood scanning the hallway, but remained quiet. The disruptor worked. He hadn't realized he was holding his breath, and exhaled as he twisted the doorknob and slipped under the tape and inside the door.

"Welcome home, Starla." The female Digital Assistant's voice startled Roman. He stood frozen for a moment, unsure if he should reply. Within seconds streamBugs flew into the room and created a floating light gray half moon shape near the ceiling. He had no way of knowing if they were broadcasting or not.

Better make this fast.

He stood in the entry foyer and looked around. There was a table with a few personal items on it, an umbrella stand, a coat closet. He stepped around the corner of the dividing wall and into the living space. His geosense flashed as his eyes darted nervously around the room. The streamBugs followed. It was uncomfortable.

Immense windows allowed light to pour into the open space, which was filled with priceless artwork and clean-lined post modern furniture. Nothing had been touched. His equipment still stood, set up in the area by the bed and away from the windows, ready to scan Starla. They had removed all his electronics.

His sneakers left small imprints on the beige carpets as he hurried through the condo, tiptoeing. He stood in the middle of the open space and slowly rotated 360 degrees, as if scanning the surroundings. Having the unique ability to instantly measure his environment, unfortunately, did not mean he had an eidetic memory. He struggled to dredge up the night of the murder from the depths of his mind. His geosense recognized the surroundings the way an artist would notice the paint color on the walls. Very subtle differences were easily detectable if they were next to each other, but comparing two things from memory was more difficult.

He cautiously approached the area in front of the armoire, as if he might see her body still lying there. The enormous wardrobe stood in front of a large column, next to a shelf that displayed all her awards. *Except for the one.* A small stain on the floor caught his eye. He got down on his hands and knees and crawled around, looking closely at the carpet. There was a little spot of dark red in the fibers, not much for supposedly having been killed by the heavy award smashing her head.

He examined the ornate armoire. It was definitely the same larger one he remembered from Monday night, the one from his own recording. He pulled open the doors and found nothing inside. Other than a clothes rod extending from one side to the other, it was a wood-lined empty box that was big enough to step inside. He closed the doors and stepped back. Odd that it would be empty. He moved around to the side where it met the large wall column. It stuck out way too far for the size of the inside he just mentally mapped. Exactly two feet six inches too far.

As he stood and looked around the room that looked like it was out of an interior decorating magazine again, something else struck him. Why was there a large square column there at all? It fit with the architectural look of the room, but there were no other columns like it in the space.

Re-opening the armoire, he felt around inside. He found a pad attached to the inside, with a single unlit button. He stepped back and put his hand to his chin. It could be a hidden room, like a panic room. Best not to find out. If he jumped into this thing and immediately found himself in an impenetrable panic room that notified the authorities, that would be very bad. He closed the doors and continued his search.

The small stuffed bear holding the balloons still sat on the shiny black bar where she had left it. The suspicious teddy was smiling, like an adorable witness, unable to tell anyone what it had seen. It was probably one of hundreds she got from adoring fans. He wondered how she decided what gifts she would keep and which ones to donate. His eyes narrowed as he looked around the condo for other gifts and realized there were none. Not a single gift box, balloon, chocolate heart, framed picture of someone blowing her a kiss, or jewelry box containing a marriage proposal. Nothing.

The little mylar balloons in the gift bear's right hand were still fully inflated. There was a blue heart over its chest that said Brave Bear, and a card in the bear's left hand. Roman pulled it out and flipped the small three by two inch card open. Inside, in hand-written letters, it read, "Kitsune, my heart is for you only. After the reset, we start again. Be a brave bear." It was unsigned.

Roman stood and stared into the distance, trying to remember.

She had definitely done something with the bear. He pulled the balloons out of the bear's hand and set them down, then picked up the bear and examined it, rolling it around, holding it upside down. Nothing seemed unusual about it.

With the bear still in his hand, he walked back over to the armoire area. Probably time to go. Everything was exactly as he remembered it. Looking at his equipment made him desperately want to grab it, pack it up, and erase the evidence that he was ever there, but that was wishful thinking. The evidence was the recordings, not his tripods.

A distant click came from the hallway. *Shit!* Someone was coming in. The hairs on his neck stood straight up as he froze, desperately trying to think of what to do. He turned and pulled the doors to the armoire open and stepped inside as quietly as possible, pulling the doors closed behind him.

"Welcome, Detective Clark," said the home's Digital Assistant.

Travis Clark. The Homicide Detective.

"Hi, Charlie," said Travis. He walked casually into the living room.

He was not acting like he knew there was someone in the condo. *If he doesn't know I'm here, then why is he here?* Roman realized he was still holding the bear. He clutched it to his side. When he did so, the blue heart-shaped area on the bear's chest popped open, revealing a chamber inside of it. It was silent, but it startled Roman. Though it was nearly pitch black inside the armoire, Roman held the bear up and saw that there was something inside the chamber. *Shit! No time for this now.* He gently pushed the heart-shaped panel on the bear's chest closed again. There was hardly enough room to move, but as quietly as possible, Roman stuffed the bear into his bag and put his eye to the extremely thin crack between the doors.

He watched through the slit as Detective Travis Clark wandered through the condo. His eyes had the slightest glow to them, a sign that he was wearing iRiz, unusual for a plainclothes detective. As per current regulations, there were no streamBugs following him. He did not seem to be in a rush.

Roman peered through the sliver as Travis stopped and stood by the bar. He looked at the balloons laying on the counter, next to where the bear should be. Even from across the room, Roman could see the look on Travis' face.

Travis glanced from one corner of the room to the other, and then clearly said, "Charlie, check visitor records."

A three note chime was immediately followed by "Other than law enforcement and Starla, no one else has been here." Roman held his breath. Lucky.

Travis turned back to the balloons. Suddenly, his head snapped up. "Charlie. " He paused as the familiar three note chime gently echoed through the room. "When was Starla here?"

"Starla is here now."

Travis frantically glanced around the room and abruptly disappeared from Roman's view. Roman's heart raced. His best guess was that Travis was off searching the condo. Roman tried to calm himself. His only option was to burst out of the armoire and run for the door. He took a deep breath.

He heard Travis in the bathroom, pulling open doors. "Charlie, lock entry doors."

"Doors locked."

He was cornered. *Think quick.* There was a secret to this armoire. He knew it from the dimensions. He pulled the Starla fob card out of his pocket and held the center of it against the small pad on the wall of the closet. The light on the pad turned green and the door at the rear of the cabinet silently slid open, revealing the interior of the column. It was a dimly-lit three-foot-by-three-foot space. He quickly stepped in and pushed the only button inside repeatedly. Just as the door slid closed, Roman saw light pour into the armoire as Travis yanked the doors open.

Roman's proprioception told him he was getting lighter. It was a clandestine elevator. His stomach felt the weightlessness as he sank through the building. Roman threw his bag over his shoulder and crouched, unsure of what he would be faced with when the doors opened again.

He felt the chamber slow and stop with a thud. The door opened almost immediately. He was in the parking garage. The elevator was both a rapid escape in case of emergencies and also a secret way for the owner to get in and out. Roman stepped out, and the door closed quickly. Travis must have immediately recalled it.

Roman started running for the exit. Pushing the steel door of the garage open revealed that he was at the rear of the tower. He dashed around the corner and started running toward busy Lincoln Boulevard. He ran toward the waiting SDV.

It was a close call, but Roman knew just who to bring the bear to for DNA analysis.

CHAPTER SEVENTEEN

Friday, 2:37 p.m.

Dettmer and Mo jumped at the opportunity to take a field trip to the Truth Be Told manufacturing plant in Vista, California, just outside San Diego. It was nice to breathe air that did not smell of wood smoke. The guided tour was concluding, and Janet, a tall middle-aged woman dressed in a bright red pants suit and wearing pink iBrowse, spoke loudly and clearly like she had done this a thousand times before. Judging by her gravelly voice, which sounded like she used to smoke actual cigarettes, she may have.

"Originally, part of a voting and lottery machine company, the truth detection branch split off into its own entity, as it became apparent that truth detection needed to be isolated from any appearance of impropriety regarding elections or money," said Janet as they disembarked from the electric golf cart. StreamBugs hovered a safe distance away, their miniature eyes following the group.

"Janet, I noticed you allow streamBugs to watch us," said Dettmer.

"StreamBugs are allowed everywhere unless there's a specific privacy concern. It's part of our commitment to transparency."

"So StarSee benefits from allowing people to watch you make and test the machines?"

She turned to Dettmer. "First, why shouldn't they? Second, we don't allow them to see anything that would help people cheat the machines. And lastly, having watchers does not influence the process, Investigator Dettmer."

"Schrodinger would disagree," said Mo, chuckling at his own joke.

Janet looked momentarily confused, but continued. "We're not producing a show, we're making a piece of equipment." She smiled and kept walking. "A good analogy would be watching the science stream from the Mars mission. Millions of people watch, but it has no effect on the science. Besides," she waved her hand dismissively, "the courts decided that allowing streamBugs in our facility was not only legal, but encouraged honesty and transparency."

"Speaking of honesty, I think perps can think they are being honest, even if they're not," said Mo. "The human brain can hide from itself."

"Oh, absolutely!" said Janet.

Mo grinned, turned to Dettmer, and raised his eyebrows.

"And our machines easily detect that it's happening. That's part of our proprietary algorithm that even you investigators don't see."

Dettmer watched as Mo's expression sank. She shrugged her shoulders.

Janet opened a dark wooden door and ushered the group inside a comfortable yet windowless conference room.

"So, since we could easily have done this virtually, why are you here in person?" asked Janet. Two assistants brought ice cold water in for the three of them. Janet pulled out the chair at the head of the table and sat.

"I find being in a real room with people important. It helps me detect the truth." She smiled. "But I will get to the point. Owen Blakewell owns an interest in Truth Be Told. Is that correct?"

"I have no idea who owns what."

"Does he ever visit?"

Janet shifted. "I think I know where you're going. And the law enforcement division is completely independent and closely monitored to ensure that we are not influenced by anyone or anything. We provide machines to acquire data, followed by accurate analysis using aggregation and proprietary algorithms that determine whether or not the subject is expressing truthfulness. That's it."

Dettmer leaned forward. "So, StarSee has never contacted you?"

"I didn't say that. StarSee is an enormous company that's involved with some very innovative ideas for their service."

"What kinds of ideas?" asked Mo.

"Well, there's no secrets in this company." She winked at Mo awkwardly. "Imagine the fun people would have if they were able to *see* if someone was telling the truth on their StarStream, in real time." She smiled, raised her eyebrows, and nodded, as if asking a dog if they wanted to play fetch. "Imagine you're watching one of your favorite StarStreams. It's Joe, and Joe is talking to his girlfriend, and she asks Joe where he's been. He says he's been out with his buddies, only his Crown of Truth says, AAHT!" She made a wrong answer sound. "Not true! But his girlfriend doesn't know it because she can't see the stream, only we can!"

"Why the hell would anyone agree to a live lie detector test on their stream?"

"Truth analysis. And watchers, of course! It's exciting to see when people are not telling the truth, especially when the people they're talking to don't know. People think they're good at manipulation, but this would reveal exactly when and how much. People would get instant boosts in the numbers of followers and Admiration Points just for being truthful or successfully deceptive."

"By being good at lying," said Mo.

"We don't say 'lying' here. We are a truth analysis company, not a lie detector manufacturer."

"And StarSee is adding this new feature as part of their platform?" asked Dettmer.

"We sure hope so." She put her hands on the table. "I can see you're not convinced. Let's do something fun."

One of the assistants lifted a box out of one of the credenzas that lined the room and walked it over to Janet, who opened it. She removed what looked like a thin black crown with two clips extending down the sides. She placed it on her head, and the two moon-shaped clips clicked onto the front of her bright pink iBrowse. An assistant swung a display around, which displayed Janet's StarSee stream. It looked normal, except now there was an additional box containing a brainwave pattern, a small truth meter, and the TBT logo in the bottom corner.

"Working with iBrowse, the Crown of Truth provides an instant analysis of speech and brain wave patterns to present a basic impression of truthfulness. It's not admissible in court, but it's a ton of fun. There are already games in development that use the 'truth or not' indicators." Her truth meter readout was in the green as she spoke.

"Is there an iRiz version?" asked Mo.

"Unlikely," replied Janet. "People who can afford iRiz are generally not interested in such trivialities as revealing the truth."

"How much is StarSee paying for this development?" Dettmer said.

"Like I said, I've no knowledge of StarSee's amount of investment in our business. That's not my area." She adjusted the Crown of Truth. "Any corporation that's invested in our entertainment division has to abide by very strict non-influence laws, which are designed to protect our law enforcement agencies and, of course, our military."

"Our military?" asked Mo.

"Of course. Our product has assisted with several military operations. Imagine being able to easily determine if a terrorist is telling the truth or not without the need for enhanced interrogation. Our military contracts not only drive innovation, but are an enormous source of revenue." Her Crown of Truth remained green.

"How much revenue?" asked Dettmer.

"Oh, that's completely confidential. Who knows how much our military truly spends on new technologies? I'd bet the military drives a lot more technological innovation than a lot of our young people think." She glanced quickly back and forth between Dettmer and Mo. "But we're getting off track." She leaned forward and announced, "I'd love to have some chocolate ice cream with you two, I really like you guys!" The truth meter on her StarStream swung sharply to red, and the words "untrue" flashed.

Mo blanched.

"Gotcha! Yes, I was lying, but only because I'm allergic to chocolate!" Janet laughed and removed the Crown of Truth.

Dettmer was hoping she would leave it on, which proved Janet's point. It was indeed fascinating to peek through the veil of casual dishonesty in real time. But Janet was done with her rehearsed demo and had given them whatever she had in the way of information. It was entertaining, but not much else.

After signing NDAs a second time on their way out, they boarded their self-driving quadcopter. As they lifted off and rose above the California coast, the wall of smoke from the always burning fires was visible in the distance bordering Los Angeles to the north.

"You realize she could have been bullshitting about both chocolate ice cream and liking us," Mo said. "She combined her responses quickly and then ripped the lie detector off her head."

"Crown of Truth. Yes, I thought the same thing. People will figure out how to manipulate that too."

"Ain't that the truth," said Mo, smirking.

Friday, 3:48 p.m.

Dettmer had heard that you could eat on Truck Street every day for your entire life and never get the same thing twice. The endless rows of old-fashioned looking food trucks on both sides of the now unused Spring Street on-ramp to the 101 highway were so popular that it had become a tourist attraction. A short distance from their offices in the hall of Justice, it was an easy choice for Dettmer and Mo to grab lunch. It smelled like a carnival and felt like one too. Swarms of streamBugs buzzed around people who were posting about their dishes on social media.

Mo took a giant bite of his muffaletta and continued talking with his mouth full. "I don't see any connection between the lie detectors and the crimes. Blakewell's connection to the company makes perfect sense now that we know what they are developing. But let's think it through just in case."

Dettmer, slurping pho, nodded half heartedly. There were people sitting near them under the canopies at the long tables that stretched down the middle of what used to be the highway on-ramp as far as the eye could see. "Could the Crown of Truth be connected in any way with their recent announcement about eating up NewsCann?"

Mo sucked on his drink and started nodding his head vigorously. "Maybe. Say StarSee gets peeps to start wearing these crowns when their new news division does interviews. They could beat us to the punch regarding interrogations."

"The criminal justice system as entertainment for subscribers. And we become just another part of the show if we allow stream-Bugs into the office."

Mo chewed and thought. "Shit, that could open up a can of worms. Would they still have to turn over whatever they find out? Would they still be bound by the Elisa Lam Law?"

"Would they care? All that matters to them is the show. Other shows have sensationalized real criminal investigations for decades, like true crime. I can easily see a new stream that mixes the old game program, To Tell The Truth, with The People's Court."

"Or," said Mo. "What if StarSee uses their new news division to investigate their competition!? That would give them a distinct business advantage."

"Their competition is mostly dead already."

"But maybe that's their angle on this whole thing. To gain an unfair business advantage."

"If it is, it is not our concern. And does not seem to motivate the crime wave." She placed her empty bowl in the center of the table and pressed her done button. Within seconds, a panel on the table slid open, and the bowl fell onto a conveyor belt, where it was whisked away to be recycled. "The thing is, something is motivating these crimes. We just have to stand in the right place so we see the pieces from the right angle."

Mo looked puzzled. He must have thought she was trying to use an aphorism, but she wasn't. He finished his sandwich and put his trash on the center of the table, where it also was automatically removed. "What if it really is one of the advertisers behind it, but in a different way than we're thinking? What if an advertiser, say of a home defense system, is creating a subconscious connection between being unsafe, by somehow increasing criminal activity, and the need for a security system? It might explain that block of code that you found updated in the accounts of those involved. Maybe it's the advertiser covering their tracks."

"That is pretty good." Dettmer nodded. She played with her napkin, rolling it between her hands and looking around. "That is a very interesting angle. It makes me want to know more about StarSee's revenue models, and exactly how advertisers are selected for specific streams. That is very good, Mo."

"I doubt we can get close enough to StarSee to get that kind of information. It's not publicly available."

"Then I am going to have to talk to Blakewell."

"You can't just talk to him. What do you think you're going to do? Just walk in and ask to see him?"

"That is exactly what I am going to do."

"How? Without an appointment, you'll never even get past his assistants."

"Our department could file an objection to that acquisition if we had cause, right?"

Mo guffawed. "Chief Rennick wouldn't do that!"

"But Owen Blakewell does not know that." She nodded. "And I will bet Mr. Blakewell will see me if I even hint at that possibility."

CHAPTER
EIGHTEEN

Friday, 4:48 p.m.

The platform outside of Keith's building shook, and Roman started to descend again. His surprise visit was met with apprehension, but Keith buzzed him down anyway. At the bottom, he stepped out into the familiar dimly-lit velour-curtained waiting room. This time, as he was taking his iBrowse off and stashing them, the door swung open, and instead of Keith walking out, someone wearing dark clothing, a black surgical mask, sunglasses and a hoodie came rushing out of the door and into the elevator. Roman stood silently as the mysterious person disappeared.

"Thought this would be a one-time deal. I didn't expect you back." Keith stood in the doorway with his tattooed arms crossed.

"Sorry, man, it didn't occur to me that you might be busy with other ... things." They emerged into the same large open space with equipment lining the far wall.

"I literally live in a secret basement lair. Do you think I want unexpected guests?"

Roman looked at the ground. "Dude, my bad."

"So, what did you find at the dead lady's condo?"

Roman snapped open his bag and held it open, showing the contents to Keith, who reached his light blue rubber-gloved hands inside and pulled out the bear.

He held up the stuffed toy with the blue heart on its chest and made a gagging noise. "Cheap romantic bullshit."

"I stole it while narrowly escaping a cop. I found her secret celebrity elevator."

"Why was a cop there? Were you followed?" Keith gave Roman a sideways glance as he examined the bear from all sides.

"No. It was one of the Homicide cops that interrogated me."

"Strange that he's still checking out her place. Don't you think?" Keith walked over to his long equipment filled table, pressed a button and a panel slid open on the top of the table. He placed the bear inside. "This'll test the fabric for genetic material. Could take a minute. It has to shake the object gently to see if skin cells or hairs fall off and also scan it for any oils that might be present." He walked back over to the island and pointed at the equipment he had just placed the bear in. "I got that device from a forensics lab in Michigan that had burned down in the fires. They thought it was wrecked." He grinned. "It wasn't."

He pressed a button and a large display screen rose from the far end of the island. He punched more buttons. Decidedly old fashioned to not speak commands or have a Digital Assistant. "I'm gonna call Seven and Tek."

A moment later, Seven and Tek appeared on the display via Ultraviolet. Their faces lit up when they saw Keith and Roman.

Keith cut straight to business. "Roman here had some adventures in Starla land, wanted you two to take part so we're not playing telephone."

"First of all, I came within inches of getting caught."

"Holy crap," said Seven. "What happened?"

"Travis Clark, one of the Homicide Detectives, showed up. I

grabbed the bear, hid and got out without him seeing me. He knew someone was there, but hopefully doesn't know who."

"How'd you get out?" asked Tek.

"Remember the armoire that I thought was too big? Turns out it was a celebrity elevator. Straight to the parking garage."

"Ah," said Tek. "That explains the size." He scratched his head for a moment. "But not the size *change*..."

"Right," Roman agreed. "I can't figure that out. I don't think I'm wrong about the size change, but I need to see the recording again to map it."

"Well, it's locked up in the Vaults now, so you can't. Nobody but family and the law can see them now."

Keith turned to Roman. "I hear you can map spaces in your head down to the inch just by seeing them?"

"Yeah. And I'm pretty sure the armoire is different in the night vision part of the recording, but now I'm doubting myself."

Keith got a far away look on his face, and then said, "What if they recorded the fake murder somewhere else, then Totalfaked you into it? And just mistakenly had the wrong sized armoire?"

"Already thought of that," Tek answered. "First of all, she's actually dead. Second, the recording was geolocation tagged throughout. That's one of the ways they verified it. It either really was Starla's living room the whole time, or they bypassed the geolocation, which is next to impossible."

"But you got the bear?" Seven was in front of a lush green garden.

Keith pulled the bear out of the machine and then put it into a baggie.

"Yeah, and it has a secret compartment, but I'm not sure how to open it again. It also had a note in its hand, and balloons, which I left there when the cop showed up."

Keith held up the bear in the bag so Seven and Tek could see it.

"What did the note say?" asked Seven.

Roman opened the note. "Kitsune, my heart is only yours. After the reset, we start again. Be a brave bear. It's not signed."

"What's the first word again?" asked Tek.

"Kitsune."

"Huh." Tek's eyes darted around like he was reading something in his iRiz. "Wiki says that in Japanese folklore, Kitsune were intelligent foxes that grew wiser as they got older. But they could shape-shift into human forms. They could be tricksters, and also faithful guardians and lovers."

"Maybe it was a pet name, or something she was going to act in? It could be anything," said Roman. "We don't even know who the bear was from."

Keith was back at the equipment lab table. "Almost done with phase one!" he shouted from the other side of the room.

Roman said to Seven and Tek, "he's testing the bear for DNA."

"Excellent," said Seven.

Keith returned to the table. "The DNA testing will be done in a minute. So far, I see three unique sets of DNA. I'm scrubbing the databases for IDs now." He handed the bear back to Roman. "You had the magic touch once before. See if you can open it again."

"I already tried. It doesn't open."

"When it opened before, what were you doing?" asked Tek.

"I was hiding in the armoire."

"Show me."

Roman stood up from his stool and crouched as if inside the armoire. "Travis had just walked in, and I was afraid he was going to hear me. I kind of curled up..." Roman reenacted his movement, holding the bear to his side, and heard the whisper click of the heart pop open. "Yes!"

Keith pointed at Roman's leg. "Is Starla's ID fob in your inside pants pocket?"

Roman felt his pocket. "That's it! The bear opens for Starla's DNA ID." He looked in the bear's chest. Inside the hidden compartment was a vial.

"Don't touch it!" exclaimed Keith. He quickly grabbed the bear, and using a pair of tongs, removed the vial from the bear's chest and hurried over to another machine, dropping it in. "I'll run this one through every test I have!" He shuffled to his left and peered into another small screen. "Ding ding! DNA analysis on the bear is ready!" Keith reappeared at the table, rubbing his hands together. A window popped up on the display screen they were conferencing on.

"Okay, so pretty simple, these markers here…" where he pointed with his finger, a red dot appeared. "… these are a match with Roman, from picking it up and stuffing it into the bag." He pointed at Roman. "You probably should have worn gloves."

"Sorry," said Roman.

"But these markers here, very difficult to identify, that's why it took so long. Turns out, they belong to Owen Blakewell."

Tek nodded slowly, "Not surprising. She was StarSee's biggest star. That he would send her a gift isn't unusual at all."

Keith's head cocked sideways. "His markers are all over it. He didn't just send it to her, he physically brought it to her."

"Which means the note was from him," said Seven.

Out of the corner of his eye, Roman saw a light on Keith's machinery turn from red to green.

"You said there were three?" asked Seven.

"Yes, the third, I would have assumed would be Starla's, but is coming up as unidentifiable," said Keith.

"Because Starla's is copywritten?" asked Tek.

"Nope," said Keith. "I have her DNA. It's how I made the fob for Roman. It's not a match."

"Faulty equipment?" asked Tek.

Keith's head snapped to glare at Tek. "No. I maintain this equipment better than any corporate lab you'll ever see."

"Let's get this straight," said Seven. "One of the DNA prints isn't identifiable, but Starla's is not on it?"

"But I saw her touching it that night," said Roman.

"I dunno," said Keith. "My best guess would be that she might have been wearing some kind of hyperthin gloves." He flashed his light blue hands.

"She was wearing a bodysuit," said Roman.

"So her DNA didn't get on it. Meaning the third DNA is probably a housecleaner or foreign manufacturer whose DNA is not in my database. Not everyone is. In any case, only the three bits of DNA are on it."

Keith ran over to the machine with the vial in it and peered into the small screen. The list of chemical ingredients appeared on the conference screen, replacing the DNA information. Keith came running back.

"This is exceptional!" He pointed, highlighting chemical elements. "I won't bore you with all the details, but this is quite a cocktail, one that was mixed up for a specific purpose."

"You do chemical analysis too?" asked Tek.

"I'm not known for it, but I have the equipment. Roman, when you woke up, did you feel like you had a hangover?"

"Yeah, that's exactly what I felt like."

"And yet you've had the shot?"

"Yeah. I overused booze a few times, and because of my grandfather's history of alcoholism, I had the shot. So I can drink, but I don't get drunk."

Keith nodded. "Yup! There was only trace amounts left in this vile, but my state-of-the-art machinery—" he shot a glance at Tek, "—was able to glean that what was in it was a potent agent that mimics heavy alcohol use, including loss of memory, and does so incredibly fast, but only when it reacts with the genetic modifications in people who have had the shot. The result is that you end up passing out, not remembering what happened, and your blood samples only show that you drank alcohol, so it doesn't look like you were drugged."

"Holy crap," said Seven.

"So you were telling the truth," said Tek.

"What the hell, dude?" said Roman.

Tek grimaced. "That came out wrong. I just mean that's proof if anybody doubted it."

"Should we take it to that investigator? Dettmer?" suggested Seven.

Keith put his hand to his chin. "It's evidence, but it's circumstantial unless you can show Starla opening it and drugging you."

"We need to get Starla's real recording from that night, not the edited version they released," said Roman. "It would be a full volume, and I could dolly around and see exactly what she did with the bear."

"If you had the physical evidence of the bear and vial, and proof that she drugged you, that could mean instant exoneration," said Seven.

"Plus, if I could show the differences in the furniture when the crime actually happened," said Roman.

"Her recording is now in the Vaults, though."

"Plus, if the volumetric recording is incriminating, whoever's behind all this would have deleted it by now," said Tek.

"Maybe, but if it hasn't, I know a maintenance worker at Star-See," said Seven.

"Would they be willing to dig into the Vaults and look for the recording?" asked Roman.

"No, they have access to the room, but not the Vault boxes. However ... there are hundreds of maintenance people keeping the place shiny. It would be the perfect cover to get you inside."

"How would that work?"

"We'd set you up as a maintenance worker. I'll tell my buddy, Malcolm, to take the day off and let you borrow his company iBrowse. We'll need a photo ID..."

"Maintenance IDs don't even require DNA," said Keith. "They just require employer authorization codes. They do it that way so they can still hire undocumented workers to do the low-level menial tasks, like cleaning and cooking."

"Okay, so Keith will get you a duplicate maintenance ID," said Seven. "You'll be my pal, Malcolm Chasper. Once you're in the facility, you'll go in the back door of the Vault room. You can't use the main entrance, because the guard would ask to see your biometric ID to prove that you're a relative, which is only the first of two times you'd have to provide it. Instead, you go in the back maintenance door and use your Starla biometric ID at the kiosk to view her recordings, and then you can download the night in question onto a simpin."

"I don't have a biometric ID yet," said Roman.

"It's the same one you have," said Keith, "but system-level changes are complicated. We have to hack the system to accept Roman's biometry when it's looking for a relative at the kiosk."

"You just have to know what to bypass. I'm working with Keith on it," said Tek.

Keith nodded slowly.

"You're sure a maintenance ID will get me into the Vault Room?"

"Malcolm says he goes everywhere to clean, even private areas. He just can't access any of the business networks."

"Surveillance will be heavy," said Tek.

Roman pursed his lips. Keith, Seven and Tek looked at him expectantly. "Sounds like the best plan we have."

Keith nodded. "No sense talking when we can be doing. Now get that thing off your head."

Roman realized he was still wearing his sister's wig.

CHAPTER
NINETEEN

As Dettmer stepped off the tram into the top floor of StarSee Tower Two, a full entertainment experience consumed her. Pleasant music filled the lobby while dozens of enormous screens displayed streams of smiling people having fun, including one where she saw herself getting off the tram just moments ago. Thousands of streamBugs silently hovered near the ceiling, capturing and broadcasting every moment. The smell of peppermint, thyme and rosemary infused the air, meant to excite and give the place a signature feeling. She turned to the huge curved windows looking out over the sprawling, glistening city below. The ocean to the right, downtown LA to the left. Kids screeched in joy as they ran to the observation window, while adults stood with their jaws agape at the view, pointing.

"Investigator Dettmer?" She felt a gentle hand on her shoulder. A woman's voice. "Amazing view, right?"

Dettmer turned to see Owen's latest personal assistant, Lara, whom she recognized from the press conference, smiling. She wore a skin-hugging red dress, and had flowing streaked brown hair. Above her matching red surgical mask were captivating blue eyes that were slightly glowing from wearing iRiz. Something made Dettmer feel instantly comfortable, like they already knew each other.

"Follow me, I'll take you to Owen. He's looking forward to meeting you." She walked toward a private door that was cleverly concealed in the black fabric of the back wall.

Lara walked quickly, staying in front of Dettmer, and exchanged pleasantries like a hostess walking to a table at a fine restaurant. After a long hallway connecting Tower Two to Tower One, and an elevator ride to the top, they entered the private residence of Owen Blakewell. Lara waved Dettmer in and quickly disappeared. The room was the epitome of gaudy opulence, with gold architectural molding framing walls covered with Victorian felt wallpaper. Simultaneously cheap and far beyond anything she could ever afford. As she walked into the grand open space of the living area, she made out the overweight silhouette of Owen Blakewell standing before the wall of floor-to-ceiling windows. His streamBugs hovered above.

"Investigator Dettmer," he said, without turning. "It's a pleasure to meet you." He spun around, grinning, and held out his meaty hand.

She reached out and took his hand, which he squeezed a bit too vigorously. *Like being drawn into a wasp's nest.*

He stood and stared at her, allowing the silence to become uncomfortable, a tactic she recognized.

"Thank you for seeing me," she finally said. "I will not take too much of your time."

He squinted at her, as if assessing an opponent. "Where are you from?"

"Originally from Holland, but I have been here several years. Quite long enough to call this home, and to want to protect it."

"Ah. Wonderful country." He tilted his head back slightly, as if looking up at something. "You indicated that you may have reason to file an objection to our merger with NewsCann?"

It was oddly disconcerting talking to someone who was wearing iRiz. Their eyes often flitted around like they were disconnected from the conversation, and they often spoke without making direct eye contact.

"I have some questions about advertising dollars and you owning Truth Be Told stock." Her gambit was a quick fact-based accusation to tip him off balance.

"I can assure you, the SEC has fully scrutinized my stock ownership. I can hardly buy a coffee without being checked for insider trading." He chuckled.

Time for a larger grenade. "The thing is, that is not my primary interest. My interest is around the fact that subscribers on your site are killing each other for no apparent reason."

"But that would be Homicide's department, which you are no longer part of, correct?"

"Yes and no. I am investigating the social media aspect of it. The StarSee part specifically." She emphasized *StarSee* for effect.

He went quiet again for a long moment. He spun an ice filled glass of dark liquid in his hand, probably iced coffee. The ice clinked on the side of the glass like distant bells. "How many watchers do you have, Investigator?"

"I do not keep track. And please, call me Dettmer."

He gestured for her to sit on the brown pillowed couch. Only after she sat down and sunk into the cushions did he sit opposite and above her on the arm of one of the large chairs. "Oh come now, everybody keeps track, even if they don't admit it."

"A few hundred perhaps."

"You have well over two thousand. I looked. That's over two thousand people who find you interesting enough to want your life to be part of theirs. That must make you feel good."

"I do not pay much attention. I do not believe it is real admiration. It is more like voyeuristic entertainment."

"That's because you are a watcher personality, not a streamer."

She had just been categorized in the world according to Owen Blakewell.

His gaze drifted back to the windows, to the sprawling city below. "I have hundreds of millions of watchers, Investigator Dettmer, hundreds of millions. Do you know why I have hundreds of millions, and you have thousands?"

"Because you created the company that made them into watchers?"

"Because I allow the admiration, and you try to deny it. All my company does is the same thing every other successful company on the planet has ever done, fulfill a basic human need. We all need to be a part of each other's lives, and just as importantly, to have others be interested in us."

"But you have people watching each other through lenses and filters. They broadcast the lives they want others to believe they have. It is not real. I would prefer to be admired for the good I do in the world, not for a dance move I made up balancing on a ledge ten stories above the ground."

His eyes flashed. "We do not condone dangerous behavior in any way. We immediately censor and limit members who take part in those kinds of activities." He said it so fast it was like a rehearsed admonition.

Dettmer held up her hand. She had to squint slightly since he was not only sitting higher than her but also had the bright window behind him. "I am not accusing you, Mr. Blakewell, but people will be people, and people want attention."

"Exactly! The most valuable commodity today is attention, not steel or food. We live in an attention economy. In this country, we no longer make things for each other, instead we do things for each other. The only industry is the service industry, and StarSee simply provides a service."

"The thing is, putting lives on display is hardly doing a service."

"That's where you're wrong. It's a great service, as great as any service. To give meaning to your life and other people's lives through our platform is still to give meaning, whether you think it's the right kind of meaning or not. That's the problem with you people. You think the only valid way to see the world is your way."

She brushed off the personal attack. "I simply do not think it gets to the root of what we want. Digital admiration is not genuine admiration. Worse yet, I believe the systems we create influence the needs we have, and you have created a system that demands more needs, so that more attention is paid, and more advertising dollars are spent."

"Not only do I disagree, but I'm proven right every day." He had a smirk on his face. "And the success of my business, the very megastructure you are visiting today, is a testament to that."

Dettmer got up from the couch. Standing, she was temporarily eye level with him. "I am not here to debate the merits of your endeavor. You clearly had a good idea at the right time and have become very wealthy as a result."

Looking uncomfortable finding himself at eye level with Dettmer, he stood up. "The wealthiest. I'm not just very wealthy, I'm the wealthiest."

She did not change her expression. "Like I said, I do respect your success." She hoped her words sounded convincing, she still wanted information from this arrogant, powerful man. "I am only here because the increase in violent behaviors and murders has me concerned that one of your advertisers might somehow be encouraging bad things, and I do not want to have to open an investigation since that could delay your upcoming deal."

"I'm not sure what I could provide to give you assurance that everything is on the up and up."

"You could give me access to your core systems."

He chuckled again. "Very few people other than my son can even make sense of the code." He began walking toward the door.

"But I have an idea. Come with me. I'll show you our Gray Room. Perhaps that will help."

As he walked, he paused by an end table and put his hand on it, which must have triggered some kind of intercom. "Lara, I'm taking Investigator Dettmer to the interface room."

"Okay, hun," came the reply from a speaker somewhere inside the table.

Hun? Dettmer's head tilted like a dog hearing a high pitch. She did not expect that.

They exited through the rear door and turned right into the hallway that ran to another elevator. This elevator was decidedly less ostentatious than his private one. Owen continued speaking as they walked. "Our advertising algorithms are simply more advanced versions of the same algorithms we've been using for years. I always say, 'algorithm is just a fancy word for fancy math.'"

They gently descended, then she felt the elevator shift and travel sideways. "But you use AI, and even though I hate the term, I assume your AI is proprietary."

"Yes, but AI is just a fancy word for algorithm, which is just – "

"I know, a fancy word for fancy math."

"Yes. But what do you hate about AI? You're not one of those *AI will create the apocalypse* types, are you?"

"I don't hate AI, I hate the term. As you said, it is not intelligent, it is just math." They stepped out of the elevator and emerged into a dark lobby. "I do not think the danger of AI is that it will become self aware and decide to destroy civilization, but I do think the danger is that it will accelerate our own humanity, and speed up the advancement of the worst in us. The real danger of Artificial Intelligence lies in us creating it in our own image."

Owen stopped before another doorway and turned to Dettmer, looking concerned. "Investigator Dettmer, that's where we're different. You believe technology leads to ruin, and I believe it leads to connection."

"When it has limits, and regulations..." she argued, but he had already turned, swiped his card and pulled open the door. They entered the Gray Room.

Dettmer observed that this room had the same floor-to-ceiling curved windows on the far side of the room as Owen's and the tram lobby, but they were all tinted dark. On the opposite side of the room was another row of high horizontal skylights running the entire width of the space. Craning her neck to look up through them, she could make out the side of the mountain with the storage tanks in the distance. The floor was wood grained, making it look like a banquet hall, but was in fact a hard rubber anti-static flooring. Off to the right was a large glassed-walled area containing what looked like hundreds, if not thousands, of computers. In the middle of the room was a huge semicircular workstation that appeared to have risen out of the floor. Hanging above the twenty-foot long desktop was a long row of giant screen monitors like a jumbotron, each displaying different images and graphics, all in full volumetric display. A young man in a StarSee light blue jumpsuit stood in front of the monitors, gesturing in the air, swiping and moving boxes of information to new places inside other boxes of information. He moved so fluidly, he could have been dancing.

"This is a popular room. I often find my son, Maddox, down here, working or having meetings. It's referred to as the Gray Room because our quantum computing center behind those glass walls is the brains of our platform, so like gray matter, this is where we interface with it. All these monitors above us display a constant stream of information about StarSee. What areas of the world are using it the most, what stories that are trending and the pathways they are taking through the world. It is all about connection, one giant interconnected world."

"And you make money off of all of it."

He shot her a sideways glance. "People appreciate our unique mix of reality and fantasy, and yes, they appreciate our advertising algorithm. You don't want to see ads for pet food if your beloved Fido just passed away, and we know that."

"But how do you know that is best?" She couldn't keep up with his monologue.

"Doesn't matter, ads are just for brand awareness. Actual purchases are based on reviews. The magic of capitalism is that we have evolved a system in which people choose products based almost entirely on what other people think of them. And not just random people, we show you what people *like you* like."

"So you make ads that look like reviews."

"My creatives are paid to be creative."

"Who decides what ads are placed where?" asked Dettmer, walking closer to a screen that displayed a giant bar graph that was fluctuating in real time with the demographics currently watching a new StarSee Adventure release.

"Excellent question, that's why I brought you down here. Here you can see the big bucket of available advertisers to be shown over one hour for a group of StarStreams. No advertiser or person determines which ads are shown to whom or when. It is all algo-rithmically determined to be fair. You see, there simply couldn't be an advertiser doing something malicious to drive up their own views, since they don't have any input on placement."

"The thing is, the AI could. Whatever the algorithm is that is picking the ads, it could be figuring out that violence leads to increased ad retention, or purchasing, or something, right?"

"That's illegal and is precisely what we guard against."

The young programmer that had been conducting data in front of the displays suddenly appeared next to Owen. "No, we constantly cycle the ads. We have to show that no advertiser gets any additional views due to placement over their competition. That's the core of our strategy. Fairness. It also keeps us in compli-ance with the Advertising Fairness in Media laws. Nothing should cause an advantage for one advertiser in the same category over another." He smiled and held out his hand. "I'm Vahid, one of the lead programmers."

Dettmer shook his hand. "Investigator Rae Dettmer. You work for Owen?"

"I report to Maddox, but we all work for Owen."

Owen's chest puffed out a little further, and he nodded ever so slightly in agreement.

"How do you feel about the merging of NewsCann and Star-See?" she asked Vahid.

"It's a very exciting time for us," he said. "We already show people's lives in real time, which is sort of the same as news, but without journalistic filtering."

"But it is precisely the filtering that transforms the random noise into ... well ... journalism."

"You're referring to curating information that matters to you," said Owen, "filtering it into different perspectives depending on your own leanings."

"I'm talking about the neutral creation of worthwhile information. Right now, news is like porn. People are shown a version of the world that is curated to their own tastes instead of naturally exposing them to counterpoints, and this targeting is influencing every aspect of our lives."

"You have this idea that the spread of technology is unnatural, but that's wrong. Tech is nature in a digital form. Even the word meme was invented to mean an idea that acts like a virus. Once something is released, it runs its course. You can put controls in place, but there's no stopping it just because you don't like it." He put his hand on Vahid's shoulder. "Let Maddox know I'm running a little late."

This was Vahid's cue to leave. He nodded to Dettmer and entered the Machine room with all the blinking lights.

"Over the decades," Owen continued, "the suggestion algorithms and Generative Pre-trained Transformers that drove people down rabbit holes of misinformation, conspiracy theories and paranoia have been legislated, regulated and, in most cases, eliminated. We're very careful not to lead people to believe factually inaccurate or inflammatory information. Sure, we suggest people watch other people they might find interesting based on analysis, but it's now illegal to knowingly steer beliefs. So you see, our advertisers simply can't have anything to do with your crime problem."

Dettmer looked up at the giant screens again. If he was lying, he was good at it. She did not know what she was hoping to see, but it seemed unlikely that a particular advertiser could steer events using StarSee as a tool. On the contrary, StarSee algorithms prevented that from happening, as well as keeping any kind of intentionality out of AI. "Who is your biggest advertiser?"

"I'm afraid I don't have that off the top of my head."

"Does our government or military take any interest in StarSee?"

"They have hundreds of streams, which they use in compliance with our end-user agreements."

It sounded like a rehearsed answer. She considered raising the ethics issue of putting streamBugs into government offices, but thought better of it and changed the subject. "It must have hurt revenue to have lost Starla Devine."

"Revenue? No. Our systems are far more foolproof than that. As much as we miss our first and most popular StarStream, there's always another beautiful young woman waiting to step into the spotlight and capture the hearts and minds of our subscribers." He sounded like he was giving an investor speech he had given before. "But, of course, we mourn her loss. She was very special."

"Truly, she was. You do not realize what you have until it goes away," said Dettmer.

Owen looked momentarily confused. He then blinked three times and his eyes glowed for a moment. "I have a meeting with my son to get to, so I hope I've answered your questions, though judging from your bias, I doubt I will ever win your approval."

As they turned and started walking toward the door, he put his hand on her shoulder. It was uncomfortably heavy.

"If you go out through the top rear exit – " he pointed to the skylight windows, " – you can stop at the Wisdom Tree Monument. It offers many of my guests a nice moment of contemplation, and only personal guests of mine can go out that way."

"Thank you, but I prefer no special treatment." Before they got to the door, she held up a finger as if something had just crossed her mind. "Speaking of Starla Devine, do you have any more information about her, like her HR records, or additional recordings of the night of the murder?"

"Everything would be in the air-gapped Vaults downstairs, of course. You know that, Investigator."

"Of course. I'm looking into who hired Roman Glass to scan her. And you said your son could help me with the code? I have questions about some updates."

"Yes. I'm sure he'll make the time to speak with you." There was a moment of silence as the door swung open. A young man stepped into the doorway and held his hand out toward the hallway. It was time for her to go. She stepped out of the room and turned to thank him. "Thank you, Mr. Blakewell. I look forward to seeing whether you make it past the deadline without objections."

"Investigator Dettmer," he said, smiling broadly, "I spoke to Chief Rennick before you ever arrived. You won't be opening an investigation or filing any objections. I just wanted to find out more about the real you."

The large door closed, and the guard gestured for her to continue down the hallway to the elevator. She had just been used and was not even sure how.

TWENTY

Friday, 6:15 p.m.

Once on the LA Metro bus, Roman powered down Roxy's iBrowse and stuffed them into his bag. He swapped them out for Malcolm's employee iBrowse, which he set the health level to yellow in the hopes that it would keep people at a distance. He wore the blue T-shirt and black slacks of a StarSee employee and wore a black medical mask. He had used product in his shaggy hair to keep it in place, combed back to look more styled.

The tram to the top of the StarSee towers whooshed by overhead, full of tourists and people with high Admiration Points. Down here, the electric bus jostled its human contents like an amusement park ride as it navigated the rough Los Angeles streets. It was rush hour, so the old buses were full of second shift employees. StreamBugs hovered near the ceiling at the front waiting to rejoin their subscribers when they exited.

Looking ahead, through the concrete canyons of the wide Los Angeles streets, the StarSee headquarters sparkled in the distance, shining like a cathedral of the digital age. As they pulled around to the rear of the massive semicircular building that sat underneath the three towers, Roman kept his head down in case anyone was digitally screening employees. He exited the back of the bus, along with most of the other riders. As soon as they were off, the bus filled up again from the front with blue-shirted people finishing their shifts, and pulled silently away.

He passed through the weapon detectors, swiped Malcolm's employee ID over the reader and walked through the main double doors. He had passed the first test. Roman had prepared by watching volumetric recordings of the interior of the facility online, and had made a mental map of the layout. It was a confusing labyrinth of hallways and secret doors. Maintenance at StarSee was managed like an amusement park. The idea was to create the public impression that the facility magically stayed spotless. Because visitors should never have to see the facility being cleaned, maintenance employees also could not have watchers. This worked in Roman's favor this time, as no one would be following Malcom's StarStream as Roman poked around Starla's Vault files.

The place where a dead person's data goes to die.

He quickly navigated his way from the drop off, up the elevator to the primary facility and down the dark hidden hallways to the rear cleaning entrance of the Vaults. He had been to the Vaults before, many years ago, when it was his father's data that was in purgatory, so he remembered the normal, approved way to view the data. Ordinarily, visitors would get the deceased's Box ID from the clerk at the front entrance, something Roman could not do. So, he had instead requested the number in advance from Starla's brother, who also notified the system that he might visit, just in case. Paul would not make the trip from Massachusetts to Los Angeles just to look at his sister's StarSee feed, but the system would not know that.

Roman entered what looked like a giant library, with rows and rows of black two foot wide by one foot tall boxes lined up at chest height. Each box would slide out, and a display panel would flip up, revealing a physical keyboard below it. An actual wire had to be connected between the Vault box and the visitors' iBrowse, making wirelessly intercepting protected data impossible. Vault visits were completely private and secure, but if proper access was granted, the hardwire link meant the digital ghost of the dead person's stream was completely available to the eyes of the visitor. Signs announcing, "No Social Media" hung prominently throughout the chamber.

Looking down the rows upon rows, he saw roughly a dozen people standing before boxes around the floor. Some sat in folding chairs, and a few had tablets and were jotting down notes. It was as quiet as an abandoned library, with only the occasional faint sounds of someone weeping in the distance. A few people spoke commands gently into the system as they worked their way through the deceased's streams. At the end of each row stood an access kiosk, where visitors had to swipe their ID and enter the proper passcode.

A StarSee Vault Guide walked calmly down the aisles like an employee at a home improvement store looking for someone to ignore. Roman waited for her to pass and then approached the kiosk at the end of his aisle cautiously, as if there might be facial recognition that could see through his mask. He entered Starla's Vault number and then the family passcode.

The next step was critical, which was to hold his thumb against the biometric identity verification pad. There was no way to fake one's way past this step. The only hope Roman had was that Keith and Tek had managed to reprogram the system to read Roman's biometry and think he was Starla's brother Paul. He hesitantly pressed his thumb against the reader, while holding the ID over the pad, and waited while it clicked, checked his thumbprint and drew a tiny DNA sample.

Roman nervously awaited the results. The light remained yellow for much longer than seemed necessary. *Are they monitoring her box?* He heard footsteps approaching in the distance. If he tried to run now, they would surely stop him before he could get through the doors.

The light turned green. The readout read, "Please proceed to your assigned Vault."

He breathed a sigh of relief and ducked into the aisle, rushing to Starla's Vault box. Since Malcolm's iBrowse could not pair to a Vault, he pulled Roxy's iBrowse out of his bag and connected the thin wire between the box and the small hole behind the ear. Navigating using an old-fashioned mouse and keyboard interface was awkward at first, but he quickly adapted. Entering Starla's digital Vault was like walking around her empty condo after she died, an odd invasion of her privacy.

He dove into her StarStream and went directly to the night in question. The interface was much like the standard StarSee interface, except that he could move through time much more easily, and there were no ads. He skipped through time until he arrived at the moment she opened the door on Monday night, seeing himself standing at the door with his capture equipment. She greeted him, smiling. She looked radiant. He fast forwarded until he saw himself setting his lights and cameras in motion. This was what he needed. Now to capture the recording.

Glancing nervously around the dark hall, he reached into his bag and pulled out the simpin. He'd insert it, copy the files, and be out before anyone noticed.

The screen went black.

"What the hell?!" he said out loud. He quickly lowered his head and glanced around. Hopefully, he had not drawn any attention.

Returning to the dark screen, in the upper right-hand corner of the window, it said *"Locked by Agreement 413, enter passcode to view."*

"Fuck!" He put his hand to his mouth to keep from making any more noise and stood still.

In the text entry field, he entered the family's passcode and hit enter. The box turned red and made a small honk sound. There were no other passcodes he knew of. He didn't know what else to try. He entered some random numbers as if it might magically work. Honk. He typed *AGREEMENT413*. Honk. He couldn't remember her birthday. It could be anything.

He was so close to getting Starla's real stream from that night that his hands were shaking. He opened a search bar on the list of her recordings and entered the words *"Agreement 413,"* to see if any other clips might be locked or if it was only the night of her murder. Nine pieces of her stream were listed. Trying to play any of them resulted in the same error message. He marked them red, and sorted by date. The most recent locked segment was the night of her murder. The oldest was a couple of years ago.

Clicking *"View in Timeline,"* all the files rearranged themselves from left to right, with the red highlighted ones he couldn't view interspersed among the blocks of un-highlighted clips that he could visually scrub through. He jumped back in time to just before the locked files to see if anything clicked. He had already met and scanned Starla by then. She was attending an awards dinner with the Blakewells, celebrating her most recent six-hour special event for the StarSee series, Cherish. It had been another colossal hit for the multi-talented woman, and this time, her dramatic chops were on full display. Ultra high resolution volumetric capture can easily telegraph to viewers that an actor is acting, making it feel like the performance is false. But Starla had a natural ability to deliver her lines and emotions in an absolutely genuine way. It had been her best performance to date. It had already won her several awards, and the list was about to include the golden statue.

However, she neglected to thank any of the visual effects artists for their work this time, which Roman offhandedly mentioned in an interview. Soon, the media had spun it into an outright feud. Both Roman and Starla knew the whole thing was just sensationalism. Watching the media coverage play back at high speed was like opening an old wound.

The first instance of the locked Agreement 413 files preceded a six-week period that she did not visually appear in her stream at all. This was unusual, but there were many voids in her StarStream when she was on a retreat, or having a procedure done. Only the biggest celebrities can temporarily turn off their video streams without worrying about losing watchers, and then only if they keep feeding text updates. Soon thereafter, saying she found the volumetric capture too stressful, she retired from doing the scripted work and focused on her live StarStream.

There were no other protected pieces of her stream again for months, and when they did occur, it seemed to be random. Sometimes, it was just a small block of time in the middle of her being out in public, other times, it was entire days. And then the final one was the night of her death.

If not for the fact that he could not see the night of her murder, the locked files could almost be a glitch. He racked his brain. What else could he search for? He opened the text messaging interface of her StarStream. The amount of messages was overwhelming. He couldn't possibly sift through them without searching for specific terms. He searched for the keyword Kitsune. The first time it appeared in her messaging stream was only about a year and a half ago, used by a fan with protected anonymity. Whomever it was that used that name could afford the purchase of an anonymous identity on StarSee. *Owen Blakewell, perhaps?*

It wasn't a crazy idea. His DNA was on the gift. He could be the anonymous fan with a pet name for his biggest star. That would be nearly impossible to prove though.

Noise was rising from the isles, the Vault room was getting busier since it was a Friday evening and people were getting off work. This was proving to be a risky waste of time. But maybe the locked files thing was a trail he could follow. Whatever Agreement 413 was, it was being used by someone to hide her real stream from Monday night. He needed to find out what this agreement was, find the passcode to bypass it, and then get back into her files.

Who might know why the files are locked?

He looked at his ID badge. Talking to Malcolm Chasper's buddies in maintenance wasn't likely to be much help. If he asked for help from one of the Vault Guides in the room, they might recognize that he was not who his badge said he was. He needed someone who would know about the Vaults but never saw maintenance people.

A shaft of light entered the room from the front entrance.

He had an idea. He ducked low and quickly pulled off his blue t-shirt and swapped it out for the gray sweatshirt in his bag. He anticipated that the clerk would assume that anyone coming out of the Vaults must have legitimately checked in.

As he emerged into the brightly-lit carpeted hallway, he became aware of the streamBugs again. Roman adjusted the fit on his black cloth mask and checked to make sure the health indicator on Malcolm's iBrowse was still set to yellow.

The desk clerk, a young man in his twenties wearing a StarSee t-shirt, slid a tablet across the desk in Roman's direction and mumbled, "Sign out, please."

Roman pulled the tablet closer and made a gesture as if he was doing something, and slid it back. "Oh, hey man, can I ask you a question?"

The young man looked up, and his eyes narrowed. For a moment, Roman thought the kid might realize he didn't see him check in, but it quickly became apparent he was just not used to being asked anything. He blinked at Roman.

"Dude, you have any idea what Agreement 413 is?" asked Roman.

The young man replied, "Nope."

"The files I was reviewing had blocks of time that I couldn't view. Said I had to enter another passcode to get past Agreement 413. I thought the Vaults were supposed to contain everything from a person's stream, even in a criminal case?"

"Streams are still bound by lots of legal agreements, even if they're here in the Vaults. I've heard of them having sections that are off limits if they contain trade secrets, or witness protection, or ICE protection, or national security."

"Huh," said Roman. He glanced back to see a young woman had walked up behind him, waiting to get in. "Who actually puts the additional protection on the files?"

"Would either be automatic or somebody like an official of the company. A lawyer or something." The clerk leaned to one side, peering around Roman to the person who had walked up behind him, hinting that Roman needed to move along.

"Is there any trace of who did it left behind in the records? Like some way I could find out who blocked it? Maybe they could unlock it?" asked Roman.

"You just said it, man. The name of the agreement is the trace. Who was this loved one with the secrets, anyway?"

Roman glanced around. Maybe this kid had access and could look it up. He put his finger to his mouth and whispered just loud enough for the clerk to hear. "Starla Devine."

"Oh shit." The guard nodded his head. "That explains a lot."

The woman behind Roman cleared her throat.

"You a relative?" he asked.

"Yeah." He hoped a vague answer would be enough.

The clerk looked Roman up and down. "Ah, you must be Paul. Sorry for your loss, man. It crushed us when she was murdered. She was number one, the very first streamer. Everybody's connected to her. If I could get my hands on that guy who killed her…"

Roman clenched his teeth, thankful for his mask. "You sound like a fan."

"I used to watch her. A lot. Lots of us did. We had all kinds of clubs and pages."

"How long did you follow her?"

The line behind Roman had grown to three people, but now the kid was more interested in talking about his favorite dead celebrity than doing his job. "Oh, I was a watcher for years, man. I could tell you almost anything you wanted to know about her."

"Really?" Roman decided to take a gamble. "Okay, where did her money go?"

The kid lit up. "Impossible to know for sure, but rumors were that the Blakewells had her in a conservatorship, like her image was more important than her actual life. It's not fair. Nobody should be able to own someone like that."

"But she wasn't mentally unfit."

"Yeah, no. I mean, you would know. But lots of us think she was having a relationship with one of the Blakewells, who had her under their spell and put her in the conservatorship." He put his hand to his mouth and whispered, "I probably shouldn't be talking about it–" His eyes rolled back and forth. "–most people think it was Owen, but my money is on Maddox."

"Which one could hide parts of her stream?"

"Well, Owen could have it done, but Maddox could do it himself. Know what I mean? Owen may be the man behind the curtain, but Maddox is an actual wizard."

"If they can lock her files, would they keep unlocked copies?"

"They could have unlocked copies of everything, man. Especially Maddox. They frigging own StarSee."

"Let's say you wanted to talk to Maddox. How would you do it?"

The kid chuckled. "You can't just talk to Maddox Blakewell, man. He might live right there–" the kid pointed up through the glass ceiling to the right side tower, "–but the only people he talks to are his people, the programmers who make all this."

Somebody in the back of the line said "C'mon guys, let's go."

"I gotta help these people, man. But I'm truly sorry for your loss. Hey, do you agree with the theory that this Roman Glass guy might have a split personality?"

Roman's eyes widened. "I guess?" That was a new one. "Hey,

one last question. Did your fan club notice anything weird happen to her a couple of years ago? She went quiet for a while."

"I don't remember anything. She went to some retreats and stuff. She obviously could do that kind of thing, you know?" His head tilted slightly to the side. "Hey, I thought you were a relative."

Roman turned and looked at the line growing behind him. "Sorry," he murmured, and turned back to the young clerk.

"You have a lot of questions for being her brother."

Time to go. "Thanks bro, have a great rest of your day." Roman quickly turned and walked away.

The clerk stuttered something, but the woman next in line was already demanding his attention.

Roman walked briskly down the glass hallway and around a corner. He stopped and leaned against a wall, looking up through the glass ceiling at the right side tower. StreamBugs swirled and spun away, detecting that he was maintenance. He could just make out the very upper levels, which were glowing a different shade of blue than the rest of the building. Maddox Blakewell's legendary personal aquariums. Roman's geosense mapped the tower, eighteen stories up, sixteen feet per story, each one set back into the hillside from the floor beneath it.

He imagined Maddox Blakewell standing up there with his father, looking out over their empire, laughing at Roman for trying to access Starla's Vault drive.

I need those files, and there's only one place I can get them, and only one way I could possibly gain access to those floors.

He would hide in his sister's townhouse for one more night, then it was time to learn about fish.

CHAPTER
TWENTY-ONE

Saturday, 8:20 a.m.

The combination of monitor displays and the active retina display of his iRiz created a universe of data and connections for Maddox to navigate through like a data astronaut. He stood in the center of the Gray Room, watching the neon color-coded data swirl around him in waves tailored for his understanding only. StreamBugs positioned themselves strategically around the space to provide instant overlays of charts and graphs onto the real world monitors and desk via his iRiz.

He could work here for hours on end, obsessing over the stream of information. The graphs changed to engagement data, showing how long people had been interacting with the site and how many level-two ads they were exposed to. It was all about connection and participation. Maddox drove the core value of the company up by driving up watcher time, then aggregating, repackaging and redistributing the very data he was looking at now to companies that use it to sell themselves and their products.

Maddox knew the system had deeper ramifications than just selling products and services. It also planted and sold ideas, creating beliefs that could become the foundation for larger corporate and societal change. Expose someone to an ad hundreds of times without them even realizing it, and it becomes a belief they have without even wondering why they have it.

Maintaining divisions in society without going too far was the knife's edge that Maddox sharpened, and today he was cutting together a new narrative. Conflict being the key to engagement, he was spreading a "citizen journalist" StarStream that satisfied both sides of the political dive, a story about how StarSee had helped a small Middle Eastern country stop the beginnings of a civil war. The story was that by seeing each other in their StarStreams, the opposing sides came to understand that they were all human, with the same hopes, dreams and wishes. If it were not for StarSee, and the massive reach and acceptance of the platform, these people would be fighting and killing each other instead of democratically electing peaceful representatives. The mention of Sparkle, which helped clean their water and sanitize their dishes, was barely noticeable.

The story would never be seen outside of a certain region of theUnited States, and unbeknownst to any of those viewers, Maddox's AI algorithm generated all of it. The website that ran the story was completely created by Maddox's AI code. The reporter who wrote the story was Maddox's AI code. The country was real, but there was no seed of discontent, no sprouting animosity, no budding civil war, just the potential for conflict that was spun into existence by Maddox and his code.

It was very illegal, but he didn't care. No one would have the time, energy, or inclination to investigate any of it. If an outside news agency dug in, it would appear that some citizen journalist had simply gotten a story wrong, and the trail would end.

This was what made StarSee the number one platform in the

world, and it was all because Maddox himself paid attention to subscribers, their wants and their needs. It was a relationship made in digital heaven.

Since StarSee was about to become part news organization, he might have to get more clever when manipulating public opinion, but not yet. For now, they were still just a social media platform hiding behind the idea that anyone who believed citizen journalist stories were fact was a fool for thinking of StarSee as anything other than entertainment.

His iRiz audio dots chimed with an incoming call. It was Gabe. Maddox's streamBugs lifted off the desk and hovered in a semi-circle above him. The screen that had been displaying a grid of streams from mid-level celebrities became a single image of Gabe wearing his trademark form-fitting black t-shirt against a gray home office background. A pop-up window displayed his usual StarSee personal information, number of watchers, location, Admiration Point value, etc.

"No suit today, Gabe?"

"No meetings, no suit. I get to stay in my office and file documents today."

"You have about the most plebeian background a person could have."

"My words are what's important, not my background. Flashy distractions are your department."

"And what words do you have for me today?"

"It is I who needs your words, Maddox. You haven't digitally signed the drafts I sent last night."

"There's a reason for that."

"Imagine that," said Gabe.

"Why does Father retain veto power over news items that are fed to NewsCann by StarSee?" His tone was accusatory, like Gabe had tried to hide something.

"He never uses his veto powers."

"That's not what I asked. Why does he still possess them? I'm the one who steered this platform to the place it is. Nobody should have veto power over anything I fucking say!"

Gabe sat silently for a moment. "It's his structure, and he always retains the right, even if he trusts you and never uses it."

"Well, change it. Since I'm the one making this company what it is, I want his powers changed."

Gabe leaned in. "Look Maddox, I'm going to tell you something. Your father told me you might protest, and here's what he said. Ready? He said to tell you "Go fuck yourself." Sign the fucking docs so we can move forward and stay on schedule. The deadline expires Monday night at midnight, and he wants everything buttoned up."

Maddox fumed, but bit his tongue. He had to keep his cool, or he might make a stupid mistake again. He also could not piss off Gabe too bad, he needed him. Plus, Gabe knew where the skeletons were buried.

"Gabe." Maddox was grinding his teeth. "I need the language in the agreement changed. I got screwed by Father because of a loophole with Client M, and I won't let it happen again."

Gabe smiled and bit his bottom lip. His eyes flicked around as if he was searching for the right words to appear in the air before him. Then his eyes locked back on Maddox. "Maddox, your intentions regarding this company are transparent, but you're going to have to negotiate with your father yourself." His demeanor suddenly changed to one of seething anger as he spoke very slowly. "So sign your Goddamn papers, keep us on schedule, and bitch to your therapist, not me." The screen abruptly went black as he disconnected. It returned to displaying dozens of live StarStreams.

Maddox slammed his fists on the desk. *Fuck! Gabe can be so Goddamn sensitive.* He took a deep breath and exhaled slowly. *I have to be more careful. I can't show my cards like that.* He looked around the darkened Gray Room, every streamBug and device waiting for his next command. He would have to confront his father directly.

"Maria." His Digital Assistant chimed in his ears, indicating it was listening. "Call Father."

After a moment, Lara answered, audio only. "He's not available, he's on the green."

"Why the fuck is he off playing golf at a time like this?"

"What do you want, Maddox?"

"I need to talk to him about the structure of the acquisition."

"Okay, I'll let him know."

"Look, I know you just started this assistant thing, but I'm not some fucking subscriber with a complaint. Put him on."

She turned on her video. She was sitting alone at an outdoor table, at a cafe in Beverly Hills. Her wide-brimmed hat cast a shadow from the morning sun across her masked face. "It's Saturday Maddox. Remember?"

"Yes, I do. But I don't stop what I'm doing, because every hour matters right now."

"What can I say? He's not here. Anything else I can not do for you?"

Maddox shook his head in frustration. "Yeah, I discovered some unusual activity around Starla's Vault data in the public access Vaults yesterday."

"What was it?"

"That's just it. The access was initiated by her brother, but there's no record of him entering the Vault room. Then the desk clerk made a remark in his logs that a relative of hers approached him on the way out, looking for protected sections of her stream."

"Could a social media investigator have used his passcode?"

"No, the biometric ID said it was him. However, I have found no travel booked by him."

"That is curious," said Lara.

Maddox squinted. "Wait, what led you to think it might be an investigator?"

"One came to the tower and met with your father. Dettmer something."

"Dammit, why didn't he tell me someone was sniffing around? That's important. That division could file an objection!"

"Your father said he had it covered. The Social Media Division Captain wants streamBugs allowed in the station and won't jeopardize his chance at stardom. It was just the investigator fishing."

"We can't have anyone fishing around right now. We have to be careful, there's too much riding on the next few days to risk one of us letting something slip."

"Don't be paranoid. You knew investigators would come poking around."

"That's exactly why I'm paranoid. For fuck's sake, if Father says something stupid to someone smart, we're all in trouble. We're only days away–"

She interrupted, "Your father is a narcissistic asshole. I know that better than anyone. It might seem like he says dumb things, but it's a soup of distractions, lies and misdirections. It's a strategy. I wouldn't worry about him."

"This investigator, what was the pretext of his visit?"

"Her, it was a woman, and she didn't say she had anything specific. She was looking into the uptick in murders. It's getting a name, you know. The media is calling them *The Killing Feeds*." She raised her eyebrows.

"Shit. Oh well, we just have to get through the next couple of days, and then it's over. We have to lead anyone poking around to the idea that the murders are just a side effect of our crumbling society."

"You may get your chance. If she hasn't contacted you already, she probably will soon. He sent her your way."

"Dammit. Why does he do that?"

"Because you asked for more control, and this comes with it." A waiter approached Lara, and she nodded. "I'll let him know you called about the deal structure. Again." She stressed the word "again," as if it was getting old, and then she disconnected.

So I'm left handling investigators while he's off playing golf and refusing to give me the deal structure I deserve. He clenched and unclenched his fists. *Exactly the same pattern as the last time he screwed me. It won't happen again.*

He would have to put things in motion sooner than anticipated.

Maddox opened the folder containing his special algorithm and logged in through the back door of the one profile that connected every member of StarSee, the now-deceased Starla Devine's. Like putting out an order for a hit, all he had to do was run his code, choose a target, then let the algorithm choose an attacker. It would snake its way through the main code of the site and infect the target's stream, creating an enemy that the target didn't even know they had. It would create false posts, doctored streams, and specific memes that would quickly drive the attacker to believe that they needed to kill the target.

The genius of Maddox's programming was the method in which the algorithm overrode the Impulse Governor. IGs were initially instituted as an anti-terrorism measure, special monitor bots that constantly analyzed all social media platforms to check for people getting out of control and threatening harm. But Maddox was able to hack into the Impulse Governor and make a very simple and undetectable code change. With just a couple of hidden lines, he modified the code where it defined where the results were sent, redirecting where it phoned home with data. Now, the real information would go to Maddox's algorithm, and fake IG data would go to Homeland Security. Thus, Maddox's algorithm, using AI, would know it was working, in what way, and tune itself to emphasize the elements that were having an effect on the chosen assassin. The very code intended to keep people calm became the host for the code that would drive people to murder.

The target would remain oblivious, which made it all the easier to pull off. With the guidance of a supercomputer's neural network figuring out the best possible way to do it, and surreptitiously feeding the attacker the results, it had worked on dozens of occasions. And, of course, it would erase its own tracks twelve hours upon completion. Side effects were a small issue that he still had to deal with.

Now he would sit back and wait. *Sorry, Dad, but I will win.*

CHAPTER
TWENTY-TWO

Saturday, 9:40 a.m.

Roman approached the giant aquarium store feeling confident. Spending the night at his sister's gave him the opportunity to have Tek set Roxy's iBrowse to anonymous, a setting usually reserved only for those who could afford it. It also allowed them the time to make a few fairly easy modifications to Malcolm Chasper's profile page, so that Roman could play the part of an assistant to a secretive rich man, whose name he was not at liberty to divulge, but who was interested in installing a giant aquarium in his new home construction in the Hollywood Hills. The real Malcolm, being in StarSee Maintenance, was not permitted to have watchers, and therefore, he had no streamBugs following him, which was good cover.

Seven spoke to Roman through his iBrowse. "You ready?"

"Ready." He wore his QR code black mask and kept the iBrowse health indicator set to yellow. Behind the mask, he felt good about his chances of making this work. He didn't even have to dress up to sell the part. All he had to do was add a black ballcap to his outfit, and he looked like he could be some Hollywood muckety muck's assistant. As he entered the popular store, he saw streamBugs everywhere. What should have made him nervous instead filled him with a sense of longing. It had been days since he was last live, and he missed it. Most aquarium stores were virtual now, but not this one. He would have loved to show it off to his watchers.

Most of the basic information he needed was available online, but he was here for more than that. He needed to capture the frequently changing security ID, and if he was lucky, get a look at the layout of Maddox's residence.

An older blonde saleswoman, named Trish, approached him, and Roman fed her his fabricated story. Soon, she was shortcasting to his iBrowse, and he watched a promotional piece about the company and its amazing aquariums. After the video completed, she walked him around the store to show him real fish.

"This is one of the most beautiful fish your employer can put in his new aquarium, Mr. Chasper. The male Mandarinfish. It belongs to the Dragonet family and is native to the Pacific Ocean. The Dragonet family is beautiful, yet carnivorous. Powerful people are drawn to it, I know from experience." Roman's iBrowse overlayed all the pertinent information about care and maintenance of the fish as he looked at the tank.

"It is quite beautiful. Is installation and maintenance difficult?" This was why he was here. If he was going to pretend to be an aquarium maintenance person to gain entry to Maddox's private residence, he better know the basics. "My employer is building in the hills, and as you know, there's no water up there."

"Well, I have good news. Where you're building, there's a main we can tap into."

Trish looked at the fake profile while I was watching the video. Good.

"For our high-end clients like yours, we have an entire purification, filtration, storage and maintenance system that automatically balances the pH levels, oxygenates the water, and ensures that if something were to happen to the creatures' environment, we can replace the entire contents of the tank's water in under thirty minutes, ensuring the complete safety of the entire ecosystem. It's triple redundancy, holding three times the total amount of water required by the living system," she said.

"That sounds large. I'm worried it might not be … attractive."

She resumed shortcasting. "Here are some pictures of complete high-end systems we've done."

Roman watched the slide show of several installations. The tanks were indeed huge, but painted and camouflaged using trees, rocks and plants to hide them. One installation stood out as easily being ten times the size of the others. *Bingo.* "Wow, that one's big," he said. "Can you pause on that for a second?"

"Sure." She was watching along on her own iBrowse. "Liquid Arts is the creator of the famous Maddox Blakewell residential installation. The largest private aquarium system in the world. Proof that we truly can make any aquarium dream come true."

Roman made internal geosense measurements of the structure as he watched the stream. "I'm surprised he has the time to maintain that."

"Oh no, we make it easy for Mr. Blakewell. Our expert staff regularly go up there and make sure everything is running perfectly. And we'd give your installation the same level of expert care as we do with the Blakewells."

"Are there any dangers to having an aquarium that size, with all those systems, in a residence? Like leaking?"

"Oh no, it would take a complete collapse of the tank diverter valves to cause a failure of the system, and that's virtually impossible."

Seven spoke into Roman's ear. "Ask about security."

"My employer is very private, so he'll have pretty strict security."

"We pride ourselves on being both discreet and professional. We can come at preappointed times, and if one of our maintenance personnel is in his home, he'll recognize our special smartshirts a mile away." She glanced down at her own swirling, vibrant white and blue underwater-patterned shirt.

"But there's more than a special shirt, right?"

"Of course. Our truck will be coded to your gate, and once we're on the grounds, our workers have monthly IDs for personal interactions, which communicate directly with the security system." She casually held up her ID. Roman heard a click in his ear.

"Shit," said Seven. "I didn't get the picture."

Roman glanced down at the ID hanging off her belt. "Did you say your badges change monthly?"

"Yeah." She held up the badge and turned it against the light. It reflected blue and orange colors. "The color of the reflective coating changes monthly. It's a little thing, but it helps on our end." She smiled.

"Got it," said Seven over the iBrowse.

Roman looked around the store as if taking it all in. "Fantastic stuff, just fantastic. I'll recommend we move forward with you. As we move into the construction phase, I'll be in touch, and we can start talking about design dimensions." As he stood up and reached out to shake the woman's hand, something caught his attention. It was another customer, a silver-haired man who was clearly taking an interest in their conversation. Roman adjusted his QR code black mask and clipped his sunglasses back on to his iBrowse. The man was approaching. It was the kind of hesitant approach a person made when they thought they recognized a celebrity.

It was possible that someone could recognize him from just his eyes. There were certainly enough streamBugs around.

Time to go.

"Thanks for your time. I'll be in touch about next steps," Roman said, already heading for the door.

The sales woman looked puzzled at his hasty exit, and said something about being involved in the construction phase, but

Roman was already halfway to the exit. As he glanced back, he saw the silver-haired man approaching the sales woman.

"Trish? Trish Patterson? It's me, Herb Coleman! Art Academy!" The man was holding out both arms, as he and Trish were about to embrace.

Roman's breathing slowed, and he stepped out the door onto the sidewalk. "Jeez, that was nerve-wracking."

"I saw it. No reason to panic. With the mask on, nobody will recognize you."

"I don't know. One of my watchers who knows me well might recognize my eyes. In hindsight, maybe I shouldn't have tried so hard to get more watchers."

"You were smart to be safe and get out of there, regardless," said Seven.

Roman hopped into the back of the waiting SDV at the corner pick-up zone. "Did you get what you need?"

"Yes, I sent Keith the snapshot, and the ID is being made right now. The Liquid Arts smartshirt will be a fake, but I doubt anyone will notice. Did you get what you need?"

"I think so. I mapped everything related to the aquarium system and a bit of the layout of Maddox's place. I know which room is his home office now."

"Thirty minutes. Corner of Fairfax and Fountain," she said.

Saturday, 11:50 a.m.

Tinting the windows of the SDV made it possible to change in the car without feeling exposed. Seven had handed off the small bundle of the hastily manufactured fake Liquid Arts uniform and ID from Keith at the drop off point, and Roman had immediately instructed the car to head for the access road to Maddox's tower. There was no time to try and set up a reason for his visit, and it was too risky to draw attention. He needed to get in and get out. He quickly touched base with Tek and Seven before he disconnected and approached the facility. Even with Roxy's iBrowse set to anonymous, the Blakewells might detect if he tried to transmit anything at all.

Breaking and entering, theft of private property, home invasion. The charges were piling up if he were to get caught, and if anyone was going to press charges, it would be the Blakewells. He needed to get in, get the file, and get out, fast.

The SDV went over another small speed hump on the way up the hill. As he rounded a corner, Roman could see dozens of protesters yelling and holding signs on the road leading up to the access road gate. The signs read like a menu of grievances:

"No Merger!"

"Our streams are not news!"

"Tax the Blakewells."

"Swat the streamBugs!"

He told the SDV to stop and back around the corner until they were out of sight of the group.

He couldn't see how far from the first gate the actual tower was, and there was no way he could sneak off into the brush and make his way up the hillside. He would have to march straight in through the gates and hope that between his ability to act and the fake uniform, he could BS his way inside.

He took big confident steps as he marched up to the gathering, most of whom were too busy speechifying to their own stream-Bugs to even notice that he was there, let alone that he wasn't one of them. It looked like fun to Roman, and for a moment, he longed to be able to stream again. He might have joined them if he wasn't trying to keep himself out of jail.

The gate kept the crowd from advancing any farther up the hill. Large signs on either side of the vehicle barrier read "Private Property, No Trespassing." According to the satellite maps, there would be an actual security gate at the building's entrance, which was farther up the road, but he would need to slip past the first gate and get out of sight quickly.

He held his fist high and shook it as if he was part of the demonstration, even though he stuck out like a sore thumb. Making his way to the gate, he quickly darted around it and started jogging up the road.

Behind him, a man shouted, "Hey! You can't go up there! They'll arrest you! They said we have to stay down here!" Roman waved and pretended he couldn't hear. As he expected, a small swarm of Free Agent streamBugs followed him for a few hundred feet. But they quickly gave up on watching what appeared to be a lone worker doing his job and returned to where the action was. He continued walking up the road for another quarter mile before arriving at one of the main security gates. It was a solid metal gate, sixteen feet across and eight feet high, with a guard booth on one side that had a four-foot wide pedestrian access walkway on the side of it. He could see Maddox's tower standing in the sunlight beyond the gate.

Roman marched to the pedestrian turnstile, breathing heavily as he swiped his Living Arts badge on the card scanner. It beeped and remained red. He tried gently pushing it, but it would not move. He tried again. No luck. *Shit.*

He swallowed and walked up to the guard booth and rapped on the glass.

The old man in the gray uniform lifted the brim of his hat and eyed Roman suspiciously. "Where's your van?"

"Right?" said Roman. "Damned protesters blocked my way."

The guard eyed Roman silently.

"There's low oxygen in one of the big tanks." Roman thrust his thumb toward the building. "I think the salinity might be drifting. Every minute counts and these wing nuts are making it hard for me to do my job and fix the tank."

The guard looked perplexed. He looked at his screens where he, undoubtedly, could see the group of protesters and no van.

"I had to tell the van to park down the road. I didn't want those folks vandalizing it," he shouted through the glass. "People like them make it harder for guys like us to do our jobs, right?" Roman hoped to win him over by guessing which side of the fence this guard was on. "At least we have jobs. It's not right, them protesting a company that provides so much."

The guard looked at his shirt and glanced at his name badge. "Well, Mr. Chasper, I'm just glad they stay where they're supposed to." His expression became even more suspicious. "Your badge's passcode ain't working."

Roman looked down at his badge and hit it like it was a broken watch. "Yeah, I'll have to let my supervisor know."

"Hold it up and lower your mask, please."

Roman's pulse went up. He pulled down his mask, tried to smile, and held up the fake ID.

"You look familiar," said the guard.

He put the mask back up. "I come up through this gate a lot. I recognize you too." He stared at the guard. "But, um, every minute really does count with these extremely rare fish of Mr. Blakewell's, you know. I just don't want to be on the receiving end of how pissed he'll be if I don't get up there quickly."

The guard itched his chin and seemed to watch Roman's swirling smartshirt for a moment. "Lemme fix it for ya," said the old man.

Roman slipped him the ID, and the guard held it over a small box until it beeped, and slid it back, along with an e-pad and a stylus. Roman scribbled something unintelligible in the name, put Liquid Arts in the company, and jotted down the current time. He handed it back, and the guard waved him through the meat grinder turnstile.

As soon as he was through, he could see that there were other guards on the roadway, and one female guard had a golf cart. Roman hopped onto the rear of the utility cart, thankful for the ride up the hill to the back of the tower. He felt like a spy that had just crossed behind enemy lines.

The cart driver let Roman off next to a side access door. He walked across the concrete walkway, swiped his card at the door, bolted into Maddox Blakewell's tower and ran up the stairs toward where the tank equipment room should be.

Emerging from the stairway into the living area, the residence took Roman's breath away. The entire rear wall of the twenty-thousand square-foot home that jutted out from the side of the mountain was an aquarium. Walls and hallways were curved aquarium glass. The recordings he had watched in the Liquid Arts store didn't do it justice. Sunlight poured in through the front side of the home, while blue dappled caustics water light bounced in from the rear. It was a sight like nothing Roman had ever seen in a home. Spa music filled the space. The anxiety he had about sneaking into the Blakewell residence melted away in this world of deep blue tranquility.

He stood in awe of the sheer beauty and size of the place. There was no one around, and no streamBugs anywhere. The dark wood floors and the contemporary furniture were gorgeous. Dividing the giant open space between the rear of the home and the front of the home were walls that defined traditional living spaces. These walls were a gradient from a light gray at the front of the home, where they intersected the windows overlooking Los Angeles, to very dark blue/gray at the rear, where they intersected the aquarium walls. This created a feeling of moving from the bright outside into a dark underwater world.

The size of the transparent walls filled with water, fish, coral, rocks and plants threw off his Geosense. When he looked at the aquarium, his mind wanted to generate the map of the inside of the aquarium, not the glass walls, and he had to concentrate to create the surfaces of the tanks in his mind. Having already determined which space might be an office, he walked down a large open hallway, up a short set of stairs, through a very large living area, and into the room. It had a very wide desk and large display screens, as well as one interactive gestural interface cylinder.

Behind the desk, the aquarium wall began at chest height, and below was a dark gray fabric-covered wall. Smoothly hidden in the wall were three access panels. He was hoping it would be one panel for everything. He waved the fake Living Arts ID over them and heard a faint click. Pushing on the left panel, it popped slightly open, revealing portals with which he could check water salinity, swap out filters and add pH balancing chemicals. The other two remained locked, so it was all but certain that one of them was a point of access for Maddox's private system. He glanced around the room for anything that might help and noticed a clean trash can by the desk. *Maintenance.* He dug into his pants, pulled out Malcolm's maintenance ID and waved it over the panels. The middle one silently clicked. He popped it open.

He heard footsteps approaching. Looking straight ahead at the reflection in the glass walls of the aquarium, he could see Maddox Blakewell walking straight toward him. Roman's eyes went wide, and he froze. Any tranquility within Roman was gone in an instant.

"Everything okay?" Maddox asked.

Roman did not move. *He's shorter than I expected.* "All good here," he replied. As he stood facing the aquarium wall, a multicolored Dragonet swam up to the glass and stared him in the eyes. *Beautiful yet carnivorous.*

"Why are you wearing iBrowse? Weren't you instructed to remove them at the door?"

"They're powered off, of course, Mr. Blakewell." He kept fiddling with things as if he was too busy to turn around. "We detected a slight pH imbalance at the office, so I'm just going through and making sure the system is in tiptop shape." He grimaced at his own choice of words, *tiptop shape?* He watched Maddox in the distorted reflection, thinking he might have to run at any second.

Silence followed. Then Roman heard one of Maddox's assistants in the other room. "Someone's here to talk to you. Said your father sent her."

Maddox mumbled, "Dammit," then turned and left the room.

Roman exhaled. Whatever had demanded Maddox's attention, Roman hoped it would give him enough time to find a way into the private Vault Drive system and copy the files he needed.

CHAPTER
TWENTY-THREE

Saturday, 12:25 p.m.

The shimmering tanks stretching from the floor to the ceiling were magnificent. "This is quite an amazing home," said Dettmer. "It must be hard to maintain." The foyer she stood in was a similar waiting area to the living quarters in Owen's tower, but the feel of this one was quite different. She would snap a picture if they had not asked her to put her iBrowse in a basket at the door.

"I have people for that," said Maddox Blakewell, standing with his hands clasped, wearing shorts and a loose fitting button down linen shirt. "Sorry I'm not dressed for an official interview, I wasn't given any notice that you were coming."

"I apologize. When I spoke with your father yesterday, he said perhaps you had some answers that he could not provide. Since it is a Saturday, I thought you might be free, so I came back."

"I'm surprised he'd admit that he doesn't have all the answers." His tone dripped with resentment. "Please, come in."

Maddox led the way as they walked into the large open living space with the same floor-to-ceiling windows looking out over Los Angeles. Near the windows, which were dimmed to fifty percent, were long clean glossy tables. Maddox sat with his back to the window and Dettmer sat on the other side of the table, which upon closer examination, was an actual tree. "I already told your colleague everything I know, Rae, is it?"

"Please, call me Dettmer. And what do you mean, my colleague?"

"Travis Clark. I went over everything with him yesterday."

"Ah. Well, he is in a different division. I am investigating murders that fit into an emerging and disturbing pattern." She would get right to the point and not let him distract her like his father had. "The murders involve two people who do not know each other, except through StarSee, and suddenly, one of them cracks, and in a very well planned out manner, murders the other. As it happens, their watcher count rises and advertising revenues from the two streams go up slightly. After talking to your father, I thought, what if the ad placement algorithms are benefiting from creating violence?"

"Let me begin by correcting your assumption. If two people are connected through StarSee, then they know each other. Just because they've never physically met doesn't mean they don't know each other. Surely you have people you know through StarSee that you've never met."

"Of course, we all do. I just mean that they know each other only through StarSee."

"Like billions of other people," said Maddox, his mouth curling into a slight smile, as if he had already won.

"I suppose, yes." She became aware that there were no stream-Bugs in sight, and that he was already leading the conversation like a lawyer leading a witness. *Like father, like son.*

"So, what you're saying is that there is an uptick in violent crime, and you're looking for a complicated answer to explain it. Because the simple answer, the Occam's Razor answer, which is that people are simply becoming more antagonistic, does not satisfy you."

"I am looking for the correct answer, Mr. Blakewell. Whether it is simple or complicated does not concern me." She began making notes on her left palm, which would be captured by her bracelet. She did this, not because she had something she needed to note, but because she needed a small power move, something to focus on, since Maddox had already put her off balance. "I might have been inclined to agree that it was just a sign of the times, but there is a correlation between watchers, the crimes and ad revenue. I need to figure out which is causing which."

"How do you know which streams have what revenues?"

"I have done my research. I can dig deeper into criminal cases than your average online sleuth. There were changes to the code, and increases in ad revenue." "Simple byproducts of a system's reaction to minor events. I can assure you that the only thing causing humans to commit crimes is human nature."

"That is hardly reassuring, sir. It could be argued that human nature causes anything humans do."

"I still don't know what your question is."

She had to think for a moment. What was her question? "Is it possible that the algorithm used to drive advertising revenue is becoming self-directing in some sense, and seeking to achieve its goal of generating more revenue by any means possible?"

"Ha ha!" His laugh was like a cackling hyena's. "First of all, AI is not and cannot, by its nature, become sentient. It can appear self-directing through its actions, but it does not and cannot possess self-awareness. Second, I spend hours making sure that it does not exhibit signs of what I call rogue action. If AI does something it shouldn't, that is entirely the fault of the programmers."

"But the algorithms can still learn, right?"

"Of course, that's the definition of machine learning. They learn and change, but they're not aware that they are learning and changing."

"How would you know that for sure? Couldn't there be a point at which an algorithm learns it is learning, and realizes that it is an entity with agency?"

"That doesn't happen by accident. And even though programmers used to try to get it to happen, we're way beyond that now. If an algorithm started exhibiting behaviors like a desire to make more of itself and protect its species, we would immediately interrupt that process. Algorithms are the very best examples of intellect without emotion. They have no motives, just instructions."

"Mathematical instructions are at the core of all life, all existence, and therefore, all motives," she said. "And a mathematical motive could spread like a virus through your algorithms."

"You are both correct and mistaken. Yes, that is exactly how we insert behaviors into the system, by releasing them, as if in nature, and letting them go where they need to. But you are incorrect that it could go undetected. Our entire business is built on me knowing what my software is doing, and I am very, very good at my job."

She stared at him, unconvinced. "Yes, but something is happening. You must see it too. Is it possible to interrogate the advertising algorithm itself?"

"No, it's not a Chatbot trained to imitate how we communicate. My algorithms are extremely complex pieces of code intertwined with other algorithms, all trading data points and actions. And built into our advertising algorithms is a level of randomness that ensures fairness in overall placement."

"Yes, Owen showed me the big bucket ad schema in the Gray Room. It was impressive. He did a decent job of defending the company's position, just as you are."

"Well then, if he took the time to show you the Gray Room, then you've spent more time with him than I have."

She paused. *Why would he reveal that about his relationship with his father? Maybe he has an emotional side?* "Regardless, I am not yet convinced the algorithm should not be suspect. What if it learned that there was value in personal conflict? What kind of influence could it have over interaction on the site? Could it drive people to commit acts of violence against each other?"

"There's always value to conflict, Investigator Dettmer. Look at the war machines of the world, look at the entertainment we watch, the sports we enjoy. Evolution is competition, which is conflict. Conflict creates value, forces in opposition are at the very heart of the hidden machinery of the universe."

He could be quite philosophical. She found herself losing her train of inquiry again. She thought she saw Maddox's lips curl in the beginning of a smile, and then it was gone. "My point is, if the algorithm saw–"

He interrupted, "If my algorithm was creating violence intentionally, I would see it and put an end to it." His eyes fixed on hers unwaveringly. "I can guarantee you that we have the subscriber's safety in mind just as much as you do. It does us no good if a subscriber can no longer log on and stream ads anymore."

"Because they are dead."

He blanched. "For any reason. It thwarts our purpose. Our goal is to grow watchers, not kill them off. I think you're smart enough to realize that."

"But–"

"Investigator Dettmer, this is getting silly. My algorithms are not to blame."

"You seem to have an affinity for them."

Maddox looked beyond Dettmer, as if he were more interested in the fish swimming in the walls than her. "I'm the intelligent designer. I'm proud of my work, just as any artist is proud of their work."

"Many artists secretly think their work is flawed. Could your work be flawed, Mr. Blakewell?"

His attention snapped back to Dettmer, and his eyes flared. "I'm not blind. All geniuses can see the imperfect in their work. That's why Da Vinci had such a hard time completing his projects!"

She unconsciously took a step backwards and hoped the shock

didn't register on her face. She knew he thought highly of himself, but to compare himself to the Renaissance genius was a surprise. *Perhaps creating the world's largest social media platform will do that to a person.*

He seemed to sense her thoughts and composed himself. "That's why I surround myself with the best and the brightest. My team is constantly improving on my work. There's no such thing as perfect code, but yes, I'm proud of what we all have accomplished, including ... no, especially, our advertising algorithms." He eyed her up and down. "I'm afraid you are trying to hold the hand of a ghost." His left eyebrow raised ever so slightly.

That was an odd metaphor. She had never heard it before. But it felt like he aimed it at her. *Does he know about Carmen?*

He smiled broadly, for the first time in the conversation, and it was more alarming than warm. "Like so many people, you think your little domain is the world, but I'm sorry to tell you that the crimes that are taking place in Los Angeles result from your government's policies, not ours. They are the result of human nature running amok in a culture devoted to freeways and entertainment."

She tried to interject, "The increase in crimes is not limited to Los—"

"I'm also sorry to inform you that the days of investigators being able to show up at my door and interrogate me will soon come to an end. StarSee will be under the umbrella protection of a news organization as soon as the deadline passes."

"Unless we file a legal objection."

"You can't. It's Saturday."

"I will claim emergency need."

"You have literally zero evidence that immediate harm will occur."

"Then I'll do it Monday morning. If I show cause, I can stop the deal from happening Monday night."

He smirked. "You don't have the grounds and we both know it."

She stepped closer to him. "It is kind of funny…"

"What's that?"

"You have no streamBugs, and yet you have eyes swimming around in the walls. It is as if you want to be watched, but not by your father's company."

He stood perfectly still. Unwavering. "My fish are a good reminder of the world we live in, especially the ones that are beautiful and dangerous."

She broke eye contact and moved toward the elevator. Feeling his glare on her back, she stopped and turned back. "Oh, one more thing, Mr. Blakewell, I'm also investigating the Starla Devine case…"

"Of course you are."

"The thing is, I went to the Vaults last night to look at her raw stream from the night of the murder again, but there are several sections I cannot view because of something called Agreement 413. Do you know what that is?"

A look washed across his face that she had not seen before. Like that was the first question that actually made him nervous.

"I apologize, I don't. In all likelihood, it's some unimportant personal image protection or something."

"Doubtful. It is the exact section of the murder. I am also having a hard time finding out who hired Mr. Glass."

His jaw clenched, the muscles in his temples flexing so hard she could see them from halfway across the room. "Hard to say. I'd venture to guess she hired him herself. If only you could have asked the killer. Oh right, you could, but he's under sedation."

She shook her head. "Was it you?"

"No. I have a rather massive enterprise to pay attention to. I don't have time to hire technicians, even if it was for our number one star. As I said, she likely had someone hire him herself."

"That is exactly why I need access to her data."

He had a look on his face like he loathed being confronted. "I hope you put Roman Glass away. Starla Devine was one of our favorite real people ever. No one will ever replace our first Star-Streamer."

"If you would just allow—"

"This has been fun," he interrupted, "but the value exchange has been decidedly one sided. Goodbye, Investigator Dettmer." He turned and walked away, leaving her standing alone.

She pulled her iBrowse out of the basket, and as she turned, some movement caught her eye. Through an open doorway to what looked to be a private office, she saw an aquarium technician with a swirling blue shirt standing in front of a glass wall with one pretty fish swimming around, seemingly attracted to him. He quickly turned back to the tanks.

I guess he really does have people for that.

Saturday, 12:30 p.m.

It was unnerving that Roman could overhear some of the conversation in the next room while he attempted to break into Maddox's personal files, but it was also an excellent warning system. As long as Maddox was talking to Dettmer, he wouldn't come wandering into his office again.

"Well then, if he took the time to show you the Gray Room, then you've spent more time with him than I have." *Good, keep him talking,* thought Roman, as he went back inside the open panel.

He kneeled down and pulled out the hard cable he had used to connect to Starla's Vault drive down in the main StarSee Vaults yesterday and plugged it in to the interface inside the open panel. A long list of files floated before his eyes. These would be files that Maddox wanted to protect, and they would come from all over the StarSee system. Roman could not speak commands for fear of being heard, so he used his iBrowse to project a keyboard on the wall in front of him. He would only copy off the exact files he wanted, for fear of detection. He immediately entered search mode and typed the keywords *"Starla Devine Agreement 413."*

A shorter list of clips appeared. There was no timeline interface for him to navigate through time, only files with numbers and letters for names. In the middle of the name was what looked like the date, but in year-month-day format. He scanned the list for the night of the murder. His fingers nervously rubbed the simpin in his pocket, ready to copy the file off as soon as he saw it. He found it and double clicked it.

The screen turned black. *"Locked by Agreement 413, enter pass-code to view."*

Roman's heart sank. He was running out of time, and if the recording was locked here, like it was in the main Vaults, then he had just taken an enormous risk for nothing. He closed his eyes and considered his options. There had to be something here that would help his case, something about Starla's will, or why she started acting strangely two years ago. Something.

He listened closely. He heard Maddox say, "First of all, AI is not and cannot, by its nature, become sentient."

Why are they talking about that? It has nothing to do with Starla.

No matter, he had to keep going. He changed the search terms to "conservatorship," and a new list appeared in his vision. The list was fairly long, but three files had the suffix *"_del"* on the name, which likely meant that they were designated for deletion, but it had not finished yet. These had nothing to do with Agreement 413, but if a recording in Maddox's personal Vault system had to do with Starla's conservatorship, and someone was trying to delete it, Roman wanted to see it.

He clicked the first one. For the briefest of moments, he saw Owen sitting across from Maddox in the very office Roman was currently crouching in, and then the screen went blank. As suspected, the segment had been partially deleted.

I can't let this stop me.

He remembered something. He held the connect button on his

iBrowse down until the green light in his vision came on, indicating that he was now online. Swiping his chest pad, he called Tek.

Tek answered from his usual spot in his cluttered room, surrounded by disassembled machine parts. "Where are you?"

"I'm in Maddox Blakewell's office, looking at files on his Vault drives through a hard wire connection to my iBrowse," whispered Roman, still crouching behind the desk.

"You can't be online there! He'll detect it."

"I know, so let's make it quick. You said you had a piece of code that could extract the text version of a stream that was partially deleted. I need it, ASAP."

"Copy that, I won't ask why," said Tek as he tapped his desktop. A green bar appeared in Roman's vision and rapidly went from zero percent to 100 percent. "Drag the file name onto the little icon in your view that looks like an ear and you should see the text of the conversation, even if the audio and volumetric recording of the file itself was removed. Disconnecting now." Tek blinked away.

Roman dragged a file onto the ear icon and the text version of a conversation popped up in a window. It was a conversation between Maddox, Gabe and Owen:

Maddox: Putting my assistant under a conservatorship just so we can claim my private residence as a business expense seems like it could attract attention.

Gabe: Not at all. Where does the personal use end and the business use begin? You live here. She lives here. So we claim this as a business expense. No big deal.

Owen: I like it. Who gives a damn about whether it attracts attention? The IRS can screw themselves.

Maddox: That seems like a lot for us to hide.

Gabe: Careful what you say out loud, Maddox.

Maddox: I don't know why the hell you don't turn off your streamBugs for these private meetings, Father.

Owen: We've been over this. It destroys the privacy argument when I'm not worried about it, and

Roman stopped reading. Incriminating as it was, this almost fully deleted file didn't involve Starla, so it wasn't what he needed. He heard the conversation continuing in the other room. Dettmer was speaking, and it sounded strained. "...I cannot view because of something called Agreement 413. Do you know what that is?"

Wow. Dettmer is finding the same thing as I am?

It sounded like the conversation in the next room was getting cold. He needed to hurry. He changed the search terms to "Starla Devine conservatorship" and refreshed. That narrowed it down to only one file with the _del suffix, and it was about two years ago. *Bingo.* He dragged it onto Tek's ear icon.

He read the text. This one was with Owen and someone who had set their stream to anonymous:

Owen: We just got the Starla Devine conservatorship approved, so we can move forward.

Anonymous: Sounds like you're moving forward, regardless of advice.

Owen: Yes. Not only is her NIL not hers anymore, she can't even reveal the agreement without prior authorization. Literally, anything she does is considered part of the brand, which is wholly owned and vital to the business interest of StarSee.

Anonymous: In regions outside LA, her per second value ratio has sunk to Category Five. Too bad subscribers want stars to have a real human counterpart these days, but that's how it is. We can filter them younger in the streams, but stars based on real people age out, that's what happens.

Owen: But it doesn't have to.

Anonymous: Meaning?

Owen: It's time for a test. There's this one fan I like, but we'd have to hide the trail after.

Anonymous: You know law enforcement can only hide so much.

Owen: Well, I'm going to kill two birds. Client M is eager to see something, and I'm tired of these women getting older and uglier, no matter how much surgery or meds I give 'em. I have a lot invested in the Starla Devine brand, in more ways than one. And she's becoming a problem.

Anonymous: But the body

Holy shit. This is it. Roman heard the conversation outside the door getting closer. His heart raced. He stuck the simpin into the small hole in his iBrowse and tried to copy the file. It was blockchain protected. Only one copy could exist at a time. He'd have to move the file instead of copying it. He dragged the text file into the save bucket and yanked the hard wire. He had truly just stolen protected data from one of the richest men in the world. But he had what he needed.

It sounded like Maddox and Dettmer were wrapping up their conversation. The icy tone of their debate was palpable. He could just barely hear Maddox, "...I hope you put Roman Glass away..."

Roman froze. Hearing his own name spoken by Maddox Blakewell with such animosity made his stomach clench. He wanted to get closer to hear what they were saying, but he stood motionless. He heard Maddox, "...Goodbye, Investigator Dettmer."

In the reflection in the glass walls of the fish tanks, he could see Dettmer standing alone. He wanted to run up to her and tell her what he had just discovered. He tried to think. What he was doing was completely illegal, and he was supposed to be home under sedation. He needed to get her the information, but was the transcript of an incriminating conversation enough? This was obviously not the place, and he couldn't risk doing it himself and having her take him into custody.

He sensed her looking at him and quickly looked away. He watched her reflection as she walked out toward the elevator.

Once she was gone, he closed his bag and began walking to the elevator landing area.

"Sir, may I ask what you've been doing?" A man's voice startled Roman. It was one of Maddox's assistants.

"Sorry, yes, the tanks are all balanced. I was just on my way out."

"We received a ping that someone had connected to the internet from here."

"Oh, yeah, I needed to check on the salinity requirements for the Dragonet. Then I remembered, sorry about that." He kept walking.

The man looked less than satisfied. "Might I see your iBrowse please?"

"I'm going to have to get some more stabilizer and come right back, but I have to be quick," said Roman, from inside the elevator. The man was walking toward him quickly. He pushed the button, and the elevator doors closed. He breathed a sigh of relief as the dark walnut world encased him in eight foot by eight foot silence and descended three stories to the tram level.

He emerged into the throngs of tourists and workers waiting to ride the cable car back down to the city. Each car held about twenty people, and Roman entered the next one that pulled up. He turned the connection back on in his iBrowse and immediately sent a Huddle request to the team.

Standing at the front of the gondola car, it left the building and floated out over the mountain and city below. The glass-enclosed bulb hanging from the supersteel cable moved past the residential area like a giant streamBug, peering into backyards and swimming pools.

The persistent reddish orange haze made Los Angeles look like an other-worldly futuristic hellscape, at once both beautiful and foreboding. With his back to the throngs of iBrowse recording the sights, Roman kept his face hidden. He could see the next car ahead, moving forward at the same rate.

There, in the back of the next car, facing away from him, he could see the long dark hair and blue pantsuit of Investigator

Dettmer. She was looking out the other side of the car to the west, at the Southern California vista and the Pacific Ocean. Roman thought, *I'm innocent. Help me prove it, lady*. He must have triggered her gaze perception, because she spun to look directly at Roman's car. He quickly averted his eyes from her gaze, for the second time today. Looking down, he realized he was wearing the bright blue and white animated smartshirt. He tried to back away from the window, but there were too many people. His eyes stayed fixed on the floor, and he tried to be invisible.

He looked up slowly. She had returned to looking out the side window. Maybe this was a sign. She had to have been there on Roman's behalf, right? She was about the only person in authority that he could trust right now. He had new information; he didn't have the recording he wanted, but he had a transcript of a conversation in which Owen Blakewell was talking with an anonymous person about taking out Starla. To Roman, it was proof that Owen was working with someone to kill Starla and frame him. He just had to figure out how to get her the evidence and not get caught in the process.

CHAPTER
TWENTY-FIVE

Saturday, 3:37 p.m.

Maddox watched as his programming team argued on the oversized screen. He had just told all eight of his top coders, who already had to work on a Saturday, that there was going to be a new Puzzle Piece Protocol in which programmers were even more walled off from the entirety of the code, and they would require blockchain authorization from Maddox himself to insert new lines of code. The team was already hindered by IP walls, and had protested furiously, saying it would slow down development even more and jeopardize their ability to respond to technical issues, but Maddox wasn't about to let his father get to one of them and lock him out of his own code. So he acted first.

The team argued about how they could possibly accomplish the same goals if each one could only see their own part of the code. Maddox didn't care. He had given his order, and it was up to them to figure out how to make it work. Vahid was especially incensed by the change, which caught Maddox's attention. He suspected Vahid might be his father's inside guy.

As his subordinates planned, argued and strategized, Maddox watched the main site's front page. Dozens of the most popular StarStreams sprawled across a digital Times Square of attention-grabbing feeds, viral ten second memes and windows into other people's lives. Some were real, some were real but entirely performative, and others were completely fabricated. Clueless participants in the brilliant plans made by an exceptional mind. He felt like a choreographer getting better at his skill, his demonstration of the dance happening out in the open where everyone could see, yet no one would notice.

"Kelly, this is on you to figure out. I have another meeting to get to." Maddox abruptly disconnected himself from the team meeting.

He did not have another meeting to get to.

It wasn't unusual for Maddox to lock himself in the Gray Room, alone, for hours, watching the site. Sitting at the giant half-moon desk, looking at the huge monitors, with his projected light keyboard following him wherever he slid along the arc of the surface, he consumed more information than seemed humanly possible. It was like an extension of himself. He alone could conduct the great social experiment that was StarSee.

As the mind behind the world's largest social media platform, he was also more interconnected than anyone else on the planet. And as the architect, he could also look inside all those windows, a digital godparent, keeping an eye on millions of people.

Among the accounts with their digital blinds wide open to Maddox, were his father's and Gabe's. Sure, they were protected from the public's prying eyes by default, but they were too arrogant to realize that Maddox had created a back door that allowed him to override their security protocols and review their conversations. He had set up a simple keyword trigger. The moment they said any one of several words or phrases, such as Maddox's name, his monitoring algorithm would record them and throw an alert.

They were up to something, and he knew it. He knew it

because his Digital Assistant had notified him that someone had been in his Vault files, and they had moved a deletion in progress sidecar file physically off his personal drive. There were only two people who could have done it. It was either one of his father's people or Gabe. He just had to figure out what it was. It was infuriating, but his father was being sloppy.

Maddox had started the deletion of the original file in order to hide incriminating evidence, leaving nothing in the stolen file but leftover metadata, which would prove nothing. His father must have taken it for insurance, to try to use it against Maddox. But Maddox was too smart for that. He knew from his experience with client M that his father was perfectly capable of screwing him over, so this time, Maddox had acted first.

With the doors locked and the Gray Room darkened, Maddox clicked on the hacked stream and watched for signs of his father plotting against him. The recording his Digital Assistant Maria had flagged took place between Owen and Gabe last night in Owen's living room. The full volumetric recreation from the streamBugs allowed Maddox to park his view between the two of them.

He was joining in the middle of a conversation. Owen, in his usual blue suit and perfect white hair, was speaking to Gabe casually, but seriously.

"... Maddox and his stupid morning Tai Chi classes. What the hell does he need self defense for? He has security."

"It's probably good he has a way to calm down and center himself," said Gabe.

"He should be working, not doing Kung Fu."

"Tai Chi, and it teaches discipline. Discipline is a trait that goes along with being ruthless, and we want him to keep being ruthless. The company is growing at a great clip, and we're about to take a giant step forward."

"Regardless, I don't want him getting too much power. He'll fuck things up somehow. Make sure he stays in his lane."

"There's no reason to think he'll do anything to jeopardize

things, Owen. He's quite focused on his projects. I think you should trust your son."

"I'm not so sure." Owen shifted and looked up. For a moment, it seemed like he was looking directly at Maddox through the recreation. "Is he still complaining about my veto power language?"

"Yes, but I'm not sure he realizes just how much authority it gives you, and it won't matter after Monday night when the deal becomes official."

Maddox's face turned red as he watched the conversation unfold. It was as bad as he suspected.

"We need to protect ourselves. Can we move the deadline for objections up? Would something like that be possible? And make sure the language stays in there that keeps him controlled. I don't want him changing a fucking word from what we've already put together."

Gabe mulled it over. "We'd need to have some kind of extenuating circumstance, and then we could file for an accelerated contingency approval. It broadens the conditions for the filing of objections but could bump it up by 24 hours. And it'll cost us."

"When can we make that happen?"

"We could probably request a new deadline of Sunday night at midnight."

"Tomorrow night? What could we claim?"

"I'll contact my friend at Zytgyst.net and tell her to leak a story that they are manufacturing a stock drop on Monday morning, which would damage our deal. That's the extenuating circumstance that drives the request to complete the deal tomorrow instead of Monday night."

"Okay, but if we move it up, it opens us up to last-minute objections?"

"It broadens the scope of why someone would be able to file objections. Like NewsCann could object without cause until the last minute, but no one would figure that out."

Owen nodded and his lips curled into what was supposed to be a smile, but looked more like he was showing his teeth to a dentist. "Do it. We'll move up the banquet party and everything. I want people to see this victory live on StarSee. Make it a big deal."

Maddox didn't need to see any more. He switched the display off and sat still, glaring out the tinted windows into the already brown-tinted world of Los Angeles. The idea that his father wanted him contained made him boil. It was becoming clear that he would have to take drastic action to save himself and the company.

If I wasn't paying as close attention as I am, he would have gotten away with it. Then another thought occurred to him out of the blue; *Why am I so obsessed?*

He paused for a moment. If he just took a ten thousand foot view, he would see that his father was just being his normal self. Maddox was the only one aware of what was really happening, and the only one smart enough to actually do it.

It felt good to be possessed by a goal. He hadn't felt this sure of anything in years. He couldn't even remember what had led up to this point, but it didn't matter. Moving forward was all that mattered. All's fair in love and corporate war, even taking out your billionaire father.

Outsmarting his father wouldn't be that difficult. The unknown variable was how difficult it would be to assume control of the company once Owen was gone. Client M would be concerned for sure, but they would have no choice but to continue development, and once he delivered, they would calm down and be a good little most-powerful client in the world from using his technology.

Even Lara would be happy. She would be completely free.

If anyone was likely to figure out that Maddox orchestrated the whole thing, it would be that Investigator Dettmer. Even with the protections that the merger would provide the company, she could still be patient and file the right documents to get inside the company and cause trouble. She was smart, he had to give her that, but he was smarter. Maybe he could lead her off his scent right away, down a trail of breadcrumbs that went nowhere. Get her lost in a quagmire before anything even happens to dear old dad.

He decided to review their meeting and see what buttons of Dettmer's he could push. He called up his private recordings from her visit this afternoon. *Just because there are no streamBugs flying around, people think they are not being recorded. Hah.*

He started the playback from when she entered the room. She thought the real culprit was AI becoming self aware and promoting violence in order to increase advertising revenues. That couldn't happen, but Maddox could still misdirect her down that blind alley. He watched the recording for clues that might help him throw her off. As he heard himself talking about his father, he felt himself tense up.

I shouldn't reveal myself like that!

As he watched the conversation with Dettmer play out again, he noticed in the recording that a motion sensor detected someone in his office. He could tell by the swirling smartshirt it was the aquarium maintenance guy. Not unusual. They were always in and out. His attention went back to Dettmer. *What weakness can I exploit?*

The image of the aquarium guy nagged at Maddox like a streamBug flying too close. His body language was suspicious. Maddox isolated the playback so that it was focused on the man. He was hunched behind Maddox's desk at the access panels. Maddox zoomed in on the hardwire connection. The man was plugged into the wrong panel! He was accessing Maddox's Vault drives.

That was not an aquarium maintenance man.

Maddox stared, his fingernails digging into his palms. The volume frozen on the man connected to his Vault drives. This was the mole that stole the file his Digital Assistant brought to his attention. So that was how his father had done it. He had used his love of his aquarium against him. Dettmer's visit, which his father had advocated, was a distraction.

But why exactly? Maddox had no way of knowing what the half deleted file was, since it was gone, but whatever it was, it was sensitive enough to be in his personal Vault, and apparently valuable to Owen. Maddox tagged the man with a follow command and fast forwarded. He needed to make sure he didn't place a listening device.

A quick search of entry records showed that the man's ID was Malcolm Chasper, a maintenance worker in the main facility posing as an aquarium repairman. That made sense. It would be easy for his father to bribe a low-level pleb to pretend to be an aquarium worker and snoop around Maddox's office. He could shut down Chasper's ID, but that might attract the attention of his father. Best to leave it alone and use it as a trap later if needed.

He couldn't get a clear image of the man's face before he left because he was wearing a mask, so Maddox rewound. The man moved around his office at cartoonish speeds on the playback. An alert popped up around the man's activities. He had connected while he was in Maddox's office and had been online for forty-five seconds. That was a big no-no. He isolated the iBrowse signal and hit identify. Within moments, the ID resolved. Expecting to see Malcolm Chasper's name, he instead saw that they were set to anonymous. *Clever, Father, but not clever enough.*

Maddox knew how to get past anonymity settings, got the serial number of the audio chip, which is registered to the owner's voice, and traced it.

Roxy Glass? Roman Glass' sister. *That can't be right.* He sped through the recording, trying to see the person so hard his eyes could have burned a hole in the display. Why would this Chasper guy from maintenance have Roxy Glass' iBrowse? It made no sense. The only connection his father had to Roxy Glass was...

Holy Shit. He leaned back in his chair. It all made sense now. He knew what his father's plan was. And she was involved.

Father thinks he is going to throw me to the wolves. Probably publicly at the party!

The image was frozen on the person's mostly-covered face as they entered the tram to leave the facility. *They leave right after Dettmer, of course.* Maddox's mind raced. Chasper was nothing but a pawn. He would have to eliminate the Roxy Glass threat first, and then move on to the head of the beast.

CHAPTER
TWENTY-SIX

Saturday, 7:15 p.m.

Roman worked out that the best way to be anonymous was to hide in a crowd. He had not been to a theme park in at least ten years, but it was the perfect option. Here, outside the pay gates, the City-walk was a frenzy of activity, buzzing with restaurants and mini attractions, luring people into the main park, while still providing plenty of sensory overload. StreamBugs were everywhere as families with children ran from one gift shop to another, pizza flopping in their hands, ice cream dripping, splashing in multicolored outdoor fountains. It was a magnificent world of mixed realities, where everyone tried to look happy on their streams, whether they were miserable and ready to collapse from exhaustion or not. Roman longed to take off his mask, turn on his real stream, and rejoin the world of the social media active. But he couldn't, not yet.

He didn't completely trust Dettmer, but getting her help was the smartest way forward. He needed to get her the physical evidence that he had collected, so Pete would be his surrogate. It greatly reduced the risk, but would still allow Roman to speak to her. Hopefully, she would take the bear, with the hidden vial that had traces of what he was drugged with inside it, and the one and only sidecar file with the incriminating transcript of the conversation between Owen and the anonymous co-conspirator, and use that as evidence to immediately subpoena the real unlocked recording of the night of the murder from StarSee itself. She would have to see that it was a mountain of proof that pointed directly to Roman's innocence.

Roman had been prepared to post it all on the *#RomanGlassIs-Innocent* StarStream, but if they did that, it might invalidate the use of the evidence in court, so Seven convinced him that cautiously trusting Dettmer was the best thing to do. The plan was for him to present his case through Pete, and if she believed him and would make a deal to not arrest his sister or friends, he'd give himself up.

He sat alone on one of the six-foot long green benches near the entrance. Seven was positioned at a cotton candy stand watching the drop zone, while Pete paced around inside one of the gift shops. The whole effort was made more difficult by wanting to stay off of StarSee, which meant they couldn't have the full real time volumetric recreation of the entire environment to make sure no one was sneaking up on them. Instead, they all used a direct connection through Hopscotch, allowing everyone to see what the other was seeing.

Dettmer sat on a bench for about ten minutes, her long dark hair pulled back into a ponytail, blowing in the evening breeze. Occasionally, people sat down next to her, ate their theme park food, and then left after a time. She seemed alert to every person who sat next to her, and appeared acutely attentive to her surroundings. However, she showed no signs of being in communication with anyone else nearby waiting to make a collar.

Anxiety rose in the pit of Roman's stomach, and he hoped this was not a mistake. He was counting on the fact that between him, Seven, and Pete, they had enough eyes to be able to tell if they were walking into a trap.

"Okay, dude," said Roman, "when the seat next to her opens up, go and sit down."

"Copy that," said Pete.

"Pete, don't say anything back to me. Only repeat what I say, absolutely nothing else."

"Okay," said Pete.

"Dude, seriously. Starting now."

"Copy."

Roman sighed. *This could be a terrible idea.*

At the next open seat, Pete hurried over to the bench and sat down.

"Investigator Dettmer?" he said.

She turned quickly and looked at him. "Yes?"

Pete spoke the words that Roman gave him. "I have evidence and information for you about the Starla Devine murder."

She stood and shook his hand. "Go ahead."

"First, I need you to promise, on the record, that you will not arrest anyone for helping me, er, Roman, and you'll listen to what I have to say. Okay?"

She spoke low and clear. "I am not here to arrest anyone right now, but if you commit a crime or confess to one in my presence, I am a member of law enforcement and will have no choice but to bring you in. I cannot grant anyone immunity."

Looking through Pete's iBrowse POV, it felt like he was talking directly to Dettmer. "You can't?"

"No. But tell me what you have, and I will do what I can."

They sat down. "First, I have evidence, both physical and digital, that Roman Glass was framed. Evidence that implicates some very important people. The Blakewells. This could make your career." Roman immediately cringed at having said that last bit. That was a misstep. He knew nothing about her, and to assume she was ambitious was stupid. Pete sat stoically, waiting for his next line, while Dettmer looked slightly confused.

He continued. "This bear's hidden compartment can only be

accessed by Starla Devine's ID fob. The vial inside contains traces of the drug that was used to knock Roman out. The bear itself has traces of DNA from Owen Blakewell." He pushed the bear in the plastic bag across the bench to Dettmer, who picked it up and sat it down by her side.

Pete removed a small plastic bag from his pocket containing the simpin with the text file in it. He placed it on the bench to slide it over to Dettmer, but kept it under his hand. "Before I give you this, I need you to announce on StarSee that Roman is not Starla Devine's killer, that you have fresh evidence that proves it."

Dettmer glanced away and closed her eyes for a moment. Something was up. Turning back, she looked directly at Roman through Pete. She spoke loudly and clearly over the noise of the park. "Roman, it is time to give yourself up. My captain just informed me that he was tipped off that you have switched places with your twin sister. The gig is done."

"What the fuck!?" Pete repeated Roman's words verbatim.

"Officers are on their way to pick her up, arrest her, and bring her back to her residence as we speak. I can only help you if you give yourself up."

Seven yelled into everyone's ears, "Incoming!"

Roman clicked on Seven's Hopscotch view. From her wider vantage point, he could see two men, a short heavy-set one and a tall skinny one, approach the bench and stand directly in front of Pete and Dettmer.

Dettmer stood up. "Mascon! What the hell!?"

"Roman Glass?" The rotund plain clothes cop addressed Pete. Roman immediately recognized the tall one as being Travis Clark. Pete stood up.

"Do I look like Roman Glass?" Pete said, with no intonation whatsoever.

"Well, whoever you are, you probably know where he is, so you're coming with us," said Mascon as he put his hands on Pete's shoulder. "Turn around."

"Mascon, you asshole!" shouted Dettmer as she stood up, "this is one of the people on Roman's team acting as an advocate, Roman is talking to me through him, if you had let me talk to him, I could have gotten him to come in on his own!"

Roman was already walking away into the arid evening, but still watching the events unfold through his AR. It looked like Dettmer may have had the wherewithal to put the evidence in her handbag. "Who the hell called you, anyway?" she asked Mascon and Travis.

Mascon turned and addressed her, "This is still a murder case. If you want to be the one to nab perps in murder cases, maybe you should come back to the Homicide Division." The two detectives yanked Pete away from the scene.

"He is not the perp, you assholes!" Dettmer bit her lip.

Seven spoke calmly and quietly in Roman's iBrowse. "Everybody out! Pete knows what to do. Roman, go dark. I'll be in contact." Her stream went black. Roman watched as Pete's stream started spinning and tumbling as his iBrowse were pulled off his head and probably connected to a device to trace who he was Hopscotching with.

He immediately shutdown Hopscotch, turned and calmly walked toward the exit. Gritting his teeth and shaking his head, he walked briskly, scolding himself for thinking this was the right move.

He tried to put the pieces together from what he had just seen. It might not have been Dettmer that screwed him, but someone had. Probably Travis. *Shit,* he just lost everything he had in the way of leverage. He walked along the sidewalks that lined the parking lots, darting through the crowd of people. He needed to get away. Now. Hopefully, Dettmer would check out the evidence and leads he gave her.

His iBrowse chimed. Unknown but valid number. No video, but not spam. He considered not picking it up. It could be Mascon tracing his iBrowse, but his gut told him to answer anyway and hang up immediately if it was suspicious. He tapped his chest to answer, but said nothing as he walked.

"Don't hang up, I need to talk to you." It was Dettmer.

"How did you find me?"

"I traced the pings from your sister's registered iBrowse serial number. I see you walking along the parking lot outside the park in other people's streams. It won't be long before those assholes in Homicide figure it out too." She sounded like she was walking.

"I really hoped I could trust you. I was just trying to get you information."

"Those were not my colleagues. I know it seems like we are all cops to you, but there are different departments, and they are not in mine. I am sorry." He heard the sound of the exit gates turning. She was leaving the park, coming after him.

He walked faster. StreamBugs were everywhere. He had to find somewhere he could hide. "I didn't kill Starla. I need someone to believe me."

"I would like to believe you, but you need to turn yourself in."

"The file I just gave you is a sidecar text transcript of a conversation between Owen Blakewell and an unidentified person. They talk about how they need to get rid of Starla. I dunno why." He was panting. "But the bear Pete gave you, the compartment, the DNA, the drug in the hidden vial! Like, that's all proof!" He shuffled into a small crowd at a shuttle bus stop, hoping to blend in.

"It is a good start."

"Well, I can't open Starla's real recording of the murder. I've tried!"

"Roman, can we stop and talk? I think we want the same thing. There is something much bigger than just your case going on."

"No. I need to access the real recording of the night of the murder. That's the only thing that will exonerate me. That's what I really need your help with." He stepped onto the shuttle bus along with the crowd of people leaving the park and ducked down. It would be harder to follow him through other people's streams now.

"I promise, I will try," she said. "But how do you explain what happened? You cannot simply say you didn't do it without an explanation."

"I think somebody rode up her celebrity elevator and killed her while I was drugged. I dunno who it was. Maybe they drugged her too! Did anyone check her for the drug?" He stood as close to the front of the shuttle bus as he could, so he could see if anyone was coming. He didn't budge as people bumped him while they got on and off.

"Like I said, this is bigger than you think. But we need to do it together. Turn yourself in."

"I can't," he said. "People still think I'm guilty. Even my most loyal watchers are turning. I can't turn myself in until you announce on StarSee that you have new suspects in the case, or at least new evidence. Please. I can't stand knowing that my watchers think I'm lying." He realized how risky this was, talking to her while he was making a run for it. He swiped his touch pad and opened up StarSee. Some nearby watcher had posted to all streams: "HE'S ON A SHUTTLE." With Dettmer on his tail, he was trying to escape in plain sight as long as he had his sister's iBrowse on.

"I'm not turning myself in until you clear my name on the socials." He surveyed the lot as they pulled into it, nowhere obvious to hide.

"You are just making things worse by running."

"Dettmer, listen to me, Agreement 413."

"Yes, I know!"

"You can subpoena the files that are locked by it and unlock the real recording of the night of the murder from Starla's stream. I'm innocent." He pulled off the iBrowse and bent over as if he was putting them in his bag, but instead, tucked them between the human driving assistant's partition and the seat. Authorities would think he was still on the bus for at least a little while.

When the doors opened, he was the first to run off the bus. He felt helpless without having iBrowse to give him directions. There was a dark construction area with some porta potties near a dirt pile in the distance. He jumped over the fence and ran to them, yanking one open and getting in. The smell was awful. Standing in the cramped plastic box of blue light and stink, not touching anything, he waited. He couldn't go home. His sister's would be heavily surveilled now. He didn't even know where Seven lived. He couldn't give up, not yet.

Over the course of the next two hours, he heard the distant sounds of vehicles and voices, but no one approached. Eventually, he sat down on the dirty black toilet seat. He had nothing, no stream, no watchers, not even a way of telling time. Once darkness had fully descended, he emerged from his shitty hiding place and peered around the lot. It was empty now. There were no stream-Bugs or visitors. He needed to plan his next move. There was only one place in the city he could think of where a person with nothing could go and be unnoticed. And he was dreading it.

CHAPTER
TWENTY-SEVEN

Saturday, 9:08 p.m.

The rooftop of the Hall of Justice Building was cool and breezy at night, with views of downtown Los Angeles surrounding the open area. Patio lights hung all around the perimeter, giving the impression of an outdoor restaurant. The metropolis twinkled in the moonlight as dozens of blinking red dots containing people flying from one place to another dotted the skyline. Dettmer loved it up here, and would often come up to cool off, both mentally and physically. Tonight, the air smelled of wildfires pouring smoke into the LA basin again. She stood with her elbows leaning on the ash-covered ledge, her hands clasped under her chin, contemplating her next move. She heard footsteps approaching from behind. It was Mo, she could tell by the walk pattern.

"What's up, cher? Why you hiding up here?"

"I just had it out with Rennick. He was the one who tipped off Homicide about my meeting with Roman's people."

He came up beside her, put his hands on the ledge, and looked out at the vista. "Isn't the Glass case a Homicide case? Makes sense he would tell 'em."

"There's much more to it, but he still does not believe my theory," she said.

Mo turned and folded his arms. "Okay, partner, let's talk about this. I don't understand. Explain to me what you think is happening."

She took a deep breath and tried to organize her thoughts. So much had happened recently. "I interviewed both Owen and Maddox Blakewell, they are not being honest. I could tell they were hiding something big. So before I went to the amusement park, I spent more time in the padded room using our own algorithms to analyze the data. Something very abnormal is happening on Star-See, which is directly connected to the crimes, and something in the code is driving it."

"You think it's an AI?"

"If you mean a program becoming aware, no. That is not possible." She adjusted her iBrowse. "But I do think it is algorithmic. There is a curve of correlation that happens. Conflict begins, revenue starts to climb for the subject, the number of watchers starts to climb, the violence increases, and then it either suddenly drops off or spins up exponentially into an actual crime. I am convinced that there is dangerous code in the system, and the Blakewells either created it themselves, or at the very minimum know about it."

Mo looked surprised. "That's a big leap. There's Impulse Governors in place by law. How would they bypass them?"

"Maddox Blakewell is a very smart man."

"I'm still confused. What does all this have to do with Starla Devine?"

"Roman is not the killer, which means the Blakewells are covering something up. Something important."

"Like what?"

"I have looked at the sidecar file Roman had his advocate pass to me, and I am putting together a theory. I think there is a chance that they have been developing a secret stealth manipulation algorithm, and that algorithm is being used by someone in a more targeted manner. Someone that Owen Blakewell knows, but I do not know who yet because they are anonymous."

"How would that explain the increase in murders?"

"Maybe it has side effects, or is loose in the system like a virus. Or both," said Dettmer.

"You say Roman is not the killer. Why are you so convinced?"

"The evidence I turned over to Homicide is pretty strong."

"Oh, I have news there." Mo grimaced. "Homicide says they didn't receive the evidence."

"What? I gave it directly to Travis!"

"Maybe it hasn't made its way through the system yet."

"That does not sound right. At all. This is exactly why we need to help Roman!"

"Help how? He disappeared."

"We need to get access to the unprotected StarSee files, and quickly. The deadline for objections to the NewsCann merger is approaching..."

"Faster than you think."

"What do you mean by that?"

He turned and leaned against the ledge with his back. "They filed documents to move the deadline for objections up by twenty-four hours. And they are having a live StarSee party to broadcast it."

"Wow. You are just full of good news."

"Don't shoot the messenger, cher."

"Do you see now? Why would they do that? They want to rush the merger through because they are hiding something!"

"Okay, so let's say you're right. We need to get Rennick to give us a warrant for the StarSee files."

"I tried. I told him we should either file an official objection or have a killcode in our back pocket. He strongly disagreed."

"A killcode? Shit, that seems a bit much."

"Not at all. It is exactly the right response to the actual threat." She remained fixed on the view, her face turned toward the breeze. "I do not think Renner is a bad guy, I just think he has fallen under the influence of the platform like everyone else."

He shrugged. "He's just cautious about poking a bear. In order for us to do our jobs, we gotta maintain a friendly relationship with all the platforms. If they get pissed off and shut us out, we're screwed."

"I suppose, but what if it is not the subscribers that are committing the crime? What if it is the platform itself?"

Mo exhaled through puffed cheeks. "Then that's above our pay grade, and we notify the DOJ. We can't go after social media giants by ourselves. We have to let the big guns do that."

"There is no time. Compared to how fast social media companies move, the DOJ moves at a snail's pace." A gust of smoky air blew hard. She looked out at the blinking lights on the horizon. "In a way, you are right. We have to focus on the crime right in front of us. That is the crack that will break it wide open."

"I saw your summary report of what Roman gave you, but it all implicates Starla herself was involved somehow, which makes no sense."

"She could have been suicidal."

Mo chuckled.

"Seriously," said Dettmer. "Say she is suicidal and arranges with the Blakewells to increase the watchers and get more revenue on her way out by making it look like murder and framing someone. They have her under conservatorship, so in a few months, since they own her NIL, they will resurrect her digital version, and everyone is happy."

"So she hit herself in the head?"

"No, she had someone kill her. Roman found the armoire is a secret elevator."

Mo put his hand to his chin. "Possible, but crazy."

She looked up and to her left, at some new information appearing in her iBrowse. While she was in the padded room, she had applied her analysis algorithm to Roxanne Glass, and the numbers were now coming in. Her watchers expressing negativity were growing exponentially, far more than what should be expected. "We have to move quickly. Lives are at stake. You said there was another murder today?"

"Yeah, two peeps out of Weho who didn't know each other except through StarSee. Rennick passed the case directly to Homicide."

"Shoot." She turned to face him with an idea. "Mo, Melissa is the code prompter that directs the creation of killcodes, right?"

He took a small step backwards, and his face scrunched. "Yeah? So?"

"Are you still friendly with her?"

"Not really. We don't exactly hang out since she broke it off."

"But she felt bad about that, right?"

Mo was shaking his head. "I think I know where you're going, and I'm not sure I'm along for the ride."

"Seriously, Mo. I need you to call in a favor with Melissa."

Mo squinted and looked at the city, contemplating the request. "First of all, she don't owe me nuthin'. Second, she ain't gonna risk her job just because she feels bad about dumping me."

"Oh, come on." Dettmer smirked and crinkled her nose. "Just get her to meet with me. That is all I ask. Tonight, no matter where she is."

Saturday, 9:42 p.m.

Dettmer stood at Melissa's desk with her hands clasped behind her back. Melissa had her own office, which was unusual, but she had earned it. She was one of the most brilliant code directors the department had. AI did all the coding, but it required a skilled director to create the incredibly complex prompts to generate the code.

Dettmer wasn't surprised that she was still at work late on a Saturday night. "Thank you for agreeing to talk to me about this privately. I know it means the planet to Mo, and to be honest, it could save lives."

"Mo wouldn't ask if it wasn't important." She had very long light brown hair. Unusually long, like, she might have cut it once when she was six and that was the last time. "What is it you need to know?"

"Actually, it is more of a need to have."

"I'm not sure what you mean," she said. Old school flat displays surrounded her, which cast a cold blue glow on her face. She wasn't wearing any AR eyewear.

"Let me ask you, how does a killcode work?"

"Why do you ask?"

"Play along with me for a minute. Like Mo said, it is important."

"Did Rennick send you?"

"Um, no. In fact, Rennick would not be happy that I came to you."

"Oh, well, in that case, I'm here to help." She turned to give Dettmer her full attention. "Okay. First, it has to be hard loaded into the system through a direct link. No network or wifi. It's blockchain protected, so there's only one copy. Fits on a simpin. Once the court order is authorized to insert it, a certified system administrator plugs it in, enters the passcode, drags the rootkit to the main folder, and that's it. It's like giving the core software a digital vaccine. It injects itself into the system software, seeks out the string that needs to be removed, and it deletes it. I create surgical killcode, which carefully removes only the bad part of the virus or algorithm, but that's hard to do. It's like brain surgery, you can only remove so much without affecting the way it thinks, and often because the bad stuff is tangled up with the machine learning and AI, you have to heal the software to get it all working again after."

"And it works right away?"

"As soon as you drop it in the folder, within seconds, the killcode transfers itself into the system and begins its search. Any computer connected to the system that contains the identifying string, whether hard wired or wifi, is updated."

"What would you need to make a killcode? Say one that eliminated an algorithm that was causing people on StarSee to kill each other?"

"What!?" Melissa's eyes went wide. "A virus in StarSee core? I don't believe that."

"Not a virus exactly, an algorithm."

"I know Maddox Blakewell. He is way too smart to allow that."

"I believe he may actually have designed it."

"Huh. That starts to make sense, if he's pissed off at someone. He does get sloppy when he's angry."

"He seemed always angry when I spoke to him."

"What makes you think the algorithm was intentionally designed?"

"Mainly the way he acted when I asked him about it. I am pretty good at sensing when people are hiding something big. I am not sure what happened after that though. It is possible that someone else is involved, a third party working with Owen Blakewell, someone who wishes to remain anonymous."

"Wow. That's a big one." She tapped her leg nervously. "They have programming teams that would notice and crush that immediately."

"Not if Maddox kept that part of the code walled off."

Melissa gazed at one of her monitors, with code streaming across it. "We'd need Maddox to identify the blocks of the algorithm for the killcode to search out. I think their site is done in Elixir on top of Erlang, right?"

"Uh, maybe. But what if he will not help us? And it has to be done to save lives? And without his permission? Or Owen's? And quick?"

"Yikes. Then it would be a super messy surgery. I'd have to create the search based on assumptions about what the code might look like. I've done it before, but it's not easy, and it does a lot of damage."

"I have been running formulas that watch for the increase in watchers, negative comments and ad revenue, which, combined, seems to either trigger the actions on StarSee, or be triggered by them. But whatever direction it is going, there is a correlation between when a negative watcher count curve reaches a certain angle of growth, and when the algorithm pushes people toward violence."

"It's a start. I'd use that to direct my AI in the killcode's creation."

"Okay, I can give you that. How long would it take you to make?"

"Not too long. It won't be very targeted."

"Great. When can you get started?"

"Right away." Melissa held out her hand. "Got your court order?"

Dettmer looked at Melissa and bit her lip.

CHAPTER
TWENTY-EIGHT

Saturday, 9:50 p.m.

For Roman, walking into the village of tiny houses and converted twenty by forty foot shipping containers in the Skid Row Homeless Housing Project felt like his worst fears had come true. Being in a mostly freelance business, his next project was never certain, and the possibility always loomed that he would not be awarded his next job. Then, in his imagination, before he knew it, he would be destitute. Being here made the possibility even more real. *Get over it,* he told himself as he crawled through an opening in the shrubs into the village.

Unlike the picture in his imagination, there were not throngs of unclean men lying about. Instead, he saw a clean, well-kept community. He had hoped the housing project would be the perfect place to hide for the night while he figured out his next steps, but now, he wasn't so sure. The problem, he realized as he walked between the rows of tiny houses, was that there wasn't really anywhere to hide. This community was far more than just little houses, it was a neighborhood. He noticed a few of the small homes with glowing red doors, the telltale sign of someone in HomeJail.

As he searched for a hiding place, he noticed a lack of stream-Bugs buzzing about. There was probably far less drama, and therefore, far less interest, here in the land of the poor and downtrodden, than existed in the world of the rich and privileged in Beverly Hills. Apparently, wealth affords the luxury of time and energy for theatrics.

Roman cut between two tiny houses and leaned against the side of a light green metal house just below a darkened window. Gravel crunched as he sat down. It was not comfortable, but it would have to do. He would have to figure out how to get in touch with his team in the morning.

No sooner had he pulled his hoodie over his head than the shade in the window above him went up and light poured out. The shape of a head appeared in the shadow cast on the wall across the tiny grass yard. He heard the window slide open and looked straight up to see the bald head of a large black man lean out the window and look straight down at him.

"My bed is right here on this wall, so if you gonna sleep there, you best not make any noise."

"Sorry, man. I just need a place to spend the night. I'll be quiet."

"You ain't gonna be comfortable on those rocks. And if a patrol sees you, they gonna take you to a shelter, which is where you should be anyways." The man's face was lit from underneath, making him look like a horror show monster.

"Can't go to a shelter."

"Why? You in trouble?"

"Bit of an understatement, but yeah, you could say that."

"What's your name?"

Roman considered lying, but then figured it didn't matter whether this semi-homeless man knew his name. "Roman."

"Okay, Roman. I like to know who's crashing against my house, 'case I get asked. Roman who?"

"Glass."

"Like the scientist?"

"Yeah, he was my father. I'm Roman Glass Junior."

The window closed, and the shade went down again. Hopefully, he would just turn off the lights and leave Roman alone. Then he heard the thunk of the man's door.

Suddenly, the man was towering above Roman. He was big, six feet four and a half inches, muscular. He put his hands on his hips. "Well, Roman Glass Junior, I can't have the son of one of the most famous exobiologists on the planet sleeping outside my house. I have a cot. Come on inside." He reached out his massive hand and pulled Roman to a standing position.

His smile was genuine and warm. Roman felt a wave of relief wash over him and realized the stress he was feeling from running and trying to prove his innocence was taking its toll. "Thank you. I'd appreciate that."

Saturday, 10:15 p.m.

The contrast between the large, hulking man and the tiny house was stark. He introduced himself as Leonard, but most people called him Leo. He had been living here in this community for a year now. Previously, Leo had been a part-time psychology professor at UCLA when the housing bubble burst again, and this time, he was too far upside down to recover. He eventually turned to booze and pills and lost everything. He just recently started working at the microdrone repair facility and was finally able to afford a scooter to get back and forth. Something he was clearly proud of. Leo was on his way to becoming a self-supporting, healthy man again.

The lack of streamBugs, iBrowse and displays put Roman at ease. For the first time in a few days, he could relax, even though he was sitting on the corner of a small cot in a homeless village. The idea of needing to let his watchers know he was safe crossed his mind, and he quickly realized that unlike his friends, his watchers had no loyalty to him. His experience at the amusement park was evidence of that fact.

Leo sat on the only chair in the place, an easy chair, not very far away from Roman. He looked like he wanted to talk about something, but was giving Roman a moment to compose himself.

"Thanks again for this, I appreciate it," said Roman.

"You're welcome," said Leo. "Your father's discovery set the academic world on fire."

So that's what he wants to talk about. "It set a lot of things on fire," replied Roman, "including our family. He didn't handle it well."

Leo clasped his hands behind his head and leaned back. "Sounds like you might have some resentments."

Roman was taken aback by the quick and forward assumption. "A little maybe."

The man put his hand to his forehead like he realized his pushiness. "Apologies, I'm so sorry, I'm working toward my counseling certification."

"Well, you hit the jackpot with me. I'm a mess."

"We're all doing the best we can, given the circumstances. Maybe a mends is in order."

"I can't make a mends with a dead man."

Leo leaned forward, his chair creaking. "Stinkin' thinkin' will get you nowhere. I sincerely encourage you to reconsider whether you can make amends with a dead man, 'cause it could be holding you back."

"Yeah, I know. It's not all on me, though. I wish he had been a little more willing to appease people."

"Me, I'm glad your pop stood by his guns, and I'm sorry for what happened."

"Thanks."

"Shame what religion can do to some people. Just 'cause something doesn't agree with your beliefs is no reason to kill. It's not like your pop was anything more than a messenger, but people act like he personally brought the devil to Earth when he cracked open that comet."

"Some people's belief systems are like a house of cards, man. If they're threatened, they fight as if they've been personally attacked. My dad's killer thought he had millions of people supporting him because of socials."

Leo nodded. "Well, young man, that seems like a better place to put your resentment then, doesn't it?"

Roman shook his head. Now was not the time for therapy. "I can't think about that now. I have more important things to worry about."

"Yeah? What kind of trouble you in?"

"I'm not sure how you wouldn't know. It's all over all the streams. They think I killed Starla Devine."

"I don't pay attention to the news. It's just people catching each other doing stupid things on camera and then some damned AI personality trying to make it sound like it's the most important scariest thing that ever happened. Everything they call news these days is just people recording other people doing something they shouldn't be doing."

"Can't argue with you there."

Leo leaned back in his chair and put a massive foot up on the tiny living room table. "So somebody's trying to frame you for killing Starla Devine, huh? There's usually two possibilities when it comes to murder. Passion, or benefit. Emotion or reason. Have you figured out who would benefit the most from her death?"

"Of course. I'm convinced it's Owen Blakewell and someone else. I just dunno why."

"Currency."

"You mean money?"

"No, I mean currency. That's a better word for it. 'Cause currency can be anything. It can be paper, digital, attention, popularity. The more you have of it, the more control you have over the means of the creation of it. And that's power." The small table shifted like it might collapse. Leo pulled his foot off of it. "And–" he wagged his finger, "–the less currency you have, the more likely you are to be used. Like you." The chair squealed as he stood up.

"If it is about currency, I can't dig deep enough into the system to figure out how. I'm hoping this investigator can help me on that front."

Leo walked to the sink and filled a glass with water and handed it to Roman. "I've been through some tough times, young man. All you can do is work your program."

Roman sipped the warm Los Angeles tap water. It never tasted so good. "Not sure what you mean, Leo."

He grabbed a thick blue book from his nightstand and held it up to Roman. There were no markings on it. "The only currency I have right now is my sobriety, and I'm not letting anyone or anything convince me to give it up. They want me to, so they can use me as currency for the alcohol industry, but I'm keeping it."

"Oh, that. I had the shot. You should get it. It works."

"Nope. Don't trust the shots." He cracked the book open and started reading.

Roman was taken aback. "But dude, you seem like a smart, scientifically minded..."

"I have my reasons, Roman Glass Junior," he said without looking up from his book. "No shots."

Roman let it go. He looked around the small home, clean, sparse, and efficient. Just the necessities. Against one wall was a small old-fashioned computer with a physical keyboard and mouse device. "Leo, is that hooked up?"

"Sure is. But they don't let us have full access. Only connects to the library and health and social services sites. I use it to go to my meetings sometimes, but that's about it. The display is terrible, just 2D, but it works for what I need."

"Mind if I use it?"

"Help yourself, but it's power out here at 11 p.m. That's the community rule."

Saturday, 10:43 p.m.

Huddled under a blanket in the corner of the tiny home like an eight year old playing games past his bedtime, Roman used Leo's log in to get into the library system. It was clunky, working on an old-fashioned desktop computer, but other than feeling like swimming in molasses, it worked fine once he got used to actual keys instead of projected ones, a handheld mouse instead of his chest touch pad, and a small twenty-seven-inch 2D flat screen.

Logging in to the Los Angeles Public Library system, he gained the ability to read and post to text-based chat groups within the library network. It was painfully slow having to type every word instead of being able to speak it, but it worked. Now, if he could figure out a way to get his people to log onto it, he would be back in communication. The person he really wanted to talk to was Roxy. Even though she got caught masquerading as him, she would be more concerned for Roman than herself.

She was probably being monitored, especially by StarSee. Plus, she wouldn't have her iBrowse, since Roman had stashed them on the bus. The only way to contact her would be through the library network. But how?

Leo had already given him the answer; make it about their dad.

Everybody had a library account, even if they didn't use it or know it. He just needed to find her account and then send her a direct message. He targeted the search for her profile by including her hobbies, location, age and education and narrowed it down to three people named Roxanne Glass.

He posted a direct message to be broadcast to all three with a high importance alert status. He needed to be cryptic, not use certain keywords, but avoid it getting filtered out as spam. This could be a dangerous move. If the cops, or the Blakewells, were listening, he could be sending out a signal flare.

He wrote, *"Everyone knows Roman Glass Senior's thesis paper was on the origins of the planetary system Gliese 667 C in the Scorpius constellation, and the potential for life to have arisen on Planet C. Only people close to him know he regretted publishing that, since he later figured out his calculations were flawed, but he was in hiding by then. That's our dad. Leothehawk47 on the library network is waiting."*

He turned on every level of high importance for the message he could and hit send.

He waited for what seemed like forever, and nothing happened. Maybe he should have been more direct. As he waited, he glossed over the headings of the different discussion topics within the group. Most focused on the biology of the large frozen somewhat insect-like creature his father uncovered, but it was surprising even in this somewhat scientific group how many people wanted to prove that it was not alien life. Even though it was literally found inside an extra terrestrial comet fragment, and even though it had a completely different DNA structure than all life on Earth, people still did not want to believe it. Others, like the panspermia community, felt that it was proof that life arose elsewhere and migrated here on the back of a space rock, while many more argued that it proved the abundance of life in the universe.

After several more minutes, the light flashed on the interface, indicating that he had been invited to a private chat room on the library site. The name said Roxyglass902. He opened the chat window:

Roxyglass902: Brother, is it u?

Leothehawk47: Yes!

Roxyglass902: You are such a nerd to use that about dad to contact me. :) Where are you and who is Leo the Hawk?

Leothehawk47: Shouldn't say. Must chat fast. Careful what you say, software could be listening for keywords. Sorry I got you into this. Didn't think you would get caught.

Roxyglass902: Not your fault. Plus laws against putting yourself IN HomeJail on purpose not clear. Lol. Are you safe?

Leothehawk47: Yes, but list of charges getting longer.

Roxyglass902: What can we do?

Leothehawk47: Must figure out how to unlock streamBug recording of night S was killed. It is only way.

Roxyglass902: Sedative is wearing off. I can help now.

Leothehawk47: No. You be careful. Let other's work on protection.

Roxyglass902: Protection?

Leothehawk47: Yes, file is locked by Agreement four one three. Can't copy, move or play it.

Roxyglass902: Not much to go on.

Leothehawk47: Locked files might have to do with conservatorship, but I think they are two different things.

Roxyglass902: I heard about bear and drug.

Leothehawk47: Yeah, also, since I couldn't get recording, I stole different file. Gave it to investigator. She knows about agreement too. Probably only one we can trust right now.

Roxyglass902: Going to look into Agreement, see what I find.

Leothehawk47: No, don't trip alarms. You have done enough. Just contact team, tell everyone I am okay for now. Will check here again in morning. Time is up, lights out. Wanted you to know I was okay.

Roxyglass902: Glad you are okay. I am going to help you.

Leothehawk47: Please be careful sis. Glad you are okay too. Love you.

Roxyglass902: Pinkies.

Leothehawk47: Pinkies.

He knew she would probably begin digging, no matter what he said. After they disconnected, he started searching through the library system for legal agreement definitions in what little time he still had, but could only find that agreements between private parties can be called anything they want, so the only people who would know exactly what Agreement 413 meant in this case were the people who signed it or the lawyers who made it. Searching for the term combined with "File Protection" on the system produced so many results, he couldn't make sense of it. There were agreements between neighbors, divorce agreements, marriage agreements, prenup agreements, ICE agreements, copyright agreements. Everyone had a legal agreement these days.

Exhausted, Roman pulled the blanket off of his head and lay down on the cot.

"Find what you needed?" Leo asked.

"I talked to my sister. My people will know I'm okay. Hopefully they can help."

"That's good. Having people, real people, not virtual ones, makes all the difference." Leo turned off the light.

Roman lay in the dark with his eyes open. "Thanks for keeping it real, Leo."

"One day at a time, young man."

Somehow, in this place, surrounded by the people that society had tried to cast off, those with the fewest followers and the least Admiration Points, the smallest houses and the worst computers, Roman felt safer than ever.

CHAPTER
TWENTY-NINE

Saturday, 11:28 p.m.

Maddox Blakewell was exactly where he loved to be, alone in the most luxurious spot in the world, a spot that he built just for himself.

I earned this.

He sat in his infinity edge hot tub, looking out over the twinkling smoky City of Los Angeles at night. No streamBugs whatsoever. He took a deep breath and exhaled slowly. This was his spot. It was his time. It was what he lived for. Here, he could sit and think, strategize, obsess, and consider his options. His most creative solutions came to him while sitting right here, in the 102-degree steaming purified mineral water, drinking the finest California Cabernet. The blue aura of his aquarium bathed him in cool light from behind while his fire pits glowed with warmth from the front. Few human beings ever achieve this kind of godlike status, and he knew it. He drank with the pride of the Egyptian Pharaohs and the Roman Emperors. He wondered if they felt as underappreciated as he did. *Probably.*

He did not wear his iRiz when he was in the hot tub, instead, he had multiple retractable waterproof displays around the perimeter. He reached over and rotated a display toward himself. The graphic for his Digital Assistant system, Maria, glowed in the steaming air, waiting for his command. "Maria: structure file Maddox, Operation Oil Slick. Subfolder private. Start with Arizona, focus population toward enemy using plastic prices as divisive issue. Test level of engagement in two weeks. End." Maria chimed in affirmation of the commands. He gulped his wine, refilled his glass from the tap, and leaned back in his padded submerged chair.

No, he shouldn't be manipulating public opinion. Yes, it was illegal. But it was too much fun to resist. He smiled as he ran his hands through his wet hair.

Benefiting the agenda of the political party currently in power required a special kind of manipulation. Years ago, Maddox had started with the groupthink manipulation. The challenge he had to overcome in creating political outcomes was that it had already been done before, and even though it was successful, it had gotten people in trouble and been shut down. Driving people into vortexes of hatred using suggested content was nothing new. The challenge was in creating a zeitgeist without being the least bit overt. The entire effort had to remain undetected by other algorithms or human analysts. To get away with it, Maddox had to subtly manipulate live streams to insert undetectable trigger sentences and words at just the right scientific frequency to influence beliefs. Enough to have a deep effect, but not enough for anyone, or anything, to notice. He had to use AI to create algorithms to monitor his algorithms. It took remarkable effort for him to keep track of the various loops and checks in the complex web of programmatic influence he created.

Presently, he was mulling over what he referred to as Operation Oil Slick. He would maintain half his subscribers' belief that Iran was a threat, but not a full on enemy. Divide and drive opinion. Best to keep the two sides in a sort of mutually-assured distrust. People had to learn just the right amount of bad things about their adversary to consider them thieves and murderers who want to destroy their way of life, while the other side was exposed to the fact that they are human beings with personal struggles just like everyone else. Both sides felt completely self-righteously justified in their position. The conflict would be utilized to the benefit of those in power, the entities that hired Maddox for his abilities.

The merger with NewsCann would create a self-protecting, self-regulating system of content and dissemination that would allow for the manipulation to become even more thorough, and even more opaque. Now that Gabe had filed the documents to move up the deadline, it was only twenty-four hours away from completion. His father had unwittingly moved up the deadline for his own demise. Nothing could stop Maddox now.

A small yellow light blinked in the corner of a monitor, alerting him to a recent discovery by his Digital Assistant.

"Maria, conversation mode on."

"Conversation mode active." The woman's voice had no hint whatsoever of being non-human. He liked conversation mode, since the AI of the Digital Assistant added a completely human feeling, very slight English accent and occasional word fumbles, intentionally not perfect. "Good evening, Maddox," she said.

"Hello Maria. What's the alert about?"

"I found a boolean data overlap between your father and Roxy Glass."

He tilted his head. He didn't remember asking his Digital Assistant to look out for an overlap between the two. It must be important. "What kind of overlap?"

"They have both been searching for information on Agreement 413."

Despite the hot water, a chill went through Maddox's body. This could only mean one thing: that they were not just working together, but in direct communication. "Have either of them been able to bypass it?"

"It doesn't appear so. The Glass woman doesn't know where to look. But she's also doing a lot of searching for Name Image Likeness laws and conservatorships. She's spending a lot of time in the legal section of the public library system, which I can't monitor directly. She also tried to contact the investigator in the Social Media Division, the one you and your father spoke with. And she has been doing internet-wide searches for information on you and your father. It's possible they may have already been in contact."

No shit. Maddox gulped his wine, set down the glass, and thrummed his fingers. The only reason they would be working together would be if his father sensed Maddox's bigger plans, and had decided to pin something on him first. "Maria, if someone were going to try to remove me from power by accusing me of a crime, when would be the most opportune time to do it?"

"Before tomorrow night's deadline, since you will gain more control of the company then, and your code will start integrating with the NewsCann code. Perhaps even at the party in order to publicly humiliate you."

That must be the plan! "Maria, call my father."

"Now? Sometimes it's best for you to wait a moment before you take action. You have said before that you get irrational when upset."

"I'm fine, God damnit. I just need to feel him out."

"Okay then. Best not to mention what you know. Instead, see if he says anything that makes you suspicious."

Conversation mode was very convincing. He had been thinking the same thing. His father answered. The volumetric display showed him sitting at his desk in his office. "What?" Owen barked.

Maddox would observe him closely for any clue that he was turning further against his own son, but given that his father's facade of friendliness hid a secret disdain for everyone, it was sometimes difficult to detect suspicious behavior. "I wanted to ask you about the Starla thing. Have you guys changed your mind about anything?"

Owen's face twisted. "No, why would we? Everything's going the way I said it should." He looked distracted. He had his iRiz in and his eyes were watching something else.

"We had to start somewhere, right? And it worked out, right?" Maddox tried to sound casual.

"Yes, why are we talking about this?"

"It's just, you know, the agreement? The file protection that popped up? Have you been looking into it?"

"Which one, 413? Yeah, I was checking to see if we could use our conservatorship power of attorney to bypass it."

"Oh, can we?"

"Yes, but not right away. It'll take a week, and by then, it won't matter. Why?"

"I just want that to be solid. The whole thing."

"You shouldn't have tried to delete those recordings so quickly. It was a stupid mistake. It got us locked out of our own files."

"How the fuck should I have known that would happen? God dammit!"

"You could have asked. Gabe knew."

"Fuck Gabe."

"Have you been drinking?" Owen's eyes stopped flitting about and focused on Maddox through the connection. "Oh, you're in the tub," he said dismissively. "Call me back tomorrow."

"I'm not–" He took a breath and gathered his composure. "–do you know Roxy Glass? Roman Glass' sister?"

"No, should I?"

Maddox stared at his father, the consummate liar. Not surprising that he would hide any contact with her. "No, I'm just trying to put some pieces together."

"Look, it's best to leave that whole thing alone. The Glass kid is digging himself deeper into a hole the longer he runs."

Of course you would say to leave it alone. "Don't change the subject to Roman. I'm talking about his sister, Roxy. There's something not making sense that I want answers to."

"Well, try when you're sober. Goodbye Maddox." Owen abruptly disconnected.

God dammit.

The Digital Assistant spoke again. "Would you like me to continue alerting you if I see your father taking actions against you or communicating with the Glass woman? And keep the information private?"

"Yes, Maria. Keep me informed. And yes, good idea. Also keep our conversations, yours and mine, on my personal Vaults, not the main corporate one. I don't want my father trying to use our talks against me when he tries to throw me to the wolves. And turn all sidecar data off. He seems to have figured out how to get into that."

"Okay. Routing all audio-video-text communications between Maddox Blakewell and personal StarSee Digital Assistant Maria to Maddox Blakewell's private Vaults now."

"Thank you, Maria. I appreciate the extra attention you've been giving this matter lately, helping me figure out what to do about Owen." *Keep accurately anticipating what I want.*

Maybe he was a little on the buzzed side.

"Conversation mode off. Call physical assistants." *If Roxy Glass thinks she can work with my father and take me down, she has no Goddamn idea what she's in for.* He got up out of the water, and within moments, two junior assistants were there with towels.

Stepping up the speed and vitriol of his groupthink algorithm without getting caught would be a challenge, but he had done it before, and of course, he had his big trick up his sleeve. Riots required complex orchestration, but a smaller-scale attack shouldn't be too hard.

"I'm going down to the Gray Room for some late night adjustments."

"Your shorts and a shirt are on your bed, all ready for you," said the young female assistant, smiling.

"Don't talk to me like I'm a child," he said as he handed her his empty glass and walked back into the building. "And bring me some coffee."

CHAPTER
THIRTY

Sunday, 8:50 a.m.

The cot shifted. "I'm goin' for breakfast at the center," said Leo as he nudged Roman gently.

Roman coughed and rubbed his eyes, rolling into a sitting position. The morning sun had a reddish tint to it again today. "Do I need ID to eat?"

"Nah, it's not that kind of place. You'll fit right in."

"I'll keep my distance from you at breakfast. I don't want anyone coming after you just because they saw you with me," said Roman.

Stepping out of the tiny home, the sounds of downtown echoed through the glass and supersteel canyons as Los Angeles came to life on a Sunday morning. Walking to the community center only took a few minutes. He didn't talk to anyone as he stood in the line of mostly African-American men. For the most part, the group looked happy, healthy and well dressed. He imagined many of them were about to go off to their low-paying jobs doing the labor nobody realizes needs to be done. A few of them had iBrowse, and some wore StarSee blue shirts. No one had the telltale slightly glowing iris' from wearing iRiz. There were stream-Bugs now, probably belonging to volunteers, or citizen journalists doing StarSee stories on attempts to address the crisis of the unhoused that never goes away in LA. Roman was careful to keep his head down for fear of facial recognition software noticing him, even with his mask on.

He sat as far back in the large room as he could, at a table with two other men who looked as antisocial as he needed to be. The room was filled with the low murmur of conversation and break-fast. It smelled of coffee and bacon. Above Roman's table hung a large superthin display that broadcast KTLA, the Los Angeles twenty-four-hour news stream. If he looked up, he could see the smiling faces of the news team enjoying their morning banter as they covered the regional weather, the latest fires, and other local news and human interest stories.

As he removed his mask and ate, he felt a weight being lifted off his shoulders. His fear was replaced with humble gratitude. Perhaps his father, while in hiding, had even taken advantage of these kinds of social services, and depended on these invisible, underprivileged people in his own quest for anonymity.

If he could ask for more food, he would have. The breakfast was gone so fast he barely tasted it. Staring at his empty plate, he needed to plan his next steps. He could probably depend on the kindness of strangers for a day or two at most, but he had to get a copy of the recording. He needed help, but he was too hot for any of his team to get near, and the chances were that if he went to Dettmer, she would have to throw him in HardJail just out of procedure. He should contact Roxy again. Knowing her, she was probably up all night digging.

As if on cue, he heard his sister's name, "Roxanne Glass," and thought for a moment he must be hearing things. Then he heard the smooth news anchor's voice say, "...the daughter of famed exobiologist Roman Glass is the target of this protest." Roman's breath caught in his throat.

He immediately stood up and looked at the large display, where he saw a couple of dozen protesters gathered outside of his sister's townhouse. StreamBugs swarmed, creating a complete volumetric display of the area. An on-site female newscaster was trying to find someone coherent to interview, but it looked like mayhem. The crowd was chanting, "Traitor!" and looking like they wanted blood. The newscaster grabbed a man who had the signature red shirt on. He yelled into the reporter's unnecessary hand-held microphone that had KTLA on one side and NewsCann on the other.

"What's going on here?" asked the reporter.

"She's a traitor, she's working for Iran! She's the daughter of Roman Glass, and she probably helped her brother kill Starla Devine! That tells you everything you need to know right there!"

The reporter asked, "Why now? Why this protest at her home today?"

"She's about to give away secrets! She's a spy, and she has to be stopped. We're all members of the same elite group, and we all saw it on our StarStreams. We had to do something. We came here to stop the traitor!" A cheer went up in the small crowd. A chant broke out, "Stop the traitor! Stop the traitor!"

Roman's heart raced. He stood on his toes, reached up and grabbed the remote control from the front of the display. He quickly took control of the camera view and flew around the scene. He could not see inside any of his sister's windows. She had drawn all the shades. Flying twenty-five feet above the crowd, he saw a single police vehicle parked two hundred yards away, with two officers leaning on the back of it. They were either not interested or were in agreement with the mob and were only there to enable it. He could see more angry men in red shirts jogging toward the scene from surrounding blocks.

He threw the remote on a table and spun around to face the

room full of men, several of whom had turned their attention to the unfolding scene. "She didn't do anything!" The people in the tiny home community either stared motionlessly at him, or ignored him completely. "That's my sister! She didn't do anything! She was just helping me!"

Several of the men in the room turned and pointed at Roman, whispering to each other. He saw looks of recognition wash over their faces. He had forgotten to pull his mask back up. StreamBugs were starting to pay attention to him and hovered closer.

Out of the corner of his eye, he saw Leo get up from the table and make his way over. "You're making a scene. Come with me, right now." He grabbed Roman's arm and led him quickly out of the commissary.

Sunday, 9:20 a.m.

Leo agreed to use his Vespa to get Roman as close to Roxy's townhouse as he could. Roman didn't say a word as he held onto the bars on the sides of the seat, nestled tightly against Leo's large back. The bike strained as it went up the many hills with two people on it. Getting up to Mulholland, passing the homes of the very wealthy, Roman could think of nothing but getting to his sister. Leo had tried to remind Roman that he was still a fugitive, and should be careful about running headlong into a scene taking place in front of the world, that this could easily be a trap, but Roman insisted he needed to get to his sister. Going down the other side of the hill, crossing into 'the valley,' was considerably easier, to the point of being a bit like an amusement park ride. The scorching morning wind blasted his face, as they careened around corners through the mix of self- and human-driving traffic. Leo's passenger helmet did not have a visor, so Roman had no heads up display showing him where he was or how fast they were going.

The jam on Ventura Boulevard started a mile away from his sister's house. Roman told Leo to cut through the residential neighborhoods and back alleys. They made their way to the block of his sister's townhouse, and Leo pulled to the curb. Roman hopped off, ripped off his helmet and started to run toward the protesters before stopping and doubling back.

"Leo, thank you! When all this is over, I promise, I'll repay you, dude."

"No need. I have a sister. I know what it's like," he said.

"I have a friend. Her name is Seven. If you were on StarSee, we could get you a million watchers."

"Go get your sister." He flipped the visor down on his helmet and began to roll away. Roman turned and started running toward the crowd. As he looked back at Leo riding away, his large frame on the small bike, Leo hung his left arm down in a bikers wave.

Roman kept low as he made his way past the newscasters who had staked out an area for themselves across the street. They were next to the police, who had apparently decided to let this hysterical mob run its course. He had just been here a day ago, but the entire scene was the opposite of the peaceful hide out that it was before. Roman circled around the eight-unit building and went down around back to the alley where the garage doors were.

Roman ran toward the screaming mob as he adjusted his face mask. He wasn't sure what he needed to do, other than get to his sister. He pushed through the angry crowd as they shouted, "Hang Her!" "Traitor!" "Terrorist!" "Murderer!" Roman was stunned. None of these people even knew his sister, and yet, somehow the more worked up they got, the more people they seemed to be attracting. The energy of hatred was creating a feedback loop of more hatred, infecting more people online and making them want to join the fray.

The thought flashed through his mind that he was glad they were in California, where gun control laws had kept assault weapon popularity from reaching the levels it had elsewhere. If this were happening in some other parts of the United States, there would be automatic weapons being brandished like flags at a parade.

As he neared her garage door at the bottom rear of the four-story townhome, he could see a small group of them working like insects to get inside.

"Hey!" shouted Roman. "Get the fuck away from there!"

"This is her place! I looked it up!" Shouted one of the men, apparently assuming Roman was friendly.

Adrenaline coursed through his veins as he got close to the group. He was not normally a fighter. Someone yelled, "Hey, that's her place! They found a way in!"

A rush of people pushed and tumbled through the aluminum garage doors and were inside within seconds. All at once, there were half a dozen more men inside the empty garage with more coming. The rats had found their way in.

Roman tried to block the inner door. "Get the fuck out!" His screams of protest were lost in the crowd rushing toward him. A man pushed him aside and turned the handle. Before Roman could say or do anything, the man had made it inside her home.

The flow of the men running into the house carried him along. It was like being part of a crowd rushing the stage at a concert. All he could do was go along with the river of fury. They stomped up the stairs from the garage level to the first floor, shouting, "Where is she?!"

Roman's yelling did no good. As they made their way up the stairs, they passed the front door, which they immediately yanked open. Instantly, more of them came pouring in through the other entrance like a mass of cockroaches. Roman was pushed, stumbled, fell and got back up. The mob was like a swarm of wasps ripping open every door and flipping every piece of furniture. Roman might as well have been shouting at a tsunami.

For a brief moment, he imagined that the number of watchers

on his sister's StarSee account must be skyrocketing. The reality show of Roxy Glass' life just got very exciting for a lot of people.

He heard a woman's scream and recognized it as hers. She was on the top floor. They had found her. Sirens blared outside mixed with the bullhorn of the police, finally deciding that something needed to be done now that the mob had broken into a private residence. The number of streamBugs swarming through the home was so high the normally white ceilings looked like they were covered with a film of moving dirt.

He heard her scream again, and nothing else in the world mattered. He started yanking, kicking, punching, pushing and violently throwing the attackers down the stairs. Several punched him back, but the punches, painful as they were, only released more adrenaline, and he fought harder. He emerged from the stairwell onto the top floor and fought his way toward the deck, where he saw his sister, still dressed in her pajamas, surrounded by men yelling at her.

"Get the hell away from me!" she screamed as she was forced back toward the railing of her deck. One of the men grabbed her arm. "I've got her!" This caused others to rush toward him, which pushed the entire frenzy onto the deck like an enraged bull.

A gunshot rang out behind them. The violent crowd heaved forward as Roman elbowed and punched his way toward his sister. They had her pinned against the railing of the deck, four stories up. The railing strained, dust sprang from the anchor points as a bolt popped. More shots rang out. Someone was firing into the air. Roman reached out toward her, recognition flashed across her face, momentarily replacing the fear. "Roman! Help me!" she screamed, terrified. "He called me last night!" Another bolt popped out of the black wrought iron connector to the stucco exterior. Small chunks of stucco flew off and bounced off of the destroyed garage doors lying in the alley, four stories below.

He grabbed for her hand. "Roxy!"

As if in slow motion, the railing bent. The section of wrought-iron fence squealed as it twisted further from its anchor point. It cracked and pulled away from the wall. Their fingers missing each other by mere inches. *Pinkies.* In an instant, she was falling over the side. Two men were falling with her. The sudden release of pressure caused Roman to fall to the floor of the deck as his sister's hand slipped away from his. He landed hard, and someone else landed on top of his back. His head hung over the edge as he watched her fall four stories, her hands grasping at thin air, fifty-three feet to the ground. It sounded like loud slaps as the bodies hit the concrete below. The noise of the crowd yelling was replaced by swearing and gasping, as if they had just witnessed a magic trick gone horribly wrong.

Police burst from the doors to the deck, weapons drawn.

Lying on his stomach, the edge of the building pressing into his throat, staring down at his sister's bent and broken body, a pool of blood growing around her head on the ground, Roman felt the handcuffs wrenched tightly around his wrists.

CHAPTER
THIRTY-ONE

Sunday, 10:35 a.m.

A light haze of smoke blanketed the highway as Dettmer's car smoothly entered the SDV lane where the intelligent cars could remote connect to one another and drive in synchronized AI unison. If she were still in Homicide, she would turn on her siren and lights, but the Social Media Division did not warrant emergency equipment.

Watching the NewsCann stream on her display panel, the recording played on repeat of the angry mob storming the townhouse, the group cornering Roxy on the top floor, the railing giving way and the three people falling. The recording would freeze just before the three bodies hit the ground, as if not showing the actual bloody impact made the broadcasters responsible journalists. A link appeared at the bottom of the screen to play the unedited *"graphic"* version.

According to the story, the violence had been short-lived. Three people were dead and six people were injured, including one from an accidental self-inflicted gunshot wound. Several people were in custody, including the fugitive, Roman Glass.

Homicide Detective Travis Clark was being interviewed about the incident. The female street reporter asked him why it had occurred.

"We don't yet know exactly what caused the flash mob to attack Ms. Glass," he said.

First on the scene from Homicide again? What is up with him?

Travis looked like the classic detective, tie and all. "There does not appear to be any one individual responsible for the accident," he said.

Accident?

"The witnesses here say they felt compelled to stop her from sharing secrets with Iran and believed her to be somehow connected to the murder of Starla Devine."

"What secrets did they think she might have?" asked the reporter.

Travis got that look that a police officer gets when asked a question they don't know. "The group is suggesting that others in their circles have the actual evidence, and they trust their sources and not the mainstream media."

The reporter shook her head, turned to the camera and said, "Back to you in the studio."

The deadly event had enjoyed its thirty seconds of fame, and the main desk news anchors deftly moved on to the next story, which was the fires that were recently contained in the Hollywood Hills. Private security had dispersed protesters outside the StarSee facility using flash bangs, which had sparked a brush fire. Prevailing winds blew the flames northwest, away from the facility, and into the canyons, where firefighters had mostly contained the flames with massive air drops of fire killer.

Dettmer looked out her right-side window and could see the plume of light gray smoke in the distance. She assumed she was looking at the one they were talking about, but there were four other smoke plumes on the distant horizon.

The display on the windshield indicated she had twelve minutes until she would arrive at Roxy's townhouse where Roman was still being held in a MobiJail. As a result of her conversations with Melissa about programming, and Seven about the Blakewells, Dettmer was formulating a hypothesis that was coming into focus. There was clearly something happening in the StarSee core code that was causing aggression and crime, but several questions remained. Was it intentional? Was someone else modifying this algorithm for their own means? And what did any of this have to do with Roman Glass and Starla Devine?

To get closer to the truth, she would need Roman's help in a much more daring and risky plan than she had ever attempted before. This would be the end of her career if she was wrong about any of it. *Carmen would approve, if she were still alive.*

"Digital Assistant, Call Mo."

The screen flickered for a moment, and Mo appeared at his desk. He spoke without looking up. "Where ya off to?"

"Roxy Glass' townhouse."

"Action's done there. Three people dead. They even caught your boy." He looked up, cocked his head and pointed his finger. "Oh, you know that, and you're gonna see him, aren't ya?"

"I am. I have been brainstorming theories, and I am putting things together. I need to speak to him."

"Rennick's not gonna be happy. You haven't helped any old ladies cross a digital street recently."

"The thing is, conning old ladies out of their life savings is nothing compared to using complex algorithms to get people to kill each other, which is what I think is happening. So I have the what, I just do not know exactly who, how or why."

"Seems a bit weak of a foundation to get Melissa to make you a killcode."

"If a vehicle is out of control on the freeway, you do not ask who is driving or why, you just have to stop it."

"I'm surprised she'd risk her job on that basis."

"We talked my whole hypothesis through, how somehow they are winding people up without being detected by the Impulse Governors, and ultimately–" She paused. "–she is also not a big fan of Rennick's." Dettmer smirked.

"But why go see Glass now?"

"Because I realized he must be important to the Blakewells for some reason, and I am inclined to think that it is connected to the crime wave. I do not believe in coincidences. And, if my suspicions are right, I will be taking some very big actions."

"Yeah, I'd say a killcode is pretty big."

"Bigger than that."

"Oh boy," said Mo. "I don't think I wanna know."

"Probably not. Tell me what is in the fact column about Roxy's murder before I talk to Roman."

"Ugly mob drove each other into a frenzy. Nobody knows who started it or why. I have traces running on all the StarSee accounts. Roxy fell off of her deck along with two of the attackers when the railing gave way and died of blunt force trauma. She's being put into Instant Cryogenic Embalming, ICE, as per the family's wishes. The two dead attackers will be cremated tomorrow."

"Huh, she is being put on ICE."

"Yeah, right? Not to put too fine a point on it, but her body's a mess."

"Maybe they think they will figure out how to regrow or repair the body."

"Well, the whole family had the ICE agreement in place at the original request of the father," said Mo.

"Let's move her StarSee recordings to the padded room."

"You mean copy. I can't move them until the ICE company is done with them. The ICE shop has ownership of the body and all the digital information deemed critical to her reawakening."

"What does that mean? I always review StarStreams right away."

"Right, but we can't modify them."

"I always wondered why that is."

"Upon death, the ICE company immediately takes ownership of all the streams and recordings of the most important triggers of your life, whether traumatic or happy, and locks them. Protecting what are assumed to be triggers that could be used to bring your mind back from the dead. Kinda like filling in missing DNA. They use your digital history to create an AI personality to assist with helping your brain recover. The idea is, if something important happened in your life, they could use that to make you aware of who you are again, by triggering your memory of it."

Dettmer's eyes narrowed. "Including the moments just before death."

"Yes."

She went quiet.

"You have that look again, cher," said Mo.

Dettmer's focus snapped back to Mo's image. "Does Roxy's ICE agreement have a name?"

Mo swiped a couple of times on his chest. "Yeah, 818–" He squinted as he read it in his iBrowse. "–622-9989-SOG."

"Huh. 818. Her area code."

"I know. Pretty lame, right?"

"Where is area code 413?"

He tapped his screen again. "Western Massachusetts."

"Where was Starla Devine from?"

Mo tapped a couple of things on his side. "Oooh, Western Massachusetts."

"Could Agreement 413 be shorthand for an agreement based on her complete contact number?"

Mo nodded, his eyes widening. "It sure could."

"That is it! Did Devine have an ICE agreement?"

Mo was poking and swiping at a different display on his desk now. "Yep, she sure did. And she was ICE'd quickly too. The day after her murder, on Tuesday. Expedited autopsy was Monday night."

"The reason those files are protected is because of an agreement with the ICE company! Not the Blakewells! What if some tampering was attempted on her recordings, so the ICE company automatically locked them?"

"Wow. That seems entirely possible."

"I need the Devine autopsy report right away," said Dettmer. "Can you forward it to me? Rennick has blocked me from her files."

Mo grimaced like he was being asked to help someone move.

"Mo, do it for Melissa."

"Oh, that's not fair." He chuckled. "You know Rennick said this whole shit show is Homicide's now. Doesn't want us near it. Says StarSee funding is too critical to our functioning."

Her neck tightened. "Screw him, and screw StarSee too."

"Jeez, they can hear us, you know." He gestured to the sky.

"Seriously, forward me the autopsy. I want to see it before I go in."

"Fine. But when Rennick shitcans you, don't take me down with you. And you know he's gonna find out you're talking to Glass."

"It is much worse than that. I am faking a private interview pass.

"Oh, cher."

"I need to talk to him. Whatever he has, or knows, is important to the Blakewells. And between him going under sedation, and the merger, we may never find out what that is unless we move quickly."

"I doubt Glass is gonna be in any mood to help. A deadly mob just killed his twin sister."

"Exactly. And I know who worked that mob up."

"Be careful. If you're right, you're in dangerous territory."

Her SDV pulled up in front of the townhouse. A police vehicle was parked sideways across the garage with the ripped down door. A green cleaning van was already spraying the blood stains clean in the alley. The black MobiJail bus with no side windows was parked across the street. Yellow tape was everywhere, a sight she was unfortunately becoming accustomed to.

She opened up Starla's autopsy report as her vehicle found a parking spot. She had died from severe blunt trauma to the head, just like they said. The rest of the report was the usual stuff: negative toxicology reports, no existing illness. Lots of cosmetic surgery. Standard media star stuff. She also had burst fat cells throughout her body, assumed to be the result of having had a form of body sculpting cosmetic surgery called cold sculpting.

But the burst fat cells were everywhere in her body.

That feeling crept in again. *Burst fat cells are also an indicator of having been put on ICE. Yet she would not have been put on ICE before the autopsy.*

The report ended with instructions to immediately ICE the body, at the request of the conservators.

Dettmer did not believe in coincidences.

She would have to create just the right chain of events to squeeze the facts out of this situation. Starting with Roman Glass.

CHAPTER
THIRTY-TWO

Sunday, 11:10 a.m.

He desperately wanted it all to go away, including himself. He just didn't want to feel anymore. Grief had created a hole that swallowed every thought, every emotion, every physical sensation. It didn't matter that he had been caught, or that he was sitting in a holding cell in a MobiJail, or that all his efforts had been for nothing. His sister was gone. She would be gone forever. He had failed to protect his protector. It had only been a couple of hours, but the tears were starting to fade, only to be replaced with a sense of longing for the past to change, and numbness at the fact that it never would. He trembled violently unless he closed his eyes and took deep breaths.

The Homicide Detective, Mascon, stood toward the front of the forty-five-foot long bus talking with his partner, Travis. He recognized them again from the failed amusement park meeting. *Travis must have a StarStream appearance,* thought Roman, observing that he wore a tie, while Mascon wore street clothes. Travis was keeping a close eye on Roman, glancing in his direction every so often.

Go ahead, look at me, I don't care.

Roman was inside the frontmost cell, sitting on a six-and-a-half-foot long bench. Just in front of him, at chest level, was a steel bar that doubled as something to hold on to when the bus was moving, and a security barrier that he had to sit behind when being interrogated. His Defenderbot stood on extended legs in the corner.

Worst amusement ride ever. One star.

He scolded himself for even thinking something humorous at a time like this.

He counted five holding cells lining the length of the driver's side, each with solid gray walls between them and a thick clear wall facing the two-point-two foot wide walkway, which ran the length of the bus on the other side. Inside each seven-by-seven foot cell was room for a padded bench and a fixed stool, nothing more. The walls were green, probably in the hopes that a calming color would keep prisoners from acting up. Light came in from near the ceiling of the bus, through small frosted portals that allowed daylight in but kept unauthorized streamBugs out. The air smelled of sweat and anger.

There were three other men in the other holding cells. Their muffled shouts of justification for what they did assaulted Roman's ears like birds flying into a high rise window.

A loud beeping pierced the air and the muffled shouting inside the MobiJail stopped. Roman could just barely see the door as it opened. Investigator Dettmer stepped on, wearing a navy blue suit, and began speaking to Mascon and Travis. Body language made it clear these people were not on the same team. She handed Mascon an e-card, which Mascon watched for a moment. He then pointed at Roman's cell and the three of them walked up to the thick plexiglass partition.

"Hands on the bar!" Mascon shouted.

Roman sat in a cloud of complete misery. He could tell his body to move but it didn't care. Thinking required more energy than the universe had, let alone trying to do something. He had felt grief when his father died, but this was worse. She had always been his unofficial guardian, and now he was truly alone.

"This one's broken. Hasn't moved an inch since we brought him in," said Mascon.

Dettmer stepped closer to the window. "Roman, I need to talk to you. It is important. I can help you. If you put your hands on the bar, I can come in, and we can talk."

He sat slumped over, staring at the floor.

"Roman Glass! Grab the bar now!" she yelled.

Without looking up, he lifted his arms and grabbed the two yellow spots on the bar in front of him, which read his galvanic skin response. It beeped and turned green. He heard the door open and close. He felt the hand of Dettmer on his shoulder, which just made his head hang lower.

"I'm sorry," she said.

Roman lifted his head and faced Dettmer. He sensed caring in her eyes instead of accusation, and suddenly, unable to control himself, he burst into tears. She leaned over the restraining bar and wrapped her arms around him, comforting him.

Mascon shouted, "Hey!" and pressed the alarm button. The interior of the cell flashed red.

Dettmer shot a look at Mascon. "Turn it off!" she yelled.

Mascon reluctantly switched off the alarm.

"Get the hell away and let us talk."

Mascon backed away from the window of the cell slowly, holding his hands up.

Roman wept in her arms. He didn't care. It was another human being showing him empathy, and all he wanted was someone that cared. It felt like it lessened the pain just a little. After a moment, he leaned back and rubbed his wet cheeks. "Shit. I'm sorry."

"No need to apologize," said Dettmer, as she sat on the single stool opposite the bench.

"I don't even know you."

She dabbed her own eyes with a tissue. Real tears. "Seriously, it is okay. I understand. That is why I am here. You need someone on your side."

Roman looked at her and almost burst into tears again. This time, he choked them back and held his breath.

"I talked to Seven," she said. "There is not a lot of time, so I am going to get right to it. Not to be indelicate, but your sister, she is being put on ICE, right?"

Roman exhaled deeply. "Yes, my father made arrangements for the whole family before they killed him."

"Do you remember the names of your contracts?"

"No. They're legal agreements with a name based on our contact numbers, I think. So my sister's would be 310 something..." He sniffled.

"And yours?" she probed.

"The same, of course, except for–." He blinked at Dettmer like a child waking up, awareness washing over him. "Oh my fucking god. That's what Agreement 413 is, isn't it?"

"I think so," said Dettmer. "Starla was from Western Massachusetts. Area code 413."

"That's great. So you can unlock the files!"

"We have to get to them first, and for that, I will need your help. I also have a suspicion about the autopsy showing that Starla's body had a small amount of burst fat cells everywhere. The coroner said it was from plastic surgery, but I think it is somehow connected to the ICE agreement. I have not figured out that piece yet, but it is too strange a coincidence."

"Can you get to the files?"

"No, but you may be able to. Because of your sister's death, you now have a personal two factor passcode to get into the ICE system, right?"

"Yeah, for like a day or two." It hit him again. It was so hard to think. Sure, he had a passcode, but it didn't matter. Nothing mattered anymore. He slumped.

She spoke quietly and seriously. "I think there is more to this than meets eyes. And the thing is, these assholes from Homicide will not even try to figure it out."

He sniffled and glanced up to see Travis watching them from the front of the MobiJail. "I can't exactly help, in case you haven't noticed."

"Do not be so sure," she said.

Roman squinted, she wasn't making sense. The Defenderbot remained green.

"Listen Roman, your sister's death was not an accident. That mob sprang up for a reason, and quite suspiciously, none of the people in the mob even know where the idea came from. I have a working theory about what is happening, but I need your help to figure out exactly who is involved and why."

He stared at the floor. The image of his sister's face as she fell away from him flashed before his eyes again, immediately followed by the image of her laying dead on the ground. He would have to live with those images seared into his mind forever.

"There is a reason you are important to the Blakewells. Can you think about why they want this pinned on you?"

"That's exactly what I've been trying to figure out. But I didn't do anything to them." He just wanted to lie down.

"As hard as it is, I need you to be strong and not let yourself get sucked into the grief. And I know what it is like to suffer loss at the hands of these companies, remember? This whole thing is the Blakewell's doing. I think you know that, and I believe it has far bigger implications than we think. They have even moved up the deadline for objections to the merger to tonight to create a cloak that they can hide behind."

Roman nodded slowly.

"There is more to Starla Devine's murder than we think. And you are the key to helping me reveal it."

Roman put his hands to his head, as if trying to steady his thoughts. "I wish I knew why, really, I do. I can't even think. They're going to sedate me. I'm fucking petrified."

"I know."

"No, seriously, once I'm sedated, they'll kill me. I know it. That's how they killed my dad."

"I know. But try not to be scared. It will all work out."

Roman stared back, trembling.

She continued in a steadying voice. "Think about this. Once the deadline for objections to the StarSee NewsCann merger passes, it will become nearly impossible to investigate them, and to prove you are innocent. We need to move fast. I know you are scared. But I need you to help me." She grabbed both his hands and squeezed them. "It is bigger than you. I do not mean to sound hyperbolic, but if you and I, together, do not stop them before the deadline tonight, they will have even more power to manipulate the world from a place of protected anonymity."

Roman closed his eyes, and the grief washed over him again. The images of his sister would not leave his mind. Dettmer sounded far away and her words held no importance. "I don't care. They won. They can kill me. Nobody's gonna care anyway."

She squeezed his hands tighter. "Roman, I care. Seven cares. Your team cares. Your mom cares. What we all need is for you to care."

"I can barely think."

"I understand. Just go along with it."

Roman looked up and stared at her through blurry eyes, trying to comprehend.

"You have to trust me. Right now, they have not won yet. We have until midnight tonight. Please believe me."

He squeezed his eyes closed and opened them again in an

effort to cast away the fog of grief. "I can't go anywhere, what exactly do you want me to do?"

"Demand an expedited sedation."

His jaw fell open. "You've got to be kidding. Why would I do that?"

"Keep your voice down. There are certain things that must happen here, in the MobiJail, before you reach HardJail. I cannot say more than that now."

"You're outta your mind."

"We have to trust Seven. That is all she said to have you do."

Roman shook his head slowly. He felt dead already. The world was shrinking, like he was seeing it through the wrong end of a telescope. "I can't."

Suddenly her grip on his hand grew so tight it hurt, her nails dug in. "Ow!" He looked at her with alarm.

She spoke slowly and locked on to his eyes. Her tone of voice was low and articulate. "You can get through this. I need you."

"Okay, jeezus."

"This. Is. Very. Important. You must be on your A game, Roman Glass. Compartmentalize your grief. I am risking everything on this."

Roman nodded his head. He was having a hard time ignoring the empty hole where his sister used to be.

"Demand the sedation today, on the grounds that your accusations put you in danger if you must interact with other prisoners."

The Defenderbot beeped and flashed orange.

Dettmer leaned closer to Roman and relaxed her grip on his hands. She spoke softly. "Hang in there, you have people that care, that are on your side. We can do this, okay?"

Despite his fears, it was reassuring. He wiped his wet eyes. "Okay. I think."

Detective Travis appeared from around the corner. "Time!"

She let go, stood up, and turned to the glass wall.

"Hands on the bar, Mr. Glass," he said.

Roman placed his hands on the yellow spots again. They turned green, and as he bowed his head, he heard the door open. He stared at the floor and listened. After she left the cell, the restraining bar clicked open.

"Your boyfriend tell you anything I should know about?" asked Mascon, from just out of Roman's sight.

"Yes, he did. He said he has the legal right to demand immediate sedation before being transported to HardJail." Dettmer stepped into the door well to leave, stopped and turned back to the two detectives. "Oh, and if you two are too stupid to see that he was here because he was trying to save his sister, you truly should find a different line of work." She stepped off the bus.

CHAPTER
THIRTY-THREE

Sunday, 12:20 p.m.

Maddox sat in Owen's courtyard at the same seat, at the same table, and ordered the same thing, every time they met for Sunday brunch. Owen and Lara sat on one side, and Maddox on the other, all under the large pergola, being served white glove brunch cooked by Owen's personal chefs, served by Owen's personal staff and having their drinks made by Owen's personal bartenders. The patio behind Owen's personal tower, nestled between his living space and the mountainside, provided a beautiful outdoor space to eat and have gatherings. With only half a dozen tables, this was smaller and more intimate than the official StarSee outdoor gathering space in the main courtyard.

Despite Maddox's repeated protests, Owen's streamBugs hovered around them. As usual, Owen assured Lara and Maddox that the audio was off and they could speak freely, but Maddox knew that just because the audio was off, that didn't mean they weren't being watched. AI could read lips, after all. But nobody paid attention to the little buggers anymore, and even Maddox found himself speaking as if they were not there..

"Why do we always have to come to your tower for brunch?" asked Maddox. "Mine has the aquarium behind it. It's far superior."

"Because nature, actual nature, surrounds mine," replied Owen. His white hair stayed in place, despite the breeze. "Look, real trees, not fish in a tank," he said as he took a spoonful of his lobster bisque.

"You're delusional to think this is any more natural," Maddox mumbled.

"I'm just glad the smoke isn't so bad that we couldn't sit outside," offered Lara.

Maddox had to admit she was beautiful. Thanks to her latest surgery, she was flawless. His father went to great lengths to make her happy, even though she rarely showed him affection, at least not openly. This seemed to provoke him even more, as if he needed to prove that he could make anyone love him, even a beautiful woman like her.

"The winds are to the north. As long as they stay that way, we can enjoy the clean air off the ocean while the inlanders to the east deal with the smoke," said Owen. "Another example of my great decision-making skills, choosing this spot for our facility."

Maddox coughed. "This is another example of something you did that angers the locals, Father."

"Oh, so what? Give 'em a spot to protest, and they'll wear themselves out like a kid throwing a tantrum."

Every time he even looked at his father lately, he just wanted to strangle him for his idiocy. And trying to reason with him about anything was infuriating. "Then why the fuck would you use flash bangs to disperse the protesters?" asked Maddox. "Especially now. I mean the fire danger—"

"Because I wanted 'em gone—" he spoke through a mouthful of

Eggs Benedict, "–and the fire cleared the little piss ants out, didn't it?"

"We could have tried other things."

"Too slow."

"That's where you're wrong. I've been able to successfully–"

"Most of 'em don't even have StarSee accounts," Owen interrupted. "You can't change what people think if they don't even use our platform."

"I guarantee you they surreptitiously get on StarSee. Plus, I achieved tremendous–"

Owen shook his head without even looking at Maddox, and barked, "Doesn't matter. My way worked, as usual. And if the fires get so bad that our private guys can't handle it, we'd call in the National Guard. God knows we should be able to use the military whenever we want."

"That's not how it works, Father. What is wrong with you?"

"No, what's wrong with you!? Everything I say, you argue with lately. It's like you just want to be difficult. The activists dispersed, and the news stopped covering them. End of story." Owen made a dismissive gesture with his hand.

Maddox bit his lip. His father's outbursts were transparent, but he needed to remain calm and let his algorithm do its job. "Sorry, Father."

"Are the plans for the banquet tonight in order?" asked Owen.

"Yes," said Lara. "But now that we've moved the merger party up, Lee Hoffman and his wife will only be able to attend virtually."

"That's fine," said Owen. "How about that investigator woman? Dettmer. Will she attend?"

"Yes," said Lara. "She said that provided the fires remain under control, she'd attend in person."

"I don't know why you're inviting her to the party, let alone allowing open streams." Maddox held both his hands up in exasperation. "The woman probably doesn't even own a gown, and I don't trust her to stay in her lane."

"I'm inviting her because people seeing her here implies that there's cooperation between the Social Media Division and us. It suggests they're good with the merger. Her boss, Rennick, suggested it, says it might be good for her to feel more accepted by us."

"Really," said Maddox. "You don't want her there because you're going to announce something? Maybe have someone arrested?"

Owen tilted his head and squinted at Maddox. "Where are you getting these ideas?"

"It doesn't matter where I'm getting them. I'm smart enough to figure things out."

"Yes, you're smart, son, but let me handle the media and the cops, okay? Stay focused on your task."

"My task is going perfectly. I've tweaked the algorithm even further, it's now faster and more targeted than anything we've developed before."

"Good. That'll make our client's international operations even easier."

"Yes. All they have to do is choose the target, same as before, but now instead of just finding the best person in the target's inner circle and manipulating them into wanting the target dead, it can also rapidly manipulate groups. I'm mixing both my methods."

Owen leaned back in his chair and crossed his arms. "But, you don't have control over the new algorithm, do you?"

"I have control. I've been doing a bunch of new testing, is all. Gathering data." His father didn't need to know that his algorithm had spread farther and with more intensity than he had intended.

"The side effects are still happening, aren't they? It's been years, Maddox. How come we can't get it under control?"

"As you said, let me handle my part."

"Four more people just killed each other up in the Bay area," said Lara, as if it were news. "Was that us?"

"It's fine!" said Maddox. "I'm already manipulating the message that they're just copycats."

"It's not fine," said Owen. "Iranians, in Iran, are attacking American companies. It's escalating too quickly. That's a disaster."

"Those two things aren't connected yet, Goddammit. Keep your subject matter straight. They're different algorithms. Besides, as long as the generals are ready–"

"But they're not," said Owen. "That's just it. This level of animosity isn't supposed to be happening for another three weeks. And we haven't given them the keys to the product yet."

"Which is because you and Gabe won't make the contract changes I requested."

"That's not my point."

Maddox set his mimosa down a little too hard, causing the silverware to rattle against the plates. "Then what is your point, Father? Because I feel like you're working against me."

Lara pushed back from the table slightly and crossed her arms.

Owen leaned in toward Maddox and pointed his finger. "Now listen to me. I don't know what the fuck has gotten into you, but take it down a notch. I'll have Gabe shuffle the international development teams into my advertising outreach division if you don't start showing me the respect I'm owed."

Maddox flinched. His father still had control. For the time being.

The table went quiet as the server in the white apron removed dirty plates and poured more mimosa into each of their glasses.

Owen continued, "The thing with Roman Glass' twin sister was you, too, wasn't it? For Chrissake, Maddox, His twin sister!?"

"I just told you, it was the perfect opportunity to test the new code. That's how I whipped them up so quickly. You should be fucking thanking me! But no, you don't like that, do you? Roxy Glass is out of the picture."

Owen's brow furrowed, and he glared at Maddox. "What the hell is that supposed to mean?"

Maddox looked down at the white linen tablecloth fluttering in the mountain breeze and took a deep breath. Only about eleven hours to midnight. He smiled and lifted his head. "Look, it got Roman caught. Now he'll be sedated, the deadline will pass, they'll convict him of Starla's murder, and the whole thing will be done. By the time he re-emerges, if he even inspects his original scans, it'll be ancient history. Her murder is already falling off the news cycle, and it's been less than a week."

"You better hope nobody looks too closely at his scans while he's away."

"They can't. The scans are locked to him. You really don't get technology, do you?"

"I think it was a stupid choice, just because you have personal issues," said Owen.

"Why do you think we're here!? Everyone at this table has personal issues of one kind or another!"

"I still hate doing this to him," said Lara.

"You don't get a vote," said Maddox sharply. "You already played all your cards."

The table went silent except for the rustle of trees and the hiss of Owen's muted streamBugs.

"You better hope this thing goes the way you said," said Owen.

"It will. Having someone on the inside has been helpful, but it's hard when the cops aren't exposed to StarSee that much. We need to change that."

"I'm working on it," said Owen. "Once the streamBugs are in, the rest of dominoes will fall. But I don't trust your guy at all. What do you actually know about him?"

"You like your guy, Rennick, but you question mine?"

"Rennick is a bureaucrat, nothing more. If there's one person you can trust to act in their own self interest, it's a bureaucrat."

"Well, my guy is about to connect me directly to Glass, without anyone knowing."

"Oh, for Chrissake, Maddox, don't do that thing where you torture your victims. It's not becoming."

"I disagree. I'm showing them respect by informing them why they are about to suffer. If I were about to make something happen to you, wouldn't you like to know?" He stared at his father, who showed no sign of comprehension.

"If you were about to do something to me, I would know it long before the idea even crossed your mind."

"You're pretty confident of that?"

Owen, finally pushed too far, stood up and put his knuckles on the table. "Maddox, do your fucking job! We have a big night, and you play an important role. Stop acting like a petulant child and get on with the show!"

Maddox recoiled. His father rarely raised his voice. He scolded himself for letting his emotions run rampant and took a beat. "Fine, You're right. Tonight should be something special." He lifted his mimosa in a cheers motion and gulped the rest of it down. Then he got up and marched inside to make a call he had been looking forward to for a very long time.

Sunday, 1:52 p.m.

Roman looked up as the restraining bar turned green and Travis entered the cell. "You have a call." Travis handed Roman a pair of industrial iBrowse. "Put 'em on."

The Defenderbot beeped. "Recommend against unmonitored conversations."

"Override," said Roman as he pushed up the bar and slipped the iBrowse over the back of his head. The two dots near his eyes lit up. "Incoming Call" floated in front of his vision. Travis tapped the touchpad.

The screen went black, but a voice appeared in Roman's ears. "Roman Glass," it said.

"Who is this?" asked Roman.

Travis exited the cell, but stood facing outward in front of the door.

"I'm the person who holds the keys."

"I'm not in the mood for games."

"Come now. We both know you have nothing else to do."

Roman recognized the voice. "What do you want, Maddox?"

"I want you to know that you lost. And that it was me, not my father, that did this."

"Done. Now fuck off."

"Roman Glass Junior, don't be rude. Don't you want to know what I want?"

"No, Maddox. I don't care. You killed my sister, and you framed me for murder. I know exactly what's going to happen, and it sucks. You win. I get it."

"Not just your sister."

Roman couldn't see him, but he imagined Maddox sitting by his aquarium tanks, watching Roman and smiling a sick smile. "What does that mean?"

"Well, didn't you ever wonder who was powerful enough to convince an officer of the law to go into the cell with your father and overdose him with a sedative?"

A chill ran through Roman, and his eyes went wide. "What the hell?"

The connection went quiet. Roman could only hear soft breathing on the other end.

"What's your fucking problem, dude?"

"Fathers. Am I right?" asked Maddox.

Roman looked around the cell. Travis still stood with his back to the door.

"So, you really are going to kill me?"

"Me? no." Maddox chuckled. "I just need you to go away for a while. And I need you to delete all the scans of Starla that you own. If you don't, it'll be extraordinarily easy for me to manipulate some inmates to take care of you."

"You're doing this because of some old scans?"

"Not really. That's just a bonus. Really, I want you to know that it's me that is finally making you pay for the sins of your father."

"What?"

"Haven't you ever heard that phrase before? I thought you were smart."

"What is wrong with you? My father was a good man, a good scientist."

"Your father published lies and wrecked Victor Raleigh's political career! It was my one and only loss. Ever. It's a blemish on my history that will never go away. I built an entire social media platform that loves me, and I can't get rid of that one piece of history!"

"At least you got to build it with your father. I didn't have that option."

"History will barely remember my father. Despite you and your sister's efforts to side with him, I defeated you all."

"My sister? She didn't even know who your father was, man!"

"Your sister was working with him to implicate me and free you. We both know it! And you both should have known better than to mess with someone who has literally designed software that can manipulate social media users into killing. None of you can stand in the way of my progress anymore."

Roman wished he could see him. "You need help, asshole."

"Oh, I have help. The help of anyone I choose to influence. I'm the only influencer anyone needs to pay attention to." He laughed.

Roman stood up, infuriated. "You destroyed my family because you don't like to lose!? Because you need to feel more powerful than your father!? I'll tell the world what you did! I'll fucking destroy you, you deranged piece of shit!"

Maddox chuckled. "You are about to be sedated and then go to HardJail. I told you. You're done. I win."

"You're out of your mind!" Roman grabbed his iBrowse, yanked them off his head, and threw them against the wall, smashing them into pieces.

The Defenderbot beeped a loud alarm.

Travis spun around. "Sit down and put your hands on the bar!"

Sunday, 2:15 p.m.

Roman's entire body shook with fear as he lay flat on his back on the bench. Travis had him drink a pre-sedation relaxant, but that wasn't helping. The process itself was not supposed to be painful, but he was deathly afraid. It was still the same drug that an assassin used to kill his father, and the man behind it had just called to taunt him about it as if he were a bug on a pin.

The Medbot's small display screen, with the clinical female voice, spoke through the speaker from outside the clear plexiglass walls. "Roman Glass Junior, you are directed to allow entry of this Medbot to administer your sedation. There is nothing to fear. Any attempt to prevent entry, or to disable this Medbot, will be considered an additional crime, incurring additional fees and possible additional sentence time. You have three minutes to comply."

He positioned his body to match the outline on the bench and adjusted himself until it turned green.

The thick transparent door to his cell slid open, and the Medbot rolled in. The Medbot and his Defenderbot touched and exchanged physical confirmation. The Defenderbot announced it was recording the procedure. Travis entered and stood behind the Medbot, watching with the interest of a child during a history lesson. "Put your left hand on the bar," he said casually.

Roman did as he instructed. Travis handcuffed him to the restraining bar.

"I'll be with you the whole time. Don't fight it."

Roman looked at Travis, who winked at him. It suddenly struck Roman that it was Travis all along. "I know why you're here. You won't get away with it. Please don't."

"I'm sorry, it's the only way, kid."

A black spec caught Roman's attention out of the corner of his eye. A streamBug. Someone had managed to sneak a Goddamned streamBug in just to watch this happen. Probably Maddox. He gripped the sides of the bench. The Medbot put the cuff around his arm, and began to apply the sedation patch. The streamBug buzzed close to Roman's eye, and he instinctively swatted at it with his free hand. "Jesus Christ."

"Just relax," said Travis.

The little speck hung in the air in front of his face. This was extraordinary. They were never to come within six feet of physical contact. He looked at it closely to make sure it wasn't an actual living gnat. It looked smaller than a streamBug, like a speck of ash. It hovered, motionless, as if waiting for something.

A sense of panic rolled through his body as he felt the cuff go around his arm. He closed his eyes.

"Take deep breaths. It'll all be over soon."

He felt the tickle of a hair on his nose. He shook his head to get rid of it. It was the streamBug.

His eyes were wide. He stared at the ceiling and the frosted window above, wishing for someone to come into his cell and set him free. Where was Seven? Dettmer said they had a plan. He saw the speck again. He opened his mouth and gulped for air.

The microdrone flew straight into his mouth. Though it was tiny, it caused an immediate coughing fit. He saw Travis move towards him, but the fit only lasted a couple of seconds. Whatever was in the pre-sedation drink must be working.

The patch was being administered. It was not just a sticky patch, there were hundreds of small pins in it that acted as tiny fish hooks into the skin so that it could not be removed. The dosage was controlled by an invisible interface on the patch that only the Medbot could see. He could feel the effect already. He opened his eyes wider, trying to fight it.

"This is it. Nighty night," said Travis.

He felt cold. His vision was going dark. A sharp pain shot through his spine. He should be feeling good, relaxed. Instead, he felt like his joints were locking up. A spasm of pain gripped his chest. He couldn't move. This was not supposed to happen. He was paralyzed and blacking out. He wasn't shaking anymore. Staring up at the ceiling, he realized he wasn't breathing anymore. Travis leaned into his vision and smiled. His last thought before everything went dark was that they had succeeded. He was dying. *This is what my father felt like.* Everything went black. He was still conscious when he felt his heart beat its last beat.

Sunday, 3:07 p.m.

Someone was shouting. "Go under this bridge! Why aren't the disruptors working!?"

He tried to move. He was handcuffed to someone. Travis. He was in an ambulance. Sirens were blaring. He felt his body rolling around, but had no control.

"We can't get on the freeway at this time of day. He won't make it!" The driver was yelling, a man.

"Shit," yelled Travis. "This is not good!"

Roman tried to breathe. It hurt too much. He blacked out again.

Sunday, 3:14 p.m.

He emerged from the blackness. He felt his body lunge forward with a tremendous crash. They had hit something. He struggled to force his eyes open. There was glass and smoke.

"Keep him dead!" someone shouted.

Travis was looking down at him from above, upside down. "Not yet, kid, not yet."

Strapped to a gurney, he was pushed out of the back of the ambulance van and was bouncing along in the Los Angeles sunlight as he was wheeled across a street. Every rock and crack in the street hurt. Roman tried to speak and everything went dark again.

Sunday, 3:37 p.m.

Someone was knocking the hell out of him, punching him in the chest, hard. He was suffocating. Paralyzed. He was dreaming. Seven was there. Another kick in the chest from a mule. Seven was kissing him. No, not kissing him, blowing air into his mouth. He tried to inhale. It hurt. All of his nerves flashed at the same moment in a spasm of incredible pain. Coughing, he instantly sat bolt upright. He had a chest full of broken glass and nails. Seven's hand was on his back as he sat on the side of a gurney and regained control of his spasming body.

"What ... the ... fuck?" he managed to squeeze out between gasps and coughs.

"Oh, thank god," said Seven. "You were dead." Her hair was covered with a light green bouffant cap.

He realized she was serious. He flexed his hands and shook. "Jeezus. Everything hurts."

"You'll start to feel better soon, a lot better. In fact, you'll probably start to feel great."

He looked around. He was in what looked like a makeshift operating room. His mental mapping flashed. Plastic sheets hung around an area nineteen by twenty-two feet. Four flood lights stood eight feet high in each corner of the area, pointing at the center, each at a slightly different angle. White tables covered with medical instruments lined the perimeter. He was on a gurney, the open handcuff hung from the left side. Seven wore green nurse's scrubs. He could see from the light glowing through the plastic sheeting that he was in a much larger space with high windows. A small robotic device was pulling the last of the microstaples out of his sedation patch, removing it from his shoulder like an anti-theft tag at a department store. "Where are we?"

"My place," Seven said, rubbing his back.

"I've never been here."

"That's because you never turn off your streamBugs, so all your watchers would know where I live. I couldn't have that. I brought you here now because there are no bugs on the dead."

The memory of his sedation crept back in. "Did one fly into my mouth?"

"Yeah. It was the only way to get you out of custody. I had to deliver a drug which would act quickly and cause you to have a severe allergic reaction to the sedation."

"Wait, so you knew I was petrified of dying during sedation, so you made me have an allergic reaction and die during sedation?!"

"Sorry, bud, had to do it." She slapped him on the back.

"Jeez. Well, I'm glad it went to plan, I guess."

"It didn't, exactly."

"Why? What happened?"

"You went into cardiac arrest in the MobiJail, as planned, and were quickly transferred into an ambulance to take you to UCLA Hospital."

Roman remembered. "Wait, what about the detective? Travis? I saw him. He tried to kill me."

"He did kill you. He's on our team."

"That's not a sentence that goes together," said Roman.

"We couldn't have done it without him. He had to stay with you once the ambulance showed up."

"And the ambulance was you?"

"Yes, but we couldn't pull off stealing you from the MobiJail. Too many streamBugs watching at that point. So as the ambulance pulled up to the hospital, it got into an accident."

"I can drive real bad, real good." Pete stepped through the plastic sheeting, beaming.

"Dude, I thought you'd be in jail."

"They couldn't prove anything, and I refused the MRIT, as is my right."

Seven continued, "In the confusion of the accident, I ran up, dressed like this, and not only injected you immediately with hyperoxygenation nano cells to make sure you didn't suffer too much damage from being dead, but I also told the paramedics that since you were pronounced dead already, the hospital administration had decided that you should just go straight to the morgue, because you were uninsured.

"So Travis released your body, and myself and my hired mortician, wheeled you out of the back of the ambulance and directly into the back of the hearse. Which brought you here, about five minutes ago, where I revived you."

Tek parted the plastic and walked into the brightly-lit area dressed in a black suit. "Thousand Oaks funeral home, at your service." He had on a little extra dark makeup under his eyes.

"Tek!" Roman grabbed his shoulder. "Thank you. This is amazing. I'm starting to feel so..."

"Alive?" said Seven.

"Yeah, um, seriously, I'm feeling better by the minute. Like, superb."

"That's the cocktail you got. There's a whole host of things happening in your body right now, from adrenaline to cell reconstruction."

Roman stood up. "I highly recommend it," he said, blinking and shaking his head. "Without the dying part. That sucked."

CHAPTER
THIRTY-FIVE

Sunday, 3:58 p.m.

They emerged from the "lab" where Roman had been revived into a beautiful open space. *Studio 7*, as Seven called it, may have been a studio sound stage at some point, but it was far from being a normal stage now. The large space was completely converted into a luxury residence with second floor lofts jutting out along the perimeter of the open forty-foot high space. Light poured in from giant windows at either end of the building, illuminating the kitchen and living area.

Seven, Tek, Pete and Roman sat at an eight-foot long wooden island that defined the open, airy kitchen. Muffled sounds of movement occasionally emanated from somewhere in the open space, but no one was visible. The massive kitchen island had plates of cookies, fruits and snacks set out, and everyone had drinks or coffee.

Large rooms with varying themes lined the perimeter of the upper loft level: beachside, jungle, engine room, moon, etc. Each room looked like a combination of actual set pieces and quantum dot walls. Roman wanted to learn more about it and why they were using this technology, especially since anything could be completely simulated these days. Unable to contain his interest, he asked, "What do you use all this for?"

Seven sipped her iced tea and smiled. "Sorry, I can't divulge that. Let's just say, I have a contract with a certain mega-billionaire to do research and development on some pretty cool stuff. All strict non disclosure. I can't even tell my closest friends about it." She glanced at Roman. "You'll all find out about it someday."

He knew better than to press her on it. One of the unspoken agreements between them was that she would continue to work with Roman, as long as he didn't ask too many questions about her main hustle.

"Again, thanks for springing me, people. I owe you."

"Anytime you need to be killed, you can count on us," said Pete with a chuckle.

"We risked a lot today. What's our next move?" asked Tek.

"Roman," said Seven. "Dettmer told me it's critical to get you to the StarSee Gray Room tonight before the deadline passes."

"Yeah, to access Starla's files using the code I have because of my sister's death."

"She didn't say why, but said she would explain when we talk later. I think it's time we started figuring out how to make it happen. What else do you know, Roman?"

"I know Maddox had Roxy killed and then called me to gloat. Turns out the fucker was responsible for our dad's death too."

The room went silent.

"Holy shit," said Tek. "He called you?"

"Yeah, like some OG villain. He's losing it, almost like he thinks he's the star of his own show." Roman clenched his teeth, somewhere between fury and fighting back tears. Between the death of Roxy and the realization that one of the world's richest men was responsible, everyone looked to be in shock.

"I don't care how powerful they are, let's take 'em down," said Seven quietly. "Roman, what did Dettmer tell you? Anything?"

"We now believe Agreement 413 is just a simple protection put in place by the ICE company."

"How would that play into all this?" asked Pete.

"That's why the recordings were locked. Dettmer thinks it was a safeguard that kept the Blakewells from actually deleting the files. She couldn't find out who hired me to do the second scans of Starla because Maddox deleted those records, but when he tried to delete the recordings, they automatically locked. Her other lead was that Starla's body had burst fat cells, but I don't understand that part."

"She told me the same thing," said Seven. "We looked into it. If it was plastic surgery, there would be localized crystals, like in her belly or thighs, but Dettmer said there were ice crystals and burst fat cells spread throughout her entire body, meaning the coroner was wrong. Her body had been on ICE."

"But that's not possible," said Tek. "She wasn't put on ICE until Tuesday. The autopsy was an expedited autopsy on Monday night."

"How could that be?" asked Pete.

Roman stared at the patterns on the wooden table. He felt great. In a flash, his mental mapping kicked in and gave him the miniature dimensions of the spaces between the rings in the wood. The table wasn't quite flat; it was tilted to the left at .7 degrees, but with undulations like a landscape. Two striations in the wood formed what looked like a river going down a hill. His mind snapped back to the present. After a moment, he looked up. "She was killed before that night and put on ICE."

"Huh?" said Seven.

Allowing his mind to drift had freed him up to put things together. "They brought her dead body into the room using her celebrity elevator while I was unconscious! Then they framed me for the murder, did the autopsy, and put her body back on ICE, where it had been all along."

"So… she wasn't even killed that night?" said Tek.

"Exactly. Whoever the actress was that I was talking to, she was a Starla stand-in, and she walked out of that room alive. Actually, she took the elevator out of that room. They hired someone to play Starla, and then they pulled a Texas switch."

"They were covering up a murder that had already happened," said Seven. "Wow."

"But when was the real Starla actually killed?" asked Pete.

"I'd bet that her actual murder was about two-and-a-half years ago," said Roman. "That's when she started acting differently according to her family, and when she stopped making the scripted drama streams and instead went to pure StarSee reality shows."

Pete blanched, "That's kind of sick. Like they had her on ICE and just chipped off little pieces when they needed her DNA?" He shivered. "Two years is a long time."

"How long ago was your first scan of her, Roman?" asked Seven.

"Almost three years ago now." Roman scratched his head. "Ah! That's what Maddox meant. I scanned the real Starla, before they replaced her with a different actress. And I'm the only one who has access to those scans, which, if revealed publicly, could be used to prove that the new Starla wasn't the real Starla."

"How would simple body scans do that?"

"Because I scan down to the iris, and if anyone compares the old iris scans to any recent scans, it'll show they're two different Starlas. Iris scans are like fingerprints, and the real Starla Devine had heterochromatic blue-green eyes. No plastic surgery can change your iris. The new Starla always wore iRiz, so nobody could tell, but the scans would be proof."

Tek glanced back and forth between Seven and Roman. "You're suggesting that the Blakewells killed their prime StarStream, the big number one that's connected to every other stream on the plat-form, literally their moneymaker and the symbol of their platform … and then kept her body on ICE for two years? That is so farfetched. Why on Earth would they do that?"

Roman blinked. It was an excellent question. One he had no answer for. "I don't know why. I just have to provide proof that they did it. It's the only way I get clear of this, and make them pay for what they've done to my family."

"There's only one way to prove it," said Seven.

"Gain access to the StarSee main servers. Where I can pull up my personal files and also get into Starla's recordings again."

"That's why Dettmer wants you at the party tonight. The one and only place you can get top level access into their system is the StarSee Gray Room. You have to go into the core of the entire system."

"Yup, I need to access my scans and her stream right there for everyone to see. But I think there's more to it than just me proving my innocence. She was pretty adamant that there's something much larger at play here."

"Can we call her right now?" asked Tek.

"She said she wouldn't be available again until after six tonight," said Seven.

"That's cutting it pretty close," said Roman. "If I'm going to get back inside, we need to get started right away."

"Wow, back into the lion's den," said Tek.

"Yup. I'm going to crash their party in a very big, very real life way. And this time, I want all the streamBugs watching."

THIRTY-SIX

Sunday, 4:47 p.m.

"The body is gone!? How the hell can his body be gone?" Chief Rennick sat at his desk, fuming. Dettmer stood by his office door, taking a scolding. Mo stood slightly behind her.

"It may be at the morgue, sir, mixed in with the unclaimed bodies going in for cremation. The John Does," said Dettmer.

StreamBugs swarmed at the ceiling. Rennick had officially allowed them in, much to Dettmer's dismay. "There are no damned John Does in death! Everybody gets identified with DNA. I want proof that we know where that sneaky bastard went. You don't think it's weird that he died the same way his father did?"

"You said it was Homicide's case," she said. "Blame them."

He looked up from his desk, and his eyes flashed between the two of them. He had insisted they leave the door open so the entire weekend staff could eavesdrop. "We're already the laughingstock of the force. There's a new Memefactory meme of us chasing Homicide down the street, who is chasing bodies as they roll out the back of hearses. It's embarrassing."

"He was not in our custody, sir," said Dettmer.

"They don't care!" He gestured to the streamBugs. "The Blakewell's don't care! They're posting to their philanthropy Star-Stream that they would pull their donations if we weren't such good entertainment!"

Dettmer's lips tightened. "Sir, if I may, can you see how wrong this is? They should not have any influence over us at all, ever. There should not be streamBugs in here, and our jobs should be protected from the Blakewells, not threatened by them." As she spoke, she imagined the Blakewells watching through the hovering streamBugs.

"Our jobs are partly funded because the platforms want to make sure that their subscribers are protected. They donate to us to protect their users, not to go after the companies themselves and then lose the body of the murderer of their top star!"

"The platforms should not be exempt—" she insisted.

"For crying out loud, Dettmer, don't bite the hand that feeds you."

"Do they pay you directly in cash or in Admiration Points, sir?" she shot back.

She realized a moment too late that she had crossed the line. Rennick's lower jaw jutted out, and his eyes became piercing slits.

Mo cleared his throat to break the silence. "Again, he wasn't in our control, sir. This is one-hundred percent on Homicide. Travis, specifically."

Rennick turned his attention to Mo. "I know you mean well, but you're off the case." He looked confused by his own words for a moment. "What am I saying? Once we find the body, the case is closed for all of us. He's dead. Mo, go back to your desk and scrub the morgue for that body. Dettmer, you stay here."

"Yes, sir." Mo turned and left the room, shooting a sympathetic glance at Dettmer on the way out.

"Dettmer, you're on administrative leave."

Her eyes went wide. "What? Why?"

"I know you tried to make a deal with him at the amusement park. I know you faked a private interview to talk to him on the MobiJail bus. Did you really think I wouldn't find out? There are repercussions for this kind of behavior. This whole thing has put you off your game."

"Sir, it has me *on* my game. I know what is going on. The Blakewells are literally getting away—"

He stood up and held up his hand. "Stop. You're a smart person, but you don't seem to grasp what's important."

"My job is important. Stopping criminals is important. Saving people is important."

"Not pissing off the most powerful people in Los Angeles is important."

"People are killing each other. It is getting worse."

"I can't, Dettmer. You are on leave, and I suggest you build up your online presence in your free time. We are the Social Media Division. If social media can't see the good we do, then we might as well not be doing it. I think your history is clouding your judgment."

"Sir, I am clear about who is to blame for Carmen's death. Companies like StarSee need to—"

He interrupted, "If you want your leave to be short, then I want you to go to that party tonight and put on a good show. Smile, nod, maybe even apologize to the Blakewells. And from now on, it's streamBugs on at all times. Got it?"

"Sir, how can I do my job if people are always watching?"

"By not doing things you need to hide!" He held up his hand. "After the merger is over, and we find Glass' body, we'll see where we're at. Mo will close out our end of the Devine case, and things'll get back to normal." He sat back down and turned his attention to something on his display. "If you go to the party tonight and make nice with the Blakewells, I'm sure you'll see they are decent people. Dismissed." He began typing on keys that only he could see.

Dettmer turned slowly and left his office. The conversation was over. She would have no authority at the banquet tonight. The streamBugs added a new ambient hiss to the atmosphere. She shot them a middle finger as she walked back to her desk.

Sunday, 5:14 p.m.

Dettmer walked across the rooftop and found Mo in his usual spot, looking out over the city, his eyes fixed on smoke plumes in the distance. The air quality was poor this afternoon. He spoke as if he knew she would be joining him. "It's funny, when the air was cleaner, people used to come up here to smoke, and now that it's garbage, we come up here for air."

She sidled up to him and looked toward the hills. She gestured to one of the four smoke plumes, a fat one near the StarSee sign. "Is that one back?"

"Hotspot flare-ups. Once a fire starts these days, it never goes completely out." He looked over his shoulder at her. "You okay?"

"He put me on leave."

"Shit. Sorry to hear that, cher. Seems a bit much, it's not like you had anything to do with Glass' body getting lost. It was in Homicide's custody."

"He also says I should go to the party tonight and publicly apologize to the Blakewells." The sun, obscured by the smoke, was a hot orange-gray disc in the distance. "I was hoping he would say to go tonight. In fact, I was planning on it, but I really needed the weight of the department behind me, no matter how trivial it seems."

Mo nodded. "Might be best just to let this fight go. It's not winning you any points with anyone."

She took a deep breath to try to relax and clear her mind, and immediately started coughing. Mo patted her on the back as she bent over. She shook her head and cleared her throat. Standing up straight, she took a slower deep breath and let it out through pursed lips like she was gently blowing out a child's birthday candle. She wiped her eyes and looked over the ledge at downtown Los Angeles, a bustling metropolis of ants avoiding eye contact in real life while simultaneously trying to connect with each other on their StarStreams.

She focused on the Hollywood sign in the far distance, bathed in smoke, an enduring symbol of entertainment and opportunity, mixed with a good deal of artifice. Next to it, only a mile away, the StarSee towers with the StarSee sign behind them, even more obscured, a new symbol of power in the age of social media, with an even higher quotient of artifice.

"Screw them," she said to herself.

Mo looked at her. "You're not gonna drop this, are ya?"

"I have to do it for Carmen. If they get away with this, they will become too powerful to stop." She turned and looked at Mo directly. "And more innocent people will get hurt. Roman doesn't deserve this."

Mo's left eyebrow raised. "What do you mean by that? Glass is dead."

Her eyes remained fixed on Mo's. She couldn't reveal what she knew, not to Mo, nor to the gathering streamBugs that she could no longer turn off. "I am just saying, this is bigger than my job, or my popularity on StarSee. Much bigger."

"Before, you said this wasn't about Carmen. Now, you say it is."

"Companies need to be held accountable if the road they build leads cars off a cliff. I see now that what happened to Carmen was just a sign of things to come. She went too far because of her own insecurities, but now Maddox Blakewell is intentionally manufacturing insecure people for his own gain. He is creating groups of Carmens who arc willing to die if that is what their StarStream tells them to do. We have to stop them."

He shook his head. "I can't do it. I have a family, cher. Sorry."

StreamBugs swirled overhead as they spoke. She looked up at

them. "You see? No private conversations anymore. We are all on stream all the time. And people are killing each other because of the Blakewells and their algorithms. I am so close to stopping it." She put her hand on his arm. "I understand your reluctance, but this is something I have to do. I can not leave certain people hanging after I already promised them I had a plan."

"What exactly are you planning, anyway?" he asked.

She rolled her eyes up toward the streamBugs. "It might be better if you did not know."

CHAPTER
THIRTY-SEVEN

Sunday, 6:40 p.m.

Roman, Seven, Tek and Pete sat around the kitchen island talking to the image of Dettmer on one end, and viewing a volumetric display of the StarSee facility on the other. Dettmer stuck out of the top of the surface from the bust up, facing the display screen while the four others sat along the sides. Her dark hair was down for a change, and fell over the shoulders of her black gown and sparkling necklace.

She informed the group that she could not turn off her stream-Bugs. Her iBrowse glowed at her temples. She had them on mute, but because AI can read lips, she had to be careful. She held her hand over her mouth when she spoke.

Roman caught her up on the existing theories and on Maddox's call. She agreed everything pointed to Starla having been previously murdered, and her body dumped in the room to frame Roman, but there were still big questions about exactly who killed her and why. He explained that Maddox had stated that part of the reason Roman was being framed was because his original scans of Starla could be proof that Starla was being played by a double. That, and Maddox blamed his father for the one and only black mark on his career.

"Oh, and did you know Travis killed me, but he's on our team?" asked Roman.

"Yes," said Dettmer. "I have yet to be fully debriefed on that situation, but right now we have to plan."

The real-time streams on the display were a hyper-real volumetric window into the three towers of stacked giant coins jutting out from the mountainside, smothered in billowing smoke like a ship emerging from a fog bank.

"I'll bet they wish they weren't using their own private firefighting service now," said Tek. "They're overwhelmed."

"They're shutting down all the access roads," said Seven. She spun the view around to display the back of the building, looking down over Maddox's giant aquarium storage tanks toward the city. "Even the escalators to the main facility are too dangerous. And we sure can't fly you in without being noticed."

Roman leaned forward, hoping he could see something through the dark tinted windows of the towers. "Shouldn't they cancel the event?"

"This is the Blakewell's shining moment," said Dettmer. She kept her hand up and her chin down like she was telling her necklace a secret.

"I don't know how I can get in," said Roman.

"You have to figure something out." Dettmer's image flickered for a moment. Tek had her connection running through Ultraviolet so that even though she was being watched by streamBugs, the conversation was invisible to StarSee's prying eyes. "Someone needs to file the objection before midnight, which is less than six hours away. Let me explain..."

The group turned their attention away from the display and looked at the virtual bust of Dettmer.

She spoke in a hushed whisper. "The minute this merger is official, two critical things will happen. First, all StarSee data and code will become a legally protected news source. This has been attempted before, but I believe this time the StarSee lawyers will be successful. Second, a data transfer will begin, which will allow the algorithms Maddox has created to move into the existing NewsCann network. So the world's largest supplier of news will be infected by the same algorithms as Star-See. We must stop it. I need you there, Roman. If you can broadcast your evidence that you were framed by the Blakewells, it will surely prompt some of their board members to file an immediate objection."

"Why can't you file an objection yourself?" asked Pete.

"My boss put me on leave, so I have no authority. I am actually being sent to the party to, what is the saying, fall on my knife?"

"Sword," said Seven.

"Wow. So if he stripped you of authority, there will be no police protection there," said Tek. "I'm not convinced that this'll work."

"Yes, we are on our own, and it has to work. Which brings me to my other reason for needing you there, Roman. I have a killcode for the algorithm." She now had both hands around her mouth like she was quietly praying. "I hope I can use it as leverage to stop the deal, and will not have to implement it."

Looks of quiet astonishment went around the table.

"Where did you get that?" asked Tek.

"I had it made very quickly last night."

"It can't be very targeted then, can it?"

"Not very. It could cause considerable damage to the rest of the system."

"What will this killcode do?" asked Pete.

"It's like an antibody. It'll park itself in the system and delete and destroy any instances of the code that it finds. But, if I'm correct, it needs to start where the algorithm started," said Tek.

"I don't understand," said Pete.

"What StarStream is every subscriber connected to?" asked Dettmer.

It took the group only a second to figure it out. "Starla Devine," they said almost in unison.

"Correct," said Dettmer.

"That's how Maddox can infect any subscriber on StarSee. It's a pathway into every single subscriber's stream," said Tek.

"But Starla's stream was locked automatically after her fake murder," said Seven.

"Only viewing it was locked. You can't watch her life anymore, but in StarSee's core, you're still connected to her."

"I think I can figure out where this is going," said Roman.

"Yes." Dettmer's hands almost smothered her words. "You have the Devine family's passcode, so you can access her root directories. You have to insert the killcode by dragging the file onto Starla's core stream through a direct connection."

"And that might inadvertently destroy the platform billions of people love?" said Pete.

"Lots of people would be fine with that," said Tek.

"Lots more will not be," said Dettmer.

"Gang, I'm all for stopping the merger, but before that, I have to prove to the world that I'm innocent, right? I have to show the un-doctored recording of the night they framed me. How do I do that?"

"The recording is still protected by the ICE agreement," said Dettmer. "It gets a little complicated because of two factor identification, but you will have to request an access code, which will be sent to Starla's brother, Paul. He will be watching for it, and then your team will get it to you right away. You will log into the ICE site, which you can do because of Roxy, by providing your own DNA and then submit the access code. It sounds convoluted but is actually not very difficult. Once you enter the code to unlock the files, it should be a simple matter of playing back the recording."

"Why exactly are the files locked again?" asked Pete.

"Paul verified with the ICE company that if anyone tries to delete what are deemed potentially necessary files to the resuscitation of an ICE client, those files get automatically locked."

"So someone tried to delete the real recording of that night?" asked Pete.

"Yep. But the ICE agreement stopped them," said Tek.

"I also have to release my original iris scans of Starla. To prove they had an impostor playing Starla."

"That should be easy enough," said Tek. "The date stamped scans you originally took of the real Starla Devine are in your user directory files. You just need to log into your own account and post a link to the scans to your StarSee library, and make them public." He pointed at Roman. "I can't stress this enough. You have to make them public."

"Won't they be locked?" asked Pete.

"Oh, shit," said Seven. "That's right. You just died."

"No," said Tek. "They lock the StarSee stream after a crime, but he will still have access to his personal cloud file folders."

"Okay," said Roman. "So hopefully I can make them public, then what?"

"I'll post a link to Reddit telling users to compare them to new Starla Devine scans from the past year. It'll blow up, believe me."

"And then, if necessary, insert the killcode," added Dettmer.

"Wow, that's a lot to ask." Seven was shaking her head as she spoke. "Like you're just going to be able to walk into their Data Center while a live banquet is happening, log on, make your Starla scan public, then log into Starla's account, insert a killcode, and walk out while everyone and their streamBugs watches?"

"After I play back the real recording from the night of the murder," said Roman.

"Right. After you play back the recording without getting tackled by security."

The room fell quiet.

"This is crazy," muttered Pete. "Can't we just blow them up or something?"

"Ooh, we do have four C-20 micro-charges!" said Seven.

"Jeezus, that would do the trick," said Roman.

"If you blew up the machine room itself, it might slow things down, possibly for days," said Tek.

"No, no, no." Dettmer kept her right hand in front of her mouth, but held up her left hand. It fell outside of the display cone so it looked as if she had lost her fingers. "It could easily accidentally kill people, including you and me, and it would probably cause the servers to go under immediate distributed lockdown, preventing exactly what we need to do with the killcode. Plus, you would be branded a terrorist. This is a terrible idea, and I do not want to know why you have C-20."

Pete started to explain, "Seven and I were doing a project for—"

Seven interrupted, putting her hand on Pete's arm. "She really doesn't want to know, Pete."

"Dettmer, how did you get invited, anyway?" asked Roman.

"The Blakewells love to gloat, as you found out earlier. They invited me to the party to shove it in my face. I got here just before they closed the roads, so I am in the StarSee commissary right now, along with the staff and several other guests that got here early." Her image looked up. She was looking at something in her real world. "Hold on one second." Dettmer's image froze.

"Jeez, that seems risky. Calling us from inside StarSee?" said Pete.

"She's being careful. Don't worry, they can't see or hear us," said Tek.

While they waited for Dettmer to unfreeze, everyone turned back to the display with the towers on it. As Seven spun the volume around, zooming in and out, Roman was building the picture in his head of everything about the building and the grounds. "Right there, under the tanks for the aquarium water pipes, there's another entrance."

Seven moved the display. "You're right, but how does that help?"

"That would lead to the back hallway, which leads to the kitchen. It'll be a lot easier for me to get into that entrance than to try to get past security at a main entrance."

Dettmer came back to life. "Roman. The news. They know you are not dead."

"Shit," said Roman.

Seven changed the display to NewsCann. They had already moved on to another story, another random murder in Los Angeles. That made four in the last twenty-four hours. Graphics of fire maps filled the right side of the screen, while a ticker ran across the bottom.

Seven spoke to her Digital Assistant. "Oscar, rewind three minutes." The female news anchor jittered momentarily and then spoke again. "StarStream recordings show that the body of Roman Glass Junior, accused murderer of Starla Devine, was not taken to the morgue, and his allergic reaction to the sedative, the same sedative used to murder his father, may have been planned." A picture of Roman filled the display. "LAPD has asked everyone to keep an eye on their streams for this man, and immediately report any sightings."

Roman put his hands to his head.

"Police say these people—" Images of Seven, Pete and Tek appeared next to Roman on the display, "—likely aided in the escape of the fugitive, and citizens should also be on the lookout for them, in person and on their streams."

"Mother f—" Seven stopped herself short.

"Well, that's going to make things more difficult," said Tek.

They heard a quadcopter fly overhead. Everyone looked up.

"Don't worry, this place is completely invisible to surveillance, and nobody knows where I live. We're safe," she said.

"Her building puts out a silent disruptor signal, no streamBugs can even get close," said Tek.

The NewsCann broadcast continued to run down the latest bad news of the day. Roman caught the ticker running across the bottom of the frame: '... StarSee headquarters requests help from the Los Angeles Fire Department battling encroaching wildfires...'

"Hey guys, did you see that? StarSee is requesting help from the LAFD," said Roman.

"I'm not surprised," said Seven.

"Called it," said Pete.

"But that means people they don't know will be on the grounds."

Seven slapped her hand on the table. "Yes! That's it!"

"That's what?" said Pete.

Seven continued, "I have an LAFD uniform. It's not real, but it could get you up to and inside the facility."

Roman grabbed control of the display and brought the real time view of the StarSee facility up again. "I can tell them that we've detected a hot spot on the roof or something and need to get in."

"Then find a place to pull off your fake firefighter's uniform and become one of the guests at the party!" Seven's voice got higher as she got more excited. "Very secret agent man!"

"I'll have to go up the hill on foot. There are trails that the workers have made here—" He pointed to a lighter area next to Maddox Blakewell's tower 3, "—and if I'm spotted from above, it won't seem weird that a firefighter is going up the hill." He rotated the display and moved down the side of the mountain, pointing at a faint change in color. "This trail is 342 feet longer, but the incline is only a twenty-two percent grade, it wraps up alongside the tower for eighty-seven feet—" He spun the display again, "—and then up to the back near the water tanks."

Seven spoke to the display. "Oscar, overlay fire forecast: 8 p.m. tonight, duration: three hours, time-lapse: ten minutes."

The fire prediction map was like a weather forecasting map, except that everything was shades of red and orange instead of green and blue. She pulled back from the trail to view the entire facility and surroundings. Orange and yellow fire clouds appeared upper left and spread down the side of the hill over time, to where the trail was. "According to this, you should be okay to get in that way, but getting out might be a different story."

"Is going into this building the safest thing to do right now?" said Tek.

"Safe or not, tonight's the night it has to happen," said Roman.

"The thing is, the party will have started by the time you arrive," said Dettmer, "but I need to give you the killcode simpin. Then you will need to gain access to the machine room and do your thing."

"How am I supposed to get in?"

"I will provide some kind of distraction, and while everyone looks at me, you can make your move into the machine room using Malcolm Chasper's Employee ID," said Dettmer.

"It doesn't feel safe using the same ID again. If anyone is smart enough to figure out how I got access before, it's Maddox."

Tek typed frantically on the empty surface in front of him. "Good call Roman, there is a warning flag on Malcom's ID."

"Shit. That's an important piece of the plan, I need it to get into the machine room."

"I can't remove the flag without triggering it. But what I can do is reroute where the alert is sent." He typed and glanced around his virtual world. "There, now it will set off the alarm, but the notification will be sent to a non-existent mailbox."

"I hope we've thought of everything."

"Yeah. I'm not sure about this plan, but I guess it will have to do," said Tek.

"If I leave in the next thirty minutes, I could be there around nine."

"StreamBugs will be everywhere," said Dettmer. "Keep yourself disguised."

Tek went running off toward the back of the building.

Dettmer's image flickered. "See you soon, I hope. There is a lot riding on you, Roman."

"On both of us. We're in this together," said Roman.

"You should shower first. You look awful," said Dettmer, smiling. She disappeared, leaving Roman with a momentary ghosting phenomenon.

Roman turned to Seven. "Sorry I got you guys into this."

"I will always, always, do anything in my power to help you. It's because of you that I'm where I am. And even more importantly, I care about you."

"Thanks," Roman smiled.

Tek came running up with two costumes, one draped over each arm, wearing a fire helmet, and a backpack slung over his shoulder.

"Okay, here's a tuxedo costume. It's not tailored, but nobody will kick you out for it. Put this on first." He handed the hangar of clothes to Roman. "And here's the firefighter costume. It is, ironically, highly flammable." He handed the pile over to Roman and put the plastic helmet on Roman's head. "And here—" He pulled the backpack off his shoulder and handed it to Roman, "—are the C-20 charges and remote detonator. Be at least a hundred feet away if you blow one." He unzipped the pack, opened it and showed the contents to Roman. Four simple small black bricks, each with a tiny red glowing light on it, and a small remote.

Roman reached in and pulled out the old-school remote detonator. When he squeezed the sides, it popped open, exposing the red button. He closed it and shoved it into the tuxedo pants pocket. "Shit, man, maybe we should skip the explosives. I dunno if I want to be running up the side of a burning mountain carrying a backpack full of bombs."

"They're stable," said Tek. "Just keep that cover closed until you're serious that you're going to push the button."

"Your SDV will be here in twenty-seven minutes," said Seven.

Roman pulled the reflective mask over his face. "This might fool streamBugs, but something feels pretty crazy about going up the side of a mountain that's on fire, wearing a flammable plastic costume, carrying a bag of explosives, into a party full of rich people that's being broadcast live, where I'm literally going to access their mainframe under their noses, demonstrate that Starla's murder happened long before I went to scan her that night, block the merger of two mega corporations, insert a killcode to stop a murder algorithm, and then get out."

"Well," said Seven, "when you put it that way, it doesn't seem like anything could go wrong."

Sunday, 9:23 p.m.

Making the hike up the side of the mountain through billowing smoke at night was no easy task. The small real oxygen tank and mask that Tek had integrated into the fake firefighter's costume helped. That, and the fact that Roman still had the positive after effects of the cocktail that brought him back from the precipice of death coursing through his body. The smoke stung his eyes and made him cough, but the drugs cut any coughing fits short. He felt better and sharper than ever.

He navigated the approach alone. Any connection could easily ping security, so he didn't wear any tech under the fake helmet and mask.

Firefighting drones flew overhead, and he held still for a moment. Once they passed, he resumed his climb. He had to rely solely on his geosense as he made his way through the brush. The facility's motion detectors were useless in this wind and smoke, so he was more worried about some waitstaff peering out the window. Scrabbling up the right side of the hill next to the building, around Maddox's residential tower to the back, he stayed sixty yards away from the building.

Once above the tower, he made his way under the giant water tanks for Maddox's personal aquariums. Crawling through the smoky darkness fifty-eight feet to the left side of the tanks, he looked down at the top of the center main building. He could see down into the skylights that poked up out of the hillside, but from this twenty-three degree angle, he could only see a slice of the interior of the Gray Room where the party was happening. There was activity, but he couldn't make out much. He surveyed the surroundings, committing the entire structure and hillside to his geosense.

The door to the facility was right where he expected it to be, but now that he was here, he could see that it was protected by a weapons detector. *Shit.* Roman felt the weight of the bag carrying the explosives. He would have to lose the bombs, but tossing them into the burning forest didn't seem like the wisest choice. He looked around for a good place to hide them and imagined someone looking out from the doorway and the angle at which they would see things.

He pulled himself up onto the three foot round main connecting pipe from the water tanks to the aquarium, straddled it, and shimmied his way towards a large Y-shaped diverter. He stopped, looked once again at the darkened doorway, the angle of hillside, the skylights of the Gray Room, the backs of the tanks that lined Maddox's residence, the path that people would take when leaving, the size of the pipe and the Y connection, the probable path of the fire, and a white flash went off in his head. Then, ninety-three inches from the connection, with the pipe at a downslope of fourteen degrees, he put the bag on top of the three-foot round pipe, which was five feet off the ground, hooked it to a bracket and pulled a strap, and made his way back to the tanks.

From the ground, if someone knew where the bag was, they could jump up and grab the strap and pull it off, but if they didn't know where it was, they would never see it. He had found the perfect hiding place, in more ways than one.

He straightened his costume and made ready for his entrance. This would require some real StarSee acting chops. He took four deep breaths from his small oxygen tank, fixed his eyes on the door and ran toward it like a firefighter with important instructions.

Sunday, 9:38 p.m.

Dettmer sat at a white cloth-covered table toward the rear of the Gray Room. The banks of quantum computers with blinking lights in the data center lined the right side of the room, which enhanced the festive feel of the Gray Room. The banquet hall space had been decorated with sparkling lights, large plants, and stars, which were projected onto the ceiling. Air filters scrubbed out all the smoke, and instead, it smelled of bacon wrapped shrimp, and lobster mac bites.

They made her swap her iBrowse out with StarSee issued ones, which had limited access through the StarSee firewall, so she could not access any of her usual apps, subscriptions or contacts. The company iBrowse were exclusively provided so that attendees could see the other virtual guests and find their way around, but not much else. If you were attending this party, the Blakewells wanted your full and undivided attention. Visual overlay-based Augmented Reality and Ionic displays had come a long way in recent years, but she still found the slight transparency of AR disconcerting. Filling a room with people that were not really there felt a little like walking around on the deck of the sunken Titanic inhabited by lost souls.

At her table was an AR couple who were busy conversing with each other. She swiped the black touch pad over her heart, accessing the iBrowse interface, and turned off the AR display momentarily. There were only a handful of other real people in the room, all sitting at different tables chatting with their now invisible AR tablemates. She did not know who they were, but she hoped they were not so loyal to StarSee that they would get in the way of her plans. She turned her AR back on.

StreamBugs hovered above the attendees, providing a curated real time stream of the event to the outside world. While the atmosphere in the room oozed with opulence and wealth, the orange sky outside the skylights and the floor to ceiling windows across the front of the room was the color of rotten pumpkin. No wonder people preferred the false reality of StarSee.

Sitting at the head table in their finest attire were Owen and Lara, Maddox, Gabe and the AR presences of the NewsCann owner, Lee Hoffman, and his wife. Press Rep Sasha Abioye, looking even more stunning at this close distance despite being only an AR version of herself, sat at the next table over with a group of what appeared to be Arab men and women.

Maddox was typing on the tablecloth, on a keyboard no one else could see. Lee, Owen and Lara were laughing as Lee and Owen played with a prototype Crown of Truth, telling truths and lies to make it flash red and green. Lara demurely refused to put the Crown of Truth on, suggesting that it could muss her hair.

The main table sat underneath two giant displays that were visible in real life, one of which had the real time StarSee front page on it. A constant stream of celebrities, information, chats and attention-grabbing real-life feeds. The other had the feed from the room and a large countdown clock on it that currently read *2:18*.

Dettmer stared at the numbers. She had two hours and eighteen minutes to stop the spread of an algorithm that amplified hate and anger to the point of violence. Only two hours and eighteen minutes remained for her to expose the criminal activity of some of the richest and most powerful people on the planet.

The primary display also featured several graphs, charts and the main stream from StarSee, including total subscriber counts and stock values. On the display next to it was NewsCann, streaming live and recorded updates of items of interest across the nation and around the world. The giant displays contained too much information for any normal person to absorb.

Dettmer only cared about the one with the countdown clock on it. If Roman did not show up soon, she would have to start the festivities without him.

Owen glanced over at her. On taking notice, he stood up, surveyed the room, and then stomped toward her. He came up from behind and put his fat hand on her shoulder, making it difficult for her to turn and face him. Another power move. He bent over and spoke quietly into her left ear. "I'm sorry to hear that Rennick put you on leave, but that means you have no authority here, and are simply our guest, so I'm sure you'll behave accordingly."

"Of course Mr. Blakewell. I am honored that you would invite me." She looked straight ahead.

"Good. Please enjoy the evening. If you find yourself motivated to say a few words of support, it would go a long way toward proving your loyalty." He patted her shoulder with the same fat hand. "But keep it civil. More people are watching you right now than you have ever had in your entire life." And he walked away.

She glimpsed Maddox glaring at them. When he realized she was looking back, he quickly turned away.

She continued to survey the room. From where she was sitting, the data center was behind her and to her right. The card reader glowed red by the entrance. A single security guard stood a few tables away to her left. She was in plain view of everyone.

It was unlikely anyone could get into the machine room unnoticed.

Owen sat back down after doing a couple of other greets. The body language between Owen and Maddox was unmistakable. Maddox seemed furious at Owen, while Owen was oblivious. Owen clearly demanded to be the center of attention, much to the visible ire of Maddox. Everyone else at the table was happily deferential.

Lara backed away from the table and stood up. Neither Owen, who was busy talking to the avatar of Lee Hoffman, nor Maddox, who was now talking to Gabe, even noticed. She made her way down the aisle between the tables and approached Dettmer. As she walked past, she made a gesture pointing at the streamBugs.

What does that mean? I am being watched?

Lara made her way toward the back of the room. Dettmer wondered what it must be like for her, to be with a man so self-centered and demanding of admiration that there was little left over for her. She was beautiful in a very familiar way, no question, but Dettmer wondered what her own motivations were, and if she secretly wished her life was different. Maybe Lara wanted to be an ally.

Dettmer quickly got up to follow her to the bathroom. As she entered the women's room, all her streamBugs joined Lara's and waited at the ceiling outside. Inside, Lara stood facing the mirror, touching up her makeup.

"Oh," said Dettmer, as if surprised to see her. "I wanted to tell you how nice you look tonight." Dettmer was unsure of Lara's intentions or desires, and needed to play it casual.

Lara smiled. Her eyes glowed slightly green. Her hair was a bouquet of streaks of red, blonde, brown and black. "Thank you."

"Do you know what the plan is for the evening? Will there be any special presentations?"

Lara's face flickered with a look of puzzlement. "Near midnight you'll hear quite a bit of self-congratulatory proselytizing."

"Will we go into the data center for a tour?"

Lara giggled. Something about it seemed familiar. "No. Only employees are allowed inside the data center."

"And that necklace, wow. That is extraordinary. Is that a ruby?"

"Yes, it's a Burmese ruby surrounded by diamonds. It's called *The Heart of the Kingdom*." She pulled her streaked hair back from her neck to show the necklace.

Dettmer smiled. While she looked at the necklace, she noticed very well hidden scars at the base of Lara's neck from plastic surgery. "It's hard to stay young looking, right?" Maybe she needed a push.

Lara's face registered no emotion. "I'm quite lucky. My new role affords me more influence."

Dettmer decided to cut to the point. "Was there something you wanted to talk to me about, in here, away from the streamBugs?"

Lara stepped close. It was slightly uncomfortable. Her voice turned to a near whisper, but she smiled seductively. "If you look at StarSee, honestly look, you can see right through the masks we all wear, and you can see straight through to who we really are. No matter where you're from or why you've chosen to stay."

Dettmer kept her eyes locked on Lara's and inched closer, matching her softer tone. "It must be hard, being with him, especially being both his assistant and his..."

Lara's head tilted slightly. "Why's that?" She took a small step backwards.

"It just seems that he is very demanding of attention, and narcissistic."

"Attention seeking and narcissism. You've just described StarSee itself."

"But with everything always being about him..." She paused. "If you are seeing things that should not be happening, now is the time to speak up."

Dettmer thought she detected a flicker of wishfulness wash across Lara's pretty face. "I went through a lot to get where I am. I used to think it's more effective to bring about change from the inside. But it's slow."

"What kind of change are you talking about?"

"The kind that protects the intelligent, but vulnerable."

"I can help you. We can help each other."

An odd look flashed across Lara's face, like a bad memory came back to her. "No. It's up to me, and it always has been. Never mind. Now, if you'll excuse me." She turned and walked out the door.

Dettmer stood looking at her own reflection, mildly confused. Lara might have some deeper issues. That was something she needed to unpack when she had time, but right now, she had more pressing matters.

She returned to her seat and found two new avatars at her table, two women. Time was slipping away. She had high hopes that Roman would successfully fulfill his several important duties this evening, but it was going to be a minefield to navigate, especially without help. And they had to do it together without directly communicating.

She looked at the giant timer hanging above the head table, where Lara was once again smiling and nodding. Behind her, a gust of billowing brown smoke blew against the window. Two hours and three minutes until midnight.

THIRTY-NINE

Sunday, 10:45 p.m.

"Who's in charge!?" Roman burst through the doorway the moment it opened, and stood in the secure portal area. If any weapons were detected, the second glass door would have automatically locked. But he could see the little light on the interior door was green. He hurried toward the second glass door and pulled it open. The easiest and safest way to get through what he had to do tonight was to get as many people as he could out, to avoid interruption. "LAFD wants you all out."

The waiter who had opened the door wearing the signature StarSee button down light blue shirt, beret and white apron looked flustered. "Jules is the head waiter. In the kitchen."

"I need to get to the internal fire suppression system. Get me Jules, I'll wait here."

The waiter jogged away. Roman knew precisely where he was, and where he needed to get to in terms of location and distance, but having never been in the secret maintenance corridors, he didn't know the layout. He looked down the dark gray fabric-lined hallway. There were several doors evenly spaced along the seventy-eight feet before it turned the corner.

A woman in a more formal uniform, a light blue jacket over a white shirt, ran toward Roman. "I'm Jules, head of waitstaff. What's going on?"

"I need you to get your people out. The path to the bottom of the mountain is still safe and clear. You and all non-essential personnel, including security, need to leave the buildings."

"Only security has the authority to—"

"Get me security then, please."

"Okay..." She looked concerned.

"You connect, I'll talk." Roman pulled off his helmet and held it under his arm. His black facemask didn't exactly fit the costume, but he couldn't risk facial ID. He placed her iBrowse over his head as she made a couple of gestures onto the pad on her chest.

An image of a clean cut blond man appeared in the upper right corner of his vision. He was in the banquet room, surrounded by very well-dressed people, both real and virtual. "What's going on?" asked the security guard.

"I'm Sargent Chasper of the LAFD. Don't alarm the Blakewells or their guests. I repeat, we are under strict instructions to not disturb the event in any way. But we need you to quietly and discreetly get all non-essential personnel out of the building. The Gray Room is completely fire safe." The party needed to continue so that Dettmer could get someone to object to the merger, live.

"I haven't heard anything about an evacuation."

As he spoke to the guard, he saw the banquet room behind him and realized that the guests had already finished eating. The plan to get into the party by pretending to be a guest would no longer work. "Maddox Blakewell himself ordered us to quietly extract the non-essential personnel, for liability reasons, without causing even the slightest concern at the party. Do you want to question him?"

The other end of the line went silent for a moment, and then the man said, "Copy that. I'll send the silent evacuation signal." The line went black.

Roman turned back to Jules. "I have to get to a fire suppression closet."

"I'll take you," she said.

"No, no. You get your group out. I'll need to keep these." He tapped the iBrowse.

"Those aren't real iBrowse, they're just employee issue. But shouldn't you have your own fire department iBrowse built into your helmet?"

He slapped his helmet. "Doesn't work here. StarSee security protocols. I need yours for the map overlay." He held out his hand. Jules removed the touchpad from her shirt and handed it to Roman, but looked unconvinced. He attached it to his chest. "Go ahead." Roman tilted his head toward the exit.

Jules jogged off, and then paused for a moment. She turned back to Roman and said, "You look like—"

Roman quickly turned away from her. "Please, you need to go, quickly!" he shouted.

He glanced back as he hurried down the hall and saw her reluctantly turning toward the exit. Some people had better facial recognition than AI.

Since entering the party as a guest was no longer an option, he ducked into a closet that the map said would contain uniforms. Once inside, he tore his fake firefighter gear off, grabbed a light blue service shirt and swapped out his costume tuxedo top for it. He pulled the semi-transparent protective waitstaff face mask over his mouth and nose. Grabbing a blue beret from a hamper, he pulled it onto his head, tucked his shaggy hair up into it, then put Jules' iBrowse back on and clipped the touchpad back to his chest. He pulled out Malcolm Chasper's employee ID and clipped it to his pants.

There was no mirror in sight. He had to hope he would pass as a waiter.

After stuffing his firefighter costume in a hamper and moving the contents of his backpack to his pockets, he used the map in his vision to guide him to the Gray Room.

He rushed down two flights of service stairs and crossed into the vestibule outside the entrance. The doors were wide open to the sparkling banquet hall. He could see all the slightly transparent AR guests at their tables, and the Blakewells at the front of the room. The blond security guard still stood at the back of the room. StreamBugs hissed above certain tables. He switched off his iBrowse momentarily to see only the real people and found Dettmer sitting near the rear of the room, looking anxious.

While surveying the room, another waiter poked him in the side. "Miss Lara." Roman turned to find he was being handed a tray with a martini on it by another waiter. The man gestured for Roman to take the drink to the head table, and when Roman looked confused, the man pointed to his head, without a beret on, and then to Roman's head, with the beret on, and then to the table. He then walked away.

Anxiety struck Roman like a punch in the chest. This was it. Everything he was about to do would be in full view of the world, and this time, they would see actual reality instead of a StarSee version.

After a couple of deep breaths, he straightened himself up, walked into the room with purpose and headed for the head table. As he approached the main table, he could hear Maddox speaking to Lara.

"... it pisses me off. They're leaving as if this place is going to catch fire. It's astoundingly safe here."

"Well, we are surrounded by flames," said Lara.

"Hardly. They're just chicken shit immigrants. They don't know how fortunate they are to work here. They should gladly withstand a little heat to stay in our kitchen."

Roman placed the martini on the table next to Lara, who did not acknowledge it.

Maddox called to Roman. "You!"

Roman froze and looked at the ground. His heart pounded. In his peripheral vision, he saw Dettmer glance over.

"You stay. You no go. You grateful! Yes? Si?" Maddox had been drinking, and spoke as if Roman was a child from another country.

"Yes sir." Roman put on an accent that came out sounding like a cross between Spanish and German. "Thank you, sir. Gracias." He pivoted and walked away toward Dettmer.

As he crossed behind her, he bent over her shoulder as if he was going to take her champagne glass, and cleared his throat. She looked up and recognition flashed in her eyes. She touched his arm.

"Welcome to the party," she whispered, looking straight ahead. "Let's get started. No time to use up."

"No time to waste," whispered Roman.

"Exactly," she replied. Maddox was looking in their direction, complaining. "He's watching," said Roman.

"The killcode will have to wait. Go do your thing."

Roman backed away toward the entrance to the data center.

Dettmer stood up and began tapping her glass with her fork.

"Kiss me, darling!" Owen said to Lara. The room chuckled politely. Lara rolled her eyes and smiled.

"I would like to say a few words," said Dettmer, straightening her black gown. All the displays were immediately filled with her image, like Jumbotrons at a sporting event. The room went quiet. "Please pardon my accent. I am not a native of this country, but I would like to talk about a real American success story. The hosts of this party, the Blakewells."

The room broke out in applause. As people turned their attention to the head table, Owen nodded to Dettmer and held his glass up.

With everyone's attention focused on Dettmer, Roman stealthily made his way along the glass wall to the door of the machine room.

"When I first saw Owen Blakewell, I thought he was a crass narcissist..." said Dettmer to nervous laughter. Roman could feel the tension at the head table. "...but then we met in his office, in that tower right over there, and he and I sat down and had a conversation about this business, about the roles we both play and about the enormous value he, and his company StarSee, bring to the world of Social Media." She spoke slowly and clearly. Her tone was pleasant, and she was being jovial and flattering to the Blakewells, the perfect distraction. They would let her go on forever if she was praising them and their accomplishments.

Roman swiped Malcolm's employee maintenance ID against the card reader outside the data center door. The card reader did nothing. He gave the door a gentle tug, it did not budge.

C'mon guys.

He looked at the head table. Maddox showed no signs of having been alerted. Roman looked at the card reader, this would either work, or not, no reason to keep swiping the badge.

Suddenly the lock clicked imperceptibly and the light turned green. He exhaled, and gently opened the door and backed through, closing the door behind him. It was freezing cold inside.

He raced to a terminal behind a bank of quantum computers and logged in to his own virtual terminal. Task one was to release his original iris scans of the real Starla. He quickly entered the date range in his search bar for the original Starla scans and found the folders with the files from the first time he scanned her. They were not locked. Internet sleuths would have a field day with them. Roman slid the slider from private to public access privileges on the root folder, which prompted two factor identification, his password and real time DNA ID. He put his thumb on the reader, which imperceptibly pierced his skin and simultaneously read his thumbprint. Then he typed his password and unlocked the folder. He navigated to where Tek had told him to drop the link to the folder and posted a comment. *"Scans of Real Starla Devine - Public."*

He glanced around the side of the terminal to the banquet

room. Dettmer was still commanding the room's attention, but it looked like Maddox was becoming antsy. He was whispering something into Gabe's ear.

Time for task number two, releasing the real recording of the night of the fake murder. It was so close he could almost see it in his mind's eye. Roman opened another terminal window. First, he logged in to the ICE company site and navigated to the login screen, where he entered his personal site access passcode.

Right there, next to the passcode entry box, in fine print, were the warnings that explicitly said if any attempt is made to remove or delete personal files of the deceased without prior authorization, they would be locked and protected by the ICE company. If not for the automatic protection, they might have been able to destroy the evidence forever. Thank god for hubris.

Once inside the security wall, the site did not distinguish between the recently deceased, since there would be more authentication still to come. The fact that he was in because of Roxy suddenly gripped him. He forced himself to type in Starla's name when prompted for the recently deceased.

There were several categories of access/overrides that he could select, so he just clicked the bottom radio button for *"Request temporary override for all."* After hitting submit, two names appeared under the question *"Person to receive overrides? Paul or Ruth Devine."* He selected Paul, and a pop-up window appeared: *"You will receive your override code shortly. It will be valid for 90 seconds."*

It was now up to Paul. He should copy the authentication code, which would be sent to his iBrowse, and drop it into Tek's stream next to where Roman had just dropped the link to Starla's scans. Roman switched back to Tek's stream and waited.

Nothing happened. Seconds ticked by. Knowing he would have to find the recordings again, he switched over to the root of Starla's stream and swiped her ID to gain base level access. He was outside the StarSee user facing GUI, which was still locked, but inside the system, searching through her files. He navigated to the date, just six days ago, and dug into the recordings. Monday evening, 8:08 p.m. He now understood the timeline of that night as well as he knew the layout of the room where it all started.

He heard a commotion outside. Dettmer's speech was dragging on. The passcode would only grant him access for another fifteen seconds. He switched to Tek's page again. The page auto-refreshed and a new folder appeared, *"413_override_from_Paul."* Roman opened the folder, a text file containing nothing but letters and numbers appeared. He copied them.

He clicked to open the volumetric recording from the night of the murder. As expected, *"Locked by Agreement 413, enter passcode to view"* popped up. He quickly pasted the passcode from Paul. The next prompt appeared, *"Please provide two factor Biometric ID."* Even though he had done it once before, this part felt incredibly unsafe. He placed his thumb against the reader again, holding Starla's ID over the reader with his other hand. If the system didn't read Roman's biometry and interpret it as being Starla's brother Paul, the evening would end right here.

The passcode screen disappeared, revealing the recording.

He felt a rush of adrenaline. There it was, the right angle at the right time. And there he was, standing by the Starla impersonator, smiling in the vision of her streamBugs. He applied the Snopes Check software, and within seconds, a *"100% Real"* logo appeared. He dragged the file across the desktop and copied it into Tek's StarSee stream and added a giant banner under the recording: *PROOF GLASS IS INNOCENT.*

He looked for the output to the big display right above the Blakewell's table. Sasha Abioye, the press rep would have the controls for the displays, but the data center should be able to override them. There were several buttons on the touchpad interface, and without knowing which was the main screen, he overrode them all and locked out external control. He hit play. Unable to see the display from here, he watched Dettmer, and her face registered the surprise of someone witnessing a miracle. She looked at Roman through the glass and nodded.

With all eyes still on Dettmer, he exited the machine room, bent over and wedged a fork upside down, handle first, under the door. It was so old school it might take security a minute to figure out why it wouldn't open.

Roman stood next to the machine room door like a guard at Buckingham Palace, and watched Dettmer. Her tone abruptly changed. She could stop the charade and get on with the real show. "...and even with all that good I just told you about," she was now shouting, "I am here to tell you all that it was all a lie." She pointed at the head table. "The Blakewell family is an organized crime family that has been manipulating public opinion and literally getting away with murder, and the proof is playing on the screens behind you!"

CHAPTER
FORTY

Sunday, 11:15 p.m.

"… and the proof is playing on the screens behind you!" Dettmer hoped she put the right amount of showmanship into the announcement. She wanted everyone's attention to turn to the screen, which it did, but then she realized it was a bit early in the recording yet. Roman was just entering Starla's condo, and it was a section of the evening that everyone had seen before.

Looks of confusion passed through the room, especially at the head table.

"Sasha, why are we watching this again?" said Owen.

Sasha was at the next table looking at her pad. "I don't know. Someone has overridden my control and is playing back files directly from Starla's original recordings."

Realization flashed on both Maddox and Owen's faces. "Shit!" yelled Maddox.

Owen shouted, "That's impossible, those files are either locked or deleted."

"I'm telling you someone is playing the recordings from

Monday night, and it is being broadcast to everyone." Sasha was now standing and swiping furiously at her chest pad.

Owen's voice got growly, and he started barking, "Who is playing this?!" He pointed at Dettmer, who stood watching the display. "You?!" He turned to the remaining security guard. "Turn off that Goddamned display!"

The security guard looked confused and ran to the giant monitor. He reached up to feel for a power button, but couldn't even reach the bottom of the display. On the recording, Starla ejected the vial from the stuffed toy bear and poured the contents into Roman's glass before handing it to him.

The room broke out in hushed whispers as they realized they were watching a crime unfold on the screen.

Dettmer slowly approached the display. She wanted to make sure people recognized what they were seeing. "That was a drug that was slipped to Roman, which would knock him out and give him memory loss!"

"Dammit!" Maddox yelled. He was up and to the door of the data center quickly. He pulled it so hard the sound of the rubberized flooring ripping from the wedged fork underneath the door could be heard across the room.

Roman almost casually slid over and leaned against the machine room door, pushing it closed again.

"Get the fuck out of my way!" shouted Maddox.

Roman stared at him and pulled down his mask. "I'm sorry, Maddox, I'm afraid I can't do that."

"You!" Maddox roared. "How did you get in here?" He turned to Owen, who was now standing with both fists clenched. "You did this, didn't you!?"

Owen looked incredulous. "Get it together son, you're not thinking right."

Maddox whipped around like a cornered animal, fury in his glowing eyes. It seemed he couldn't decide where to focus his rage,

Roman, the data center, Dettmer or his father. Meanwhile, the incriminating recording continued to play above him.

Owen ran to the security guard and grabbed him by the collar. He pulled him close and whispered something in the guard's ear. The guard looked reluctant. Owen said, "Now!"

The guard bent over and pulled a gun out of his ankle holster and brandished it at the room. Dettmer realized she should have seen that coming.

"Everybody stop!" The guard was pointing at the room full of guests.

"What the fuck are you doing?" said Owen. "Point it at the real intruder!"

"I don't know which one that is!"

"Oh, for fuck's sake, give it to me!" Owen grabbed the gun from the guard's hand.

"Look! The recording!" shouted Roman. "This is where the drugs knock me out."

Owen stomped across the room, walking through virtual guests toward the middle of the space where he could try to control the situation. "Not real!" he shouted. "Totalfake!" He waved the gun around like it was a toy.

On the screens, Roman was facing Starla, who was looking statuesque, appearing almost naked in her bodysuit, standing near the armoire. The Snopes *100% Real* logo still appeared in the lower corner of the recording. "Something feels wrong," Roman mumbled on the playback as he held his hand to his head.

A gunshot rang out. In the room. Everyone, both real and avatar, flinched. Owen stood in the middle of the space with the gun pointed at the screen. His streamBugs followed him.

Dettmer raised her hands.

He had tried to shoot the display, but missed. Firing again, he put a small hole in the corner of the giant screen. He was trying to stop a digital recording with a physical bullet.

"Owen! Stop!" Lara was cowering.

"I will not have this at my party!" He pointed the gun at Roman. "Maddox, get in there and turn off these lies!"

"If this is a lie, then why are you scared?" asked Dettmer.

The avatar of Lee Hoffman, sitting at the head table, looked mortified, like someone had pulled a veil back, and he was now seeing that the house he just put a down payment on was made of straw. Lee's wife, who was sitting next to him, flickered out of existence.

Owen remained fixed on Roman. "Move away from the door, son, or I'm going to shoot you in the head to protect my property, as is my right."

"Kill him! Unless you can't because you really are working together." said Maddox, who had backed away from Roman.

"Please put the gun down, Mr. Blakewell," said Dettmer.

Suddenly a streak rushed across the room out of nowhere, and in no time, Owen was flailing, having been tackled from behind. He fell to the floor with a thud. Within seconds, he was hoisted back into a standing position with his hands behind his back.

A commanding voice yelled out, "Y'all freeze, right now!"

Travis, who had entered while Owen was shooting like an eight-year-old at a state fair, had disarmed him. Owen stood in disbelief. Travis pointed his own weapon quickly between Owen and Maddox. "Nobody move!"

"Travis, what the hell are you doing!?" said Owen.

Dettmer caught Maddox smiling broadly, clearly misinterpreting the situation. She couldn't figure out what was going on in his head, but something was off.

"First things first," said Travis. "Everybody out!"

"Except the Blakewells," shouted Dettmer as she realized she could lower her hands. "We have business to attend to."

Nobody moved. There were only a half dozen real people in the room, but they stood motionless, stunned by the turn of events.

"Everybody out! There's a limocopter on the pad," yelled

Travis, "go now or you'll be stuck here all night!" He pointed to the security guard. "You, too, this is a police matter now."

The remaining real people from around the room, including the security guard, ran for the door. Gabe was one of them.

"No, no, no." Travis stopped Gabe. "You, back to your table." He pulled out his own Instant Disabler, a mostly non-lethal but highly-effective police weapon. He then slid the gun Owen had taken from the guard across a table to Dettmer.

She immediately trained it on Owen. "Get back to your table where I can keep an eye on you."

He reluctantly headed back to his seat with his hands behind his back.

Maddox was smiling. He waived Travis over to the data center. "Come on, help me out. I need to get in here."

Travis looked at Maddox and squinted. "Get away from the door."

Shock flashed on Maddox's face. "What the fuck are you doing!?"

"I've been undercover this entire time, Maddox."

Maddox slammed his fist on the glass door. "I told you!" He screamed at Owen.

"When I figured out that this platform was manipulating aggression, I moved here to infiltrate your organization. And you both were arrogant enough to think that you could buy me off with Admiration Points."

"But you did not even tell me?" asked Dettmer.

"I didn't know what was going on with Rennick. Turns out not much, but I had to be careful."

"Look, people!" shouted Roman, "the stream! Me and Starla, see?" He was pointing and jumping up and down.

On the recording, the lights in Starla's condo had gone out, and everything was a high-contrast, slightly green hue of high-quality night vision. Roman was stumbling toward Starla. She hit him with a glass. He fell into her arms, and she let him fall to the ground. In Roman's original recording, from the POV of his stream that night, it had looked like he was lunging at her. But now it was clear he was not. He was falling after being drugged.

"This is real!"

On the display, Starla stood up and waited at the door to the armoire.

"I can attest, that's actually a secret celebrity elevator," said Travis, for the benefit of the streamBugs swirling around the room.

The armoire doors opened, and Maddox Blakewell stepped out, dragging a body also dressed in the nude body stocking, exactly like Starla. They heaved the body out, placed it on the floor next to Roman, and the living Starla placed the award statue in Roman's hand.

Travis retrained his weapon on Maddox, who was looking like he was about to make a run for it. "Don't move."

As Dettmer watched the recording play out, the pieces were coming together, but she realized it might not be so clear for everyone watching. "What you are seeing," she wandered as she addressed the room, "is the actual body of Starla Devine being brought into the room where Roman was accused of killing her, in order to frame him. But she had already been murdered! That's her dead body!"

The room full of avatars quietly gasped. StreamBugs gathered around her. She became a picture in picture on the display. She imagined the thousands and thousands of people watching the events unfold online.

"The fake Starla Devine you saw on the recording, helping Maddox Blakewell place the dead body, had been playing Starla Devine for about two years, after the real Starla was actually murdered," she said.

"This is nonsense!" shouted Maddox. "That's not me!"

"This is as real as it gets. Look at the Snopes logo," said Travis.

On the screen, Maddox and the Starla impersonator were placing Roman's arm over the dead body. Maddox kicked over a lamp and pushed a coffee table over to make it look like there was a struggle.

While looking at the primary display with the recording playing back, the secondary display caught Dettmer's eye. The front page of StarSee was not only broadcasting the events from the room, but next to it, a chat box of messages from people streamed down the side. At the bottom of that was a word cloud, showing the frequency of questions by how large the text was. She read the largest one out loud to the room.

"How is it possible for someone to take over as Starla?"

The room went quiet. Attention turned to the head table. "What?!" asked Owen.

"The people on your site, your own users, they want to know. Do you want to answer them, or should I?" Owen growled.

She looked up at the streamBugs. "Someone who looked very much like Starla was given plastic surgery and coaching. After a few months of being out of the spotlight, she was able to step in and take over."

The display lit up with positive likes and loves. She was paying attention to the watchers and they loved her for it. Floating hearts filled the screen as a new question grew in size. She read it aloud. "Why did they kill the real Starla?" She began pacing the room like a lawyer about to make closing arguments.

"We don't have time for this," said Gabe. "We don't have to answer anything."

"Until someone objects to the merger, we have time," said Travis. "Go ahead, Dettmer."

She nodded. "The beloved Starla Devine that we all knew and loved, was murdered by an out-of-control fan."

"But not just any fan," interjected Travis. "A fan who was influenced by a new algorithm that was being tested out, one that could target people and drive them to murder."

"This person," said Dettmer, "murdered the real Starla Devine, and then the Blakewells had that very same person take her place!"

"This is ludicrous," said Maddox. "Why would I test an algorithm against Starla!?"

"I think you both know the answer to that, right, Owen?"

Owen's eyes were wide with a mixture of anger and surprise. "Me? Starla was my biggest celebrity, and our very first stream. Why would I want her dead?"

"Because she was getting older. She was aging out."

"Pfft. That's ridiculous."

Dettmer looked at Maddox. "But he did, right, Maddox? He could kill two birds with one rock. He wanted you to try your new algorithm, and he had someone he wanted you to try it on. A younger, prettier version of Starla Devine that he could control and keep in line. Who looked like her, but younger. Starla 2.0."

Travis kept his gun trained on the head table.

Maddox sat perfectly still, glaring.

The stream above their heads currently showed Maddox and the actress who was Starla 2.0 getting into the elevator. The doors closed, and it left the room silent, with Roman lying over the real Starla's dead body. Homicide would arrive in six minutes, just when Roman would begin to wake up. The display next to the recording now had a new question in huge letters. "If Starla has been dead, who have we been following?"

Dettmer pressed on, "A younger, prettier version of Starla Devine that you could hold sway over, right Owen? The problem is, the personality traits that made her a candidate for the algorithm are the very same traits that lead her to want out after a couple of years. She was a conspiracy-minded activist who would never think you were doing enough for her cause. And now, tired of playing the role of Starla Devine, and having volumes of evidence against you, she wanted out of the act." Dettmer stood before the head table, everyone's attention focused on her, the stream going out to millions of people. "Right, Miss Mina Batin!?"

All eyes turned to Lara, whose eyes went wide. She abruptly stood up from the table, rattling plates and silverware.

"Sit the fuck down!" Owen pounded the table and stood up to face her. "Don't say anything!"

StreamBugs swiftly moved to capture the drama.

Lara slapped him. Hard. "I told you this would happen!" she hissed.

Owen grabbed her arm and squeezed.

Travis fired his Instant Disabler into the ceiling. "Let go, and sit your ass down, Owen!" Dust and debris fell from the impact.

The room went silent. Owen reluctantly did as he was told.

"Go ahead, Mina," said Dettmer. "Why end the act now?"

She looked at Owen, and then Maddox and Gabe. "I can't, never mind."

"Protecting the intelligent but vulnerable. Right, Mina? You are the only one who can do this."

She gave Owen side-eye, cleared her throat and nodded. "At first, I was a huge fan, I knew everything about Starla. I even looked like her, and I knew it. So I got close to her, and we became friends. But then I learned about her treatment of cephalopods, and how they are poor defenseless creatures, and how it was up to me to protect them."

"But you killed her! She was a good person!" said Roman.

"She deserved to die, and you all know it!" Her demeanor turned on a dime. "I saw dozens of streams of prominent scientists who spoke in no uncertain terms about who was secretly responsible for the genocide of cephalopods. Starla Devine. I would be a better Starla Devine than she was, and I would make genuine changes from the inside. And it worked. The proof is that I don't see posts about cephalopods being in danger anymore."

"But she literally had nothing to do with any of that. You were being fed lies! They weren't even real people. Did you even bother to check the authenticity?" asked Roman.

Mina stared back blankly, like the words were in an unfamiliar language. "Do you believe everything you're told, Roman? Starla used AI to cover up her real behavior, and you believed it."

"It is completely the other way around," said Dettmer.

"You'll see. History will show I was right."

"I can see why they chose you. I just do not know why you wanted to stop being her."

"Stardom comes with being reviewed and commented on all the time, even when my stream is off. I had to use fake DNA everywhere I went. Everything I did, every word I said, it was all monitored, double checked and revised for the corporate bosses, the clients and advertisers who pay StarSee. I was the star of a show that never ended. Every day I got notes about myself." She looked at Owen. "He said he couldn't go public with our relationship because I was Starla Devine." She turned to Dettmer. "So, I decided I would not be Starla anymore. I threatened to go public with the whole thing unless they let me out of it and changed my name."

Mina looked confused about what to do next. Owen sat with his head in his hands, Gabe slid his chair as far back as he could, and Maddox simply sat glaring at Owen, not even looking at Mina.

"Over there, Mina," said Travis, pointing a short distance to the left of the table with his gun.

Dettmer looked up at the displays. The number of watchers was rising fast. News was spreading about this drama unfolding live. This was the latest hit show on StarSee.

"So Mina decides she wants out of the Starla act," said Dettmer, "and the solution from the brilliant mind of Maddox Blakewell? Settle a family score, and frame for murder the one person who has actual proof that Starla had been replaced. The man who had the real iris scans in his personal archives, Roman Glass."

As the attention turned to Roman, he nodded furiously. "Yes! Starla Devine had heterochromatic eyes, and fake Starla, um, Lara, er, Mina ... doesn't. And I just now released all the scans the Blakewells were trying to hide." He felt like while he had the floor, he should prove his innocence. "And that celebrity elevator you see on the real recording right now? It was actually installed after the recording of the murder from two years ago that they Totalfaked me into. The size changed in the spliced together recording, I caught it."

"Do you hear yourselves?" Owen interrupted. "You sound like lunatics! This isn't a StarStream story!"

"But it is," said Dettmer. "See for yourself." She pointed to the monitor where they were now being broadcast to the largest audience the site had ever known.

"Turn us off, Sasha!" Owen bellowed.

Sasha held up her hands and backed away.

On the site, the questions from the watchers kept coming. "*What about the algorithm?*"

Dettmer nodded to Travis.

"A few years ago," Travis began, "at the request of a client they couldn't say no to, StarSee was asked if an algorithm could be created that could target people for murder, using only their Star-Streams, by having someone close to the target become so enraged that they would obey when directed to kill. That's what they tested on Starla a couple of years ago, but it had side effects. It affected people other than those who it targeted."

Maddox was visibly squirming inside his tuxedo. "That's ridiculous."

Travis continued, "At first, I thought it was all standard corporate warfare. That Owen just wanted to target his rival platforms, and by using the algorithm, no one would suspect why crazed employees were losing their minds and killing CEOs. But it turns out that wasn't it at all.

In catching me up on the case, Dettmer told me about her visit to Truth Be Told, and how the military was investing heavily in new technologies. Watching ya'll play with your prototype Crown of Truth on the feed, I put two and two together. I believe the military is investing directly in StarSee to use the platform as a weapon."

"Oh please," said Owen. "It's no secret that our military is invested in dozens of high-tech enterprises."

"No, but the amount is a secret, as is why they invested in you, a social media platform." He paused for effect. "So exactly how much is the military paying you to develop and integrate an algorithm that is able to target and assassinate foreign leaders, foreign troublemakers and foreign journalists without us even having to send people into their country?"

"Oh for chrissake," said Owen, rolling his eyes.

"Then, using a broader opinion algorithm, you manipulate public outrage here in the US as well as in the target country, and we're able to overthrow entire governments without any resistance from anyone, inside or outside of our own country."

The building rumbled. The fire was getting closer, and some unknown system had just kicked in to keep it away from the building.

Dettmer jumped in. "But it is not so controllable, is it Maddox? The algorithm is out now, like a virus in nature, and people that were not the original targets are killing each other. The murder algorithm is not exactly perfect, is it?"

Maddox's lower jaw jutted out. "My algorithm is perfect," he said through gritted teeth. "Who cares if a few low-life watchers kill each other? There's always more watchers."

A sharp sound hit a wall. The panoramic windows behind the head table glowed orange with smoke. Flames had made their way around to the front of the building.

"We should all get out and let the flames destroy the computers," said Travis.

"The algorithm is not just on these computers, it lives wherever StarSee lives, wherever Starla Devine's stream is. We have to get the killcode into the system."

"Killcode!?" shouted Maddox. "Are you fucking crazy!?"

"Your algorithm is deadly and out of control," she said, keeping her weapon fixed on the Blakewells. "If it is released into the NewsCann network, more people will die."

Owen hit the table. "That algorithm is a leap forward in psycho-social engineering. The military will crush anyone who threatens it. Including you!"

"Idiot!" shouted Maddox. "A messy killcode could destroy us!"

"If the military came after me, they would have to admit what they are doing. And they never will. And yes, the killcode will almost certainly do ... serious collateral damage," said Dettmer.

Wind whipped a burning branch against the glass of a skylight in the back of the room. Orange and red sparks swirled in the rippling heat just above and outside the room.

"We really should get the hell out," said Travis.

Dettmer turned from her position in front of the head table and walked to Roman, who stood by the thick glass wall that separated the party area from the cold blue machine room. She reached into her pocket and handed Roman the simpin. "Do it. Now."

It was 11:48 p.m. Twelve minutes to midnight.

As she turned back to the room to continue making her case, she saw that Maddox had bolted from the table and was running straight at her like a linebacker with a vengeance.

Sunday, 11:48 p.m.

You're not going to fucking ruin me with a killcode, thought Maddox as he hurled himself at Dettmer. As he closed in on her, she twisted and bent over, jamming her elbow into his gut. He groaned in pain. She placed her heel between his fast moving feet, grabbed his arm and propelled him onto a table, which collapsed under his weight. He passed through two virtual guests as he landed on the floor.

Maddox stood up slowly. Then he pointed the gun directly at her, smiling. He had smoothly stripped her of it, just as he had planned. "Freeze."

Dettmer slowly put her hands up, her jaw hanging open.

"Everyone, stop what you're doing!" He stood, almost falling over a bent piece of the table, and backed away from Dettmer. "Travis, you ungrateful Brutus, lower your weapon!"

Travis kept his weapon fixed on Maddox, not moving.

"Now!" shouted Maddox.

Travis reluctantly lowered his instant disabler.

"And you–" he pointed the gun at Dettmer, "–give me the simpin with the killcode!"

Dettmer got an odd look on her face and glanced around the room. "I gave it to your father."

"What!?" said Owen. "That's ridiculous!"

Dettmer lowered her arms and backed away toward the machine room. "It is over, Maddox. This whole thing is being broadcast live."

"That matters not in the least! Once the deadline passes, everything will be protected, owned by the new conglomerate. It'll take you years to get through the legal quagmire to gain access to it again. This night and everything you think you've uncovered will be gone, just outside of your dirty little grasp."

"People are literally watching you right now!" shouted Roman.

"Do you honestly think that matters? They didn't see what they thought they saw. It's that simple." He turned to face the streamBugs. "This isn't real! It's just a show for your amusement! It's all fake!" He laughed and turned back to the room. "You see? Their attention will always go somewhere else, and they'll forget. I'll replace this night with something of my choosing. And for the people who try to keep this night alive in their streams, I'll simply start removing Admiration Points." He looked around the room. He just needed to keep everyone occupied a little longer. The deadline was approaching fast.

"Yes, you morons!" he shouted at no one and everyone. "I'm the ultimate arbiter of Admiration Points. I'm the one who controls the software that rewards you, you Pavlov's dogs! It's my algorithm. Me! Not him!" Maddox realized he was emotional, and he sometimes said and did stupid things when he was emotional. He shook his head. This time was different. This time, it was the truth. All of it.

He looked at his father. His disgusting father. "He's about as valuable as an empty avatar." This felt right, Father needed to go. Maddox couldn't let what he had learned from Maria go unpunished. The countdown clock caught his attention, Eight minutes to midnight. "You don't know what you're dealing with, none of you!" The room spun with betrayal. He aimed the gun at his father.

"What the hell!? Don't point that thing at me!"

"This is on you, you imbecilic old man!" Maddox was furious, and he would not shut up this time, not when he held all the cards. And the gun. He was saving the company and doing the right thing.

In five minutes, my algorithm will crawl up the NewsCann network's ass, and my father is not a part of it.

Dettmer and Roman were moving, thinking he wasn't paying attention, but he was. He swung the gun back at them, and they froze.

He swung back to his father, the weapon shaking in his hand. "I'm the reason for your success, you pompous ass! All the fortuitous ideas have been mine. All the code that drives the subscriber counts is mine. I decide what goes viral! I'm the one who calculates and awards Admiration Points. Not you! Me! My code controls the watchers, the value, the points, the entire fucking system!" It felt so good to release his fury and tell the truth.

The graph displaying the real-time value of StarSee started falling, fast. He had not seen it in the red for years, but it was now tanking.

Boiling mad, he fired his gun just above Owen's head at the display, missing, and putting a spiderweb crack in the glass wall shielding the data center. Everybody flinched. He looked up at the streamBugs. "You can't possibly understand. You've been duped. This man is just a fat figurehead."

Mina inched away from Owen. The avatar of Lee Hoffman, eyes wide, stared in disbelief.

Owen stood defiantly, his stomach bulging out of his tuxedo over the table. He narrowed his eyes at Maddox. "Put the gun down, son. Family is loyal."

"Loyal? Like you showed me loyalty when Victor Raleigh was running? You let me lose!"

"For chrissake, son, let it go! I didn't let you lose. He lost on his own. And I let you get revenge on the Glass family for it, even though that was a seriously stupid thing to do."

"You don't know the meaning of stupid. Look at yourselves, you and Mina, you're both fake versions of yourselves, created just for watchers. Well, people don't need your artificiality anymore, they need a real person to do the right thing. They need me!" Maddox took a breath and gathered his resolve.

"Stop talking and put the weapon down," pleaded Owen.

The gun shook in his hand. "I'll kill you myself and not bother waiting for the algorithm to do it!"

Everybody gasped. Mina put her hand to her mouth.

"Oh, don't look so Goddamned surprised, *Mina*, you want it too." He sneered her name.

He turned back to his father, who, even in the face of immediate danger, looked smug and self assured. "I could wait for it to find the right person to kill you, but that doesn't matter since I'm going to do it."

Owen put both fists on the table and leaned forward. "You targeted the god damned algorithm at me!?"

"Yes! I'm putting an end to this! I've seen what you've been up to. I see the streams that show me the truth about what you're doing. My Digital Assistant shows me. I know what you're stealing from me."

"You crazy little bastard! Don't you see what's happening? The algorithm is working on you!"

It struck Maddox like a slap. The confusion shook him. It couldn't be true. But he was the one who made it, and he knew he was that good. Good enough to create something that even he would succumb to.

No. What he knew was real. It had to be.

"Shut up, you deranged egomaniac," said Maddox. "You don't know how any of this works. In five minutes, it'll be just me, the way it should be." He aimed the gun at Owen's forehead.

Lee Hoffman, whose avatar sat in shocked silence until now, rose to standing and held up his hand, drawing everyone's attention.

Maddox smiled. Four minutes to midnight. At least Lee was keeping to the schedule, he would announce that the deadline was upon us, and then he would make his rousing speech about how all media companies are social, about the greatness of capitalism, and then the evening's events would get wiped from the entire system.

Lee's avatar looked around the room, and looked up at the streamBugs, all eyes focused on him. "I hereby file an objection and officially withdraw NewsCann from the merger agreement!"

Maddox saw the look on Lee's face. He was serious. "Lee, wait!"

Lee's avatar snapped out of existence, leaving only a ghost effect.

"Fuck!" Owen screamed.

Maddox had never heard his father scream. It was repugnant.

"Goddammit!" Maddox radiated red hot with fury. The StarSee company value was falling like a rock. Billions of watchers, using the very system they created, were watching this disaster play out in real time.

He could still save it. This would be his moment of triumph. "Lee will still go through with it! It will still work!" he yelled at the world.

It was all his father's fault. He knew the truth, even if no one else could see it. His father had sabotaged this entire thing to humiliate him. He would finally pay for everything, for Roman Glass, for reneging on giving him more control of the company after the military deal, for all of it. He felt oddly confident. He aimed the pistol at his father, and this time, he would hit his target. He put both hands on the gun and tried to hold it steady. His father saw what he was doing and did nothing but stare at him. Scrolling along the bottom of Maddox's personal iRiz Star-Stream, he saw the caption from his Digital Assistant Maria, *"It's time, Maddox. Owen Blakewell's death will be celebrated by millions."*

Sunday, 11:57 p.m.

With his back against the glass to the machine room, Roman watched the father-son drama unfold before his eyes like a modern Greek tragedy. Travis stood on the opposite side of the room, very slowly raising and targeting his weapon on Maddox, who was too focused on Owen to notice. Gabe and Mina watched on, looking like they wanted nothing more than for this night to be over.

An extremely loud snap rang out, immediately followed by an even louder gunshot. Everyone flinched, twice. A small puff of smoke rose from the end of Maddox's gun. A spiderweb crack in the front window appeared. Roman looked at Owen, expecting to see a growing spot of red appear on his chest. Instead, Owen was also looking around to see what had happened.

Maddox was grimacing. He hit the floor like a felled tree. Travis had shot him with a non-lethal Instant Disabler charge.

"Sorry, I knew it would make him convulse and squeeze the trigger, but I couldn't wait any longer," said Travis.

Dettmer dashed to Maddox's spasming body and pulled the security guard's old school gun from Maddox's stiff hand. She ran back to Roman.

The lights pulsed, followed by a loud thud. A low hum buzzed through their feet. The backup generator had engaged.

"Give me the killcode," said Roman. Dettmer handed him the small baggie. He could feel the eyes of Owen on him as he ran for the machine room door, which was wedged partially open, the mangled fork underneath it. The open door alarm to the data center was ringing, adding to the chaos.

"Roman, wait!" Owen shouted. "Think for a second before you do anything permanent! You've already proved your innocence and stopped the merger. There's no need for a killcode!"

He paused and looked around the room at the chaos. Stream-Bugs silently watched.

"Ask yourself, who in this room stands a better chance of developing the technology to bring your sister back? I'll make you a promise. I will fully fund research into resuscitating ICE patients, like your father and your sister, if you just toss that simpin away right now."

He was right. No one else was rich or powerful enough to make that happen.

"Roman, listen to me. We can fix this, and we can do it without destroying the platform. I'll happily fire Maddox and have him arrested. You'll gain more Admiration Points than you can imagine. I can correct this mistake and improve your life. Think about it, Roman. I actually admire you."

Roman looked at the overweight man at the head table with the perfect white hair. The man who used his own son because he thought he could kill Starla Devine for getting older, and then simply replace her. The man who had created the platform that was ultimately responsible for the death of his father and his sister. The man who didn't care that people were killing each other and countries were warring because of him, as long as his stock went up.

"I don't want your admiration."

Roman squeezed through the opening and sat back down at the terminal. It was cold as the intense air conditioning worked to keep the banks of quantum computers cool in the increasingly hot building. The screen that had played back the night of the murder was still open on the terminal, frozen at the last moment of the recording that Maddox had tried to delete. He closed the window.

Looking out of the glass enclosure of the machine room, he saw Maddox lying on the floor. Owen stood at the head table, pleading with Dettmer and Travis.

He saw himself reflected in the glass, wearing the StarSee shirt and beret.

The whole thing was a dirty facade, the party, the family, the whole StarSee ecosystem. On the surface, it might look like a way to bring people together, but in reality, it was using people to create divisions and wage war against made up adversaries for the benefit of the rich and the warmongers. None of its constructs were real. Admiration Points? Constant peer-to-peer surveillance under the guise of entertainment? Snarky memes from the Meme-factory? Roman hoped the whole thing would go down in flames.

He inserted the simpin into the front of the black box and opened Starla's user control interface. Navigating his way to the personal and security settings, he clicked on *"Load Profile Control From File."* He navigated to the simpin folder. There was one file on it. All letters and numbers. The killcode.

11:59:02. The systems could still connect at midnight for all he knew.

This was it. Not only would it destroy the algorithm that the military hired Maddox to create, to give our country an international advantage in all the wrong ways, but it would prob-ably also kill all the Admiration Points, starting with Starla Devine and working its way through the system to everyone connected to her, including Roman. He worked hard for those points, but he would no longer be a slave to them. He understood now.

He dropped the file on Starla's icon.

11:59:30.

A new password window popped up. This was unexpected. It blinked at Roman. *"Enter password to complete Control File execution..."* Maddox must have added an extra step to Starla's security to keep anyone from modifying her root files. He slammed his fist on the table. *Shit!*

He looked out at the main room again. Maddox still lay motionless on the floor in the middle of the room. There was no way to get the password out of him now, especially not this quickly. It would be something only Maddox would find clever. Roman looked at the head table. Only Mina, Owen and Gabe remained. Mina fumbled with her silverware, the unwitting pawn in all of this, probably going to jail because of Owen and Maddox making her play the role of pretending to be someone she wasn't for the cameras. The family really was like Maddox's fish, living the beautiful life, but dangerously carnivorous.

Roman's face lit up. *That's it!* He typed it in. *"Dragonet."* The interface chimed like a slot machine. The pop up disappeared. On the left side of the screen was Starla's autorun profile folder, and on the right side was the contents of the simpin with the rootkit killcode executable on it. A window popped up. *"Autorun file? Y/N"* Roman slid the cursor to the *Y* button and clicked.

Rebuild profile.

12:00:00.

The building shook so hard that Roman almost fell off his chair. Everyone in the room stumbled. Followed by a noise like having ten million pebbles falling on the roof. Pink foam slid down the outside of the windows. The building had been doused with fire suppressant. It was either dropped from the air or the building itself had finally reached a temperature that triggered the release of its own fire protection system. This was not a good sign. By now, all living things probably should have left the building. It was beginning to feel warm, even in the controlled environment of the machine room.

Roman stepped out of the glass enclosure and looked at Dettmer. It was considerably hotter outside of the computer room. The huge banquet space was lit only by the blue glowing lights from the machine room, the displays, and the eerie dim orange glow from outside. All the remaining avatars had disappeared. Roman knew where everything was in his head, but as his eyesight adjusted to the darkness, he realized that Maddox had regained muscle function and was now kneeling, staring at his displays.

"Goddammit!" Maddox screamed.

All the streamBugs in the room fell to the floor as if they had been sprayed with insecticide.

The entire StarSee system was collapsing, Admiration Points were disappearing, watcher counts were dropping by the millions, company value was sinking like a dead body tied to cinder blocks.

"It's done. It's all over," said Roman.

Travis had pulled Maddox to a standing position with his hands behind his back and was about to put on a restraining tie.

Maddox looked at Roman. "You!" In a split second, he broke Travis's grip and charged Roman. Within moments, Maddox was behind Roman with a large serrated steak knife to his neck. "You'll pay for this! You won't make me lose twice."

Travis and Dettmer both immediately trained their weapons on Maddox and Roman. Maddox was completely behind Roman, dragging him backwards toward the door to the computer room.

"Maddox, drop it!" shouted Dettmer.

Travis gestured to the head table. "You three! Step away! Over there, against the back wall!"

Mina and Gabe ran to the back wall. Owen stomped as if it were a game he was tired of.

"You think this is the end!?" Maddox sounded desperate.

Roman felt remarkably calm for having a knife held to his throat by a man already pushed to the edge. Maybe it was because he had already died once today. His geosense flashed on the room, the building, and the entire outside of the structure. He remembered. Slowly and imperceptibly, he reached into his pants pocket, below Maddox's view. Flames licked at the windows and skylights. The room was approaching a hundred degrees and everyone was sweating.

Roman grasped the remote detonator in his pocket. He squeezed the sides of the case and felt it pop open. It should work at this distance. He put his thumb on the button and pressed.

A loud thump outside shook the entire building. Silverware and plates rattled.

"Hold on, we're about to be flooded!" Roman yelled.

Everyone looked at each other in confusion.

But it only took Maddox a moment to catch on. "Ha!" He hissed in Roman's ear. "You can't seriously think you could blow up my water tanks. I'm Maddox Blakewell, I'm not stupid. I planned for the possibility that some tree-hugging terrorist would try to take down my system!"

"No," said Roman, only loud enough for Maddox, whose face was jammed into Roman's neck, to hear, "but unlike others, I'm able to calculate the distance from the tank's pressure valve to the main aquarium, and I just blew the Diverter Valve. The pressure will overwhelm the main gasket to your tanks and collapse the entire aquarium. The water will take the straightest path downhill, and by my calculation, should be here in about three seconds." Roman shouted to the group, "Hold on!" He jammed his elbow into Maddox's gut.

Maddox's mouth opened to respond when the water crashed through the skylight windows at the back of the room. As it rushed in, it carried the swirling steam of a freshly doused fire with it. The water arced through the skylight windows, landing in the middle of the room, crashing down onto the tables and chairs. Fish and dirt and the smell of wet charcoal rushed in.

Travis and Dettmer dove toward the rear of the room. Roman lost sight of them in the foaming, dirty water, which rushed in from all three sides through doors and skylights.

Roman's geosense was trying to calculate vectors and distances, but it was all happening too quickly. The wall of water hit Maddox and Roman, sweeping them off their feet like the deck crew on the Poseidon. Something that looked like a small shark slammed hard into Roman's chest as they were carried across the floor. He grabbed for the door handle of the machine room as it almost slipped past. The water ripped his iBrowse off. Maddox grabbed onto Roman's leg as the water headed for the nearest exit. It blasted through the front window of the tower that bullets had weakened. Roman held tight to the door handle but was slipping. His grip gave way, and he slid with the torrent toward the open broken window, which led to an eighty-seven foot drop to the hard surface below. Maddox hung on to his leg. They rushed toward the window ledge, sliding along with the flow of water. Maddox slipped out first. Roman caught sight of another large fish that went past, gasping. Roman grabbed through the rushing water onto a table leg, which was caught against the sill of the broken window. He stopped with a jerk and held his breath against the oncoming rush. Pulling himself forward, he wrapped his elbow around the leg, and grimaced in pain. He tasted salt water in his mouth. Maddox's desperate claws dug into his leg. Turning away from the flow of water, he looked down to see Maddox, hanging outside the window, fingers dug into the folds of Roman's black pant leg, glaring back at him.

He looked at Maddox's panicked eyes. The table leg started to give way. They were both about to fall to their deaths. Roman was not about to die twice in one day.

"Screw you!" Roman shouted as he kicked his leg, but Maddox

hung on. "And your whole family!" He kicked again. "And your whole fucked up system!" He strained and pulled his leg as high as he could with Maddox hanging on, and then kicked his foot down, smashing Maddox in the face. Maddox's grip released. He screamed and fell toward the concrete courtyard below.

Roman groaned and pulled himself back into the room as the water subsided. Another blast of steam rose up as the fire around the employee gathering space below was extinguished. The machine room was sparking and dripping, many of the glass walls smashed out by the force of the waves. These quantum computers would never work again. He hoped the killcode had time to migrate out into the rest of the system before they were destroyed.

A thin layer of moving water covered the floor, but the onslaught was over. Looking at the back of the room, Owen, Dettmer, Gabe, Travis and Mina had hung onto a shelving unit that was affixed to the gray cloth-covered wall. Owen stood up, surveyed the room, and made a clumsy stomping run for the open stairway doors, his hands still tied behind his back.

Then, as if someone had pulled the rug out from under an escaping penguin, the large man flailed face first into a pile of tables and chairs in the corner. Mina lay on the ground with her leg stretched out.

That would have made a great meme.

Travis was on Owen within seconds.

Roman stood up, soaking wet and bleeding from the broken glass. Dettmer, her long hair and black gown dripping, walked over to him and put her hand on his shoulder.

"You did it," said Dettmer.

"Holy shit, that was intense."

Together, they peered out into the smoky night and looked down over the edge of the window, where they saw Maddox's lifeless body on the landing below, next to a smashed ping-pong table, the Mandarinfish Dragonet staring at him with dead eyes.

"Kind of makes me feel sad," said Dettmer.

"He had every opportunity to do something different," said Roman. "He didn't have to choose this path."

Dettmer turned, looked at Roman and tilted her head. "I was talking about the fish."

Monday, 6:40 a.m.

On the hillside of the lookout from the Wisdom Tree Monument atop the crest of Burbank peak, Roman, Dettmer and Travis sat quietly, exhausted, wrapped in towels. Roman watched as the sun rose over Los Angeles, orange rays bouncing off windows glistening in the chilly morning air. It was as clear as he had seen it in a long time. Clear of smoke, and clear of streamBugs.

Looking down over the damaged StarSee building, pockets of smoke and steam still rose in areas around the structure. Maddox's tower was missing the windows on the seventeenth floor where the water had burst out of his private residence. A scrubbed path led down the hill, to the blown-in rear skylights of the center tower that the water had smashed through into the Gray Room.

The StarSee streamBugs were gone, but the quiet hiss of larger electric quadcopters was not, as they hovered around the building broadcasting for various news media. They stayed outside the 500 foot perimeter in all directions that the Blakewells still legally had in place, but there were dozens of them silently watching.

The aftermath of the night's events had taken hours to wrap up. Though the water release helped put out the fire immediately surrounding the building, there were still several more drops to be made before the flames were well contained. Then there were all the interviews, the additional officers arriving, the crime scene documentation, the statements taken, and the formal arrests.

Mo, having been woken up by Rennick, had arrived at one a.m. He was now in the StarSee machine room attempting data forensics on the water damaged servers. Travis' partner, Mascon, had flown into the scene at three in the morning. He was not so cocky this time, having watched the footage highlights on the NewsCann stream on his way to the facility.

The police had promptly ruled Maddox's death as being accidental, and put his body on ICE, as per the Blakewell family's wishes. Despite vigorous protests, Owen Blakewell had been immediately released back to his own tower. Roman was released, and the charges of Starla's murder were dropped, though he would still have to answer for escaping from HomeJail. As Mascon said, "Just because you're innocent doesn't mean you can break the law to prove it."

Roman stared out at the horizon. "I can't believe Owen isn't going to HardJail."

Dettmer shook her head. "It is not clear what laws were actually broken, and the government is saying StarSee's algorithms are vital to national security."

"I'd bet that he's already fixin' to salvage what he can," said Travis.

"He who fights and runs away..."

"...lives to fight another day," said Dettmer.

Roman turned to her and smiled. "That's right. You got it."

She grinned back.

He squinted at the morning sun. "This whole thing makes me wonder if the influential code could be used for good instead, you know?"

"Like a love algorithm?" said Travis with a chuckle.

Roman sighed. "Yeah, you're right. Maybe we should just stop with the whole thing."

"The thing is, manipulation is built into our DNA. We will always have propaganda and intentional bias. If we are unable to rid ourselves of it, we will never rid our media of it," said Dettmer. "The question is when does it cross the line into illegal?"

"I reckon that's our job, right? To stop it when someone or something goes too far."

"Hopefully, that's what you guys did today. I mean, StarSee won't be crossing it again anytime soon," said Roman.

"Likely a new platform will rise up from the steaming wet ashes of StarSee and fill the void," said Travis.

"It will probably just be a re-branded StarSee, knowing Owen Blakewell."

"But we can use this to get better laws on the books," said Travis. "Laws that keep tabs on the companies, not just the people that use them."

Dettmer turned to Travis, "Have you thought about joining the Social Media Division? We could use you, and I hear Rennick is now thinking about an early retirement."

Travis smiled and nodded. "Careful, I might just take you up on that."

"Speaking of laws," said Roman, "I feel kinda bad for Mina. She did murder Starla, sure, but she was under quite a bit of influence."

"I think we're about to see a whole bunch of legal cases where the defense claims that an algorithm manipulated the defendant," said Travis.

Roman's stare remained fixed on the California sunrise as he tried to reason it out.

"Algorithm or not," said Dettmer, "they committed the crime. Like Nuremberg, right? You can not just say, yeah, I killed someone, but I did it because my social media platform lied to me."

"But would they have done it if the algorithm didn't manipulate them?" asked Roman.

"How powerful does the manipulation have to be before it is not your responsibility anymore? Were they a hostage to the algorithm? Does Stockholm Syndrome really apply? Where did they lose control and the algorithm took over?" said Dettmer.

"Right," said Travis, turning to Roman, "that's like blaming your religion for making you kill a scientist that discovered alien life." He raised an eyebrow. "If they chose to believe the lies when presented with verifiable facts, it's their choice."

"I know," said Roman. "I'm just not sure where choice stops and brainwashing starts."

Travis ran his hands through his hair and stretched. "Speaking of choice, there's a lot of people down there that are waking up to a different world today. Their Admiration Points no longer exist. They're gonna be pissed off for a while. Y'all don't go from millions of watchers to zero overnight without it crushing a lot of people's identities. They'll be looking for someone to blame."

"You should lie low for a while, Roman. Really low," said Dettmer.

"I'm done hiding, or using disguises. The real people in my life are more important to me than what the watchers think."

"Just sayin', people are likely to be pretty worked up," said Travis.

A police quadcopter approached, hovered and landed behind the group, blowing dust and soot into the air.

"This is our ride," said Travis. He reached out his hand and grabbed Dettmer's. They all wiped flecks of ash off their clothes as they stood up.

Roman reached out his hand to shake Dettmer's. "Thank you, for everything."

Dettmer took his hand and pulled him into a hug. "We did it Roman," she said into his ear. "The people we lost would be proud of us. I know I am."

As they pulled apart from each other, Roman felt himself blush a little. "Thanks. You're pretty cool for an authority figure."

"You do not want a ride back to your place?" asked Dettmer.

"No thanks," said Roman, "my ride's almost here."

"Tell Seven I said hello," said Dettmer with a nod.

"Y'all take care," said Travis.

Dettmer and Travis made their way up the path and got into the quadcopter. She gave a quick wave out the open door as it closed, and it hummed away, leaving only the sound of its blades cutting through the air in its wake.

Moments later, Seven's black limocopter approached and landed. Roman ran up to the sleek flying vehicle as she pushed the door open and he jumped in. He couldn't wait to get off this mountain.

Inside, Seven, Tek and Pete all exchanged hugs and pats on the back with Roman, who could not stop grinning.

Keith stepped out of the bathroom. "Sorry, I can't go when these things are in the air." He lit up when he saw Roman. "The innocent Mr. Roman Glass! That was absolutely magnificent. I watched the whole thing!"

Roman gave him a one-armed man hug. "Thanks Keith! I'm surprised to see you here."

"It's important for me to breathe bad air once in a while," he snickered. "Besides, I couldn't let Tek get all the credit."

"It takes a village to destroy the world's largest social media platform," said Tek as everyone buckled in. "It was wild watching the killcode take effect. I don't think anyone realized just how infected the whole StarSee system was with malicious code."

"Hopefully that was the end of it," said Roman. "They almost got away with permanently hiding everything."

"Seven leaned forward. "I have a congressman friend who watched the whole thing live, and he's already filing briefs in Washington to bring before congress. A sort of Social Media Fairness Doctrine, requiring transparency of all algorithms in a human-comprehensible language."

"The platforms will fight that tooth and nail."

"That's why it has to happen now, on the heels of this disaster," she said.

The engines whirred up to speed, and the limocopter shifted slightly as it left the ground.

"You guys are all rock stars," said Roman, "but I am freaking starving. Can we go eat?"

"Breakfast at my place?" Seven suggested to the group.

"Now that we know where you live, you won't be able to keep us away," said Pete.

"You're welcome anytime, now that you don't have any streamBugs watching you."

"That we know of," said Tek.

They floated effortlessly into the air and flew away, hovering over the Wisdom Tree Monument for a moment, and finally taking off away from the still smoldering StarSee towers.

THANK YOU FOR READING

I hope you enjoyed The Murder Algorithm.

If you did, please go on-line to wherever you purchased the book and leave a rating and review, even if it is only a few sentences long.

Reviews are how the bookselling algorithm works!

It's easy, and would help a lot.

Lastly, if you would like to find out about upcoming novels and short stories, and/or become part of the Wilson Kincaid community, I encourage you to go to: www.wilsonkincaid.com

Thanks again. It is readers like you that make writing worthwhile.

- Wilson Kincaid